ALSO BY JAY McINERNEY

FICTION

How It Ended
The Good Life
Model Behavior
The Last of the Savages
Brightness Falls
Story of My Life
Ransom
Bright Lights, Big City

NONFICTION

The Juice
A Hedonist in the Cellar
Bacchus and Me

Bright, Precious Days

Jay McInerney

Bright, Precious Days

BLOOMSBURY

LONDON · OXFORD · NEW YORK · NEW DELHI · SYDNEY

Bloomsbury Publishing
An imprint of Bloomsbury Publishing Plc

50 Bedford Square
London
WC1B 3DP
UK

1385 Broadway
New York
NY 10018
USA

www.bloomsbury.com

First published in Great Britain 2016

A portion of this work appeared in the August 2016 issue of *Esquire* (www.esquire.com)

British Library Cataloguing-in-Publication Data
A catalogue record for this book is available from the British Library.

ISBN: HB: 978-1-4088-7658-9
         TPB: 978-1-4088-7659-6
         EPUB: 978-1-4088-7657-2

2 4 6 8 10 9 7 5 3 1

Designed by M. Kristen Bearse
Composed by North Market Street Graphics, Lancaster, Pennsylvania
Printed and bound in Great Britain by CPI Group (UK) Ltd, Croydon CR0 4YY

To find out more about our authors and books visit www.bloomsbury.com.
Here you will find extracts, author interviews, details of forthcoming events,
and the option to sign up for our newsletters.

For Anne

Every marriage is its own culture, and even within it, mystery is the environment.

—RICHARD HELL

Bright, Precious Days

1

ONCE, NOT SO VERY LONG AGO, young men and women had come to the city because they loved books, because they wanted to write novels or short stories or even *poems,* or because they wanted to be associated with the production and distribution of those artifacts and with the people who created them. For those who haunted suburban libraries and provincial bookstores, Manhattan was the shining island of letters. New York, New York: It was right there on the title pages—the place from which the books and magazines emanated, home of all the publishers, the address of *The New Yorker* and *The Paris Review,* where Hemingway had punched O'Hara and Ginsberg seduced Kerouac, Hellman sued McCarthy and Mailer had punched everybody, where—or so they imagined—earnest editorial assistants and aspiring novelists smoked cigarettes in cafés while reciting Dylan Thomas, who'd taken his last breath in St. Vincent's Hospital after drinking seventeen whiskeys at the White Horse Tavern, which was still serving drinks to the tourists and the young litterateurs who flocked here to raise a glass to the memory of the Welsh bard. These dreamers were people of the book; they loved the sacred New York texts: *The House of Mirth, Gatsby, Breakfast at Tiffany's* et al., but also all the marginalia: the romance and the attendant mythology—the affairs and addictions, the feuds and fistfights. Like everyone else in their lousy high school, they'd read *The Catcher in the Rye,* but unlike everyone else they'd really *felt* it—it spoke to them in their own language—and they secretly conceived the ambition to one day move to New York and write a novel called *Where the Ducks Go in Winter* or maybe just *The Ducks in Winter.*

Russell Calloway had been one of them, a suburban Michigander who had an epiphany after his ninth-grade teacher assigned Thomas's "Fern Hill" in honors English, who subsequently vowed to devote his life to poetry until *A Portrait of the Artist as a Young Man* changed his religion to fiction. Russell went east to Brown, determined to acquire the skills to write the great American novel, but after reading *Ulysses*—which seemed to render most of what came afterward anticlimactic—and comparing his own fledgling stories with those written by his Brown classmate Jeff Pierce, he decided he was a more plausible Maxwell Perkins than a Fitzgerald or Hemingway. After a postgraduate year at Oxford he moved to the city and eventually landed a coveted position opening mail and answering the phone for legendary editor Harold Stone, in his leisure hours prowling the used bookstores along Fourth Avenue in the Village, haunting the bars at the Lion's Head and Elaine's, catching glimpses of graying literary lions at the front tables. And if the realities of urban life and the publishing business had sometimes bruised his romantic sensibilities, he never relinquished his vision of Manhattan as the mecca of American literature, or of himself as an acolyte, even a priest, of the written word. One delirious night a few months after he arrived in the city, he accompanied an invited guest to a *Paris Review* party in George Plimpton's town house, where he shot pool with Mailer and fended off the lisping advances of Truman Capote after snorting coke with him in the bathroom.

Though the city after three decades seemed in many ways diminished from the capital of his youth, Russell Calloway had never quite fallen out of love with it, nor with his sense of his own place here. The backdrop of Manhattan, it seemed to him, gave every gesture an added grandeur, a metropolitan gravitas.

Not long after he became an editor, Russell had published his best friend Jeff Pierce's first book—a collection of stories; and then, after Jeff died, his novel, two of the main characters in which—it could not be denied—were inspired by Russell and his wife, Corrine. Editing that book would have been difficult enough, given its not-quite-finished state, even if it hadn't involved a love triangle featuring a married couple and their closest friend, but Russell was proud of the scrupulous, sometimes painful professionalism with which he'd tried to implement Jeff's intentions. The novel, *Youth and Beauty,* was generously praised by the critics—including several who'd been unkind about his debut—as books by recently deceased authors often are, especially those who die young and in a manner that confirms the myth of the artist as a self-destructive genius. Even before the book was published there was spirited bidding for the film rights. It sold well in hardcover and again, a year later, in paperback, and then its sales fell off, dwindling into the double digits a few years back, its author little more than a name associated with the period of big hair and big shoulder pads, yet another of the victims of the great epidemic that scythed the ranks of the artistic community, although, as a heterosexual, he didn't really fit the profile of the plague narrative and his fiction had more in common with that of James Gould Cozzens or John O'Hara than with the high-gloss, coke-fueled prose of his famous contemporaries. Over time his reputation faded like the Polaroids from their days at Brown. Then, gradually, almost inexplicably, the book and its author had been resurrected.

This process first came to Russell's attention with a long essay in the inaugural issue of a magazine called *The Believer,* which Jonathan Tashjian, his PR director, had shown him. The writer of the essay claimed to be part of a growing legion of fans, and cited a Web site, Lovejeffpierce.com. Just when Russell had begun to suspect that earnest young people cared much less about literature than his own generation had, a new wave of book people rose up to adopt Jeff. The appetite for his work was fed in part by its very obscurity and by the lack of availability of the books, which had fallen out of print, abetted by a sudden interest in the eighties on the part of those who were too young to have really experienced that decade. Not long after he took command of his own publishing house, Russell bought back the rights to both books and quickly reprinted them. The sales figures thus far did not begin to reflect the intensity of interest on the part of the early adopters, and Russell could only assume that these true believers would lose interest if and when the books again became popular. Still, the second-generation interest had caught the attention of a production company, which picked up the lapsed movie option, and as literary executor Russell had gotten Corrine attached to the project as a screenwriter; her critically praised adaptation of Graham Greene's *The Heart of the Matter*, released the previous year in seven or eight theaters worldwide before going to video, having given her just enough credibility to merit a first crack at the script. After two drafts they wanted to hire a new writer, but Russell had insisted that Corrine stay involved. Though they hadn't heard from the would-be producers in almost a year, the option had been renewed again just a few weeks ago.

In the meantime, he'd agreed to have lunch with the creator of another Jeff Pierce Web site, one Astrid Kladstrup. Unlike some of his colleagues, Russell believed in the potential importance of the Internet and the blogosphere, which he himself had difficulty plumbing; this was one of the main reasons he'd hired Jonathan, who lived in that world, and also why he'd agreed to talk to this young fan, although he'd possibly been unduly influenced by a photo of Jeff's latest fan on the Web site.

When she appeared in his office doorway, escorted by his assistant, Gita, she looked even younger and hotter than in her photograph, so much so that he felt guilty at having invited her to lunch in the first place. She was petite and voluptuous, her figure highlighted by what looked like a vintage dress in a shiny red fabric, the narrow waist accented by a flared skirt. She had pouty red lips beneath a lacquered brunette bob and wore heavy black glasses that seemed somehow ironic, and suddenly he felt like Humbert fucking Humbert.

He rose and walked around his desk to greet her. "Astrid?"

"Very nice to meet you, Mr. Calloway."

"Please, call me Russell." He almost said "Mr. Calloway is my father" but realized how incredibly old that joke was, how old it would make him sound, and how lame, although it was possible, of course, that she was so young that it would be new to her. "Have a seat."

"It's weird," she said, tilting her head to one side and then the other, like a parrot, as she studied him. "I feel like I know you."

"If you're imagining me as the character in Jeff's book—"

"Sorry, I guess that's pretty pathetic."

"Jeff would have been the first to insist on the autonomy of his fictional characters." Not wanting to sound pompous, he added, "When he published a chapter of the novel in *Granta* way back in '87, he categorically denied it had anything to do with us."

"You and Corrine."

Hearing his wife's name on these plump, shiny, strawberry-colored lips, he felt a twinge of—what? He nodded. "Yes. Nothing to do with us," he insisted."

"And you believed him?"

At the time in question, Russell had been furious, the characters being all too recognizable in those early drafts. "Well, I wasn't altogether pleased with that particular piece."

She nodded adorably. "Still, you look exactly like I thought you would."

"Only older," he said, trying to maintain a modicum of sanity and decorum.

"And this place," she said, waving a forefinger from side to side. "It looks like an editor's office should."

"Thanks. One of the perks of buying a venerable old publisher on life support was the nineteenth-century town house that came with it." Russell tended to speak of himself as the proprietor of the operation, though in fact his equity share was considerably smaller than his investors' and was about to shrink further if the fall list didn't start performing better. This past spring he'd had to rent out the top floor of the town house—to a couture-shopping Web site, no less—and cram two subrights assistants into Jonathan's office. His took up the back of the second floor, overlooking the courtyard and the scruffy garden out back, which looked far more impressive in the verdant months. The side walls were essentially floor-to-ceiling bookshelves that culminated twelve feet above the floors.

"So you weren't . . . always here?"

"Back in Jeff's day, no. I was working for Corbin, Dern then. I took over McCane, Slade in 2002."

"Great place. Kind of creaky and dusty and Dickensian. Sorry, I didn't mean that as an insult." She stood up and walked over to a shelf filled with photographs, focusing on the one of Jeff slouched against the door of his East Village apartment.

"That was taken in 1986."

"Wow, do you think we could get a copy for the site?"

"I'm sure we could manage that."

"This is cool," she said, pointing at the photo of Jack Nicholson, a signed publicity still from *The Shining*. "What does it say?"

"It says, 'To Russ, who gives good book.' I did the movie tie-in paperback years ago and Stephen King got him to sign that for me. I don't know why I still have it. And that's John Berryman, one of my all-time favorite poets. You should read *The Dream Songs* if you haven't."

"Is he the one who jumped off the bridge?"

"Well, yes." He was pleased the name was still out there, but hated to hear Berryman reduced to a tabloid headline.

"Who's that?" she asked, nodding toward a Lynn Goldsmith photo of Keith Richards.

"You're kidding?"

She shrugged.

"Keith Richards. Of the Rolling Stones."

"Did you publish him or something?"

He shook his head. "Sadly, no." The grittier of the Glimmer Twins was, in fact, under contract to Little, Brown for a memoir, with an advance so staggering that Russell had never even considered playing.

"What's the significance?"

"It's *Keith fucking Richards*."

After making sure she wasn't a vegetarian, as so many young people seemed to be these days—in which case it would've been out of the question—he walked her some five blocks south of his West Village office to the Fatted Calf, a self-proclaimed gastropub inspired by recent trends in ever-trendy London. Although it had been open less than two years, it looked as if it had been in business since Prohibition, with creaky, mismatched tables and chairs, its framed butcher's-eye diagrams of vivisected cow carcasses, on which each cut was carefully labeled. The maître d'—if a guy with a chullo cap and a soul patch qualified as such—led them to a rickety back table with a rough, water-stained top. Russell had discovered the place early on, thanks to a tip from an English writer he published, and had started coming before it became one of the toughest seats in town, although the lunch hour was relatively uncrowded; there weren't any office buildings in the neighborhood, and the staff inevitably seemed surprised that anybody was actually vertical at this undignified hour.

"The food's great," Russell told her. "At night it's a mob scene. Two-hour wait. They supposedly don't take reservations, but if you're a celebrity or a friend of the house, there's a phone number."

Astrid examined her surroundings with new interest. "I take it you have the number."

He shrugged. "I come here a lot."

"So, what do you recommend?" she asked, leaning forward and gazing at him as if prepared to follow any directive he might issue. He wondered if this was how professors lived, bathed in the admiration of young people, and if so, how they managed it. He'd considered the academic life, and even applied to several grad schools before dropping that idea. Now, mesmerized as he was, he was pretty certain he could keep his mind straight for a couple of hours. But he felt he'd be a shivering wreck if he had to contend with this girl for, say, an entire semester.

"The chef has somehow convinced a lot of New York foodies that an ox-tongue sandwich is a desideratum, not to mention fried tripe," he said, sounding—he couldn't help it, apparently—somewhat professorial. "But I remain agnostic, not to say skeptical, about stuff like that. I'd recommend the burger, which they make from a special blend of different cuts of beef from this bespoke butcher in the Meatpacking District, who may, in fact, be the *last* butcher in the Meatpacking District. All the others got priced out by nightclubs and fashionable restaurants that'll soon go out of business to make room for even more fashionable restaurants and clubs."

"Do you mind?" she asked, holding up a small digital recorder.

"I'm not sure I have anything all that interesting to say."

"Can I get you something to drink?" asked the waitress, a brunette with red streaks in her hair and multiple nose rings. Astrid looked at him for guidance. Although he was known to have a cocktail or a glass of wine with lunch, Russell ordered an iced tea. At some point he had to figure out her age.

"Can I get a Belvedere Bloody Mary?" she asked.

"Our house specialty is actually a Bloody Bull with house-made beef stock that's rendered here daily."

"Okay, I'll try that. With Belvedere. Make it a double."

"I should tell you we have one special today."

They waited as the waitress looked around the restaurant before leaning in and resting her palm on the table. She seemed to be judging the advisability of sharing this information.

"We're all ears," Russell said.

"Chef calls them 'crispy bollocks.'"

"You're shitting me," Russell said.

Astrid, clearly, was unfamiliar with the term, but she leaned forward, an eager student.

"Testicles," Russell said. "Deep-fried bull's balls, I'm imagining."

"Well—"

"Known here in America as prairie oysters."

Astrid had been game for the house-made beef stock, but this was clearly a step too far. She directed a look at the waitress that seemed to implore her to contradict Russell's description.

But the waitress, sticking to the party line, merely shrugged her shoulders.

"Really?" She was not a girl who lacked self-confidence, or an adventurous spirit, or the will to appear more sophisticated than she knew herself to be, but neither had she left Middletown, Connecticut, this morning expecting that she'd be invited to eat the balls of a bull, fried or otherwise.

"I think we'll get two burgers," Russell said. "Medium rare."

"Sorry," Astrid said after the waitress had receded.

"That's okay. It seems a little surreal even to me, and I've lived here for twenty-five years. So you're at Wesleyan?"

"And you all went to Brown? You and Jeff and Corrine?"

"Class of '79."

"Well, I've never really done this before, so let's just start at the beginning. How did you meet Jeff?"

"People were always telling us how we'd love each other. We were both writers, English jocks. So of course I hated him. We didn't officially meet until sophomore year."

"You got into a fistfight over a girl?"

"Now you're extrapolating from the novel."

"So that didn't happen?"

"Not exactly. It's actually hard for me sometimes to separate the fact from the fiction. Jeff's version can be very compelling. He was a good writer. A very good writer. So at this point it isn't always easy to remember what really happened as opposed to his reinvention of it. There was a punch thrown, I know that much. We were at a party and he flicked a cigarette in my beer cup. And I jumped up and tried to hit him, but I think he ducked away. That night's shrouded in an alcoholic haze. And the next thing I remember we were lending each other books and talking late into the night over Gauloises and Jack Daniel's about the Frankfurt School and *Exile on Main Street* and narrative modalities in *Ulysses*."

"Like, what books were you lending?"

He thought about it. "Céline, Nathanael West, Paul Bowles, Hunter Thompson, Raymond Carver. Carver's first collection of stories was huge for both of us."

"And when did you meet Corrine?"

"That I remember very clearly. I first saw her at a party my freshman year. She was standing at the top of a staircase in a frat house. That was my first glimpse, looking up at her, a beautiful blonde, smoking a cigarette. I don't know if I would've worked up the courage to talk to her or not, but as I watched her boyfriend came up from behind and she turned to look at him as he reached out to touch her cheek. I had no idea at the time they were going out, but I knew who he was. On the basketball team—a big man on campus. They were up there on Mount Olympus and I was downstairs with the geeks and the drunks. The next semester she was in my Romantic poetry class. I showed off big-time in class. Jeff was in that class, too, but I never talked to him. Hated him. We were competing for dominance."

"For Corrine's attention?"

"For everybody's attention, though I suppose I was especially trying to impress Corrine. And the professor, of course."

The waitress arrived with Astrid's drink, sweating in a heavy glass, with a celery stick sprouting from the ice cubes.

"You know what, get me one, too," he said.

"Belvedere bullshot?"

"Why the hell not?"

"Go for it," Astrid said.

"I am," he said, "although I seriously doubt that either one of us can tell the difference between a supposedly top-shelf vodka and the pour from the well. In fact, I *know* we can't. The well, just in case you should want to know, is the place underneath the bar where they keep the cheap generic shit; I know this because I was a bartender in Providence when I was making my way through Brown, and the idea that you could possibly taste the difference between Belvedere and the industrial stuff that alkies drink when it's mixed with tomato juice and Tabasco and horseradish is ludicrous. In fact, I doubt you could taste the difference straight up. The whole point of vodka is that it has no taste. It's alcohol and water. Period. End of story. The cult of these premium brands is ludicrous, a marketing scam that started when I came of age. We used to think we were so fucking cool specifying Absolut. Me and Jeff, back in 1981, at the Surf Club. Yeah, we were such connoisseurs. Now it's Ketel One or Belvedere or Grey Goose, but it's not what's in the bottle; it's pure marketing, and whether or not a fucking celebrity gets spotted ordering one or the other."

"So why'd you order the Belvedere?"

"Because I didn't want to look cheap."

"Have I said something to make you angry?"

"No, of course not. I'm sorry, I didn't mean to go off on a rant."

"You seem to have some major issues with Jeff."

"Oh, please, don't give me that shit. You probably weren't even born when he died, and I've had decades to think about this. The only issue I have with Jeff is that he fucking died. That and his being a junkie."

"Well, those are big issues."

"I'm sorry. I don't mean to get all worked up." At which point the waitress arrived like an angel of mercy with his drink. "God that's good," he said after swallowing a third of it. "So where were we?"

"Complaining about vodka."

"I just realized where I got that riff."

"What riff?"

"That whole vodka rant. That was actually Jeff's thing. He used to mock me for specifying Absolut. He'd make a point of ordering Smirnoff or whatever was cheapest. After he died, I stopped drinking premium vodka for years in tribute to Jeff."

"Oh, wow. That's kind of cool."

"You mean it's cool now that you know Jeff said it."

"Well, I *am* writing about him."

"And I'm grateful, really. A few years ago it made me sad to think that no one was reading him, that there were only a few of us who remembered him."

"Still, it must be a little weird, the fact that he was—I know not exactly, but still—writing about you. You and him and Corrine."

"Kind of strange, sure."

"So I guess what everyone wants to know is about how you edited *Youth and Beauty*."

"The same way I edit every book. Sentence by sentence, reading closely, asking questions."

"But Jeff wasn't there to answer them."

"So I answered them the way I thought he would have."

"I mean, did you edit the book in a way that made you look . . . better? You and Corrine. I guess the question is—sorry, but you know, it's out there on the Web and everything—did you leave out unflattering material?"

"That's a loaded question."

"Well, it must've been tempting. Didn't you ever think about turning the manuscript over to someone else? How could you possibly be objective?"

The waitress arrived with the burgers, giving Russell an interlude to refine and, eventually, mute his indignation.

"Can I bring you anything else? Mustard, ketchup?"

"Ketchup," Russell said.

"And I'll have another bullshot."

Russell considered the options. "What the hell, bring me a glass of the Rafanelli Zinfandel."

"I'll have one, too."

"You want the bullshot *and* the Zinfandel?" the waitress asked.

"Why not? It's almost the weekend."

Russell was sort of impressed. "One of the things I love about this place," he said, "is that unlike almost every other New York restaurant that doesn't call itself a diner, they'll actually bring a bottle of ketchup to the table."

"Would it be correct to put ketchup on bull's balls?" she asked, then giggled fetchingly.

"I think it would be almost mandatory. It certainly couldn't hurt."

After the waitress delivered the ketchup, they set about the business of preparing their burgers, Russell putting a careful dollop of ketchup on each side of the bun and, on the top of the patty, a smattering of sautéed onions. Astrid was equally absorbed in her own rituals.

The waitress returned with the drinks, then left.

"We're about to achieve a new level of intimacy," Russell said when he had reassembled the dish.

"Really? Right here at the table?"

"To consume a hamburger in front of another person is to shed several layers of formality and dignity."

"Especially if you lick the other person's fingers."

"I can't say I've ever even thought of that."

"You should try it," she said, and raised her index finger, shiny with grease, to his lips.

Simultaneously appalled and gratified that she was so blatantly flirting with him, Russell felt it would be unchivalrous to embarrass her and reject what was, after all, a relatively cute and harmless gesture. He leaned forward, opened his mouth and closed his lips around her digit.

"How was it?"

"Needs a little salt," he said. Was she really coming on to him, or just teasing him?

The conversation died for a time, both taking refuge in eating.

"So, there's a school of thought that says you censored Jeff's book."

"'A school of thought'? Jesus, what are we talking about here? Has Harold Bloom weighed in on this subject, or are we talking about some Red Bull–fueled trolls surfing the Web in the wee hours?"

"It's just been the subject of a lot of threads."

"Threads?"

"You know, like online conversations about a particular subject on a site or a board. I'm not, like, saying you did anything wrong. I just want to set the record straight. Plus, I'm curious, what it felt like editing a book that's partly based on you and your experience. Weren't you at least tempted to rewrite a little? Clean it up?"

"Of course I was. And sometimes I was angry with Jeff, and sometimes hurt. But he was my friend and he was a very good writer, potentially maybe even a great one, and my first and only duty was to him and his book."

He remembered wishing he could have changed the past as easily as he might have changed the nuances and even the facts in Jeff's novel. He always told himself it was fiction, even when bitterly aware how heavily indebted it was to actual events. But he was proud of the fact that he'd improved the novel, though he wasn't about to brag about that.

"But you must've changed certain things."

"Far fewer than I would have if he'd been alive. I bent over backward not to do what you're suggesting. It's one of the lightest edits I've ever done, and nothing affected the tone or the story line. You've read it—obviously. It's not as if the Russell-like character comes off as anything like a saint. He's kind of comically full of himself at times, and clueless at others. And"—he paused, but what the hell—"he gets cuckolded."

"That's exactly what I've been saying."

Somehow this didn't quite track, given her line of inquiry, but he said, "Thank you."

"What happened to the manuscript?"

"I have it somewhere." Actually he knew precisely where it was, locked in a file cabinet at home.

"Would you ever consider . . . I don't know, showing it to somebody?"

"Do you have anyone in mind?"

"Well, obviously, I'd love to see it. I mean, someday."

Another interlude of silence set in as they concentrated again on their meals, a trance of caloric surfeit, warmed by the sunlight that bathed their table and spilled halfway across the floor of the room.

"Would you object to my seeing it?"

"I'd consider that a betrayal of trust," he said. "The editor's hand should be invisible."

"The wine is really good," she said.

"The perfect hamburger wine."

"Would you think I was really decadent if I asked for another?"

"As a gentleman, I would probably have to join you so as not to make you feel self-conscious."

He asked her about school, about her classes and her reading. She asked him about New York, publishing and the eighties. He couldn't help liking her, a beautiful young girl interested in him and the things he loved, full of wine and vodka and admiration for his accomplishments, his worldliness, to the point that she actually seemed to find him sexually attractive. Outside the restaurant, she took his arm and said, "Let's get a room at the Chelsea Hotel."

He looked at her, stunned; her impish expression read to him like a challenge, a dare.

He considered it for a moment. The temptation was almost overwhelming. "I can't tell you how much it means to me that you suggested that," Russell said. "Even though I know you didn't really mean it."

"I did, actually," she said, leaning over and kissing him on the lips.

"I'll live on that for the rest of the year."

"Let me know about the manuscript," she said.

Later, walking back to the office after putting her in a cab, he felt amazed that he'd been so sensible, proud of himself but also a little sad to think that he might never again experience the incomparable thrill of exploring a foreign body.

This sense of erotic possibility stayed with him throughout the day, and that night, when he got into bed after consuming most of a bottle of Pinot Noir over dinner, the feeling drew him closer to his wife. As she read beside him, he began to kiss her neck and fondle her breasts. At first she ignored him but gradually succumbed.

He couldn't even remember the last time they'd made love, but now, for the first time in months, he found himself aroused, and worked himself on top of her. "Wait," she said, reaching into the drawer of the bedside table, fussing with some kind of lubricant that she applied even as he felt himself deflating, reaching for him, guiding him inside. They found their rhythm and he found himself succumbing to this slow, mounting pleasure. As good as it felt, it kept getting better and more insistent. Apparently he'd had just the right amount of wine to loosen his inhibitions and his quotidian anxiety without quite physically disabling him. They had slipped into a mutually satisfactory rhythm that gradually accelerated.

All at once he felt a shortness of breath that became more acute, until he was afraid that he might pass out at any moment, or worse. Even as he gasped for air he continued to thrust his hips; the term *death throes* came to mind. He was going to die in the saddle, like Nelson Rockefeller. *He thought he was coming, but he was going.* With a racing heart and a rising sense of despair, he struggled to fill his lungs. He was filled with the dread of his own eventual demise. This is how it would feel as he lost his grip on the world, this breathless dread. Even if he managed to pull back this time, it would come for him again. This is the way the world ends. Not with a bang, cheated of the final glory at least of an orgasm . . .

He tried to tell Corrine that he was in distress, but he was unable to speak, unable to bid farewell to the love of his life; and then, just when he was convinced he would die on top of her, he began to recover his breath and his panic gradually subsided. He faked an orgasm with several violent hip thrusts accompanied by a series of moans before rolling off of her, his anxiety subsiding to an almost manageable level, leaving him with a residue of dread, his relief tempered with a hopeless sense that he had just caught a glimpse of oblivion.

2

THE BEST MARRIAGES, like the best boats, are the ones that ride out the storms. They take on water; they shudder and list, very nearly capsize, then right themselves and sail onward toward the horizon. The whole premise, after all, was for better or for worse. Their marriage was seaworthy, if not exactly *buoyant*. Better off, surely, than the republic, bulging at the waist and spiritually enervated, fighting two wars and a midterm election, all of which seemed endless.

Or maybe not.

At least they'd had sex last night, the first time in God knows how long. She wished they didn't have to go out tonight, but they had a gala benefit: the third this month. How had she let herself get talked into this one? Her friend Casey had insisted, and it had seemed harmlessly distant a month ago, plus she owed Casey for buying a table for the Nourish New York benefit. That was how the system worked. She couldn't remember what tonight's worthy cause was. Something to do with South Africa? Russell was leaving from the office, where he kept his tux, because these benefits were almost always uptown, in the traditionally patrician district, despite the fact that money continued to migrate down the island; happily this one was nearby, at the Puck Building in SoHo.

She sat at her vanity, which doubled as her desk, applying eyeliner with a sense of fatalism, knowing full well that at some point in the evening it would end up on her upper lids, which had sagged over the years. Would an eye lift be a total betrayal of her principles? If she could even afford it. It kind of sucked, being nearly fifty, discovering a new laugh line that you'd at first imagined to be a crack in the mirror.

She was getting more than a little sick of black-tie benefits. Even though they usually attended as guests, rather than ticket buyers, she didn't have the wardrobe to do full formal all that often. The Upper East Siders, like Casey, her girlhood friend and prep school roommate, went to two or three a week and never repeated a dress. The younger society girls borrowed from the designers and the jewelers, but their mothers spent the equivalent of a Range Rover on dresses every month. Associating with the rich was inevitably expensive, even when they were ostensibly paying. You paid one way or another. Corrine was going to have to wear one of the two long dresses in her closet, the Ralph Lauren probably, the one she'd bought for less than half retail at the sample sale, the same thing she'd worn to the Authors Guild benefit, and hope that no one remembered it. But then, why would they? It wasn't as if the party photographers immortalized her fashion choices. And she didn't feel like she was getting all that much masculine attention, either. She examined the satin bodice in the mirror. Was it tight? Tighter than a month ago? And what about shoes and a bag? More things she wished she could afford to indulge in. She settled on the silver Miu Miu pumps to sort of go with her grandmother's silver mesh clutch.

Corrine tottered out of the bedroom, taking care with her heels on the undulant antique oak floor of the loft, with its treacherous gaps. God, she was *so* over loft living—that was one of the things they fought about, her desire to move; the fact that the kids could get a better education outside Manhattan, since it didn't look like they could afford private school tuition for both next year, after the kids graduated from PS 234. They'd be positively well-off if they lived almost anywhere outside this wealthy, skinny island. It was always about money, somehow—except when it was about sex. Young idealists, Ivy League sweethearts, they'd followed their best instincts and based their lives on the premise that money couldn't buy happiness, learning only gradually the many varieties of unhappiness it might have staved off. Russell liked, especially after a few drinks, to divide humanity into two opposing teams: Art and Love versus Power and Money. It was kind of corny, but she was proud that he believed it, and of his loyalty to his team. For better and for worse, it was her team, too.

The kids were on the couch, watching the new *Shrek* video. Jean, the nanny, meanwhile oblivious, distraught, pacing in the corner, fighting with her girlfriend on the phone. Apparently living with a woman was also difficult.

"Bye-bye, my little honey bunches. Love you tons."

"Where are you going?" Jeremy asked.

Corrine waited for Storey to comment on her outfit, but she remained absorbed in the video.

"I'm going out to save the world."

"How does going out save the world?"

"People buy tickets to fancy parties," Storey explained, "and then the money goes to, like, people with diseases and abused animals and stuff. It's called a benefit."

"Exactly."

"Why don't you just give the money and stay home?"

"Because adults like parties," Storey said.

Corrine saw that her motives didn't really bear scrutiny. She wasn't actually giving money and she wasn't even looking forward to this event. She was a fraud, a pretender, a hypocrite. But then, the kids seemed fine. Just a year or two ago they used to get distraught, try to argue her out of going out, weep and gnash their teeth, but now they seemed perfectly content to let her go. She wasn't sure this development was entirely welcome.

The elevator rattled as if in its death throes. She found a cab on Church Street, which also rattled and lurched. What was that band that Storey liked, Death Cab for Cutie?

A cluster of yellow cabs and black Lincoln Town Cars debouched sleek New Yorkers two by two into Lafayette Street at the entrance to the hulking red edifice, where they elbowed and kissed one another, funneling between the gray pillars, beneath the gilded statue of Puck, who disregarded them as he admired himself in a hand mirror. If only, Corrine thought, he might bring a little mischief to what promised to be a thoroughly boring evening.

She checked her coat, picked up her table number at reception, followed the throng into the ballroom, where, failing to spot her husband, she scanned the silent-auction items: the handbags and jewelry, the photo sessions with prominent lensmen, the trips—golf in Scotland, salmon fishing in Iceland, wine tasting in Napa, game watching in Kenya, river rafting in Zambia. Looking up, she spotted Casey Reynes at the bar. They'd remained close despite the divergences of their post–Miss Porter's lives; Casey had married an investment banker and lived in a town house on East 67th; this was Casey's native environment—the charity ball circuit. She was wearing a sea foam blue empire-waist gown accessorized with tasteful diamonds. Very few women could have pulled it off, but somehow Casey looked as if she'd been born in a ballroom.

"Corrine, oh my God, I was just thinking about you."

They exchanged kisses on each cheek, Casey dipping in for a third, as was the latest practice in her circle. Sometimes Corrine had to struggle to see her friend underneath the facade of tribal costume and customs.

"I appreciate your coming out for this."

"What's the cause?"

Casey smiled enigmatically, her forehead serene and undisturbed, but at either edge of this chemically frozen expanse a series of tiny lines, like stitches, betrayed some sort of emotion, though Corrine couldn't quite interpret which.

"It's *Luke's* charity."

"Luke? You mean—"

She leaned forward conspiratorially and hissed into Corrine's ear: "I mean *your* Luke."

As if summoned by the incantation of his name, the man himself appeared out of the crowd a few steps away, his reconnaissance of the room snapping into focus at the sight of Corrine. He seemed to recover his composure more quickly than she felt she did, striding over to greet her, taking her hand in his own and kissing her cheek, only one cheek, in the American fashion, surprising her with the familiarity, the sin-gularity of his scent, which seemed, even more than the sight of him, to elicit a chemical response, a tingling in her scalp, at the back of her neck, even as she tried to adjust to the changes in his appearance, nota-bly the raised pink scar that started just above his chin and trailed down his neck.

"What a lovely surprise," he said.

"I didn't expect to . . ."

"I was wondering if I might see you."

"I don't know if you've met my friend Casey Reynes. Casey, this is Luke McGavock." Corrine was all befuddled and couldn't remember whether they'd met or whether she and Casey had just talked about him, but then she realized they'd traveled in the same circles for years.

"We're old friends," Luke said, gallantly overstating the case. He looked in some ways the same and yet older, less robust, not only because of the scar. It had been, what, more than three years since she'd seen him? He seemed to have accumulated more years than that in the interval; his dark hair now several shades closer to silver, two crescents furrowing either side of his face from nose to lips. And yet, still, she felt a visceral thrill in his presence.

"Nice to see you again," Casey said. "Congratulations on this won-derful organization. The fact that all these jaded New Yorkers have chosen to come out for yet another benefit is undoubtedly a tribute to you."

"I'm hardly the only one behind this thing, and besides, I'd prefer to think it was a tribute to the cause." He bobbed his head up and down as he spoke, as if he were agreeing with himself, a nervous tic she remembered fondly.

"It's a wonderful cause," Casey said.

What cause? Corrine wanted to scream, but she was loath to admit her ignorance at this stage in the game. "The last I heard, you were in South Africa," she said.

"About half the year. I invested in a winery and I got more and more involved. I'm back here for a few weeks, for the benefit, taking care of business, visiting Ashley. She's up at Vassar."

"Oh my God, she's in college!"

"Well, it was sort of the logical next step after high school."

Jesus, Corrine thought, was there any limit to her insipidity? She hated it when people marveled at the fact that other people's kids aged instead of magically remaining the same as when the interlocutor had last seen or thought of them. But she was nervous and uncomfortable on several levels.

"How are the twins?" he asked.

"Good. Fine."

"They're how old?"

She had to think a moment. "They're eleven."

If only Casey were to make a dignified exit, they might be able to get beyond this twaddle. Was there anything worse than small talk between two people who'd once exchanged bodily fluids? Her confusion was compounded by the fact that one of his eyes seemed not to be looking at her. What was that about? He'd always had a somewhat manic aspect, a darting field of attention, but this was different.

"I think I'll find my husband, and get him to bid on some jewelry," Casey said. "So nice to see you again, Luke."

And suddenly, confusingly, they were alone in the midst of the burbling crowd.

"You haven't changed," he said. "You look beautiful."

"Now I'm unlikely to believe anything else you say."

"You never did accept a compliment lying down."

"Women get suspicious of compliments when they discover the purpose is to *get* them to lie down. And then when they get older, they become so unaccustomed to hearing them that they don't know what to do with them. I just spent twenty minutes in front of a mirror, and no one knows better than I how much I've changed since we last met."

"Now I recall that your lack of vanity was one of the things I loved most about you."

"I like to think of myself as a realist."

"I prefer to think of you as a romantic," Luke said.

"Once, perhaps, when I was young. Have you noticed—romantics are like fat people? You don't meet many old ones."

"You're still young in my eyes," he said. "After all, you're quite a bit younger than I, and I insist on seeing myself as youthful."

Despite the strangeness of his off-center gaze, she was recalling how much she loved their banter, when a blonde in a lavender gown suddenly appeared at Luke's side.

And even before he said *"There* you are," there was something in the ease of her comportment, in the serenity of the smile directed at Luke, and in Luke's sudden discomfort, that provoked a sinking feeling of nausea in Corrine.

"Giselle, this is Corrine Calloway. A very dear friend."

Oh, thanks for that, she thought. *Dear. Friend.*

"Corrine, this is my . . . wife, Giselle."

"How nice to meet you," Corrine managed to say, although it was all she could do to remain standing, feeling suddenly light-headed and faint.

"Likewise," she said. "It's lovely to meet so many of Luke's old friends. I'm afraid we got married in such a terrible hurry, I feel I've a great deal of catching up to do." She was very pale, with white blond hair, although an athletic physique and an air of boisterous vitality undermined the impression of Pre-Raphaelite delicacy. Likewise her accent, which seemed like a muscular, rusticated version of upper-crust English.

Corrine caught sight of Russell and waved frantically.

"Were you two school chums?" Giselle inquired politely.

"We met doing some volunteer work together," Luke said quickly, as if he were afraid of what she might say.

"After September eleventh."

"Ah, yes. At the soup kitchen. Luke told me about that. It must have been a terrible time."

"Best of times, worst of times," she said, regretting it as soon as it was out of her mouth. "I mean, as terrible as it was, it brought out the best in a lot of people." God, what an idiot she was being tonight. She realized how clichéd this sounded, which was only slightly better than glib.

To his credit, Luke was looking slightly pained. She was improbably grateful to Russell as he bumped into her and splashed some of his drink on her arm. He had this kind of overflowing physicality, a puppyish lack of coordination, a sort of comical deficit of grace that had earned him the nickname "Crash."

"Hello, my love. Sorry."

"Hello, Russell. I don't know if you remember Luke McGavock. And this is his wife, Gazelle."

"Giselle, actually."

Yes, she knew, but she couldn't help herself, and was that a look of amused complicity on Luke's face? "My husband, Russell Calloway."

"The man of the hour," Russell said, shaking Luke's hand.

"I'm grateful to you and all the other guests," said Luke before excusing himself to be towed off by a woman with a clipboard.

"Interesting guy," Russell said after they'd both been swallowed by the crowd. "Tom was just telling me his story."

"I know," she said. "We worked together for six weeks."

Russell looked blank.

"Ground Zero, soup kitchen."

"Oh, right."

Five years later—another era. "You met him once outside Lincoln Center, just before *The Nutcracker*."

Russell shrugged. He didn't seem to remember one of the pivotal moments of Corrine's life, had no idea that the complex emotional transaction of that encounter had preserved his marriage. Russell's obtuseness had been a blessing in the event; he'd never suspected anything, so far as she could tell, never noticed how thoroughly she'd withdrawn from him back then, how close she'd come to leaving.

The lights were pulsing, summoning them to the main event. "We'd better find our table," he said. She felt the familiar pressure of Russell's hand on her elbow, guiding her forward into the throng, the radiant, bejeweled women with their taut faces stretched back over their ears, and their sinking cleavage, the men in their bespoke tuxedos with faraway stares, thinking about share prices in Hong Kong and mistresses in condos in the East Sixties.

Seeing Casey, their hostess, standing at the table, Corrine wondered if this had been some kind of setup. How could she not have mentioned, when she invited Corrine, that this was Luke's charity? But what was the point, exactly? Luke was married, as was she. So maybe it was a coincidence.

"Corrine, you know Kip, of course," Casey said, indicating Russell's business partner. "And this is Carl Fontaine, who works with Tom," she added, directing her attention toward a burly young man with thinning hair and a florid complexion.

"A pleasure," he said. "I can see I'm very well seated tonight."

She wished she could say the same, but at least his enthusiasm seemed genuine. She walked around to double-kiss Tom, who was fiddling with his BlackBerry, and Kip's wife, Vanessa; they agreed unanimously that their children were doing very well, indeed, thank you.

The tables were extravagantly decorated in a safari motif—herds of toy elephants, rhinos and hippos wandering over the zebra-print tablecloths, a tropical jungle sprouting from a sisal bowl in the center. "I'm actually dying to hear all about the charity," Corrine announced, taking up the glossy magazine-size brochure on her plate that featured a picture of Luke standing amid a sea of African schoolchildren.

"Well," Kip said, "McGavock was a founding partner in the Riverhead Group, one of the top private equity firms. Big player. He retired a few years back, bought a winery in South Africa and planned to sit and watch the Cabernet Sauvignon ripen, but you know, guys like us, you can't just sit on your ass no matter how much capital you've piled up, and sure enough he finds a project."

"I don't know if I'd call her a project," said the man next to Vanessa. "More like a trophy."

"Tony, you're terrible," said Vanessa, who, Corrine knew, had once been a trophy herself, and seemed genuinely amused by this remark.

"A little young," Kip said.

"No, it's actually age-appropriate for the second wife," Tony said. "The formula's half your age plus six years."

Carl Fontaine picked up the Luke narrative: "Of course, vineyards are pretty labor-intensive, and he started getting involved with his workers. Adopted the village. Built a school and a clinic, and now he's encouraging his old friends to do the same."

Proud of Luke, Corrine wondered how much it cost to adopt a village. He really was a good man, a generous soul. She'd always known that about him. But how could he have gotten remarried without telling her?

"What's with the scar?" Tony asked.

"Car crash," Fontaine said. "Luke spent, like, three months in the hospital."

Corrine tried to conceal her distress by waving over the waiter. Perhaps the girl had been at his bedside and he'd married her out of gratitude. She held out her wineglass for a refill of Sauvignon blanc, which Kip informed her was from Luke's winery.

"It's actually surprisingly good," Russell said. "And I don't normally go for New World wines."

Did South Africa qualify as New World? she wondered. Wasn't it the birthplace of the species? The home of Lucy and all those other hominid fossils? Didn't get much older than that. She brooded through the first course, imagining Luke's suffering, listening to Tom and the older man to his left comparing notes on game camps in Africa, arguing the virtues of Kenya versus South Africa.

"Singita Boulder's incredible. Amazing chef."

"We were at Masai Mara last year. Top of the line. Saw the big five."

"What exactly are the big five?" Corrine asked.

"Five toughest game animals: lion, elephant, Cape buffalo, leopard, rhinoceros."

Vanessa said, "I thought the big five were cats—lion, tiger, leopard, cheetah and . . . panther?"

"No, no," Russell chimed in from the other side of the table. "The tiger doesn't live in Africa, and the panther's actually just a melanistic variant of the leopard." He'd never been to Africa, but he'd read all of Hemingway.

Setting aside her notion of Giselle as nurse, Corrine imagined her as a predator, stalking Luke. He'd been alone in a strange land; she was a native, on familiar terrain, hunting him down. As smart and successful as he was, he was, like most men, emotionally naïve. His ex-wife, Sasha, had played him for years.

Someone onstage was talking about what a terrific guy he was, although the din from the tables made it hard to hear. At their table,

Carl Fontaine was giving his own little speech about Luke: "Let's hope he sticks with it. These private equity guys have a pretty short attention span, they're used to the two-year turnaround—buy, slash, fix, sell. I wonder if we'll even be here in three years."

Corrine was indignant that no one was listening or paying attention. Did these people think paying $25,000 for a table absolved them of any semblance of courtesy?

The introduction was punctuated by scattered applause as Luke took the stage; she was relieved to notice that the chatter subsided. Standing silently on the podium, he waited until the room was almost quiet. "Ladies and gentlemen, friends, and former colleagues, and philanthropists. I was lucky enough to discover South Africa almost by accident. It's a country of extraordinary diversity and beauty. I went there to manage a winery but ended up discovering a people. . . ."

She tried to listen but instead found herself thinking about the first night they'd been together, at the little studio he kept in a dilapidated town house on 71st, his body stippled with stripes of streetlight filtering through the venetian blinds, the musky scent of him tinged with the residue of the acrid smoke from Ground Zero. . . .

Fully clothed on the podium, Luke was saying, "For thirty-five thousand, less than the base price of a Lexus, you can build a double-room schoolhouse with a capacity for up to a hundred children. For the same price you can build accommodations for the teachers. Kitchens are very important, so the school can get government food grants and apply to the World Food Program. Ecofriendly, hygienic bathrooms cost about seven thousand. And water-catchment systems, gutters that trap and store rainwater in so-called JoJo tanks, these are a few thousand dollars. Less than some of us spend on a suit—I'm looking at you, Ron Tashman. Is that an Anderson & Sheppard tuxedo?"

This provoked a few ripples of laughter.

"Finally we have three clinics ready to build, each providing health care for an entire village or a township, for between a hundred and two hundred and fifty thousand dollars. You can find the details in your program. Put your name on one of those. On the screen to my right you are going to see some phone numbers next to particular projects. Text us your pledge and your name will appear on the screen on my left, along with your project. Unless, of course, you want to remain anony-mous, in which case just put Ron's name down, since he's always happy to take credit. Let's start out with the water-catchment systems, at a mere three grand. Come on, Chuck Coffey, that's less than your weekly cigar budget. . . ."

Corrine opened her grandmother's purse, pulled out her Razr and tapped in the number. She'd never encountered this bidding technol-ogy before and she didn't entirely believe it would work, or so she told herself as she typed in the code and then the message *Happy H2O*. She glanced over at Russell, who was deep in conversation with Kip Tay-lor's wife. Would including his name make it better or worse? Should she just stop now? She typed *Corrine and Russell Calloway* and pressed SEND.

"We have our first pledge," Luke said from the stage. He seemed to miss a beat, pause just a moment before announcing, "Corrine and Russell Calloway have just bought clean drinking water for a school in the Transvaal. Thank you, Corrine and Russell."

Russell looked more puzzled than angry as he accepted congratu-lations from his tablemates before directing a quizzical gaze at Cor-rine. She shrugged, put on her most winsome smile. There would, of course, be an interrogation, reminders about bills and tuition, admo-nitions about charity beginning at home. It was going to wreck their budget for the next few months, probably. They gave, when they could, five hundred to Brown, their alma mater, five hundred to Oxfam and Meals on Wheels and the Henry Street Settlement, two fifty to PEN and the ASPCA. And they gave every day, in a sense, to Nourish New York, since as an executive director of that organization, Corrine was paid about half of what she would have been paid in a private-sector job; plus, they wrote a check every year for the gala. But they'd *never* given this much to any single charity. She hardly knew why she'd done it—on an impulse, as a kind of ontological squeal, a cry of "I'm here" directed at her former lover? But on reflection she was glad, and she thought she could justify it, smooth it over at home.

She had a strong suspicion that Russell was going to get lucky tonight. For him that was the good news; the bad was that she was afraid she'd be thinking of someone else.

3

STILL ON THE AFRICAN CLOCK, Luke woke up a few hours after he'd fallen asleep, thinking about Corrine. He checked the markets in Europe, cleared his e-mail and talked to his vineyard manager. Baboons harassing the pruning team—normally only a problem near the harvest, in March, when the grapes were ripe. Something they didn't have to deal with in Napa or Bordeaux. The workers threw rocks at them and the apes started throwing them back. His manager had put in an early order for lion dung from a local game park, which was effective as a deterrent.

He'd known that he would see Corrine the night before last, but he hadn't really known how he would react. Three years ago, after yet another post-breakup rendezvous, he'd taken himself to the other side of the world in no small part to get away from her.

He met Giselle at a garden party in Franschhoek, a pretty girl in a white dress crouching in the courtyard, talking to a giant tortoise with a ring dangling from a hole in its shell, feeding it an orange wedge from the drink in her hand. "We're old friends," she said when she looked up and caught him watching her. And indeed, her little gold nose ring hinted at a certain affinity. He was immediately attracted to her; only later did he become conscious of her resemblance to Corrine.

Twenty-nine years old, she'd recently broken off a long engagement with a man she'd known since childhood. That first afternoon she told him quite frankly that she was tired of all the young men in her insular social circle and that she was thinking of moving to London or the States. She'd done some modeling in Paris as a teenager, traveled in her early twenties, and ended up back home in Cape Town, where she fell in with an old family friend, who'd eventually proposed.

Luke told her about his recent divorce from Sasha, about his daughter, who'd be joining him for her summer vacation, but he never mentioned Corrine. Before proposing to Giselle, he'd gone back to New York and spent a month at the Carlyle, somehow imagining that he'd run into Corrine somewhere. He felt that if he did, it would be a sign. A few days after he returned to South Africa, he ran into Giselle at a cocktail party.

At seven-thirty the breakfast cart was delivered and he woke Giselle, who was flying back to Cape Town that morning. "All packed?" he asked as she lingered over tea in her fluffy white bathrobe.

"I think so," she said. "I'm sorry to leave you here alone."

"I'll be busy," he told her, "and you can't very well miss your cousin's wedding."

After the bellman finally came for the luggage, he walked her down to the car. "I'll miss you," she said.

"I'll miss you, too," he agreed, though in fact for the first time he could recall he was impatient for her to leave.

After the car disappeared into traffic, he scrolled to Corrine's number on his BlackBerry and typed: *Thanks for the contribution. It was great to see you the other night.*

It occurred to him that their affair had preceded texting—or at least their own use of it. Maybe she didn't text.

A few minutes later the instrument buzzed, dancing on the onyx coffee table.

Great not quite the word I'd use. Had no idea would see you. Husband not real happy about sudden excursion into philanthropy.

Don't worry, I'll cover you on that.

Too late. Already settled up on the way out.

Can I see you?

Why?

Tell you when I see you.

He stood at the big window, looking downtown, as if he might be able to spot her out there down near the tip of the island, past the MetLife, the Chrysler and the Empire State Buildings, checking the screen of his BlackBerry as the minutes ticked by. The device finally vibrated again.

Working today in Bronx.

Time to meet before?

9 AM Caffe Roma.

He wondered if he was supposed to know where it was, if she was testing him. He Googled it: a pastry place in Little Italy. They'd stopped there once, he remembered now, coming off the night shift at the soup kitchen. Cannolis and cappuccino. Holding hands under the table, the interior redolent of fresh-baked bread and coffee after a night in the acrid smoke, the airborne residue of the ruined towers, of which they both reeked. Still dark outside, the only other customers a table of revelers who'd closed some nearby bar or nightclub, soaking up the alcohol with sweets.

If Corrine was trying to be discreet, she'd picked well. Little Italy, what was left of it that hadn't been swallowed by Chinatown, was an unlikely destination for anyone they might know. A few tables away, a young French-speaking couple pored over a map. The only other customers were four strident Italians, throwing back espressos and talking with their hands—the whole place picturesque, quaint in a manner that to fashionable New Yorkers would seem kitsch: the white marble tables with their cartoonish bent-wire café chairs, the dark green pressed-tin ceiling sagging with innumerable layers of paint, the display case teeming with pale confections. He checked his e-mails, and tested his French by eavesdropping on the couple two tables away, who were deconstructing Scorsese movies.

Through the window he spotted Corrine, hurrying up the sidewalk in a peacoat and jeans, and for just a minute he could see her as a type, a New York woman rushing somewhere important, harried but not frantic, confident that she would be waited for.

"I'm sorry," she said, sitting down across from him. "I was thinking of making you wait, of being deliberately late, until I realized how childish that would be, but then I got caught on the phone with our director about a lost truckload of cabbages."

Not a type at all, he realized happily, recognizing what he took to be the singular staccato rhythms of her thought, though he was baffled by the reference to cabbages. "I'm just glad you came at all."

"Well, I didn't want your last impression of me to be flustered and tongue-tied. As I suspect I was the other night."

"I thought you were very composed."

"*Please.* I was . . . flummoxed. I had no idea what the event was, or that you were the focus of it. Kind of a shock, really. You could have warned me you were coming to town."

"If I had, you might've raced off in the opposite direction."

"I can't believe I was totally oblivious to the fact that it was your charity."

"Do you know what I was thinking about when I was up on the podium?"

"Your wife's dimples?"

"I was thinking about making love to you on that musty old couch in Nantucket with Gram Parsons singing 'Love Hurts.'"

"Gram Parsons was correct," she said. "It does hurt. It would behoove us both to remember that."

He started to sing softly: "Love hurts, love scars, love wounds and mars—"

"Luke, for God's sake." She was blushing, embarrassed by the attention he was attracting, not to mention the quality of his singing. "That was terrible. You shouldn't be allowed to sing outside the shower."

"I bought the album after that weekend. I'd never even heard of Gram Parsons."

"Shouldn't you be singing to your wife? How the hell old is she, by the way?"

"Young enough to be my daughter, but older than my actual daughter."

"Well, close enough, no doubt, that they can become BFFs."

"She'll be thirty-two next month."

"And you are, let's see, fifty-seven?"

He nodded.

"What's the rule of thumb I heard the other night, the remarriage formula? Half your age plus six years, that's the ideal equation for a second wife in this town. I guess by that measure she's just a little young."

She was smiling, but he definitely detected the edge. "I admit, when you put it that way, I'm feeling like a cliché."

"Does she know about me?"

He shook his head.

"I'm glad of that at least." She seemed to ponder this. "Cappuccino," she said. "I'd like a cappuccino to go. I have to leave in five minutes."

When he returned with the coffees, he could tell her mood had turned darker. "You know, I almost broke up my family for you," she said. "And then I don't hear from you for three years. I'd have thought, at least, we were friends."

He was taken aback at the iciness of her tone. "We were far more than friends, Corrine. What was I supposed to do, write you e-mails about the weather? It was painful. I wanted you and it didn't seem possible and I had to pull away. Hell, I went halfway around the globe to forget about you."

He hadn't necessarily realized this back then, but in retrospect it seemed obvious.

"What did you feel after that night at the Carlyle a few years back? When you ran back to Tennessee, when you stopped calling and returning my e-mails?"

"I was afraid we were just falling back into an untenable situation. Our circumstances hadn't changed. You were still married. I was sad and the situation seemed hopeless. I'm pretty certain now that I may have gotten married again in an attempt to get over you."

"So it wasn't just that you'd forgotten me?"

"I had an accident about a year ago, and it was touch-and-go for a couple of days whether I'd make it." He fingered his scar, still numb, to illustrate. "Strangely enough, when I came to in the hospital, my wife was asleep in the chair beside me, lying with her face turned away from me. All I could see was her hair—and I was convinced it was you. I even called your name." He wasn't actually sure if he'd said her name out loud, but he'd indeed imagined, briefly, that the woman in the chair was Corrine, and he wanted to tell her so.

She was staring at him intently, apparently weighing the truth of this assertion. "Was your left eye injured?"

He nodded.

"Can you see out of it?"

"Not really. Sorry, I know it's disconcerting."

"*Please.* I'm the one who should be sorry." She lifted her cup and looked down into the foam. "Do you know where the name comes from? Cappuccino?"

He shook his head.

"From the color of the coffee-milk mixture, which reminded some-one of the color of a Capuchin friar's habit."

"That's one of the things I miss about you."

"My pedantry?"

He shrugged. "That sounds negative. Your eccentric erudition, let's say."

"You didn't have all that much time to get used to it, did you?"

"It's hard to believe it was only two, three months."

"Ninety days, as it happens."

"Was that it?"

"From the day I first saw you walking up West Broadway, covered in ash, till the day after *The Nutcracker,* when we said good-bye in Battery Park. You see, I really am a pedant."

"That sounds more romantic than pedantic."

"Well, whatever. I'm off to work."

"What are you writing?"

"I'm not writing, actually. I decided there were plenty of unemployed screenwriters in the world already."

"But *The Heart of the Matter* was produced. I read a great review in the *Financial Times.*"

"I must've missed that one." She shrugged. "Let's just say it was less than a blockbuster."

"I thought it was great."

"You actually saw it?" She seemed skeptical.

"I own the DVD. Watched it three times."

"Twice more than I did."

"You were always self-deprecating, almost to a fault. It's a very rare quality."

"In this city, perhaps."

"So now you're . . ."

"I work for an organization called Nourish New York. We solicit excess food from local restaurants, food banks, farmers, grocery stores, and try to get it to the people who need it."

"Sounds somewhat familiar."

She blushed and looked away. He was touched that her new vocation connected her to their shared past in the soup kitchen.

"Did you ever write that book about samurai movies?"

It took him a minute to figure out what she was talking about; he'd forgotten that this was one of many projects he'd conceived after retiring from the firm, samurai films having been a passion for many years. "I discovered I don't have the patience or concentration to sit down and write a book."

"It's probably true," she said. "I'd forgotten how hyper you are. Like the way you tap your foot when you talk." She paused. "Anyway, gotta go."

"Where?"

"A housing project in the Bronx. We have a bimonthly distribution program for fresh fruit and vegetables. Today it's carrots, apples, cucumbers and onions."

"Can I come along?"

"Don't be ridiculous."

"Don't you have volunteers?"

"Well, yes."

"So that's what I'll be, then. I have experience, remember? You might recall I was the one who got you involved with the soup kitchen down at Bowling Green."

"Surely you fulfilled your monthly good deeds quota the other night."

"Perhaps, but I didn't get to spend any time with you."

She regarded him skeptically.

"I want to see what your days are like."

"Well, you asked for it. Let's go."

"I have a car," he said, holding the door open for her.

She shook her head. "If you actually want to see what my days are like, you'll need to take the subway."

She seemed determined on this point. He knew that look, so many of her gestures and expressions coming back to him so clearly.

After he dismissed the driver, they walked over to Canal Street and descended into the IRT, squeezing themselves into the crowded number 2 train among the rush-hour commuters. She was pressed against his shoulder and thigh, her legs enveloping his, and even in the stale, funky train car he could smell her hair. He'd almost forgotten that smell. Absurdly, he found himself getting hard. They rode most of the way in silence, leaning together, their physical contact obviating the need for speech. Whatever they needed to tell each other was too intimate to be said here.

They got off at Grand Concourse/149th Street, Corrine leading the way up a series of passages and stairways to the corner of two large boulevards, where she indicated their direction with a nod of her head.

"So tell me," she said, "did you just forget to tell your wife about me, or did you *deliberately* not tell her about me?"

"I think the latter."

"And will you be telling her about me now?"

"No, I definitely don't think so."

"Why not?"

He tried to decide why, and then whether, to tell Corrine the truth. "Because if I really told her how I felt about you, it would break her heart."

She seemed genuinely surprised by this declaration. After digesting it, she said, "Is she enjoying New York?"

"Actually, she left this morning."

They passed a barbershop with matching lurid-colored hagiographic posters of John F. Kennedy and Martin Luther King, Jr., crossed the boulevard and turned into a smaller street lined with low-rise hair salons, bodegas, clothing boutiques, liquor stores and an abandoned brownstone covered in graffiti, including the slogan ARM THE HOME-LESS.

Corrine pointed to a cluster of brick towers in the distance. "That's our objective. Four thousand residents in the poorest congressional district in America. The nearest supermarket is more than a mile away. And of course no one has a car. A gypsy cab to the supermarket will cost eight, ten bucks each way. Most of them buy their food from the bodegas, which stock no fruit or vegetables aside from a few old plantains."

As they approached the towers, a long queue of people stretched back along the sidewalk.

"Our clients," Corrine said. "Looks like a busy day."

As they walked down the line, a motley, colorful cohort attired not only in the baggy staples of American leisure wear but also in the traditional garb of at least half a dozen nations, she greeted several of them by name.

"How's your gout, Jimmy? Are you staying away from the red meat?"

"Tolerable better, though I did get me a batch of ribs night 'fore last."

To another man she said, "How'd that job interview work out?"

"Would I be in this fuckin' line if it did?"

Luke wanted to tell the guy to show a little respect, but Corrine pushed on, saying, "Come talk to me inside."

Luke followed her, hopping over a chain into a parking lot flanked on either side by open tents. Corrine introduced him to several harried colleagues and deposited him with a group of volunteers. "Georgia here will show you the ropes." Georgia was a petite Goth brunette whose grooming and wardrobe choices seemed to intentionally contradict her sylphlike physique: her hair cropped close to her skull, her ears studded with metal, her pale skin, where it emerged from her black leather jacket, heavily embroidered with tattoos.

"We're cucumbers," she said.

"Pardon?"

"Our station. We're distributing cucumbers."

"Okay."

"You always dress like that to hand out vegetables in the South Bronx?"

"When I got dressed this morning, I didn't know I'd be coming here."

"What, you thought you were going to shoot an ad for *GQ*?"

"I'll pretend that was intended as a compliment."

"Whatever gets you off, dude. Nice scar, though."

She showed him the stacked cartons filled with cucumbers, how to weigh and bag them in three-, four- and six-pound units. "The clients have a coded checklist, *A*'s the smallest bag, *C* the biggest. I'm hoping you can guess which one *B* is. When you give them their bag, you check it off their list so they don't try to come back again."

When the gate opened a few minutes later, they were besieged by a procession of supplicants, their demeanors as various as their sizes and shapes, showing degrees of gratitude from shy to effusive; some resentful and sullen, others embarrassed, a few greedy, trying to snatch up extra bags or pass through the line twice. The majority were women, the men mostly elderly, a few sulking teens among them. After an hour he was told to take a break, at which point he called his driver. When he returned to his station, one of his coworkers informed him that many of the cucumbers in the second pallet were rotten; they ended up throwing half of them out.

Corrine appeared to assess the situation. "I can't believe they pawned this shit off on us," she said. As it turned out, they were running short on the other vegetables, too, with some forty or fifty people still waiting in line, so she instructed the volunteers to cut the rations in half. With the crisis more or less in hand, she told Luke she had to get back to her office.

Hoping to persuade her otherwise, he followed past the stragglers and out into the street. For some reason, she felt particularly bad about the very last woman in line, a strung out–looking mom with matted hair and two shivering toddlers, one of whom wore mismatched boots. Corrine tried to slip her ten dollars, but instead of quietly pocketing the bill, she snapped, "What the fuck this for?" holding it out in front of her, pinched between her thumb and forefinger, as if it were tainted.

"I just felt bad that we'd run low on provisions."

"I don't need your fuckin' pity," the woman shouted.

Corrine looked stunned by her wrath. "I just thought, with your two little ones—"

"Don't you be talking 'bout my kids. Ain't none ayo' fuckin' bidness."

The next woman in line said, "Hey, sister, you don't want it, I'll be happy to help out."

"Who asked you to put your fuckin' nose in it?" After the recipient of the bill crumpled it in her fist and pocketed it, word of the cash handout spread down the line, provoking queries from those who'd received only coupons.

A skeletal man stood with his hand outstretched before her, wrapped in one of those quilted blue blankets used by moving companies to cushion furniture in transit.

Corrine was clearly mortified, all the more so when Georgia came over and said, "What's going on?"

"What's goin' on is—some people gettin' special treatment."

Corrine drew her colleague away and tried to explain the situation. "I know, I know," she said in response to the reprimand that Georgia had yet to deliver. "Totally unprofessional."

"Well, you're the boss," Georgia said in a tone of voice that transparently betrayed her actual belief—that Corrine was a slumming dilettante.

"Well, that was incredibly embarrassing," Corrine said when they were alone. "I'm sorry you had to see that."

"Don't be. I love it that you have such a big heart. So, might you consider accepting a ride downtown?" he asked, spotting his car idling across the street.

She seemed deflated by the recent fracas, less trusting of her instincts. "Just give me a ride to the subway."

"Let me buy you lunch," he said when the driver asked for their destination.

"I need to get back to the office."

"Just a quick bite at the Four Seasons—it's on the way," he said after she'd given the address. "I've hardly spoken to you the last three hours."

"I'm sorry, Luke—I've got a meeting."

"How about dinner?"

"I can't—"

"A drink, then, after work. I'll show you pictures of the village your water-catchment system will benefit."

"All right, we'll see."

"I'll pick you up at your office."

He dropped her off at the subway stop and rode back down to the Four Seasons, not entirely discouraged by his progress, but she called at five to cancel.

"I'm sorry, but I'm going to be in a meeting till six-thirty and I've got to relieve the nanny by seven."

"When will I see you?"

"Luke, honestly, I don't know what you want from me."

"Just to catch up, spend a little time together."

He was lying through his teeth. He didn't know if sleeping with her one more time would sate his desire or fuel it, but he found himself consumed with the need to find out.

4

RUSSELL HAD SPENT THE AFTERNOON hunting and gathering in search of the perfect ingredients: the heritage ducks from upstate at the Union Square farmers' market, the star anise from Fujian in Chinatown. He belonged to the new breed of male epicureans who viewed cooking as a competitive sport, and pursued it with the same avidity that others had for fly-fishing or golf, with the attendant fetishization of the associated gadgetry and equipment. He and Washington, his best friend, had serious arguments about Japanese versus German cutlery. Russell had been raised on frozen vegetables and casseroles made with Campbell's soup, and Corrine saw this as another means of distancing himself from his midwestern roots, which was just fine with her, since she'd rather have gone to the gynecologist than cook a meal from scratch. This macho cooking thing worked to her advantage.

"Where's my damn immersion blender?" Russell huffed, standing at the counter in his Real Men Don't Wear Aprons apron.

"I don't even know what the hell that is," Corrine said.

"I need it for my brown sauce."

"Has anyone ever told you you're *such* a poofter."

"What's a poofter?" Their daughter, Storey, had suddenly appeared as if out of thin air, as was her practice. A slender blond ghost.

"It's just . . . well, it's just a word I use when Dad's being kind of ridiculous and pretentious."

"So you must use it a lot. I'm surprised I never heard it before."

Corrine was taken aback. Eleven years old? One minute she's talking about Hannah Montana and the next minute she sounds like Janeane Garofalo. Russell, searching for his inversion blender, or whatever the hell it was, hadn't seemed to notice.

"Jeremy's playing a video game," Storey said, reverting to a younger persona. "It's a weekday and he's not supposed to."

With mixed feelings, Corrine went back to his bedroom to investigate. It was true that Jeremy wasn't supposed to play video games on weeknights; and also true that Storey had a not entirely admirable tendency to tattle on her brother. They'd shared a bedroom until last year, when Russell finally agreed to partition off another hundred-something square feet of the apartment so they could each have their own. It was an old railroad-style loft, twenty-two by eighty. Before they arrived in '95, someone had slapped together a master bedroom in the back with two-by-fours and Sheetrock, and when the twins were born, they'd walled in twelve by fourteen feet, and then this second, almost identical room had shrunk their open space considerably. They'd grown accustomed, especially for publication parties, to fitting sixty or eighty people cheek by jowl, but now their guests really had to rub up against one another. This project had involved posting a bond with their landlord, who reserved the right to have them remove the walls on termination of the lease. She didn't know anyone else in their circle who still rented, but their rent was lower than mortgage and maintenance payments would be if they were to buy a comparable space, not that she was sure there were many comparable spaces left—an old-school loft with exposed pipes and wiring, warped hardwood floors with gaps large enough to swallow golf balls; palimpsest pressed-tin ceiling, the fleur-de-lis squares cut and patched and painted over countless times; an ancient freight elevator that worked according to its own moods. The decor had remained unchanged for a decade: one solid wall of books, the other a collage of framed photographs and paintings and posters, including one for the Disney movie *Those Calloways,* "A Family You'll Never Forget!" Only the Russell Chatham landscape, a small Agnes Martin etching and the Berenice Abbott portrait of James Joyce were worth more than their frames.

Corrine was desperate to move, desperate to have a second bathroom, but Russell clung to an outdated vision of himself as a downtown bohemian. Their apartment could have been a diorama at the Museum of Natural History: *Last of the Early TriBeCans,* an example of the traditional dwelling of the original loft dwellers. The neighborhood was being gentrified and renovated out from under them. Construction everywhere now, new buildings and wholesale renos, scaffolding and cranes and Dumpsters on every block, steel-on-steel banging, blasting and generators chuffing all day long; it was like living in a war zone. It had fallen silent for a few months after September 11, though in retrospect it seemed as if the construction and the speculation had started up again just at about the same moment the smoke had stopped coming off the mountain of rubble farther south. New towers with doormen and spas rose from the landfill along the river, while the old industrial buildings were gutted and gilded and stocked with shiny new residents thrilled to have ceilings high enough to accommodate gigantic canvases by artists who'd lived and worked here in the seventies and eighties. Now you saw movie stars in the Garden Deli, investment bankers at the Odeon. There hadn't even *been* a deli when they'd first arrived. The Mudd Club was certainly long gone and so were the Talking Heads, though Russell was currently blasting "Life During Wartime" to inspire his cooking, an anthem of their early days in the city.

She was just heading back to investigate Jeremy's activities when the buzzer sounded.

"Jesus," Russell said, "it's not even seven-forty."

She turned back to the front door. "Didn't we say eight?"

"We always say eight. Which means eight-twenty. Everybody knows that."

She worked the intercom. "Hello?"

Static, a frequent guest.

"Hello?"

"Um, I'm here for the . . . for the, uh, dinner."

"Who's this?"

"It's Jack Carson?"

He sounded uncertain and so, for a moment, was she. "Oh, right."

Russell's new literary prodigy. "Press the door when you hear the buzzer. We're on the fourth floor."

"It's Jack Carson," she told Russell.

"I guess they don't do fashionably late in Tennessee," he said.

"Given what you've told me about his appetite for controlled substances, we should be grateful he got here at all."

"Actually, I think he's been clean for a couple months now."

Corrine waited by the elevator door, curious to see this genius, this redneck bard about whom Russell was so excited, whose book he was publishing next year. She was a little disappointed when he turned out to be a gangly kid with dark hair pointing in several directions, a mottled complexion and piercing, almost black eyes, wearing tattered jeans and a black leather jacket over a black T-shirt with a big five-pointed star and the caption *Big Star*.

"Welcome, I'm Corrine. Russell's told me so much about you."

"You wrote the screenplay for *The Heart of the Matter*."

"Well, yes, that would be me."

"I thought it was great," he said. She was pleased but flustered as he scrutinized her with those black eyes.

"How did you even come across it?"

"Russell gave it to me. He knows I'm a big Graham Greene fan. I thought it was cool the way you managed to humanize Scobie in a way that Greene didn't."

She found herself surprised at the erudition implicit in this statement—not just the fact that anyone remembered her little film— even as she realized there was nothing inherently contradictory about the accent and the sentiment; she knew she shouldn't equate southern with ignorant. Luke came from Tennessee, and they didn't get much smarter, though his accent was barely noticeable compared to Jack's. He'd called a few days ago to say good-bye; she supposed she should be happy that he was halfway around the world again, though she'd felt strangely bereft at the thought of his departure.

Russell bounded over and wrapped his new discovery in a bear hug. "How's the city treating you? So, you met Corrine. And you found us all right?"

"Well, yeah, after I spent about half my advance on the goddamn cab."

"It's a bitch, I know. Don't worry, I'll call you a car service for the ride home. Come on in, let me get you something. Storey, can you come over and say hello to Jack?"

Corrine slipped away to check on Jeremy.

"What are you doing, sweetie?" He was sprawled on his bed on his Pokémon duvet, with Ferdie the ferret sprawled on the pillow beside him.

"Super Mario Sunshine."

"What day is today?"

"I dunno."

"Isn't it a Tuesday?"

"Maybe."

"Which would be . . . a weekday?"

"I guess," he said, not looking away from the screen, where the little red man traversed a tropical island.

"And are we supposed to play video games on weekdays?"

"I thought it was like a holiday."

"It's Election Day, which is not a holiday. Holidays are when you don't have school. Now turn that off before I take the controller away."

"Let me just save it."

"What's to save? That's what you always say when you want to keep playing for another five minutes." She still wasn't sure if this "saving" gambit was legitimate or not.

When he appeared to keep playing, she walked over to the bed and took hold of the control unit in his hand. Ferdie, snakelike, opened his eyes and regarded her languidly.

"Okay, okay."

"I don't want to come back and find this going again. What's the homework situation?"

"I'm done with everything except math."

"Well, let's do math, then."

She left before he'd actually turned the game off, weary of the struggle. At the same time, enacting these little family rituals was reassuring; she'd felt thoroughly unsettled these last few days, after seeing

Luke, and eager to convince herself that she was over him, that he had no bearing on her actual life.

Storey was sitting on the couch with Jack, pointing out a passage in her book. "Are you a Democrat?" she asked. "My dad says friends don't let friends vote Republican. That's a joke; it comes from that ad that says friends don't let friends drive drunk. Everybody we know is a Democrat." The buzzer rang before Corrine could hear the answer.

"It's Hilary and Dan." Two Republicans, in fact. Just barely audible on the crackling intercom. Corrine's younger sister and her fiancé, the ex-cop, who'd finally gotten divorced from his devoutly Catholic, supremely bitter wife a few months ago. Arguing that Hilary had been with Dan for five years now, Corrine had finally gotten Russell to stop referring to her as "your slutty little sister."

"Who's that?" Russell asked, approaching from the kitchen.

"Hilary and Dan."

"Ah, your formerly slutty little sister and her police escort."

"Jesus, Russell." She nodded toward the couch.

Chagrined, Russell glanced over to see the blond crown of Storey's head just visible above the couch cushions. "Sorry."

They listened to the elevator rattling upward and finally shuddering to a stop, the doors groaning open.

Kisses and handshakes . . .

"Happy birthday, sis," Hilary said. "Oh shit, I forgot we're not allowed to mention your birthday." She held a finger to her lips. "Top secret."

"Not so secret now, thanks," Corrine said. She'd insisted that this was not a birthday party, having no desire to commemorate the fact that she was turning fifty, unlike Russell, who'd had a big bash a few months ago to celebrate his own semicentennial.

"Where are my little chickadees?" Hilary chirped.

Corrine glanced over at her husband, who was studying her ruefully. He knew how much it pissed Corrine off when her sister used the possessive adjective with reference to the kids, as if determined to reiterate her maternal claim and give them hints about their complicated origins, whether they were ready for this knowledge or not.

Storey rose from the couch and marched over to greet the newcomers.

"There she is!" Hilary lifted Storey in her arms without losing her grip on the Pinot Grigio. "How's my favorite girl?"

"Good." It warmed Corrine's heart to see how Storey stiffened and struggled in her grasp. Hilary was one of those people who just couldn't connect with children, who seemed unable to speak their language, having spent all her adult energy learning the idiom and gestures of seduction. She'd been a professional girlfriend for years, a concubine without portfolio, a groupie.

Dan rescued Storey from Hilary's awkward embrace, hugged her and set her down again. "How's my storybook princess? And where's your stinky brother?"

"I'm good. He's playing video games even though it's a weekday."

"We'd better go make a citizen's arrest," Dan said.

The buzzer interrupted this interdiction, followed by the crackling baritone of Washington Lee on the intercom. The elevator soon debouched Washington and his wife, Veronica, Russell's best friend natty in a black suit and crisp white shirt; his wife, who worked for Lehman Brothers, wearing a businessy charcoal suit. Russell dragged Jack into the group, introducing him to all as the author of the most brilliant collection of short stories he had ever had the privilege to publish.

What about Jeff? Corrine thought. What about our dead friend?

"Jack's from Fairview, Tennessee," Russell said, relishing, she knew, the idea of gritty Americana. Much as Russell liked his adoptive home, this slender, crowded island at the eastern edge of the continent, he believed in his heart that America was elsewhere, off in the South or the West, the big sprawling vistas beyond the tired ramparts of the Appalachians; that the country's literature was about the strong, silent men and women of the hollows and the heartland—although to judge from Jack's stories, which showcased babbling, toothless speed freaks, they were no longer necessarily silent.

"So did you vote for the cracker or the brother?" Washington asked him.

"Are we to assume you're inquiring about the Senate race in Tennessee?" Russell asked.

"Indeed, Corker versus Ford," Washington said.

"I think they both suck," Jack said, catching everyone by surprise.

"Well, sure, but there are degrees of suckiness," Washington said. "Last time I checked, Ford wasn't running ads that implied Corker fucked black girls." Typical Washington, Corrine noted, making assumptions about racism based on accent. Come to think of it, the kid *could* be a racist, for all she knew. But if he acted like one, Washington would eat him alive. He'd always relished playing the race card, using his blackness when it suited him; the only thing he enjoyed more than twisting liberal white people into pretzels of self-consciousness was messing with unreconstructed racists.

"Wash, *please*," Corrine said.

"Hey, I got no secrets," Jack said. "I wrote in Kid Rock."

Corrine laughed, relieved at how neatly he'd defused the situation. It was a pretty funny joke—even funnier if it was true.

Jeremy had emerged from his room, as if intuiting the arrival of Dan, with whom he had an easy rapport, and asked to see his gun, as he inevitably did.

"I thought you told me you were a Democrat," Dan said.

"So what?" Jeremy said.

"Well," Dan said, directing an impish look at Corrine, "if the Democrats win, nobody will be allowed to carry guns except criminals."

Jack said something that sounded like "Wut chu packin?"

"A Sig P226."

"That's a great gun," Jack said. "I was shooting one a few days ago with my buddy. Let me check it out."

Corrine refrained from protest as Jeremy, Jack and Dan lovingly examined the lethal black-and-silver pistol, though she hovered at the edge of the group, ready to pounce if anyone let Jeremy touch it.

Nancy Tanner showed up just as Chef Russell was complaining about her tardiness. Nancy was back in the city after a stint in Los Angeles, working as a producer on a Showtime adaptation of her last book. She looked better than ever, thin and sculpted, and Corrine couldn't help wondering if she'd had any work done out there.

"How are my favorite preppy bohemians?" Nancy said, kissing Corrine on both cheeks, and then, to Washington and Veronica: "And how's life in Cheever country?" They'd fled to New Canaan in the wake of September 11, then moved back to the city this summer in time for the school year, buying a loft a few blocks away in a converted tool and die factory, although this news hadn't yet reached Nancy.

"I think we found out why Cheever drank so much," said Washington.

"It was horrible," Veronica said. "We thought we were doing it for the kids, but if anything, they hated it even more than we did."

"And everyone thought I was the help," Washington said.

"Now you're exaggerating, Wash."

"Fucking dudes in madras shorts trying to hire me to cut the lawn."

"Stop it."

"'Hey, *boy,* can you carry my golf clubs?'"

"He's only slightly exaggerating. Even the dog hated it."

"And Mingus got Lyme disease."

"Who knew the yard was lousy with ticks."

"The *dog* got Lyme disease."

"Everybody up there has it. It's like this fucking epidemic."

"Give me roaches any day. Way better than ticks."

"I was so happy when we moved back to the city and I spotted a roach in the sink."

"I could've told you it was a mistake to move to the suburbs," Nancy said. "I grew up there."

"Didn't everybody?" Hilary said.

"We were city kids," Washington said, "Veronica and I. We both grew up in fucking Queens, man. The dream was to trade the tenement for a house with a yard. And it's like we had to live out our parents' immigrant dream of escape to the suburbs. It was encoded in us, ever since Veronica's mother fled Budapest after the revolution and my mom stowed away on a boat from Port of Spain: *Go to America, work hard, eat shit, scrub floors, and someday your children will live in Westchester.* And Veronica's mom—ever since she was a little girl she wanted her daughter to live in New Canaan. Anyway, it's over, our little American dream turned nightmare. We're back, baby. Solid concrete and asphalt underfoot. Skyscrapers and everything. Just like I pictured it. Yellow limos at my beck and call. Doorman standing at attention, building superintendent at the other end of the intercom whenever you blow a fuse or a fucking lightbulb. City life's the life for me."

"I don't know," Russell said after a slug of champagne, "nobody loves New York more than I do, but I feel like the city's getting suburbanized itself. Less diverse, less edgy. It's more like New Canaan than like the city we moved to."

Corrine said, "Let's not get nostalgic for the era of muggings and graffiti and crack vials in the hallway." She'd almost said AIDS but stopped herself in time. She didn't want to scratch that scar right now, in the opening hour of a dinner party with strangers in the house. She wasn't about to talk about Jeff. But it was too late—he was here in the room with her, with his tobacco-inflected scent—back then almost everything smelled like tobacco, Jeff only a little more so, layered over a leathery smell that she'd never encountered since. Everyone has an olfactory signature, if only we're attuned to it, and she'd been attuned to his. What they called chemistry, she suspected, had mostly to do with smell. She'd felt it again, the other night, with Luke. When we form a snap judgment, and don't know why. We're animals first. And she'd loved Jeff's scent, even though he was Russell's best friend. It had only happened on a couple of occasions. But the eventual revelation had almost wrecked their marriage. Eighteen years now—he'd died in '88, in the great epidemic.

To break the spell, she said, "Remember those sidewalk paintings that looked like crime-scene silhouettes—how you couldn't tell if it was graffiti or a homicide? Who was that artist?"

"What about stepping on crack vials?" Washington added. "On the Upper West Side it was like acorns in a goddamn forest."

"New York in the eighties," Jack said. "That must've been rad." And at that moment something in his manner, his youth, his slouching posture reminded her of Jeff.

"We didn't know it was the eighties at the time," Washington said. "No one told us until about 1987, and by then it was almost over."

5

THE SUMMER AFTER GRADUATION, Jeff is subletting a *loft* in SoHo. The word itself seems as raffish and bohemian as the neighborhood, half-deserted, inhabited mainly by painters and sculptors in search of cheap studio space. The district is zoned for light industry and it's illegal to actually *live* here, which only adds to its mystique. Jeff is cat-sitting for a girl he knows who's touring with her band for three months, and who, in turn, sublets the place illegally from a painter living in Berlin. It's just the kind of convoluted and jerry-rigged yet serendipitous situation in which Jeff inevitably seems to find himself, or, more accurately, in which he manages to place himself.

Having recently graduated from Brown, Corrine lives on the Upper East Side and works at Sotheby's. To her, SoHo is terra incognita, a mysterious southern region of the island allegedly inhabited by artists and who knows who. No one who's gone to Miss Porter's, certainly. It seems a little eerie to her, almost deserted, as she emerges from the subway at Prince Street and walks west, her shadow inching out across the buckling sidewalk, the ornate, soot-stained facades of the buildings that had once been sweatshops and factories. She passes a heavily bearded man in overalls sitting on a stoop, smoking; she would guess he's homeless except for the paint caked on his fingers and his OshKosh overalls. For all she knows, he could be James Rosenquist or Frank Stella.

She can't help feeling very adventurous coming down here on her own, almost tingling with anticipation as she approaches Greene

Street. Jeff offered to come uptown, but she insisted on seeing his place. Later she will cross-examine herself about her motives.

Russell's at Oxford on his fellowship, studying Romantic poetry. He writes her long letters about his reading and the quirkiness of the Brits and the horrors of Marmite, letters that inevitably culminate in declarations of love. They can't afford to talk long-distance more than once or twice a month. In his mind they're already engaged, but she's been very specific in telling him to see how he feels after eight months apart. It's been six weeks, and already he's worried that she'll meet someone else. She hasn't met anyone, and visiting Russell's best friend feels like a way of being closer to him.

She finds the building, with its elaborately ornamented cast-iron facade—grimy columns framing tall, arched windows, the rust showing in patches through the layers of once-white paint and city grit. Corrine, an art history major, can't help noticing that Corinthian, with its fluted columns and complicated acanthus leaves and scrolls, was the classical order favored by the nineteenth-century architects who created the neighborhood. On the sidewalk in front of the building is a splattered black human silhouette that looks like it might be a crime-scene outline of a body.

At the door, a cluster of mismatched buzzers is mounted on a sheet of plywood, one of them labeled with a scrap of yellow legal paper on which the initials J.P. are scrawled. She presses the button and waits, eventually looking up when a window above rattles open and Jeff's head emerges.

"You sure you want to come up?"

"Absolutely," she says. "I've never seen an artist's loft."

"It ain't pretty." He dangles something from his fingers. "Catch."

A key attached to a piece of dirty balsa wood clatters to the sidewalk.

"Fifth floor," he calls. "Can't miss it."

Inside, she's confronted with a vast creaking stairway composed of ancient oak planks that recedes as it ascends ahead of her, each floor taking her farther back into the building, until finally she finds herself on the top floor, where the door stands ajar. "Not exactly a stairway to heaven," Jeff says, bowing deeply and ushering her in, hunching slightly to make his height less daunting. He's wearing his standard outfit, an untucked Brooks Brothers button-down shirt over a pair of ripped jeans.

"Please don't say 'Welcome to my humble abode.'"

"I was going to say my cleaning lady died, but I don't actually have one."

"It's very . . . lived-in."

"I was also going to say this is where the magic doesn't happen."

It's a mess—clothes and books and overflowing ashtrays everywhere, but the space itself is grand, with a soaring pressed-tin ceiling supported by more columns, and huge arched windows on either end. One wall is dominated by a long graffiti mural, all swirls and distorted letters and fanciful animals, by an artist friend of his, he explains when she asks about it, who painted it recently after partying all night in the loft.

"That's such a stupid verb, *partying*," she says. "I mean, really, don't you think? It's so coy. What does it mean—does it mean drinking? Doing drugs? Having sex? All of the above?" This sounds prissy and pedantic even to her and she realizes she is nervous, though she isn't sure why, exactly.

At one end of the room, a mattress floats on the wide floorboards like a dilapidated barge, the bedding in disarray. At the other end, a door rests on two filing cabinets—a makeshift desk with a big beige IBM Selectric perched between stacks of books. Russell has been jealous of Jeff's typewriter for years—the ultimate writing machine. In between, an island of decrepit furniture suggests a living area: a brown legless couchlike object, a beanbag chair, and in the role of coffee table, a surfboard supported on either end by cinder blocks.

"Originally, Seventy-seven Greene Street was one of New York's most notorious cathouses," Jeff tells her. "When that building burned down, this came next and housed a corset factory for many years."

"Unfettered wantonness yielding to the creation of feminine fetters."

"Relentless," Jeff says, "the march of civilization."

For all its shabbiness, the sheer expanse and the architectural details give it the aura of a place where great deeds should be performed, great paintings painted, or even a great novel written—and that, she knows, is his sole ambition, though he carries himself with a self-deprecating cynicism and has so far published only a single short story in *The Paris Review*. But it's his whole identity: Jeff Pierce, the writer, the *poète maudit*. When he read *The Sun Also Rises* at the age of thirteen, his destiny was revealed. Robert Lowell is some kind of distant uncle. At Brown he walked around with a copy of *Ulysses* under his arm and studied with John Hawkes, the avant-garde novelist, who vouched for his genius. He was one of the few non–New Yorkers at Brown who visited Manhattan frequently, eschewing the traditional landmarks of his classmates—Trader Vic's and '21' and Dorrian's Red Hand—in favor of poetry readings and punk-rock clubs downtown. Somewhere along the line, he became acquainted with William Burroughs, who, he says, now lives in a former YMCA gym on the Bowery.

A black-and-white cat appears and rubs itself fervently against Jeff's leg. She remembers this about him—animals always like him. "That's Kurt Weill," Jeff says as the cat slides away.

"I might have known," she says.

He offers her a Marlboro, and lights it, and then his own, with a Zippo. It gives them something to do together, and something to do with their hands. They all smoke, all the time, everywhere—at home and in bars and restaurants, in movie theaters and on airplanes.

"Why do you always have the collars of your button-downs unbuttoned?" she asks. "Have you ever thought of getting the regular kind of collars, without buttons? It seems like it would be easier. I mean, if you're not going to button them anyway."

"Not really. I like having the option."

She's just making conversation, knowing this is one of his signatures, like his grandfather's old gold Longines, which he wears with the face on the inside of his wrist. Not that he would ever tell you himself; he does his best to distance himself from his heritage, but Jeff comes from one of those old New England families that view the Pilgrims as arrivistes. They wear threadbare blazers with Wellingtons and drive shit brown Oldsmobiles. Some have lots of money, others only the memory of it. Even those who've escaped the gravity of Boston tend in the summers to cluster in rambling shingled houses on the rocky Protestant coast of Maine, occasionally traversing the pebbly beaches to dunk themselves in the frigid waters of the Atlantic, more often sailing the surface in wooden boats. But Jeff has come to downtown Manhattan to reinvent himself from scratch, or so he likes to believe, though he's likewise determined to remain true, in some sense, to his roots, to be at once authentic and unique. His grandfather's watch might seem to complicate the self-invention narrative; on the other hand, it distinguishes the wearer from the aspiring bohemian herd. Just as William Burroughs, the famous junkie and wife killer, dresses in three-piece suits.

"So," she says, inhaling a lungful of smoke. "What does one do downtown?"

"Drugs," he says.

"Very funny."

"You asked."

His demeanor is a blend of boyish and smug, and she sees that he is actually serious. Serious, but also amused at his own cleverness, his knowingness. He wants to shock her, even as he wants to invite her into the circle of forbidden knowledge. She's smoked pot with him before, so she knows it isn't that.

"What, cocaine?"

He beams. "Ever tried it?"

She shakes her head.

"Want to?"

Of course she doesn't want to seem like a—what, a wimp, a prude, uncool? But still . . . *cocaine*? She knew some kids at Brown did it, city kids who went back to Manhattan on weekends and hung at Studio 54 and Xenon, then bragged about it back in Providence. But Corrine isn't that kind of girl, is she?

"No pressure," he says.

"What are you saying?" she says. "That we would, like, do it . . . now?" She seems unable even to name the drug, and knows that she is stalling for time, trying to decide what she feels about this totally unexpected proposition.

"Well, yeah."

She trusts Jeff and doesn't think he'd lure her into anything really dangerous. On the other hand, that's the whole thing about Jeff; he *is* more reckless than the rest of their crowd at Brown, the guy who wrapped an Austin-Healey around a telephone pole outside of Providence and walked away unscathed. That's one of the reasons they're all attracted to him.

"You have some?"

"I wouldn't offer you any if I didn't have it."

"Will I like it?"

"I personally guarantee it."

She shrugs. "Okay." This is definitely one way to cut through the awkwardness of the moment. "I don't even know how you do it," she says.

She follows him over to the makeshift desk; he clears books and papers away and picks up a framed picture, an almost-familiar sepia-toned image of a beautiful boy with flyaway hair and sleepy eyes, in disheveled Edwardian garb. Suddenly, it comes to her. "Rimbaud?"

He nods and lays the frame flat, unfolding a rectangle of shiny paper on the glass, as if creating some sort of origami.

After tipping the contents of the unfurled packet onto the glass, he chops it up with a one-edged razor blade and lays out eight identical lines of white powder.

She can't help giggling when he hands her a short plastic straw. "Are we really going to do this? I'm not sure I know how. Why don't I watch you do it first?"

He takes the straw and leans over the glass, neatly inhaling one of the white lines and then, moving the straw to his left nostril, another.

"Wow, you're good at that."

"It's like anything else. Like how you get to Carnegie Hall."

"What?"

"Practice."

"Oh, right, sorry." Why is she suddenly feeling so slow-witted?

"Your turn."

She takes the straw and bends down over the desk. As she leans forward, Jeff gathers the hair around her neck and holds it, which seems very sexy to her and also makes the thing she is about to do seem less dangerous.

She can only manage to inhale half of a line the first time. It's a very weird sensation, a not entirely unpleasant burning in her nasal passages, and then, a few minutes later, a bittersweet drip at the back of her throat. After several tries, she consumes two of the lines and feels very pleased with herself. Having been a little afraid and uncertain, she now congratulates herself on being brave and going for it. Nothing scary here. She feels almost normal, except better than normal.

"I think I'm feeling it, but I'm not sure," she says. "I feel good but not, like, stoned. You know, I've never really liked pot, to tell you the truth, that feeling of not being myself, of being kind of slowed down and dumbed down. That *dopey* feeling. No wonder they call it dope, right? But now I feel like myself. But sort of, I don't know, a really upbeat version of myself. Is that the cocaine? Because actually I feel pretty great. I feel like, I don't know, like *doing* something."

Jeff smiles and nods.

"Say something."

"*Something.*"

"You're teasing me. Am I talking too much? I'm talking too much, aren't I? Is that the cocaine? Is that what it does?"

"It comes with the territory."

"But why aren't you talking as much as I am?"

"Be careful what you wish for."

Jeff leans down and snorts another line, then kneels down to riffle through a stack of LPs on the floor beside the stereo, selecting a record and placing it on the turntable.

"I like that," Corrine says of the wailing guitars and whining, world-weary vocals.

"It's Television," Jeff says.

She looks back down at the stereo, wondering if that was a joke. She often feels this way in Jeff's company, as though she is missing out on some inside reference. Maybe the drug is messing with her perception, although, in fact, she feels incredibly clearheaded and sharp at the moment.

"It's a stereo," she says.

"Television's the name of the band. Unfortunately, no longer with us. I saw them in '78 at CBGB."

"Oh, right," she says. The singer's voice is very nasal and adenoidal—maybe he did cocaine? What *is* he singing? She listens for the next chorus. "I fell right into the arms of Venus de Milo." It takes her a minute. And then, she says, "Very clever. I get it. Better late than never, I guess. You must think I'm very uncool, basically."

"I've never thought that. I think you're amazing."

"I don't know the new music, or even the new art. I mean, I'm good up to Jasper Johns and Rauschenberg, the Stones and Led Zeppelin, but after that . . . " She shrugs. "I feel like rock and roll kind of petered out a few years ago, but that's probably just me. Is Led Zeppelin still cool? How do you find these things out? I mean, is there some committee that decides? A bunch of cool kids in leather jackets, smoking bidis, who sit around and pronounce on these issues? Whoever they are, they don't have my telephone number. And my taste in literature is pretty conventional. I tried, but I couldn't get past the first twenty pages of *Naked Lunch*. And that book you gave me last month, *Finnegan's Stew*?"

"*Mulligan Stew*, by Gilbert Sorrentino. Finnegan was Joyce. *Finnegans Wake*. Although curiously enough a character from *Finnegans Wake* turns up in *Mulligan Stew*."

"That's what I mean—a novel within a novel within a novel, all that postmodern self-consciousness. A writer writing a book about a writer writing a book. Jesus, I'm sorry, I just get lost. I like Edith Wharton and Anthony Powell and Graham Greene. I'm just not hip enough. I live on East 71st Street and I belong to the Colony Club and the Daughters of the American Revolution. You grew up in the same world I did, but you've sort of rejected all that."

"That doesn't define you. You're so much more than that. I don't believe in types, I believe in individuals. I believe in *you*. You're like no one else. I don't know anyone else at all like you. You don't judge. You're the least judgmental, least prejudiced person I know. You take everyone at his own worth. You look at a picture and see things nobody else does. You're smart. You're funny. You don't accept conventional wisdom. You're beautiful."

"You really believe all that?" Corrine is amazed. She always imagined that Jeff was judging her and finding her wanting. She thought that each of what she considered to be her secret flaws were glaringly obvious to Russell's smart, cynical, good-looking best friend. More than she's ever been willing to admit, she craves his approval, even his admiration. Actually, she wants him to love her, she realizes. That doesn't necessarily mean that she loves him, but she wants him to want her, and she certainly *wants* him, never more so than right this minute. He seems to divine this sentiment, stepping toward her and touching her cheek, cradling her face in his hand and guiding her toward his lips, kissing her avidly, almost violently, pressing his lips against hers and probing between them with his tongue, Corrine returning the ardor as she puts her arms around his shoulders and pulls him closer.

It feels as if there's no time to spare, that after so long a wait they need to seize the moment immediately. He lifts her in his arms and carries her to the bed without taking his lips from hers. They struggle out of their clothes as if they are on fire, she tugging his belt open as he scrabbles at the hook of her bra. She finds herself undoing her belt, unzipping her jeans and stepping out of them. His jeans are still wrapped around his ankles when, twisted on top of her, he pushes himself inside of her. Some sort of animal sound escapes her and then she thrusts her hips upward, finding a rhythm as she races toward her goal. She's never felt so driven, so desperate, and even the inevitable thought of Russell fails to quell—seems even to fan—her desire. She has never before come so quickly, just a little ahead of him, and it occurs to her as she returns to her body and her senses to wonder about the drug's influence, although she has imagined this experience more than once—she's been wildly infatuated with Jeff since they met—and she finds it hard to believe that she will ever regret it. Later, however, she will question the postcoital conviction that she was somehow bringing herself closer to Russell by fucking his best friend.

That just might have been the drugs talking.

6

JACK DIDN'T QUITE KNOW what to expect from a Manhattan dinner party, but so far he felt like a rube—which actually was pretty much what he'd expected. He felt like he was watching a movie, an updated version of one of those Depression-era New York flicks in which all the characters were ridiculously good-looking and witty. He wouldn't have been totally surprised if one of his publisher's friends had suddenly started belting out "Puttin' on the Ritz," although the stage itself was a little shabby, a little more *After Hours* than *Dinner at Eight.*

"We didn't know it was the eighties at the time," Washington was saying. "It was just the present. Does anyone ever have a feeling of living in a particular decade? I mean, do you feel right now, right this minute, like you're living in the aughts? Is that what we call them? Are we somehow acting out the zeitgeist here and now? Are we exhibiting aughtness? I sure as hell don't remember being aware it was the eighties back then."

"I'm not sure Russell and Corrine *ever* knew it was the eighties," Nancy said. "They were like these elegant throwbacks to the twenties, having these chic little parties. The rest of us were living in hovels, illegal sublets in the East Village and shared railroad flats in Hell's Kitchen, eating pizza and lo mein out of boxes while they were serving cocktails and canapés on the Upper East Side. Poster children for the good life, the perfect couple—while everybody else was single and searching and scruffy. Russell even had a velvet smoking jacket. It was all very Scott and Zelda, Nick and Nora."

"Now you're mixing your periods," Washington said.

"I'll have you know," Russell said, "I published a book by Keith Haring."

"You are so fucking hip," Washington said. To the others: "Russell went to the Mudd Club one night in a blue blazer and chinos. I shit you not. Everybody thought he was being ironic."

"It was authentic," Russell said. "I yam what I yam."

"Before anyone romanticizes the eighties any further," Nancy said, "I have two words: Milli Vanilli."

"Talk about authentic."

Jack decided not to ask what the fuck Milli Vanilli was.

Eventually, when they were all finally seated at the dinner table, Russell stood up and raised his glass. "I'd like to toast old friends and new, and in particular to welcome Jack Carson to our fair city." Even as he shrank away from this unexpected beam of attention, this turning of all eyes in the room on him, the rube among the sophisticates, dressed like a bum, with the manners to match, Jack thought, defensively, *Nobody says our fair city anymore, do they?* He was relieved to hear his famous Manhattan editor sounding so dorky.

"Two years ago," Russell was saying, "my assistant urged me to look at some unpublished stories posted on Myspace, and I couldn't have been more skeptical. In fact, I wasn't even sure what Myspace was."

Washington said, "He still thinks the Internet is a passing fad."

"But I eventually read the stories and I was *blown away*. It was like Raymond Carver and Breece D'J Pancake had had a love child—"

"That is so gross," Nancy interjected.

"Breece D' what?" Hilary asked.

"And at the same time, it was unlike anything I'd ever read before. So please raise a glass to our new friend and his masterful book, which I'm more than honored to be publishing."

Jack didn't know what the hell he was supposed to do or where to look. He'd never been the object of a toast before. For that matter, he wasn't sure he'd ever been to an actual dinner party before, unless you counted the odd Thanksgiving or barbecues at his uncle Walt's. This was all very . . . *civilized,* Russell and Corrine like two glamorous parents presiding over some kind of *salon.* If his stepfather could see him now, he'd say, *What, you think you're fucking special?*

After disappearing for a few minutes, Washington returned to the table, clinked his fork against his wineglass repeatedly until he mostly had their attention. "Ladies and germs, it appears Eliot Spitzer is our new governor."

"Big surprise," Dan said. "But just remember, New York isn't America."

"Thank God for that," Nancy said. "Isn't that why we all came here in the first place?"

"Better be careful comin' to my part of America with that attitude," Jack said before he could check himself. He hadn't meant to say it out loud, but in his nervousness he'd already guzzled two vodkas and two glasses of wine.

"Darn tootin'," Hilary slurred.

"Honey," Corrine said, "tell us about the wine." Apparently, this was a play she'd called more than once. And sure enough, old Russell got up and yammered on about the wine, which apparently came from Spain. Washington threw a piece of bread at him. Jack couldn't help laughing, finally recognizing at least one dinner ritual.

After Russell sat down, Corrine turned to Jack and said, "I don't know when I've seen Russell as excited about a book as he is about yours."

"Shitfire, ma'am, pardon my French, but I grew up readin' the books he published," he said, obligingly pouring on the backwoods accent for her benefit. "Gettin' published by Russell, it's like signin' with the fuckin' Yankees. Coming from where I come from, the idea that I'd ever publish a book at all was just pie in the sky."

It was becoming impossible to ignore Hilary, directly across the table, who seemed to have consumed a hell of a lot of Russell's wine, judging by the volume of her voice. "You fucking liberals are so predictable," she said, toppling her wineglass with a dismissive wave of her arm, spattering Spanish red all over the table.

"You right wingers are so fucking *violent*," Washington said, brushing a few drops from the sleeve of his jacket.

"That was an accident."

"Yeah, and so was the Tuskegee experiment."

"Hey," said Russell, mopping up the spill with his dinner napkin.

"What the hell is that?" demanded Hilary.

"U.S. Public Health Service used six hundred Negroes as guinea pigs to study the effects of untreated syphilis."

"Oh, *right*."

"Google it."

"I will."

Corrine, in despair, turned to Jack. "Is this your first Manhattan dinner party?"

"Yes, ma'am."

"Sorry, we're usually slightly better behaved."

"Back home we don't consider it a party till blood's been drawn. Last Thanksgiving my uncle stabbed my aunt with the electric carving knife."

"Oh my God! Was she okay?"

"She was fine. It wasn't plugged in at the time. They stitched her up and sent her home that night."

"Are they still married?"

"Not exactly. She shot him dead a few months later." This part wasn't exactly true. She shot him in the arm and he drove himself to the same clinic that had sewed her up at Thanksgiving, but Jack assumed he had a role to play here and didn't want to disappoint anybody.

"Oh my God," she said again.

"He had the emphysema bad, so it was only a matter of time," he drawled. As both a southerner and a fiction writer, he hated for the facts to get in the way of a good story.

"What about your parents?" she asked.

"Well, my dad left before I was born. He was a musician. My mom met him in Nashville; she was only with him for a few months before he hit the road. Then there was the meth dealer and then Cliff, my so-called stepfather, who did a little of everythin' and a whole lot of nothin'. My mom shoulda shot his goddamn ass but never did. Woulda been a service to humanity. I thought about doin' it myself. In the end, I knocked him senseless with an ax and went to juvie."

Corrine looked pained, and Jack almost felt bad. Clearly she hadn't read the stories yet.

"The French were right about the Iraq War," Russell was saying. "Back when all these jerkoffs were boycotting French wine and cheese and calling french fries 'freedom fries,' I was calling cheeseburgers *fromage* burgers and boycotting California wines."

"Big fucking sacrifice," Washington said. "You haven't drunk a wine from California in years."

"Wait," Nancy said. "I thought *Spain* was the new France."

"The point is," Russell said, "if you're going to boycott the products of a country based on disagreeing with their foreign policy, then those of us who think the Iraq debacle was the most ill-advised and un-justified shoot-'em-up since Vietnam should be boycotting American products."

"That's easy," Washington said. "America hardly makes anything anymore."

"What about Harley-Davidsons?" Jack said.

"And Levi's."

"Nope, sorry. Made in China."

"We do make cruise missiles and stealth bombers."

"Weapons of mass destruction."

"We've met the enemy and he is us."

"Fiction," Russell said. "We still do fiction really well. American literature's alive and well. When I first got into publishing, everyone said the novel was dead, that our generation wasn't reading. Since then we've seen, like, two or three generations of American novelists come of age."

"Tell it to the Nobel Prize committee," Washington said.

Hilary was regaling Veronica about the TV pilot she and Dan were trying to pitch, based on his career as a cop in Brooklyn. "This is, like, totally authentic, not like those bullshit cop shows. Dan was on the force for twenty years. He knows where the bodies are buried." This

Hilary is kind of hot, Jack thought, if not exceptionally smart—a not atypical combo—and he was fascinated by Corrine's barely concealed contempt for her.

"As a cop," Russell said, "wasn't he supposed to tell somebody where the bodies were buried before now?"

Jack went back to trying to entertain his hostess with tales of crystal meth in the land of moonshine. "The meth business, it's all in the family," he said. "You got three generations cookin' crystal in the kitchen. Course, there ain't a big age gap between the generations. Momma's thirty-three and Gran's forty-five. And they're all losin' their teeth thanks to the crystal and the co'cola. *Toothless in Fairview.* That could be the title of my book."

"Shit, round here meth's strictly a gay thing," Washington said. "Wealthy decorators and film producers trolling the bathhouses wired to the gills."

"I can't believe you said decorators," Corrine said. "That's such a stereotype."

"A gay thing?" Jack was appalled. "Meth? Fuck me. Who woulda thought? Seemed to me like us rednecks owned that shit."

Corrine said, "Didn't the bathhouses shut down in the eighties?"

Washington shook his head and poured another glass of wine, so Jack held his out for a refill.

"They're back," Washington said. "These guys start on a Friday night, do meth and Viagra and go at it all weekend."

"It's true," Russell said.

"And we know this how?" Corrine asked.

"I know a guy, Juan Baptiste. He's into the scene."

"The *Voice* columnist."

"Does the *Voice* still exist?"

"It's a giveaway now."

Jack was struggling to keep up. He had to stop drinking before he totally lost his grip in front of these people and said or did something stupid. "What voice?" he said.

"*The Village Voice,*" Corrine said. "It was the hipster alternative weekly when we first came to New York."

"Norman Mailer started it. We all used to read it to figure out what our politics should be and what music to listen to."

"Mailer's cool," Jack said, latching onto a familiar bearing. "Specially *Advertisements for Myself.*"

"I once played pool with him," Russell said.

"But then it got pretty gay," Nancy said.

"What, Mailer?" Jack asked, confused.

"No, the *Voice.*"

"God, we're dating ourselves here," Corrine said. "Let's turn on CNN and find out about the midterms."

Russell protested, complaining that they hadn't served the cheese yet.

"I hate this cheese thing," Corrine muttered to Jack.

"Cheese?" Jack wondered if that was code for something else.

"Another thing we borrowed from the French. It became fashionable in Manhattan about ten years ago. You finish a giant meal and then gorge on semirancid dairy."

"Yeah, I don't actually see the point of that," Jack said. "Where I come from, we got something called dessert."

"That comes after the cheese," she said.

Despite her age, he was surprised to find Russell's wife sexy—in a refined, untouchable kind of way. To his mind she looked as he imagined the temptress suburban housewives in Updike would look. They would be so cool and collected right up to the minute they grabbed your crotch behind the pool house while their husbands were playing croquet on the lawn a few yards away. He couldn't help imagining how sexy, because unexpected, the grunts and groans of passion emerging from such an elegant creature would be. He felt totally weird fantasizing about fucking his editor's wife, so he tried thinking about Nancy, right across the table and also pretty hot for a chick her age.

Eventually, after he reminded himself that these people were from another planet and might have totally different genitals, the group moved away from the table and Corrine switched on the television so they could all check on the elections. It looked as if the Democrats would take the House and the Senate. Russell sat on the back of the couch behind Corrine, running his hand through her hair. Jack found it kind of sweet. He'd never seen a married couple touch like that.

Wolf Blitzer announced that CNN was predicting that Nancy Pelosi would be the first female Speaker of the House in history.

"California knee-jerk liberals," Hilary shouted. She was pretty wasted. Her lips seemed to be congealing around her words.

"She ought to know," Corrine said to Russell. "She slept with half of Hollywood." She'd probably intended the remark for his ears only, but by chance it pierced a brief moment of silence in what up to then had been relentless clamor.

Hilary spun in Corrine's direction and fixed her with a blurry look of hurt reproach before storming off in the direction of the bathroom.

"Oh shit," Corrine said. "That was supposed to be sub rosa."

"Wait, check this out," Russell said, pointing at the TV screen, which showed a photograph of a middle-aged dude. Blitzer was saying, *"We've received word that American journalist Phillip Kohout has been found alive in Lahore, Pakistan, after allegedly escaping captivity at the hands of terrorists associated with the Taliban. Kohout disappeared almost three months ago while researching a story about terrorism in the North-West Frontier Province of Pakistan. He reportedly made his way to the American consulate in Lahore after escaping from a compound in the nearby suburbs. More on this story as it develops."*

"I didn't know he'd been kidnapped," Corrine said.

"I heard something about it a couple months ago," Russell said.

"Couldn't have happened to a more deserving fellow," Corrine said.

"That's a little harsh," Russell said. He turned to Jack. "An author I published. His first novel was a big success."

"After which he dumped you," Corrine added.

"Well, he screwed me out of the option on his second book. But I don't think that warrants two months wearing a black hood in Waziristan."

Suddenly, Storey, the daughter, appeared in her nightgown, looking distraught, and ran across the room to Corrine. "Aunt Hilary says you're not my real mother! She says *she's* my mother."

Hilary followed in Storey's wake, looking like someone determined to maintain her sense of righteousness even as she was starting to lose her conviction. Jack couldn't believe this shit—Storey clutching her mother's waist, Corrine lifting and enfolding her in a desperate hug and Russell advancing on Hilary.

"Did you really do that, you bitch?"

"She's deserves to know the truth. You can't hide it forever."

"You fucking cunt," Russell said, backing her against the wall.

"You can't talk to my girlfriend like that," Dan said, rushing up, grabbing Russell's shoulder to spin him around and throwing a punch that caught him squarely on the cheek, sending him back against the wall with a thud. Russell staggered to his feet and took a swing at Dan, barely grazing his rib cage.

For a moment Jack couldn't locate the source of the wail of pain that echoed through the loft, until he saw Jeremy standing in the hallway, staring at his father, who was propped against the wall, stunned, holding a hand to his cheek.

Corrine clutched Storey's head to her shoulder and marched straight at Dan and Hilary. "Please leave, both of you." As Jeremy howled again and Storey began sobbing, her fury redoubled. "Get out! Get the hell out! Right now!"

Jack hadn't noticed Washington since the onset of hostilities, until he scooped up Jeremy in one arm and pointed at Dan with the other. "You heard the lady," he said. "Get your sorry cracker asses the fuck out of here."

Jack wasn't entirely sure what he'd just witnessed, although the general tenor of family rancor and violence was reassuringly familiar. For the first time all night he felt nearly at ease. Apparently, these people weren't as different as he'd first imagined.

7

CORRINE WOKE FEELING CLOUDY AND ANXIOUS, experiencing a sinking dread as she reviewed the evening's absurd and mortifying climax. As many outrages as her sister had committed over the years, this was truly the most unforgivable.

She found Russell out in the kitchen, finishing off the dishes, a fresh blue-and-yellow bruise on his left cheek.

"Ouch," she said. "Does it hurt?"

"Only when I breathe." He poured her a cup of coffee from the French press.

"I still can't believe it. When I woke up just now, I thought, There's no way that actually happened."

"On a happier note, the Democrats took control of both houses."

She heard a thump from one of the kids' rooms. "Oh shit," she said. "We're going to have to have a serious talk. But first we've got to figure out what to say."

"Fucking Hilary."

"Really. Hilary the C-U-N-T. You were so great, Russell. I never thought I'd approve of anyone using that word. Ever. But I couldn't think of a more appropriate deployment."

"Well, I've always believed there is a precise word or phrase for every need, and that was the exact word for the occasion. And by the way, she's banned from our threshold henceforth."

"You won't hear an argument from me."

"Persona non grata."

"I think we need to talk to the kids right away."

"Yeah, you're right. But not this morning. Too much to process. I'll come home early tonight and we'll have a family dinner."

Sometimes, just when she needed him most, Russell came through for her, and she suddenly experienced a little shudder of guilt about her recent preoccupation with Luke.

The kids were unusually quiet, and even manageable, as if fearful of what might happen next. Russell took them off to school, promising to get home early. Corrine poured a second cup of coffee and tried to plan her day. She had to go to the office and organize Saturday's food giveaway in Harlem, but she also knew that she wouldn't really be able to concentrate—the combination of a little too much wine at dinner and being completely distracted by the situation that Hilary had created.

How many times had she asked herself why she'd chosen her as an egg donor, her irresponsible, coked-out, slutty little sister, and yet, to question that decision was to question the children's very identity; they were, for better and for worse, hatched from Hilary's eggs, and she couldn't repent the choice without in some fundamental respect renouncing the result. She couldn't imagine loving her children more completely, and at this point days and even weeks went by when she never once thought of the circumstances of their conception, because she could not possibly have felt more like their mother. For most of human history, being a mother meant bearing young from your womb. She'd always imagined that they were out there in the void, waiting for her, these little souls, and that after years of struggle and miscarriage and failed in vitro fertilizations she'd discovered a way to reel them in. She believed they were hers; she would never allow herself to be swayed by mere biology.

But now she was scared, riddled with doubts, most specifically that they would love her less when they found out the facts, that they'd blame her for not being who they had so implicitly believed her to be, or, worst of all, that they would gravitate toward Hilary, their real mother, their flesh and blood. She'd once had a nightmare in which her sister and Russell had run away together with the children. She sometimes masochistically imagined the day in the not too distant future when one or both would ask if they could live with Aunt Hilary. She was haunted, too, by something Hilary had said that summer they'd all shared the house in Sagaponack while they were coordinating their menstrual cycles and Russell was shooting Hilary up with progesterone, sticking a giant needle in her ass filled with a substance distilled from the urine of menopausal women: "It's not natural, what we're doing." Hilary was drunk and probably coked-up after having stayed out half the night, rebelling against the strict regimen of temperance and injections they'd been observing the entire month, but Corrine sometimes worried that it was true, that they had tampered with the natural order of things.

All of these worries had preyed on her, but she'd always projected them into the future, hadn't ever suspected they'd have to try to explain exactly what had happened before the kids were old enough to understand the basics of reproduction. How to explain to them that Russell had drawn the line at adoption and hadn't wanted to raise kids that weren't genetically his own, in whom he was afraid he would not see himself. So when it became clear that her eggs weren't good, she'd devised this plan, almost unheard of at the time, to plant Hilary's in her own womb. The fertility doctor had said, when she'd proposed it, "Well, theoretically it's possible." But, as hard as she'd tried, apparently she hadn't considered all of the practicalities.

Checking her e-mails, she accepted an invitation to a screening next week, deleted spam for discount pharmaceuticals and breast enlargement. *Breast enlargement.* As if. Eye lift maybe.

The phone chirped, displaying the name and number of Jean, their part-time housekeeper and nanny. She was calling to say she had a doctor's appointment and couldn't get the kids after school. She sounded weepy, and Corrine was afraid that if she asked what was wrong, she would hear another tale of the cruelty and heartlessness of Jean's girlfriend, Carlotta, who'd been making her miserable for nearly a dozen years now, and Corrine just didn't have time for it this morning. Plus, she thought it was a good idea, today of all days, to pick the kids up herself. So she said, "Don't worry, Jean. Take the afternoon off and we'll see you tomorrow."

Corrine took the subway to her office and spent the morning talking to various food banks in the greater metropolitan area, trying to
secure vegetables that stood half a chance of not being rotten. Not
quite the workday she might have imagined for herself twenty years
ago. After her stint at Sotheby's, she'd embarked on a successful but
ultimately uninspiring stretch as a stockbroker before indulging her
artistic yearnings by taking film courses at NYU, and wrote an adaptation of Graham Greene's *The Heart of the Matter*, which had, against all
odds, and after many years, made the arduous journey to production,
and, just barely, to a few screens. In the heady months leading up to its
release, Russell had managed to get her hired to write the screenplay
for *Youth and Beauty*, the option on which had been renewed by Tug
Barkley's production company, but the project had gone dormant after
two drafts. Later she'd struggled to write about what had happened to
her in the months after September 11, but instead of inspiring a book
or movie, her experience at the soup kitchen had led her to the job at
Nourish New York.

She'd just finished a SlimFast at her desk when Nancy called.

"Oh my God, I'm so hungover."

"Did you go out?" Corrine asked. Sometimes she felt she lived vicari-
ously through Nancy, who was still pursuing the single-girl life that
Corrine had never actually experienced for herself, and that most of
her peers had resigned from a decade ago.

"I went to Bungalow 8 with that handsome young redneck that Russell's publishing. By the time I was fucked-up enough to think about
seducing him, he'd disappeared."

"He does have a roguish, rough-hewn charisma."

"Then I went to some after-hours place where some fan boy tried
to seduce me, but even as drunk as I was, I got a bisexual vibe from
him, and I have so stopped doing *that*. I mean, what is it about me that
attracts fags? Why don't they just stick to their own? I am absolutely
not a fag hag. Do I seem like a fag hag to you?"

"Of course not. So what happened?"

"I'm not sure how I made it home, but I woke up fully clothed in the living room, so I must've been alone. And now I'm literally dying. Excuse me while I go vomit for the third time."

"You're excused."

An old hand at vomiting, Nancy frequently stuck a finger down her throat when she thought she'd eaten too much, or if she felt drunk but wanted to keep drinking. Corrine wasn't entirely unsympathetic, having been there, but she couldn't bring herself to do it anymore—not often, not in a fairly long time—and tried instead to limit her intake of calories. She was relieved, too, that Nancy was too self-absorbed to bring up the Hilary debacle.

Waiting outside the school, Corrine surveyed the parents and the nannies, more of the former than the latter, and more fathers than you'd ever see at the uptown schools—Buckley or St. Bernard's, Chapin or Spence. Here at PS 234, the moms were less uniformly blond than their Upper East Side counterparts, less Chaneled and Ralphed; more messenger bags than Kelly bags. She waved to Karen Cohen and Marge Findlayson, in their puffy parkas and their Uggs, both full-time moms whose involvement in various school committees and projects made her feel inadequate. The din of construction from the giant apartment complex down the street absolved her of the need to say anything to them, and she chose a spot next to hunky Todd, whose last name she'd never picked up, who worked at home as a Web designer while his wife raked it in at J. P. Morgan.

And suddenly the kids were pouring out, shrieking and howling, hands clutching the straps of their backpacks. And while her children greeted her enthusiastically enough, they grew uncharacteristically subdued on the walk home, and even Rice Krispies Treats from the deli failed to raise their spirits significantly.

Russell came home early, as promised, with the ingredients for the kids' favorite meal, which he adamantly refused to call "chicken tenders," as it was known in certain quarters; he'd actually been known to tell waiters that *tender* was not a noun, unless it referred to a boat that was used to ferry people and supplies to and from a ship. But it was certainly not a part of any chicken. The kids would use the phrase just to wind him up, to hear Dad launch into his tirade. He was willing to call these fried strips of breast meat "chicken fingers," as long as they understood that this was a fanciful association. Whatever they were called, Corrine hated it when he made them, because the batter making and the deep frying trashed the kitchen; he was capable of getting batter on virtually every surface, once even on the ceiling, and he could have easily ordered takeout from Bubby's, just a few blocks away. But the kids were always deeply appreciative, even now that they had moved on to appreciate such grown-up fare as fried calamari and rock shrimp tempura. They still declared loyally that Dad's were better than the restaurant kind, and perhaps they were. At any rate, tonight it seemed extremely important to enact this family ritual, and she was grateful to Russell for thinking of it.

"Have you thought about what, exactly, we're going to say about last night?" he asked, mixing the batter.

Both children were still in their rooms, allegedly doing homework.

"I think we'll just have to come totally clean. Look, we knew this day was going to come. We've just been putting it off."

The battered chicken hissed and sputtered as he slid it into the oil, protesting as if it were alive. "Too good a fate for your sister," he said, nodding at the pot. "I guess we no longer boil people in oil. I don't suppose she called to apologize?"

Corrine shook her head.

"Well, I'm as ready as I'll ever be," Russell said a few minutes later as he carried a salad and the platter of chicken whatevers to the table and Corrine went to fetch the kids, finding both hunched over their desks.

"Dad made your favorite—chicken tentacles," Corrine said, urging them toward the table.

"Why's he home so early?" Storey asked.

"So he can have a nice dinner with his family."

Once they were seated, Russell inquired about their school day and received a perfunctory answer from Storey.

He cleared his throat. "Now, let's talk about last night. It must have upset you, what Aunt Hilary said."

Storey asked, "Is she really our mother?"

"No, she's not," Russell said. "Your mother's your mother."

"Are you okay, Jeremy?" Corrine said, laying an arm around his shoulders.

He nodded, his eyes suddenly welling with tears, then surrendered to his mother's embrace and sobbed.

"It's okay, honey; nothing's changed."

"Can we still live here?" Storey asked.

"Of course, silly." Russell was being solid and sensibly Dad-like, which was good, since Corrine was on the verge of absolute fucking hysteria.

"She can't take us away?"

"No one can take you away."

"Here's the thing," Corrine said, trying to keep her voice steady. "More than anything in the world we wanted to have you two, but I was having trouble with my eggs—they weren't strong enough—so I had to borrow some eggs."

"Does that mean Dad had sex with Aunt Hilary?" Storey asked.

"Absolutely not," Corrine said.

"You guys know about . . . reproduction?"

"We're *eleven*, Dad," Storey informed him.

"Well, basically, my, uh, sperm was mixed with Hilary's eggs."

"You mean in vitro fertilization," Storey said.

Russell and Corrine exchanged a look. "Well, yes, exactly. And then the fertilized eggs were planted in Mom's . . . in Mom."

"So does that make Hilary our mother?"

It was all Corrine could do to maintain her composure.

"Aunt Hilary helped, but Mom is your only mother," Russell said. "She'll always be your mother."

"She can't take us away?"

"No one can take you away from us," Russell said. "You'll live with us until you're so sick of us that you can't wait to go off to college and pretend you never had any parents at all."

So impressed was she with Russell's performance that night, and the night before, that she felt an upwelling of the love and desire she sometimes feared had gone extinct, and that had lately been eclipsed by Luke's reappearance. But tonight she felt a rekindling of the belief that this was her soul mate, the one person on the planet made especially for her, her Platonic twin. She hadn't felt so close to him in years; when they were finally settled in bed, she kissed his neck and worked her way down his chest, eager to express her gratitude. Russell seemed surprised at first, moaning and arching his back, quickly becoming hard, and she realized it had been months since she'd done this, and when she felt him on the verge, she slid up his chest and slipped him inside and didn't mind that he came almost immediately—took it as compliment, basically—and she fell asleep feeling as happy and fulfilled as she could remember being in a very long time.

8

ONCE AGAIN IT WAS THE HOLIDAY SEASON, that ceaseless cocktail party between Thanksgiving and New Year's, when the city dressed itself in Christmas colors and flaunted its commercial soul, when the compulsive acquisitiveness of the citizenry, directed outward into ritual gift giving, was transmuted into a virtue and moderation into a vice. Mendicant sidewalk Santas rang bells beside buckets dangling from chains on tripods. Doormen were suddenly eager to perform their jobs, opening taxi doors and carrying shopping bags, which were abundant, and maîtres d'hôtel greeted their regulars with extra obsequiousness. As the end of the tax year approached, the philanthropic impulse became more acute. The directors of great museums and charitable foundations awaited the mail as eagerly as did the bankers and analysts and brokers of Wall Street, whose bonuses would soon flood the streets with gold. Fantastical landscapes materialized in the windows of Saks and Bergdorf and Lord & Taylor, and legions of actors and dancers answered the call to service, signing up with the catering companies that orchestrated and provisioned the great corporate and private holiday fetes. The children became manic, fueled by sugary treats and the anticipation of gifts; the lions on guard outside the New York Public Library donned spiky wreaths. Redolent of mothballs, furs and tweeds were liberated from storage. Furtive blondes draped in sable and mink emerged from the backseats of black Mercedes and Escalades, darting across the open tundra of the sidewalk into the refuge of Madison Avenue boutiques. The once-verdant island called Mannahatta was reforested, coniferous thickets springing up on sidewalks and in vacant lots—dense stands of Scotch pine, blue spruce and balsam fir tended by upstaters wrapped in layers of down and fleece.

Russell loved this time of year more than any other, loved the city most when it was imbued with the familiar rituals of his youth, amplified or distorted as they might be, loved sharing it all with the children. For six weeks every year he nearly suspended judgment, choosing not to be offended by the blatant commercialism and the clichés, by the mercenary undercurrent of the bonhomie. He perused the *Times* food section for the latest wisdom on preparing the traditional Thanksgiving bird, varying from Pierre Franey and Craig Claiborne's roast young turkey with giblet gravy to R. W. Apple's brine-cured roast turkey and Mark Bittman's improbable, and not entirely successful, forty-five-minute turkey. The question of whether or not to stuff the bird was a perennial stickler. This year he decided to brine and slow-cook the turkey, a heritage breed ordered two months in advance from a farm near Woodstock, and to cook his mother's traditional pecan stuffing on the side. The cast in their loft included, in addition to the Lee and Reynes families, both Washington's mother and Veronica's. Much to everyone's relief, Corrine's mother had chosen to invite Hilary and Dan to her house in Stockbridge for Thanksgiving after her arguments for a reconciliation fell on deaf ears, thus sparing the Calloways the inevitable vodka-fueled domestic drama.

Then, with increasing frequency, a series of outings: *The Nutcracker* at Lincoln Center; family lunch at '21' with the Salvation Army singing carols; Russell's and Corrine's respective office parties; the Reyneses' Christmas cocktail party at Doubles. And then the selection of the tree—a ritual that engaged all of Russell's aestheticism and sense of ceremony, even as it delighted the kids. He'd inherited this fixation from his own father, who had sometimes visited three or four purveyors in suburban Detroit before finding the ideal evergreen. They walked the three blocks over to the tree sellers on the corner of Chambers and Duane. The notion of a portable forest inspired Russell to tell the children an abbreviated version of *Macbeth,* and about how the thane's demise was ordained when the prophecy of Birnam Wood moving to Dunsinane was confirmed.

"But how did the witches know?" Jeremy asked.

"That's their job," Russell said.

"There must have been an awful lot of soldiers to chop down a whole forest and move it."

"Well, I'm not sure they actually moved the whole forest. They probably just chopped off some branches to camouflage themselves."

"That sounds kind of improbable," Storey said.

"Hey, who's the editor in this family, anyway?" Russell said. "Let's have a little suspension of disbelief here. And let's pick a great tree." He surveyed the offerings with a critical eye. A stickler for symmetry, he rejected Jeremy's first choice, a sort of droopy Scotch pine, as being obviously lopsided. Storey's first choice was crooked and lamentably sparse on one side. Eventually they started picking obvious rejects just to torment him, bursting into laughter even before he had a chance to unleash scornful commentary. Despite these provocations, he eventually found the perfect tree, a seven-foot blue spruce, which he lugged, bound in twine, back to the loft. He spent the rest of the day washing off the fragrant sap.

The evening was devoted to decoration, Russell first stringing the lights and then setting the kids loose with tinsel and finally hanging glass balls and assorted handmade ornaments, including some monstrosities they'd crafted at school over the years.

On Christmas Eve, the Calloways rented a car and drove north to Stockbridge and Corrine's mother's, the residue of dread from previous visits alleviated by the sudden appearance of snowflakes dancing in the headlights on the Taconic Parkway. And that night, after the kids had opened one present each, he read from "A Child's Christmas in Wales" as they sprawled on either side of Corrine, alternately comatose and twitchy.

And then the unaccustomed benediction of a week at Tom and Casey's house in Saint Barth's, sunbathing among plutocrats and pop stars, drinking Provençal rosé the color of onion skin, eating insanely expensive lunches of lentil salad and grilled langoustines that lasted until dusk. At one of these endless feasts at a beachside restaurant, Russell was startled to see Phillip Kohout holding court at the head table, the center of a large and boisterous group that included a Hollywood actor and a Paris-based fashion designer. Later, retreating to the men's room, he collided with the writer, who was coming out of a stall, bumping him hard enough to dislodge something he was holding in his hand, which clattered to the floor—a small glass vial filled with white powder.

"Russell," he said, bending down to retrieve his stash. "This is so amazing, man. How long has it been?"

"How are you, Phillip?"

"Let me tell you, I've been a whole lot worse."

"So I heard."

"I mean, Waziristan was pretty bad, but the debriefing in D.C.—now that was a fucking nightmare."

"Looks like you're making up for lost time." Russell hadn't meant to sound pissy, but realized he did.

"Well, carpe diem, you know? That's one thing I learned wearing a hood for two months."

"No, yeah, definitely," Russell said, unintentionally covering all the bases.

"We should hook up back in the city," Phillip said.

"That would be great."

"Yeah, definitely."

Phillip took a step toward the door, then turned to wrap Russell in a bear hug. "Look, I'm really sorry about that business with the second book. It was a crazy time."

"Long forgotten," Russell said.

"We'll catch up for sure in Madhattan."

And all too soon they were back in the city, returning tanned, dulled and sated, awakened from the dream by a brisk slap of cold air on the jet bridge at JFK.

Then, a snowstorm on Valentine's Day: It had been coming down heavily since they woke; school had been canceled, much to the chagrin of Storey, who was apparently expecting some pledge of troth from her classmate Rafe Horowitz. That night they left the kids with Jean and trudged, heavily bundled, to Bouley, their traditional Valentine's destination, a temple of haute cuisine that was, conveniently, a short walk from the loft. Corrine held Russell's arm with one hand and an umbrella with the other as they negotiated the heavy snow on the sidewalk, admixed with hail, which had a granular texture, like wet beach sand. Corrine had made it clear she would have been happy to stay in tonight, but Russell had insisted that the holiday be observed with a romantic meal.

He discussed the wine list with the sommelier while Corrine visited the kitchen to pay her respects to the chef, who was on the board of her organization. He had just settled the debate over the merits of Chablis versus Chasselas when she returned. He stood up as she approached; his father had drilled him in the forms of chivalry.

A few minutes later when he looked up from his menu, he saw that Corrine was crying.

He reached over and put his hand on hers. "Sweetheart, what's the matter?"

"Oh, Russell, is this it? Roses once a year and maybe an obligatory drunken fuck? We're fifty years old. Where's the romance? Whatever happened to the romance?"

Russell had no idea where this was coming from—having thought things were relatively good between them—but this kind of outburst was by no means unprecedented. And while he believed, after all these years, that he knew her better than he knew anyone on earth, he sometimes suspected there were parts of her psyche that were inaccessible to him, vast regions beyond the beacon of his understanding.

9

"IS THERE ANYTHING BETTER THAN BONEFISHING?" Kip asked as they sprawled on lawn chairs on the deck outside camp, looking out over the flats, silvery pink in the reflected sunset. Owl-eyed from a day on the water, white sunglass-shaped ovals on his sunburned face, he was wearing a multipocketed turquoise shirt and a Lehman Brothers cap.

After a nearly perfect day on the water, Russell felt there was indeed much to be said in favor of fly-fishing in the Bahamas with Kip Taylor, his chief investor, who was picking up the tab.

"It's damn good, but I don't know that I'd put it right at the very top of the list," Russell said. His hands were still fragrant from the nine bonefish he'd caught and released, one of them a probable ten-pounder, his personal best.

"Russell, don't be so predictable, for Christ's sake. Are you actually going to try to tell me, at our age, that the most important thing in life is sex?"

Russell couldn't quite decide if Kip was being refreshingly honest or simply trying to be original. "Not necessarily the most important, but certainly the most pleasurable."

"So why are you here instead of at home poking your wife? I think that's just what you think you're supposed to say."

"If I could only have one or the other, I don't think I'd pick fishing."

"After twenty-five years of marriage you still find it exciting?"

For purposes of this discussion, Russell had been thinking about

sex in general, or in some earlier incarnation of his marriage, not necessarily conjugal relations in the present tense, though they'd enjoyed
a bit of a revival in that department recently. "It comes and goes," he
said.

"How often?" Kip demanded. "*Honestly.*"

Russell sometimes felt that Kip believed his wealth entitled him to
the truth, as if it were a commodity like any other. His questions often
took this form, an interrogative followed by the imperative *honestly*.
"Maybe once a week," he said. This was, in fact, a wildly optimistic estimate. Twice a month, maybe.

"I'm on my third marriage and I've come to the conclusion that on
average sexual infatuation lasts about five years."

"Good thing you have fishing, then."

"Honestly, I get a bigger hard-on closing a serious deal than fucking my wife. And you'd probably rather find the next Hemingway than
fuck yours. Hell, I'd rather *read* the next Hemingway, if the truth be
told. Or reread *A River Runs Through It*. You ever hear the one about the
three stages of marriage? When you first get married, you're having
chandelier sex, swinging from the light fixtures. Next you have bedroom sex, once a week, in the bed. Then finally you have hallway sex.
Know what that is?"

"What's that?"

"You pass each other in the hallway and say 'Fuck you.'"

Russell issued a perfunctory snort.

"So, good-looking woman is in a department store," Kip said, now
on a roll. "She's with her two kids, and she's yelling at them, 'Stop
touching this, stop fooling around,' basically cussing them out, and
eventually she's at the cash register, still yelling at them, when the guy
behind her says, 'Those are fine-looking young boys. Are they twins?'
And she looks at him and says, 'No, they're not twins, they're nine and
eleven, you idiot. What are you, stupid? Anybody can see they aren't
twins.' And the guy says to her, 'It's just that I can't imagine anybody
fucking you twice.'"

After a self-appreciative pause, Kip said, "Ah, yes, kids. That youthful sex drive is nature's reproductive imperative. But once the kids

come along, they destroy it. It's amazing anyone has more than one; the little buggers seem to be programmed to behave in such a way as to discourage parents from ever doing it again."

Russell nodded, suddenly feeling guilty that he hadn't thought about his own children all day.

"But you need distractions, of course; you need your visceral pleasures. God knows I do, being semiretired. Fly-fishing and single-malt scotch," he said, hoisting his glass and sniffing it appreciatively. "It's either that or you start screwing your masseuse."

"I turned down a proposition," Russell said, "from a hot college girl a few months back."

Kip looked intrigued. "On what grounds?"

"I'm still trying to decide," he said.

"There're only three," Kip said. "Fidelity. Fear of getting caught. Or lack of interest." Kip was fond of categorical pronouncements.

"One and two, I guess," Russell said, although he had to admit that while Astrid Kladstrup had certainly stirred his loins—and in a perfect world he would have liked nothing better than to have exercised them—at this point in his life he just didn't think it was worth the trouble.

"But I'm not sure you can parse out the reasons that neatly," he added. "Guilt and fear of getting caught can erode your interest—your carnal enthusiasm. It wasn't lack of interest so much as lack of the kind of overwhelming drive required to surmount the guilt and the fear of getting caught."

"That's what I was saying earlier," Kip said. "Sex no longer rules your life. There was a time you would've been all over that. God knows I was. Secretaries and waitresses were my big hobbies then. Why do you think I got divorced twice?"

Russell had, in fact, been unfaithful to Corrine in the past, not often, but more than once. He wasn't proud of it now, and he just didn't want to feel that way again. He wasn't certain whether this meant he was getting wiser, or merely older.

"So who was this?" Kip asked. "Some girl at the office?"

"No, although I've made that mistake before."

Kip looked surprised, and Russell realized that this was the first time he'd ever admitted to any kind of extramarital activity in front of his business partner. Their friendship was relatively new. They'd been acquainted at Brown but had fallen out of touch in the years after both moved to New York. They started socializing five years ago, after a chance encounter at an uptown dinner party, where they discovered that Kip's son was the same age as Russell's twins.

They'd both been English majors, but after a year in Paris, failing to write a novel, Kip had joined the training program at First Boston, and later started a hedge fund while maintaining his subscriptions to *The New York Review of Books* and *The Times Literary Supplement*. He kept up with contemporary fiction, and Russell was flattered to learn he'd followed his career. Kip confessed he'd always wondered what it would be like if he'd pursued a literary career, and had always watched the alumni review for notes on Russell's progress. "You know, the road not taken." Kip's son hit it off with Jeremy, and Russell shared Kip's passion for fly-fishing, though he'd never been able to practice it much farther from home than upstate New York before Kip started taking him along on his trips. It had been on the North Platte River in Wyoming that their business partnership had been conceived, though it took them several months to find the appropriate vehicle.

Russell was chafing in his old job, working for a philistine at a once-illustrious publishing house that had been purchased by a French conglomerate. He'd been increasingly unhappy since the change in ownership, and after the events of September 11, he felt the need to make his mark in the world while there was still time, and to do more than other publishers were for the writers he believed in. He'd seen too many talented authors sent naked into the world as the big houses lavished all their hopes and energy on a few flashy titles for which they'd overpaid after ruinous bidding wars. He'd recently attended the funeral of a friend who'd published four serious, well-reviewed novels, whose fifth Russell had been unable to convince his employers to take on, given the disappointing sales of its predecessors. Though it turned out the writer had been treated for depression, Russell never forgave his boss, or himself, when the man committed suicide a year later. And of course there was Jeff. . . . When McCane, Slade went up for sale after old man Slade suffered a stroke, they'd pounced. It had a venerable name and a solid backlist that threw off over a million a year. Kip assembled a small group of investors, putting up half of the money himself, giving Russell 20 percent of the company, with additional equity contingent on performance. And, in 2004, after just two years, they'd turned a small profit. Score one for the Art and Love team.

They were summoned to dinner by Matthew Soames, an Englishman in his mid-thirties whose fifth-great-grandfather had been given title to this Bahamian island by King George III. Various agricultural schemes had been tried and abandoned over the generations, until Matthew, after getting kicked out of Oxford, had finally hit on the idea of building a fishing camp on the otherwise-uninhabited island. After his first two visits, and his very first tarpon on a fly rod, Kip had invested in the camp. The accommodations were more spartan than Kip was accustomed to, but the fishing more than compensated, and Matthew's girlfriend was an excellent cook.

Tonight, Cora started them with stone crab claws. The main course was a very tasty Nassau grouper in a green curry sauce. They talked about fishing and, with an earnestness unique to fishermen and sea-farers, about the weather, until Kip sent Matthew to fetch a second bottle of wine.

"So what's your thinking on this Kohout book?" Kip said.

"An important title, no doubt about it."

"Well, getting captured by the Taliban or whoever the fuck they are doesn't seem like such a brilliant achievement in and of itself."

"No, but Phillip managed to escape, which wasn't all that easy, and in the meantime he seems to have picked up some interesting intelligence. He claims that bin Laden is in Pakistan."

"That's hardly a novel theory."

"But beyond that it's a story of triumphing over adversity. What'll make this different is that he's a very good writer, and a real writer can make a trip to Food Emporium fascinating." Russell decided not to mention the recent encounter in Saint Barth's; if he begrudged his authors' drug habits and narcissistic behavior, he wouldn't have much of a list. "I've worked with Kohout before—I basically discovered him, so I think that gives me an edge. Plus, a book like this puts us right in the middle of the cultural dialogue."

"It seems to me our business model is still sound. We cultivate new talent, mostly fiction, buy low, sell foreign rights, leave expensive wannabe blockbusters to the big houses."

Easy for Kip to say—he had a five-bedroom apartment on Park Avenue. Russell could have said he wanted to be able to send his kids to private school, or buy an apartment, or take the occasional trip to Europe, but instead he said, "Well, yes, but sometimes we might need to be flexible, be willing to assume some risk for a worthwhile project with a big upside." He realized that he sounded a little stilted trying to speak Kip's language. "Obviously, if the book goes for three or four million, we're out, end of story, but maybe we could make a preemptive offer, let's say seven fifty, and see if we can't make a deal. I think it's an important book that could put us in a different league."

This was not a jaw-dropping number to a man like Kip. For him, McCane, Slade—the repository of Russell's life's ambitions—was more or less a hobby, not that he wanted to lose money on it, any more than Russell did. Still, if Russell ever hoped to own a house or leave money to his kids, this was his shot, and that was no small part of what attracted him to the Kohout deal. For most of his life he'd worked for large corporations, in whose profitability he'd had only an indirect share. He'd acquired a few best-sellers over the years, without ever participating in the profits they generated. This had, he realized now, allowed him the luxury of choosing books according to his own tastes and interests, confident that in the long run they'd make money in the aggregate and keep him employed. His books often won prizes and garnered positive reviews, and his employers understood that these bolstered the value of their brands. But now his compensation was tied directly to his performance. After years of collecting a paycheck, he found himself an entrepreneur.

"Well, if you think we can get it for seven fifty. What kind of rights are we talking about?"

"Well, we'd try for foreign and first serial."

"Let me look at the proposal one more time."

When Matthew returned with a second bottle of white Burgundy, Russell told him, "Kip thinks sex is overrated as a human motivation. What do you think?"

"I'm English," he replied. "Of course I have to agree."

"You misrepresent me," Kip said. "I proposed that at a certain age it ceases to be the predominant, overarching drive."

Matthew bobbed his head, his weathered face glowing red in the candlelight. "Can't possibly argue with that."

"So what's your secret?" Kip asked.

"My secret?"

"To happiness."

"Who says I'm happy?" Matthew said.

"You seem to have it all figured out."

"In terms of men and women, if that's what you mean, my secret is not to get married. We've been together eleven years, Cora and I, and I'm convinced that if we tied the knot, it would spoil things between us."

"How does she feel about that?"

"She's still here. And she still has the figure she had when she was twenty."

Matthew elaborated on this theme the next day when he took Russell out on the flats. "Security and excitement are opposites, what? You can't have both."

They'd chosen the inside of the island, working the maze of creeks and swamps inshore, while Kip and his guide worked the outside. It was a primeval landscape, more liquid than solid, the border between the two blurred by the red mangroves, their dark green leaves hiding the sand, and their roots reaching out into the murk, a universe of prey and predators concealed within these underwater forests. Just an hour past low tide the backcountry was ripe with the tidal-pool stench of decay and regeneration, the effluvia of billions of microorganisms having sex and dying.

The surface of the water was still and glassy as Matthew poled across the flat toward two feeding bonefish, their silvery tails breaking the surface and waggling as they worked, grazing the shallows for crabs and mollusks, sharing the flat with two white egrets that walked with a deliberate and fastidious gait, raising their feet out of the water between steps, periodically piercing the surface with their long beaks. They paused to watch the skiff as it glided closer, spreading their wings in unison and lifting off, spooking the two bonefish, which shot across a half-submerged sandbar and settled on the other side.

By the time Matthew poled over to the sandbar, the fish were working some fifty yards away, and he made a walking motion with his fingers. Russell slid off the bow into the water and waded slowly, carefully extracting each foot from the muck with as little noise and motion as possible as he stalked within casting distance, watching for the tails, which periodically cut the surface, finally unleashing his cast, throwing two false casts to get his line out, waiting for the slight resistance of his back cast before launching his rod forward and dropping his fly six feet in front of the cruising fish. It seemed to him that his line had landed hard but miraculously; they didn't spook, continuing to move toward the fly, two gray shadows against the gray-brown mud. When they were within a few feet of the fly, Russell twitched it once and then began to retrieve, pulling in line with his left hand and holding the rod close to the surface with his right, until one of the fish broke from its course in pursuit.

In his excitement he snatched the fly away just as the fish was grabbing for it, but he stopped his retrieve and then slowly resumed as it made a second run, and this time when he set the hook he felt a solid tug. It took the creature a moment to react, and time seemed to stand still, Russell hoping he'd set the hook, and then the fish was off, stripping fifty yards of line, Russell getting his hands free of the unspooling fly line just in time to prevent the leader from snapping, holding his rod tip up in the air as the drag of the reel screamed.

"Nice shot," Matthew shouted from the skiff.

Ten minutes later, with the frantic silvery fish finally brought in and released, Russell said, "Could be Kip's right. Maybe this is better than sex."

"Another reason to shun marriage—I don't ever want to think like that."

"You know you love it," Russell said.

"What, the fishing? Yeah, but it's my job. Doesn't always do to turn your passion into your work. It's a bit like marrying your mistress, innit?"

10

SHE MET CASEY AT JUSTINE'S, a private club in the basement of a midtown hotel, a plush red sanctuary that at lunchtime was popular with ladies who spent a good deal of time and money just up the street at Bergdorf, while their mates coveyed up nearby at the Four Seasons and '21.' Casey lived in the East Sixties, and they alternated between uptown and downtown for their lunch dates. For once she was on time, chatting with some women at another table when Corrine arrived. The others all seemed to be wearing Chanel suits. Casey looked very fashion-forward, by contrast, sporting that luxe boho chic look—a below-the-knee burgundy skirt and a long, nubbly olive turtleneck cinched with a big brown belt.

"Sorry, traffic. Love your outfit."

"It's Oscar. Very down-home for him—I know. Don't tell me you took a cab? Usually I have to listen to you tell me about how fast and convenient the subway is, and all I can think of is you'll get mugged or anthraxed or something."

"I was on the Upper West Side, so it was the only option."

"What were you doing there? Are you seeing your shrink again?"

As soon as she mentioned where she'd been, Corrine realized it was a bit of a giveaway.

"Well, yes. Just a one-off. Situation with the kids."

"Should I pretend I'm not interested?"

"No, I was going to tell you. My beloved sister's been calling, trying to worm her way back into our lives."

"Tell me everything."

"I need to hit the buffet first. I'm starving."

"The chef will be delighted, if he doesn't die of shock. The food's basically decorative. Very few of our members actually eat."

After they settled back at the table with their plates, Casey said, "It's always amazed me that you have this white-trash sister." She poked at the lozenge of chicken paillard on her plate. "As long as I can remember, she was a real problem. I mean, I grew up with you, I know your family, and you're one of the most elegant people on the planet. Maybe your mom screwed the milkman or the chimney sweep."

"Don't say that. Hilary's the biological mother of my kids."

"You'd better hope nurture trumps nature."

"Thanks for sharing that."

"If you want my advice, keep her out of your life and your kids', too."

"Sooner or later they're going to want to get to know her."

"I'm not entirely sure about that, but much later would be much better."

"I can't stop worrying that eventually they might think of her as their mother."

"You raised them to have better taste than that." Casey took a sip of her iced tea and leaned forward in her conspiratorial pose. "Have you seen Washington?"

"Yes, with his *wife*." Corrine did not approve of Casey's affair with Russell's best friend, which had been going on, intermittently, for years.

Casey waved at a fierce-looking blonde with protuberant cheekbones and sticklike arms a couple of tables away.

"Who's that?" Corrine asked.

Casey leaned forward. "That's Carol Ricard. Her husband just divorced her right before the escalator clause on the prenup kicked in."

"That's sad," Corrine said reflexively.

"Not really. Apparently, he's agreed to marry her again after the divorce."

When she'd worked at Sotheby's and lived on Beekman Place, Corrine used to think of downtown as the province for all kinds of bohemian kinkiness, but lately she'd decided that Casey's coterie of uptown socialites was far more debauched and jaded.

"One time we saw her at '21,' pushing lettuce leaves around her plate, and Tom had a burger sent over to the table. It was hilarious. He made the waiter promise not to say where it came from, but the whole room was buzzing."

Corrine looked over at the skeletal Mrs. Ricard with a certain fascination, not entirely disapproving. She was not immune to the dream of leaving behind the heavy cloak of flesh. And in fact, Carol Ricard was only marginally thinner than her dining companions—or Casey and Corrine, for that matter.

"She has to shave her arms and chest," Casey said. "When your body approaches true starvation, it grows fur as a protective reaction to try to keep you warm."

"That's gross." Apparently it *was* possible to be too thin. Who knew? At least, Corrine thought, she'd never gotten to that point.

Casey lifted her by-no-means-chubby arm, decorated with several bands of gold and a Bulgari snake watch, and summoned a waiter who was hovering in the corner. "I'd like another iced tea," she told him, "and my friend will have another cranberry and soda with lime."

Corrine had been waiting for an opening. "I got a call from Luke today."

"Is he here?"

She nodded, surprised that Casey didn't seem to be.

Casey clapped her hand on top of Corrine's and beamed. "So, will you see him? And more to the point, are you going to sleep with him?"

Corrine looked around, mortified, but no one was conspicuously eavesdropping.

"He invited me out to Sagaponack for the weekend."

"This is huge," Casey said, leaning forward. "What about the wife?"

"Ten thousand miles away."

"Well, what are you waiting for?"

"I'm waiting for my conscience to have a stroke. I mean, why am I even contemplating this?"

"You're contemplating it because he's rich and handsome and he loves you."

"How can you possibly know that? He clearly cares about me and he seems to want to sleep with me, which is, I must say, a big point in his favor. He's actually been sending me these very romantic e-mails."

"He's crazy about you. Do you think it was a coincidence that you were at my table for his benefit? He asked me to invite you."

"That was a setup?"

"He really wanted to see you," Casey said, "and I suspect he wanted you to see *him* in his moment of glory. He must've heard that Tom bought a table, so he called me out of the blue and practically begged me to take you."

"And you're just telling me now?"

"He swore me to secrecy, Corrine."

"I'm your best friend."

"And as my best friend, you should realize I have your best interests at heart."

"What's that supposed to mean?"

"Only that I approve of you and Luke."

"There is no me and Luke. We're both married."

"I think Luke is over his marriage."

"That's ridiculous. You saw that girl."

"Yes, I did. And she looked a lot like you. What does that tell you?"

"That he has a type."

"Are you having sex with Russell?"

"I can't remember. Last fall we had a brief renaissance, and then once in Saint Barth's."

"I don't even *want* to sleep with Tom anymore; that's the sad part. I give him a blow job on his birthday and we call it good for another year."

Corrine would never get used to her friend's sexual candor, but she was probably the perfect adviser in the present situation; certainly Corrine couldn't imagine confiding in anyone else. "What should I do? And what the hell would I say to Russell?"

"Tell him you're going out to Southampton with me for the weekend—a little time away from the family."

"Why are you saying this?"

"Because I don't think you're really over him. And I don't think he's over you."

Corrine refused Luke's offer of a ride—a small and perhaps absurd point of honor, given that she'd agreed to spend two days and nights alone with him—opting instead for the jitney. The principal bus service between New York City and the Hamptons used this obscure term for a public conveyance because the kind of people who could afford to live in both places either didn't ride buses or, if forced to, would never identify them as such. A neologism was called for. Even those with drivers and multiple German automobiles sometimes found it convenient, and there was little stigma attached to riding the bus by another name. Corrine, considering it more sensible and ecologically sound, would have insisted on this mode of transport even if the purpose of her journey had been beyond reproach. Casey, as it turned out, was going out to the island only for twenty-four hours on Saturday, and they would drive back together Sunday.

She took the kids to school that morning and watched them disappear inside with a rising sense of panic and dread, as if it were possible she might never see them again. She was about to venture beyond the pale—and what if she couldn't return? What if something terrible happened out there? On the walk back to the apartment, she resolved to call the whole thing off. The night before, after several glasses of Sancerre, she had been certain that seeing Luke was, if not the right thing, at least what she wanted, even craved. She just needed to get this out of her system. Her yearning was palpable, and she'd gone to bed reviewing and savoring the memories of the episodes of lovemaking that had constituted their brief romance. This morning all she could think about was everything she was putting at risk, without any compensatory prospect of reward except that of possessing him and being possessed one or two or three more times, of fulfilling a desire that continued to plague her, although it had almost gone dormant until she saw him again last fall.

She was slightly ashamed and baffled by this. She'd always had a healthy appreciation of sex, and never quite stopped enjoying it with

Russell, but she'd never felt this kind of compulsive desire, unless perhaps back when they'd first started dating at Brown. Part of her had
rationalized it retroactively; she and Luke had come together in the
days after September 11, and such cataclysmic events were aphrodisiac,
conducive to compulsive and reckless behavior. But the truth was, she
was still drawn to him.

Stopping at the corner of Broadway and Reade, she hit number three
on her autodial. "I can't do it," she said when Casey picked up.

"You owe it to yourself to follow through. You need resolution. Otherwise, you're always going to wonder."

"What kind of resolution can I possibly find? Even if we make mad,
passionate love, he will have scratched that itch and then will probably
remember he's got a younger, sexier blonde back home."

"Never discount the value of mad passion. I'd give my left breast for
a good night of it."

"I know, that's the terrible thing. I really do want him."

Thankfully, there were no familiar faces on the jitney when she boarded
at 40th Street, the last stop before the tunnel to Long Island. In July
or August, it would be jammed after running down the East Side, but
today only five passengers were scattered down the aisle: an elderly couple, a weary middle-aged Hispanic woman, and a pretty young mother
in a Barbour jacket and jodhpurs with her preschool daughter. Corrine
had borrowed a galley of *The Savage Detectives* from Russell's pile in the
bedroom, and now she opened it again, determined to distract herself.

When the bus turned off the expressway ninety minutes later, she
gave up reading and looked out over the scrub pines alongside the road,
crossing the Shinnecock Canal into Southampton, finally disembark-
ing across the street from the post office in Bridgehampton. They'd
agreed it would be risky for Luke to pick her up, so he'd commissioned
his caretaker, Luis, who was waiting in a pickup. He apologized for the
state of the truck, which was, in fact, perfectly tidy, and answered her
questions by saying he was from Oaxaca and had been working for Mr.
Luke for thirteen years.

It was a short, familiar drive down Sag Main. Russell liked to call it

"Writers' Row," annotating the landmarks for newcomers as he drove them from the jitney stop: the house where James Jones had spent the last years of his life, the now-boarded-up farm stand where they bought their corn and tomatoes, the old one-room schoolhouse, the general store, the house John Irving used to live in, and, across the street, the shambling old place that had been George Plimpton's for many years, then the one Kurt Vonnegut still lived in, from which he occasionally shuffled to the general store to buy a pack of Pall Malls—at a party he'd once told Corrine that smoking was the classy way to commit suicide—and down the road was Peter Matthiessen's. Russell loved being in the proximity of all this literary talent, which he felt almost compensated for the invasion of what he called the hedge funders behind the hedgerows, though by now the writers had mostly died or moved on. It's not so different, Corrine thought, from what's happening in TriBeCa.

The late-March fields were brown, the trees gray and naked. Intermittent gusts of wind stirred eddies of crisp leaves in the road. And here she was, pulling up to the white picket fence in front of Luke's house, a century-old three-story cottage with light blue shutters in the indigenous Shingle Style, one of the originals that had inspired hundreds of imitations in the surrounding fields. By the time she'd realized it was his, he'd been in the middle of his divorce from Sasha, who had apparently claimed exclusive use of it in the ensuing years.

He was waiting in the driveway, looking impatient and vaguely nautical in his white Irish fisherman's turtleneck. She'd almost forgotten the disconcerting, wandering eye. But she was happy, even excited, to see him. Luis, carrying Corrine's bag, asked which room she'd be staying in.

"I'll take that," Luke told him.

He opened the door for her. Inside the entry hall, he dropped the bag and gripped her shoulder, firmly turning her, dipping down and kissing her. His kiss was both familiar and thrilling.

"Sorry," he said, releasing her. "I just kind of needed to do that."

She suddenly felt inordinately shy and awkward, glad that she'd come, though uncertain that she could follow through on the implicit promise of the weekend.

"Let me give you the tour," he said.

The interior was decorated more elaborately than she would have imagined, not as ostentatious and formal as many of the homes she'd seen in Southampton, with their chintzes and their Chippendale, but still more pristine and staged than she would have liked, her taste shaped by her own childhood in rambling houses in Wellfleet and Nantucket, with their jumble of objects and beach salvage collected over time, furniture with worn and faded upholstery, and random knickknacks. This was the Ralph Lauren version of her primal memories of tatty old WASP summer homes, bearing the same relation to the archetype as the McMansions out in the potato fields did to the house itself.

"Sasha decorated," he said, as if reading her mind. "With a little help from Peter Marino."

Of course—she should have known. Luke's ex would have had to have everything just so. "It's lovely," she said.

"*Tasteful*," he said in an italicized tone that alleviated her previous disappointment. And who was she, after all, to insist that his house resemble her grandmother's? It wasn't Luke's fault that her grandfather had given all his money away, that she was stuck with memories of lost privilege and a sense of aesthetic judgment that bordered on snobbery.

"Are you hungry?" he asked, and for once, she realized, she was. Ravenous, in fact.

"I'll put together some lunch," he said. "You can explore the place."

She drifted through the living room to the library, the most masculine corner of the house, examining the artifacts therein, the books and the photographs, his daughter, Ashley, being the most frequent subject—only one picture showed the three of them, Sasha and Luke and Ashley, all in white at some garden party, and Corrine was amazed anew by how beautiful Luke's ex was, or had been—like a young Candice Bergen. No one would ever ask, "What does he see in her?" She found it annoying that he'd married two beauties—it suggested a certain superficiality of character, a value deficit. She could consider herself complimented to be in that company—maybe he thought she was beautiful, too, or maybe he liked her because she was different from his wives. Thankfully, there weren't any pictures of the new one here, but neither was there any evidence of Corrine's existence, or so it seemed until she spotted the copy of *The Heart of the Matter* on a side table next to a big leather club chair. On further inspection, it proved to be the copy she'd given him six years ago, with the inscription, XI XII MMI XXCC. Her initials and kisses beside the date she'd presented it, two months to the day after they'd met.

She wandered out to the kitchen, where he was finishing his lunch preparations. "Almost ready," he said. This room felt more homey than the others, perhaps because the pine cabinets and the antique Windsor chairs around a circular table reminded her of the kitchen she'd grown up in.

He pulled out a chair, motioned for her to sit, and said, "I prepared a special treat for us," holding out a tray of sandwiches.

They looked frighteningly retro—white bread cut into triangles. "Oh my God, is that peanut butter and jelly?"

"Sorry, I couldn't help myself. You don't have to eat them. I have a Greek salad in the fridge."

It took her a moment to catch his reference to their days at the soup kitchen, a kind of private joke; peanut butter and jelly sandwiches had been the first item on the menu.

"I remember eating one of these that first day," he said, "and having this violent emotional reaction, like I was being transported back to my childhood. I hadn't had one since I was a kid. Haven't had one since, either."

"I could never actually eat one," she said. She found it kind of touching, though, that he'd made them. "Maybe I had too many as a kid."

"Ah, well," he said, bringing the salad to the table and setting it in front of her. He took a sandwich for himself and bit into it.

"What does it evoke now—childhood, or the soup kitchen?"

"Both," he said. "I can almost smell that foul smoke."

"The oven cleaner smell."

"I remember it more as burned plastic."

"That's because you have no idea what oven cleaner smells like." She helped herself to the salad. "As I remember it, you were the one who stared hitting up the restaurants. One time you drove up to Babbo and came back with like fifty veal chops."

"I think that was Jerry's idea," Luke said. "I wonder what's happened to him. Did you stay in touch?"

She shook her head. Jerry was a carpenter who'd rushed downtown as soon as the towers collapsed to help dig through the rubble; he'd returned the next day with a coffee urn and a vanful of food, eventually establishing an ad hoc soup kitchen, which soon attracted volunteers, Corrine and Luke among them. "I did for a while. We had a coffee a few months after. Exchanged a few e-mails. But it was hard. I felt like those weeks were the high point of his life, that after that he seemed kind of angry and lost. Plus, honestly, I couldn't. It just reminded me of you."

"I'm sorry."

She shrugged. "What could we do? It was for the best in the end."

"I'm not so sure," he said. "I had a lot of time to wonder about that when I was in the hospital."

"No, you were right the first time. I can't just walk away from my life, my marriage and my kids."

"Yet here you are."

"Can I ask you why you got Casey to invite me to the benefit?"

"That should be obvious by now."

"Not really."

"Ever since my accident, I've been thinking about you."

"Tell me about the accident, if it's not too . . . "

"I don't remember all that much. I was in the car alone, coming home from Cape Town at night. I got hit by a van that crossed the line into my lane. The driver drunk, of course. He died, along with his passenger. Not my fault at all, apparently. Giselle hired an investigator and a team of lawyers, but that didn't keep it from getting ugly. White survivor, two dead black men. But I missed a lot of it. I was in hospital for almost three months."

"You say it the way they do—'in hospital.'"

"What do you mean?"

"We'd say 'in *the* hospital.'"

"I hadn't thought about it." He paused, rubbing the shiny patch of skin on his neck. "I loved the idea of Africa," he said. "And I loved the reality, too. Its primal, cradle-of-life, origin-of-the-species aliveness. The smells, not just the fertile dung smell of the veldt; even the wood smoke, seared meat and raw sewage smell of the townships. It felt like the beginning of the world, where I could really start all over again. Even the fact that I was a minority, the possibility of violence, it made me feel more alive just at a time when I was feeling half-dead. My firm had acquired the winery and I'd been charged with overseeing it, pumping it up and selling it for a big profit, but when I went to visit, I kind of fell for the whole picture, Africa, the agrarian dream, the safari life."

"The girl."

"That was later. Anyway, as I was negotiating the terms of my retirement, I sold the winery to myself."

"I've never quite understood your former business."

"Private equity. Didn't you tell me that years ago your husband tried to buy the publisher he worked for in a leveraged buyout?"

"Yes, though in the end, of course, he failed."

"Well, it's the same basic idea multiplied many times over, spread over different industries. Private equity is just a rebranding of the leveraged buyout concept. We're essentially high-class used-car salesmen. We raise funds from private investors, pension funds, whatever. Then we target an underperforming company, ideally one with bad management and good cash flow. We use some of our own funds, but leverage is the key. Let's say we commit a billion of our own and our investors' money and we borrow maybe six billion from the bank. We buy it, install new management, fix it up, sell off the spare parts, pay the interest on the loan out of cash flow and then try to sell it in a couple of years for maybe ten billion. A profit of three billion. After you pay off the bank, you've tripled your original investment. That's the beauty of leverage—playing with someone else's money."

"What if you can't sell the company at a profit?"

"Well, that's what separates the good players from the others. But ultimately leverage still works for you. If the whole thing goes south, it's the lenders who take the biggest hit."

"It sounds kind of, I don't know . . . like you say, selling used cars."

"The theory is that we keep the economy healthy by fixing broken companies."

"So every couple of years you're in a whole new business?"

"Every couple years we're in ten new businesses. Or I was. I'd had enough, so I cashed out. The winery was just something we'd picked up when acquiring a larger South African conglomerate, one of the pieces the firm was selling off. I picked it up along with a game farm in the Transvaal. It's quite wonderful. You should come visit."

"How would that work? You and me and Russell and Gazelle riding around in a Land Rover, looking for the big five?"

"I was thinking more of you and me in a Cessna, flying low over the savanna. Did I tell you I've learned to fly? It comes in handy, going between the game farm and the winery."

"I'm not sure I'd feel safe with you in the pilot's seat."

"What's that mean?"

"It's just that your attention kind of jumps around from one thing to another. Maybe that's why you were so good at private equity."

"I'll have you know I'm an excellent pilot."

"Well, maybe someday I'll find out. In the meantime, let's take a walk on the beach."

He gave her a flannel-lined Adirondack coat, presumably Sasha's, but she decided not to question the provenance.

She smelled the ocean as soon as they stepped out the door, and heard the waves as they approached the parking lot of the town beach. Just a few months ago she'd walked this very beach with Russell and the kids. She stopped in her tracks, not certain she wanted to do this.

"What's the matter?" he asked.

"Nothing," she said, willing herself forward. It was just a walk on the beach, after all. Then, feeling the cold and smelling the brine, she remembered another walk on a winter beach in Nantucket five years ago, with Luke—that and the smell of wood smoke afterward and Gram Parsons in the borrowed house on a winter weekend. *Love hurts.* No shit.

The long ribbon of white sand was deserted for as far as they could see, and she finally allowed herself to take his hand. Even allowing for high tide, the beach seemed narrower than she remembered it; she'd heard something about a nor'easter. A heavy surf pounded the sand, misting them with salt.

"You can see why all those painters came out here," Luke said. "The sky has a clarity. And it's even clearer in the winter." It was true: The sky was a limpid periwinkle blue, more vivid than any she could recall from the past summer, with majestic flotillas of altocumulus drifting eastward out over the ocean, nudged by a stiff western breeze. She imagined the two of them, she and Luke, from the vantage of a ship at sea, tiny figures in a vast Turneresque setting, a perspective that seemed to both ennoble them and minimize the moral consequences of their actions.

When they got back to the house, she had almost come to terms with her desire; chilly as she was, she thought of them taking a bath together, gradually reacquainting themselves with each other's bodies, although she wasn't yet emboldened enough to suggest it.

At that moment her phone rang in her purse and she knew, even before fishing it out to look, that it was Russell, knowing with the certainty of guilt that her adulterous fantasy had called forth a rebuke. Luke watched as she stirred the contents of her purse and finally came up with the phone, just as it stopped ringing. He knew, too. He seemed to be holding his breath. She flipped it open to check the caller.

"It was Russell," she said.

He nodded mournfully.

"I'd better call back," she said.

Outside, on the deck, the wind had picked up, and she considered going back in for the coat but then decided that she deserved to suffer. Dialing her husband, she imagined, beyond the possibility of her own secret having been discovered, everything that might have gone wrong with the children in her absence: illness, injury, disappearance. So she wasn't all that surprised when Russell said, "It's Jeremy."

Luke seemed to have anticipated bad news; he held her gently as she explained . . . *chest pains, emergency room, appendicitis.*

"Don't worry," he said. "I'll get you back to the city. I just need to make a call."

She started dreading the two-hour drive, crawling along the expressway with her only son waiting, stricken, on the other end.

"We're all set," Luke said, emerging from the library. "I'm going to fly you into the city myself."

"What? Are you sure you can do this?"

He picked up her bag where he'd dropped it only two hours ago. "Let's go."

They spoke hardly at all as he raced over the back roads to the East Hampton Airport, paused only briefly at the flight desk. The plane was a flimsy twin-engine with four seats. Luke buckled her into the copilot's seat and proceeded to run through the preflight protocol, looking at ease with the panel of toggles and switches and dials. He showed her how to use the headsets, since the plane was too noisy for normal conversation in the cockpit, but she remained silent for most of the flight, consumed by anxiety and guilt, barely noticing the sere landscape between the open ocean and the sound, coming to her senses above the necropolis of eastern Queens, looking out at the Manhattan skyline rising beyond an undulant sea of headstones, surprised anew by its recent disfigurement, altered like a familiar smile marred by missing teeth.

11

RUSSELL WOKE THE KIDS, moving back and forth between their rooms until they were upright and moving, under protest. Ferdie emerged from under Jeremy's covers and followed him into the kitchen, snaking along at his heels, waiting eagerly for his bowl of ZuPreem Ferret Diet pellets, supplemented with a chopped sardine, which was supposedly good for his coat and his bones, if not his breath. He strained upward on his hind legs, like a masked bandit, as Russell stirred the fragrant mess.

Storey appeared first, dressed and ready with her backpack and her homework binder. "Can I have French toast?" she asked.

"That's a weekend treat," Russell said. "I've got yogurt and a banana and Honey Nut Cheerios here. Promise I'll make you French toast tomorrow."

"With sausage? I like the English ones you got last weekend. The exploding kind."

"Bangers." He'd picked them up at the limey grocery store in the West Village, along with some Aero and Cadbury bars for Corrine, milk chocolate being among the very few foods she craved.

"Why are they called bangers?"

"Because of the way they pop and explode in the pan."

He hated to admit it, but Corrine was right that Storey was getting compulsive about food and, lately, a little bit chubby. Corrine thought it was somehow a reaction to Hilary's drunken revelation, a theory that seemed plausible enough. They would have to address this sooner or later, though just now he needed to check on Jeremy's progress; getting him dressed and organized on time was a continual challenge. Jeremy was, in fact, still in his pajamas, hunched over his desk. "I thought you finished your homework last night."

"I just forgot some math."

"Time's up. Get dressed and get out here now."

"Hey, Dad?"

"What?" he said, trying to contain his mounting irritation. He'd failed to contain it often enough to be aware of the potential consequences, the kids' tears and his inevitable apology. Both lately seemed excessively sensitive to any criticism whatsoever.

"Are we ever going to see Aunt Hilary and Dan?"

"I don't know. Why, do you miss them?"

Where had that come from? he wondered, even as he acknowledged that for kids, there's no such thing as a non sequitur. Nonlinearity was a given.

"I guess I should miss Hilary," Jeremy said, "since she's sort of my mom."

"Well, yes and no."

"I feel bad I never liked her that much."

"Don't feel bad about your feelings. As long as you try to be understanding and sympathetic to others, that's all I'd ask. But we can't always control what we feel."

"I kind of miss Dan," he said. "He seemed like a good guy. Until he hit you, I mean."

"He has his virtues. Now come on and get ready."

"It was so cool when he showed us his gun."

"Actually, that was kind of a dick move."

"A what?"

"I mean it wasn't cool."

"I think Storey is freaked-out," Jeremy said.

"About the Hilary thing?"

"Yeah."

"Why? Has she said anything to you?"

"Not really. Just a few things."

Before he could pursue this, Storey herself was right beside him. "We are going to be totally late. Is Jeremy still pretending to be wounded?"

It was true: He'd been milking his appendix scar for all it was worth this last week, and it hadn't taken Storey long to lose patience.

He got them into the elevator with just a few minutes till the bell and hurried them down the block, scolding Jeremy when he tried to pet a passing fox terrier tethered to a pretty young redhead Russell noticed frequently at this hour. When they arrived at the school yard, it was empty, and Storey was distraught; she was a fastidious and law-abiding citizen who dreaded violating rules or schedules, whereas her brother was essentially an anarchist.

He led both children to their homeroom, the smell of the corridors almost overwhelming him with sense memories, that compound of linoleum, art supplies, ammonia, snacks and childish effluvia unique to elementary schools, so reminiscent of his own, a thousand miles and four decades away in Michigan.

Back outside, a stiff breeze off of the Hudson helped propel him along Chambers to the subway. Going down the steps, he encountered many trolls and one princess, a lovely creature in a white leather jacket whose porcelain face was framed by shiny blue-black tresses. He kept waiting to become inured to beautiful strangers, who seemed even more abundant now than when he'd first arrived in the city, yet his heart always leapt and his imagination wove unlikely narratives of erotic encounters and alternative lives. Somewhere in the metropolis was a Russell Calloway whose life was devoted to seduction. In this case, he courted and bedded the white leather angel, moved into her penthouse on Broome Street, became very rich in some undefined enterprise and retired from publishing to travel the world with her, all in the distance between Chambers and Canal Streets, where she rose from her seat and got off the train, while he continued on to 14th.

Ascending to the sidewalk, he trudged past the Starbucks on Eighth Avenue, past his office and up Ninth Avenue to the Chelsea Market on Fifteenth, entering the redolent brick cave lined with bakeries and restaurants—which had once, long ago, been a Nabisco biscuit factory before it had been abandoned to become a refuge for the homeless and derelict, a shooting gallery where Jeff Pierce went to score heroin—then waiting at the counter with Food Network execs for his latte, a filigreed heart inscribed in the foam. He wouldn't necessarily want anyone to know that he added three blocks to his morning commute because he thought this was the best coffee in the city, certainly not his wife, who already thought his epicureanism was some kind of sickness.

Walking back to the office, he unlocked the front door and stooped to scoop up three take-out menus and a brochure advertising the latest local manicure parlor. All this paper was destined for the trash, and yet when he thought about it, as he did now, he found it touching that these small businesses were popping up and reaching out to him, a Chinese or Korean immigrant with his life savings on the line, in hock to some murderous criminal who'd smuggled him into the country. And he could empathize because he, too, was a small businessman, with all his paltry capital invested in his company, only two or three flops away from financial peril, if not outright ruin. This morning he was particularly susceptible to intimations of doom because he was short on sleep and slightly hungover and especially because he was about to take the biggest risk of his career.

At his desk he wrote three rejection letters. Russell took great pride in these, and was known for them; while most editors tried to stay vague and upbeat—"not quite right for our list at this time"—he was specific about his reservations and offered constructive criticism, even as he admitted that his judgment was fallible, or at least that in the end he was a prisoner of his own taste (not that he really believed this). Usually this scrupulous attention was appreciated, although the agent Martin Briskin once told him, "Just give me the fucking verdict and spare me the sensitive lecture." And it was Briskin with whom he had to deal today.

At nine-thirty he called Kip Taylor, whose money he'd be putting on the line, to get the final clearance.

"Russell, you sound terrible. You're croaking like a frog. Pull yourself together, man."

"I'm fine, Kip. Ready to go."

"So, you think you can get it for seven fifty?"

"I'll try like hell."

"You know he'll want a million. It's the number—the basic unit."

Russell assumed he was being polite about the Lilliputian dynamics of publishing, because he distinctly remembered Kip saying that in the financial world, 100 million was the basic unit.

"Then I guess we have to be willing to walk away," Russell said tentatively.

"Is that what you want to do?" Kip asked.

"I think it's worth a million with foreign rights."

"All right, do it if you can."

This was one of the things he admired about Kip, his decisiveness. He'd started his career as a trader at Salomon Brothers, staking millions on split-second judgments.

"Russell, I have to trust your instincts. That's why I hired you. If your gut tells you to go for it, then go for it. Honestly, it's your call."

Actually, Kip hadn't hired him; rather, Russell had solicited his capital to help buy a struggling business in which they both saw hidden value, but he was willing to let this pass. Having gotten the answer he wanted, he couldn't understand why, after hanging up, he felt such trepidation and anxiety. His esophagus was burning with indigestion, his stomach suddenly queasy.

He went out to the deli and bought a toasted corn muffin fresh off the greasy grill—a plebeian delicacy that pleased him no less than last night's short ribs—gobbling down half of it as he hurried back to the office, chucking the rest, intercepting Gita, his assistant, and Tom Bradley, his subrights director, coming in together. Were they a couple? They certainly seemed a little flustered to encounter him here on the steps. Both followed him up to the second floor after Russell told Tom he wanted to review Kohout's foreign prospects before making the big call.

At ten-thirty he punched in the number. He could've had Gita make the call and ask Briskin's assistant to hold for him, but that wasn't Russell's style. Briskin made him wait several minutes before picking up.

"Speak to me."

"I want to preempt the Kohout."

"I hope you have a large figure in mind."

"It seems plenty big to me."

"You probably believe it when your wife says that about your dick. But let's hear it anyway."

"Seven fifty."

"Are you fucking kidding me? You call that a preempt?"

"This will be our top title of the year. And I'll be there with Phillip every step of the way. He's worked with me, and I think he'd like to again. He knows I'm a good editor and somebody he can trust."

"Russell, be serious. I can't go to my client with this."

"The worst he can say is no."

"He could say a lot worse, and so can I. If you were on fire, I wouldn't cross the street to piss on you for seven fifty," he said before hanging up.

Russell plodded along through the morning, unable to focus as he tried to decide whether to call back and sweeten the offer or wait Briskin out. Maybe, he thought, I should just sit tight. Maybe he'd just dodged a bullet. He had a somewhat distracted lunch at Soho House with David Cohen, the young editor he'd taken with him from Corbin, Dern. David was a keen advocate of the Kohout book and urged Russell to up his offer. The rooftop restaurant had just reopened for the season, and it seemed almost miraculous to dine outside, with the sun on your face, looking out over the Hudson, the slightest fetid whiff of which reached him on the breeze.

He'd just settled back at his desk when Gita told him Briskin was on the line.

"Give me a million," Briskin said.

"Nine hundred, and we keep world rights."

"Try again. A million and I'll give you the UK. That's the best I can do."

That Briskin was calling at all, Russell interpreted as a sign of weakness.

"A million and world rights," he said. "Final offer."

"Come on, Russell, world rights might not be that big a factor on this book."

"Then you shouldn't mind giving them to us."

"Fuck you," he said before hanging up again.

Russell's pulse was racing, his face flushed. As the adrenaline subsided, he found himself disappointed and second-guessing his tactics, but later, when his publicity director, Jonathan, and David came in for an update, he felt relieved.

"Well, it wasn't really our kind of book anyway," Jonathan said. "I wouldn't know how to play this to the reviewers."

"Maybe, but we can't just suffocate in our comfortable little niche," David said. "We need to grow."

"We do?"

"Of course," David said.

"We don't do that blockbuster thing," Jonathan countered.

How easy it is, Russell thought, to be a purist in your twenties.

Gita buzzed and said that Briskin was on the line. All at once the silence in the office was palpable. Russell picked up the receiver.

"All right," Briskin said, "we have a deal. I have to tell you I advised my client against it."

"If I didn't think we could do right by this book I wouldn't have pushed so hard. I'm going to do everything in my power—"

"Spare me the fucking speech and send over the contract."

"Okay," he said, feeling giddy and light-headed as he hung up the phone.

"We got world rights?" Jonathan asked.

Russell nodded. "I'll tell Tom to get busy on it."

"You all right?"

"I think so," Russell said, standing up and walking unsteadily to the bathroom, where he threw up what was left of his lunch.

12

"'THE LIGER IS A HYBRID CROSS between a male lion (*Panthera leo*) and a tigress (*Panthera tigress*).'" Jeremy was reading aloud to his mother from Wikipedia, psyching himself up for the day's adventure, to see an actual liger in the native habitat of one of the Wildlife Society's most generous benefactors. "'Thus, it has parents with the same genus but of different species. It is the largest of all known extant felines. Ligers enjoy swimming, which is a characteristic of tigers, and are very sociable like lions. Ligers exist only in captivity because the habitats of the parent species do not overlap in the wild. . . .'"

Casey had two extra tickets to see the liger and its trainer in the Fifth Avenue town house of Minky Rijstaefal, who was president of the society. This beast had risen from obscurity into a kind of cult fame after being mentioned in *Napoleon Dynamite,* and the society was capitalizing on that interest. Indeed, the event had quickly sold out, drawing the otherwise jaded children of the 10021 zip code, who'd already seen plenty of lions and tigers and bears, oh my, and more than a few of whom had been on Abercrombie & Kent safaris in Kenya and South Africa. For Corrine's part, she couldn't help being reminded of Luke, who was, she knew, spending the week at his game park, couldn't help conjuring a glimmer of communion in this Upper East Side expedition, or thinking about the e-mail she'd write to him about it later.

Much as Storey had liked *Napoleon Dynamite* and its supernerd protagonist, she didn't want to go. It always made her sad to see wild animals in captivity. Corrine didn't bother to point out that the liger wasn't technically a *wild* animal, since she had only the two tickets.

She wondered, too, if there wasn't another point of reference in Storey's refusal; she'd entered a stage of acute social sensitivity, having recently complained about the "snotty UES rich kids" she'd encountered at a birthday party, and the Wildlife Society event would be largely composed of that species. Jeremy, by contrast, was excited from a zoological standpoint and relatively oblivious to the sociological implications. He was lying in bed with his laptop, his neck propped up on a pillow, reading everything he could find online. "It doesn't say whether they're dangerous or not."

"Well, I assume this one isn't too dangerous, or they probably wouldn't be bringing it into somebody's living room."

He didn't seem entirely satisfied with the idea of a harmless liger. "Lions are dangerous, and tigers definitely are."

"Well, personally I'm going to sit as far away as possible."

"I might sit close to it," Jeremy ventured.

"Don't blame me if you both get eaten," Storey said.

"No one's going to get eaten," Corrine said.

"I'll just stay home and watch *Napoleon Dynamite* instead" was Storey's final comment.

Spring had finally made its debut, and while Corrine had planned to take the subway, it seemed a pity to go underground, given this unaccustomed warmth and sunshine, so she grabbed a passing cab, reasoning that she'd already saved two grand on the tickets.

When they arrived at the town house, a Beaux Arts limestone edifice designed by McKim, Mead & White just a door in from Fifth Avenue and the park, Corrine realized that she'd been here once before, years ago—a wild night back in the eighties. Minky, née Hortense, was a famous debutante who'd acquired her nickname shortly after she came out at the age of seventeen and *Town & Country* announced that she owned twenty-three fur coats. She threw infamous parties and eventually spent the latter part of the eighties in rehab. After one of her stints at Silver Meadows, she publicly renounced her fur habit, selling off her coats at a well-publicized auction at Christie's and giving the proceeds to People for the Ethical Treatment of Animals. She'd since settled into harmless modes of eccentricity, collecting and discarding exotic husbands—an Argentinian polo player, a Russian ballet dancer and an Italian/Uruguayan rancher—while devoting herself increasingly to the welfare of animals. In addition to the Wildlife Society, she sat on the boards of the Central Park Zoo and the ASPCA and was the sole benefactor of an elephant sanctuary in Tennessee and a turtle refuge in Palm Springs.

A lugubrious young Asian man in a black Nehru suit answered the door and beckoned them inside. The town house of her memory had been largely obliterated by a recent renovation, the gilt and ormolu stripped down and plastered over. In place of the former baroque splendor was a Zen temple with an ornamental pool fed by a trick-ling bamboo spout on one side of the entry hall, flanked on the other by a Ginkaku-ji-style rock garden, a stark rectangle blanketed with polished black stones the size of flattened quail eggs. A Greek kouros stood in an alcove, a torso mounted on a steel rod, sans arms and legs and head, the lack of appendages in keeping with the minimalism of the decor, although the penis had somehow survived the millennia. Directly across from the statue was a Picasso from the painter's classi-cist period, a rendering of a surreally distorted white sculptural figure against a milky blue background. Otherwise, the space was unembel-lished, a vast expanse of white wall and black marble floor, whose owner seemed to be boasting that empty space was the ultimate extravagance in this costly precinct of this expensive city. In the eighties the entire neighborhood had been decorated like Versailles, but now, it seemed to Corrine, the au courant aesthetic model was the downtown loft, as if someone up here had noticed or at least suspected that the zeitgeist had moved south. The sole architectural feature of the entire floor was a massive rough-hewn staircase forged out of bronze, which seemed to dare the intrepid visitor to explore the upper reaches of the house. The man in black pointed out that there was also the option of an elevator at the far end of the hall.

Corrine didn't choose her route fast enough to avoid Sasha McGa-vock, Luke's ex, who came in right behind her, heels clicking on the marble floor, towing by the hand her six-year-old stepson, who, like a recalcitrant bulldog on a leash, was strenuously resisting forward motion. When she'd started her dalliance with Luke, Corrine had been inordinately curious about Sasha. She was fairly certain Sasha didn't know she existed, but she'd followed her rival's social progress in the years since their divorce, via the press and intermittent briefings from Casey, and it wasn't unlike Sasha's current march through the entry hall, a triumph of will over not-inconsiderable resistance. Her affair with the billionaire Bernie Melman, an open secret toward the end of her marriage, had ended in humiliating fashion. She'd confided to all of her friends that she fully expected him to initiate divorce proceedings against his wife once her own divorce from Luke was final. In the meantime, Melman's wife decided to go public, slapping Sasha's face in the dining room of Le Cirque at lunch while advising her to "stay the fuck away from my husband." This confrontation brought joy not only to the wives of the community but also to hard-hearted gossip columnists, and the subsequent publicity seemed to mark a turning point in Bernie Melman's attitude toward his wife and his mistress. In the days after the slapfest, photographs of the Melmans engaged in public displays of affection appeared in *Women's Wear Daily* and the *New York Post*. Sasha compounded her disgrace by tearfully confronting Melman at the benefit for the Costume Institute at the Metropolitan Museum—whose theme that year happened to be "Dangerous Liaisons"—and demanding to know why he hadn't returned her calls, all this under the turned-up noses of Anna Wintour and Charlize Theron. Just when it seemed she had no choice but to get out of town, she appeared at the Robin Hood Gala on the arm of Nate Bronstein, who'd clashed with Melman on several corporate takeovers. Some were surprised that Bronstein would be interested in his enemy's discarded mistress, but others, particularly some of his colleagues in finance, felt that in scooping up Sasha he'd shown a savvy sense of market timing, acquiring a blue-chip asset at a steep discount. And last year Sasha had closed the deal with Bronstein, though it was widely noted that she continued to use the name McGavock, which suggested to more than one commentator a reluctance to bear a Semitic surname.

Thankfully, she didn't recognize Corrine—they'd met only once, in passing—and was fully engaged in the struggle to drag her stepson toward the stairs.

"I don't want to see the tiger."

"It's not a tiger," Sasha hissed. "It's a liger. Like in that stupid movie."

Jeremy observed the younger boy with an air of sympathetic condescension. "It's okay," he said. "There's actually nothing to be scared about."

Not true, thought Corrine. That little boy had plenty of reasons to be scared.

Upstairs, a flock of mothers and their young chattered en masse in the drawing room. As an interloper from downtown, Corrine was ill-equipped to decode the room and plumb the levels of intrigue in this gathering, although she did identify among them the much-photographed first and second wives of a hedge fund manager whose divorce had been chronicled in the columns—the new young wife the center of an enthusiastic audience, chattering like grackles, the old one huddled resentfully with a single companion at the outer edge of the scrum.

The room itself was less austere than the entry hall, the decorator seeming to have grudgingly acknowledged the need for some furniture—a pair of bargelike beige sofas faced each other across a prodigious expanse of white-lacquered coffee table. An orange-and-chartreuse Rothko hung over the stark black marble fireplace.

Casey waved her over to the corner that she shared with the woman they'd seen at Justine's a few weeks before, who resembled a bejeweled Giacometti in a canary yellow dress. She stood beside an actual Brancusi—a shiny marble *Bird in Space*. Even as Casey introduced them, the scarecrow glanced over the top of Corrine's head in search of more familiar faces.

"Can't thank you enough," Corrine told her friend. "Jeremy's so excited." Her son nodded solemnly in confirmation, visibly flustered by the arrival of Casey's daughter, Amber, a budding beauty three years his senior. A quadruple threat: blond, tall and elegantly thin, she had in the past year sprouted perfect pear-shaped breasts. It hardly seemed fair, with all her other advantages, that she should look so good, or that she could maintain an A average at Spence. She was destined, Corrine felt certain, to make some nice boy from Harvard or Princeton very miserable.

"You remember Jeremy," Casey said.

"Yeah, hi. Look, Mom, can we go to Jessica's house after this? Her dad has an advance copy of *Knocked Up* and we're going to watch it in their screening room."

"This is what, a new movie?"

Amber rolled her eyes. "It's the new Seth Rogen and Katherine Heigl, and it's not even in theaters yet."

"It's supposed to be really cool," Jeremy said, gazing up at Amber with fear and longing.

"I suppose that's fine. But not until after the presentation. And I want you to ask questions."

"Whatever."

"You know I hate that word."

"Okay, fine, I will ask incisive questions that make my mother look good and thereby increase her chances of getting asked to be on the board of the Wildlife Society, which is the only reason we're here. I don't even know why you want to be on the stupid board anyway. You don't even like animals."

"We're all animals, Amber. Let's go upstairs and get a seat, shall we?"

Rows of folding chairs had been set up in the library on the third floor. Jeremy insisted on taking a seat in the first row. Corrine sat, reluctantly, beside him, with Casey on her right. At the end of their row, a cameraman and a soundman were setting up under the supervision of Trina Cox, one of cable TV's Money Honeys, not to mention Russell's former partner in the failed attempt to takeover Corbin, Dern, the publishing company where he'd been working at the time. Russell had somehow conceived the idea of a leveraged buyout of his employer after learning that he was on the verge of getting fired, and Trina had been the investment banker who advised him and, quite possibly, slept with him. They might have succeeded in the takeover if the stock market crash hadn't derailed them. It was the eighties. Stranger things had happened.

Now Trina was one of several babes employed by the cable stations in the past decade to deliver business and economic news, the collective bet being that the audience for such, as with sports, was largely hetero male. Corrine had to admit she looked good. Though she hadn't been a raving beauty back in the days when she was seducing Russell—call her crazy, but Corrine certainly didn't think so—she was one of those women who'd actually grown more attractive in her thirties and forties, her face losing baby fat and gaining definition. Still, this seemed like quite a comedown from delivering the monthly jobs report on CNN. She was alternately standing in front of the camera, mike in hand, and checking the playback.

"Jesus Christ, I look like Kathy Bates in *Misery*. Can we do something with the fucking lights, please?"

"Excuse me. . . ."

One of the moms raced over and tapped Trina on the shoulder. "*Excuse me,* this is an event for *children,* as you can plainly see, and we would all appreciate it if you'd refrain from inappropriate language."

"Sorry," Trina said, turning back to the cameraman. "I meant to say 'Could we please do something with these *fornicating* lights?'"

The buzz of conversation subsided when Minky wafted into the room, her gold caftan flapping like a sail. Even as a debutante she'd been more zaftig than her peers, and the years had only added to her volume. Surrounded by stick figures, she seemed to be serenely comfortable in her flesh, untroubled by the neuroses and eating disorders of the lesser rich. Her blond bob was kept in check by a black velvet headband and she was bedizened with enormous jewels.

"My friends," she began, "thank you so much for coming. And thank you for supporting the Wildlife Society." A few of the children tittered, seemingly amused by her fluty patrician voice. "I'm particularly pleased for the opportunity to introduce these young people to our group. It's crucial that we preserve our wildlife so that you will inherit an earth where humans and animals live in harmony. Imagine a planet with no lions or tigers or elephants. If not for our society, there might have been no American bison left. Do you children all know what the bison is?"

"It's a buffalo."

"We have bison burgers when we go to Jackson Hole. Mom says they're superhealthy."

"That's gross."

Minky frowned. "What you children may not know is that by the end of the last century the bison had been hunted almost to extinction. In 1907, our founder, William Temple Hornaday, sent fifteen bison from the Bronx Zoo to a reserve in Wichita, Kansas, where the buffalo had once roamed in the millions, and gradually the species recovered in some of its natural habitats. Today we're working to save other endangered species. Who here has visited the Central Park Zoo?"

A unanimous chorus of cheers and huzzahs.

"And the Bronx Zoo?"

Only a trickle of affirmations followed this query.

"Well, today we have a very special visitor from the Bronx. Please welcome Lionel the Liger and his trainer, Dr. Michael Jost."

All eyes turned toward the hallway, which was empty. A disembodied voice was exhorting the star attraction: "Lionel . . . Lionel?"

Necks were craned; feet were scuffed. The tension was broken, briefly, by a pigtailed preschooler in a tartan jumper: "Come on, Lionel, don't be afraid."

Trainer and beast finally appeared at the top of the stairway, eliciting a collective gasp and assorted squeals, the liger resisting the pressure on his leash, batting at the silvery chain links and shaking his head back and forth. It was a very big animal, much bigger than Corrine had expected. The man holding the leash, though fairly solid, wouldn't stand a chance against a cat that must've outweighed him by a factor of three or four.

The squeals rose in volume as he succeeded in leading it into the library. After some coaxing and pushing, he managed to get the big cat to sit on its hind legs.

"Good afternoon, everyone. I'm Dr. Jost, from the Bronx Zoo, and this is Lionel, who's visiting us from his home at an animal refuge in South Carolina."

"Isn't he from Africa?"

"No, he's not, but I'm glad you asked that. Lions and tigers don't live near each other in the wild. The Bengal tiger lives in Asia and the lion is native to Africa."

"So how did the lion have sex with the tiger?" shouted one of the older boys.

Dr. Jost waited patiently for the uproar to subside.

"Well, in the case of Lionel's mom and dad, they were living together at the game refuge. His father was a lion and his mother was a tiger. And, in fact, the liger shares traits with both of his genetic parents. Like tigers, they like to swim, and like lions, they're very sociable. But they're significantly bigger than either lions or tigers. They can grow almost twice as big."

Whatever his parentage, Corrine didn't like the way this animal was looking at Jeremy. At first she thought it was just her imagination, but when she studied her son, his eyes were locked on those of the cat, who was staring back at him disconcertingly.

A late-arriving mother and son were standing in the doorway, and Corrine decided to use this opportunity to get Jeremy out of the liger's direct line of sight by moving over to occupy empty seats near the end of the row. But the cat's gaze was still fixed on Jeremy when they settled into their new chairs, a fact that the trainer seemed to register.

"Stop tracking," he said, whacking it on the side of its neck.

After shaking its huge head and yawning, Lionel returned his gaze to Jeremy. It was terrifying, and Jeremy seemed a little freaked-out himself.

"Mom, why's the liger staring at me?"

"I'm not sure, honey."

Dr. Jost continued his spiel: "What we do know is that ligers are missing the growth-inhibiting gene that keeps them at a normal size. They can weigh up to nine hundred pounds and the skulls are forty percent larger than a Bengal tiger's. Lionel, *stop tracking.*"

He whacked the cat again, and that was enough for Corrine. She grabbed Jeremy's hand and started to lead him out. As they crossed in front of the liger, it crouched and seemed to take aim for a lunge, at which point Dr. Jost tugged hard on its leash. "Behave yourself, Lionel."

Corrine shoved Jeremy ahead as she watched over her shoulder, the liger stationary but shaking its head against the straining collar. In the hallway, she took his hand and together they ran down the stairs.

"That was pretty scary," Jeremy said.

Corrine nodded. She didn't want to overdramatize, but she'd been terrified.

"Was it just me, or did that liger look like it wanted to eat me?"

"Well, let's just say I didn't like the way it was looking at you."

Standing outside on the sidewalk on a warm spring afternoon, she wondered if she'd let her imagination run wild. Just across from the town house was a large trailer towed by a pickup truck with a Bronx Zoo logo. They crossed Fifth Avenue and walked down the park side, under the porous canopy of just-leafing tree branches. She could predict the call from Casey, who would accuse her of being a crazy, overprotective mother, but she really didn't care.

In fact, when Casey finally did call, it seemed that the Calloways' premature exit was overshadowed by subsequent events. The story that gradually emerged was that Lionel, while being led to his trailer from the door of the town house, had pounced on a passing jogger, who was now in stable condition at Lenox Hill Hospital.

13

THEN IT WAS MEMORIAL DAY WEEKEND and the Calloways were packing up the borrowed Land Rover and joining the exodus from Manhattan, funneling out of the Midtown Tunnel into the so-called expressway, joining the hundred-mile-long queue of vehicles creeping toward the outer reaches of Long Island, the traffic eventually congealing like melted butter turning cold at the lower end of the lobster claw of the South Fork late Friday afternoon. Every year they left TriBeCa earlier and every year the drive was longer, or so it felt to Corrine.

The old farmhouse they'd rented for so many years, and the two acres that remained of a once-vast empire of corn and potatoes, within sniffing distance of the ocean, was on the market for $4.9 million. Even in this booming market it seemed unlikely the Polanskis would get that much, and, in fact, it had been listed for nine months when Sara Polanski had called Corrine and offered to rent it one more time if the Calloways agreed to show it, her native thrift triumphing even on the verge of the avalanche of cash that would be hers when the house sold. Already the Polanskis, who'd farmed the land for more than a century, were wealthier than some of the second-home owners from the city, after years of selling off acreage by the sea. Certainly much richer than Russell and Corrine, who'd been instrumental in getting Becca Polanski into Brown, the first alumnus of Bridgehampton High School to matriculate there, and Corrine sent Christmas and birthday cards, while Russell sent books that might appeal to one family member or another—none of which had hurt when it came time to negotiate a deal each spring.

The first weekend in June, they quietly observed their twenty-fifth wedding anniversary, as they had less significant ones, at the Old Stove Pub, a steak house on the highway. Neither seemed inclined to make a big fuss about it, sensibly agreeing to save energy and resources for their big Labor Day party; in the end, they included Tom and Casey, whose own silver jubilee was just a few months off.

Russell took the jitney from the city Thursday evenings and went back into the city every Monday morning, while Corrine, on hiatus from her job, stayed out with the kids and adhered rigorously to the South Beach diet. Russell talked to the children every day during the course of the week; toward the end of July, he and Jeremy camped out at the Books of Wonder bookstore in Chelsea, where they communed with live owls and several hundred fans waiting for the midnight release of the final Harry Potter novel. That summer, except for a few John Edwards partisans, everyone was divided into Hillary and Obama camps, and the arguments were heated around the pools and fire pits.

Tom and Casey had lent them their old Land Rover, a stylish, if not terribly reliable, vehicle in regulation hunter green, and thus they were able to spend yet another season beside the ocean, going to movie premieres in East Hampton with the actors and directors, arranging play dates with the children of a media mogul, playing grass-court tennis in Southampton with the spawn of great American robber barons. It was a life they'd been living for years, and therefore unremarkable to them, until some minor dislocation or embarrassment highlighted its absurdities. Storey's desire to keep a horse at the nearby stable, as some of her friends did, had to be thoroughly discouraged. The proximity to so much wealth could be infectious; only last year Russell had talked about buying into a bankrupt vineyard. Likewise, unless they were included by someone who'd purchased a table, they had to find clever excuses for declining invitations to the charity benefits that had spread east to the Hamptons in recent years, some of which ran to a thousand bucks a head. And yet, many of their friends and their children's friends were here, and over the years they'd carved out a place for themselves in the Darwinian social fray without violent effort or expenditure. They were well liked, and their parties fashionable—the kind of gatherings that mixed what was left of the literary and artistic communities with some of the Southampton blue bloods and the East Hampton Democratic Party politicos and the Amagansett *Saturday Night Live* crowd.

Even the hedge funders who'd bought up most of the oceanfront and the dentists and dermatologists whose houses dotted the former potato fields had a soft spot for the founding myth of a seaside arts colony, for the days when Pollock and de Kooning had lurched around the same sand dunes as Capote and Albee. The Calloways somehow managed to inherit this tradition; one of the many glossy giveaway publications that chronicled the summer scene had recently compared them to Gerald and Sara Murphy, the great host and hostess of the Lost Generation, which delighted Russell, who'd published a book about them, though Corrine considered the comparison imperfect on the detail of the Murphys' inherited wealth.

Their Friday-before-Labor-Day party had become a fixture on the Hamptons calendar, and Corrine was always amazed to find herself being courted during the summer by those who hoped to get invited. They tried to hold the guest list to a hundred, but last year at least twice that many had showed up. Certainly no one came for the food, although Russell seemed proud of the chili and cornbread and salad he made with the help of a local chef, the bulk of the budget going to booze, wine and beer. They hired three bartenders and three servers and hoped it wouldn't rain, since the crowd inevitably overflowed the house, and a tent was beyond their means. It was exhausting, but it would kill Russell to give it up.

"It's bigger than we are," he once told Corrine when she complained about the effort and the expense. She wondered if it was the kind of institution that could survive uprooting; this year's gathering would have a valedictory feeling, almost certainly their last in the old farmhouse.

———

That week, Cody Erhardt, the director, was staying with them. Once upon a time he'd been a notorious badass, a hard-drinking, skirt-chasing American ninja—also the title of his best-known movie—but at this point in deep middle age he was fairly unprepossessing, doughy and overfed, with thinning hair and a mottled pink complexion. Although he'd played a version of himself in a Godard film, no casting agent would have, at this date, tried to sell him as a macho hip direc-tor. It was strange to see him—so clearly an indoor creature, a native of editing studios and screening rooms—out here at the beach. Cody was, if not exactly an old friend, at least an old acquaintance, an avatar of the brief, lamented renaissance of American film that flared up around 1969 in the wake of *Easy Rider*. Russell had published a collection of three of his screenplays and he'd later, briefly, been attached to Cor-rine's adaptation of *The Heart of the Matter* after it had been bought by New Line. Though that film got made by someone else and ultimately played in only a few theaters, it was still a hot project when she man-aged, with Russell's help, to get herself assigned to do the script for *Youth and Beauty*. Tug Barkley, or someone who worked for him, had discovered Jeff's novel. After going silent for two years, his production company had recently renewed the option, and Corrine was working on yet another draft with Cody. The development process had been, from her point of view, painfully protracted and convoluted, though no more so, Cody assured her, than the average movie; he'd been trying to make Kerouac's *Dharma Bums* for seventeen years.

Although she liked to give the impression that she'd adapted *The Heart of the Matter* on a whim, that she'd never expected anything to come of it, she had worked on it tirelessly and was thrilled when her screenplay was optioned, pleased to have forged an identity in the Hobbesian cultural landscape of Manhattan after a stint as a stay-at-home mom, resentful of any insinuation that Russell's connections had played a part, and secretly crushed when the film disappeared without a trace. She'd thrown herself into the job at Nourish New York on the rebound. She loved the work, but when she was given another chance on *Youth and Beauty*, it felt like a new lease on life. Corrine des-perately wanted to see it made, and succeed, though she would be hard-pressed to say whether it was herself or Jeff she was hoping to redeem.

She and Cody had been working during the day and then the three of them would make the rounds in the evening. As August progressed, the social pace had become ever more frenzied; it would have been impossible to honor even half of their cocktail and dinner party invitations, even if the traffic hadn't been so clotted as to make it necessary to plot out one's course in advance, calculating likely time of transit and distance between points, weighing the relative desirability of events that were unrealistically far apart. Russell actually enjoyed this crazy whirl, at least up to a point, and Corrine was grateful that Cody was here to accompany him, allowing her to spend a few nights with the kids.

For their latest powwow, she had forced Cody to accompany her to the beach, which she hadn't seen in three days, and he'd covered himself up like a mummy, swathed in gray sweats, with a towel on his head.

The ending of Jeff's novel had always posed a problem. In the book, the Jeff surrogate—a successful neo-Expressionist painter—dies of a heroin overdose, presumably accidental, although the possibility of suicide isn't far-fetched; he is, after all, hopelessly in love with his best friend's wife. Just to complicate matters further, his best friend is his gallerist. Corrine had originally adhered closely to the novel, but the studio execs had balked once they read the first draft, and in the next draft a car accident took the place of the heroin overdose. Lately, a consensus had been building that the protagonist shouldn't die at all.

"Back in the day, the studios would have let us get away with that," Cody said one morning, "the hero dying of an overdose; they would have let us show it, for God's sake—the syringe in the arm, the trickle of blood—then pulled back on the dude gradually turning blue. After *Easy Rider, Five Easy Pieces, Mean Streets* and *Death by a Thousand Cuts*, they realized they didn't have a clue, and for a little while they let the kids have the keys to the candy store. But eventually the marketing department took over, and now they call the shots. No way they're going to let us kill off our fucking protagonist."

"Well, his death does resolve the whole love triangle thing pretty nicely."

"Hey, maybe we have all three of them move in together, remake *Jules and Jim,* which I'm pretty sure none of the marketing morons ever heard of—except it probably won't pass muster with the PG-13 police, either. So, tell me, really, did you actually fuck the guy, or was that wishful thinking on his part?"

"I'm just going to leave it up to your overheated, lecherous imagination, Cody."

"Am I the only one who thinks it's weird that Russell edited the novel?"

"It was remarked on somewhat."

"I mean, doesn't that make you cringe a little bit?"

"It was a long time ago," she said.

The day of the party dawned brilliantly clear, and the weather held, the heat of the day moderated by the ocean—audible just over the dunes all day—fading to perfect shirtsleeve temperature by six.

"We're sorry to be so unfashionably early," said Judy Levine, who, with her husband, Art, was the first to arrive. "But we can only stay a minute. We've got to go to the Aldas' and then on to the Michaelses' for dinner." Corrine could imagine that Judy must have thought herself very clever to apologize in a manner that allowed her to drop these names, which could only suggest to the hostess that it was she and her husband who were not quite fashionable enough to merit a later arrival, that the Levines were only stopping by on their way to grander events.

"At least now we'll get a chance to talk before all the fashionable people show up," Russell said, parrying the thrust. Corrine tried not to smile. He was a good host, but he was nobody's patsy. Art was kind of interesting, a writer and director from the golden age of television, though of that generation of men for whom women were anything but equals, and Judy was just a silly, social-climbing twit who couldn't possibly have improved his opinion of their gender over the course of a thirty-year marriage.

The guests came mostly in pairs, some early birds with a child in tow, others with houseguests—a new divorcée or a single friend from the city. Some of the couples came with a gay friend, and some of the gay couples had a straight friend in tow. They all observed certain sumptuary laws of the time and place; an observer of the cars lining the street might have guessed there was a prohibition on American automobiles, and the people climbing out were dressed in a style best described as expensive casual: polo shirts, jeans, driving shoes. Socks were universally shunned by the men, as were ties—although late in the evening an interloper from Southampton, obviously lost, appeared on the lawn wearing a seersucker suit and a pink tie with a sailboat motif, clutching a bottle of Macallan by the neck.

The women wore sundresses and sandals, and the early arrivals were hidden behind big sunglasses—Tom Ford was the frame of the moment—which they pushed to the tops of their heads after the sun went down in a way that they hoped was reminiscent of Jackie O. Corrine was wearing a stretchy turquoise paisley Pucci that she'd bought when Russell took her to Capri for a literary conference, and she was wondering if it wasn't just a little too tight.

She was always surprised that she knew almost every single person, except for the houseguests, who were inevitably profuse in thanking her for allowing them to come. She wasn't aware that Tug Barkley had been invited until she saw him amble up the drive wearing nothing but cargo shorts and a wifebeater, flanked by two glamazons in tiny white dresses. Tug's interest had revived the long-dormant production of *Youth and Beauty*, though she'd never actually met him. He seemed to sense she was the hostess, smiling broadly and thrusting out his hand. "Hey, I'm Tug. Thanks for having me."

"I'm Corrine," she said. "It's a real pleasure to meet you." While she considered herself immune to the charms of vapid celebrities, that wasn't how she felt at this moment. Perhaps it was the fact that this was the man who would play Jeff on-screen. Except, of course, it was more than that. "Actually, I'm working on the *Youth and Beauty* screenplay with Cody Erhardt."

"That's cool," he said. "Love Cody."

Somewhat taken aback, expecting some kind of follow-up or

acknowledgment, she explained that there were bars inside and out, and told them to make themselves at home. She was only slightly surprised to see Russell bound off the porch and greet Tug like an old friend. Russell was nothing if not gregarious, and if she sometimes thought he was indiscriminate in collecting people, she also couldn't help sometimes admiring the breadth of his acquaintance and his enthusiasm for new people, as well as his conviction that there were still friends to be made at an age when most men were consolidating their portfolios of names and faces. After all these years he still had a boyish love of parties, and a provincial's wonderment at the social spectacle of New York, with all its bright stars and unlikely juxtapositions—and this was undoubtedly New York, with a sprinkle of Hollywood, spread out on the browning lawn beside the old shingled farmhouse.

Cody, meanwhile, was chatting up one of the gorgeous young things who'd showed up with Tug. "I'm just saying every novel's unique, a reinvention of the form. A screenplay has conventions that need to be observed—action, dialogue, three-act structure."

"What's three-act structure?"

"Boy meets girl, boy and girl get into pickle, boy gets pickle into girl."

She giggled, raising her hand to her face to cover a crooked tooth.

"I haven't heard that one," Tug said, returning with three drinks in hand, one of which he handed off to her. "So I see you've met the great Cody Erhardt."

"Cody who?"

Cody looked miffed, of course.

"Shit, that just shows what's happened to this business," Tug said. "Cody here's the man. He did all these amazing movies in the seventies. Part of that Scorsese-Schrader clique. *American Ninja, Death by a Thousand Cuts.*"

The great man himself, who had tried at one time to get his pickle into Corrine, bowed in acknowledgment of the compliment.

"Oh right," the girl said. "I loved *American Ninja.*"

Burly, bearded Rob Klemp, the painter, in paint-stained cargo shorts, was talking to reedy Jillian Simms, the fashion designer, angelic in white jeans and white T-shirt, her blond hair flat against her skull, pulled back in a ponytail. What were they talking about? Sometimes Corrine wondered how these people knew one another, and how the hell *they* knew them. As she got closer, she heard them arguing.

"Come on, Obama has no résumé," Jillian said. "I mean, he's been a senator for, what? Three minutes?"

"Long enough to be right about the war in Iraq."

"Hillary's got substance. Face it, Obama's a lightweight."

Russell had loaded up a special iPod for the occasion, which seemed to Corrine to consist of Don Henley's "Boys of Summer," the Go-Go's "Vacation," the Motels' "Suddenly Last Summer," "Summertime Blues" by various artists, "Margaritaville," plus pretty much all of the Beach Boys catalog. Thankfully, he'd skipped "Big Girls Don't Cry" and "Umbrella," the ubiquitous anthems of the summer.

"Oh my God," Corrine said, spotting a newcomer. "That's Tony Duplex."

"Yeah," Rob said. "He came with Gary Arkadian. Tony's got a new show going up this fall at Arkadian's gallery."

"I haven't seen him in years," Corrine said. Tony looked very much out of place in a tight black suit over a shirt as white as his complexion.

"He disappeared up a crack pipe for most of the nineties, but apparently he's back."

"I remember," she said. He'd been great friends with Jeff, in fact.

Not surprisingly, he looked frail for his years. They were almost surely the same age, but he looked much older, his face pitted and canyoned. He showed no sign of recognition when Russell came over and introduced him to Corrine. One of those downtown bad boys who failed to leave the party while the getting was good, he'd managed to sustain his drug habit well into the nineties, by which time his critical reputation had crashed and his drug of choice had gone out of fashion. As she recalled, there'd been some kind of fight with a collector who held dozens of his paintings, and the guy dumped them on the market all at once, right before Robert Hughes wrote a withering review of his latest show. She hadn't heard his name for years; then, recently, she'd seen a picture of him at a party in *New York* magazine, and she seemed to recall a mention of his resurrection in the *Post*'s Page Six.

"Thanks for having me," he said, shaking her hand limply. Obviously he had no memory of the night she'd met him on the Lower East Side, ransoming him and Jeff from a shortchanged drug dealer with a handful of gold coins.

Kip Taylor emerged from the throng, with one hand raised in greeting, the other perched on his wife's shoulder, accompanied by Luke and Giselle McGavock. Corrine tried to mute her shock as the group approached, to compose her features as Kip and Vanessa hugged her in turn, at which point the question of how to greet Luke presented itself. He answered it quickly by kissing her cheek, as did Giselle.

"I hope you don't mind us crashing your party," Luke said. "We're staying with Kip and Vanessa this weekend."

"You're more than welcome," Corrine said, hoping she sounded less flustered than she felt.

"I told them it was the party of the season," Kip said.

"Hardly that," Corrine said.

Luke grazed her with a rueful, apologetic glance.

Ten minutes later he found her alone in the kitchen, where she'd quickly retreated.

"I didn't mean to sneak up on you," he said. "Kip only mentioned that we were coming here an hour ago."

"Why should I mind?" she said, realizing immediately that her tone was peevish. "I'm sorry," she said. "I'm just—I just wasn't expecting to see you."

"I thought about calling. I didn't know if I should. But I'd love to see you."

"Here I am."

"I mean alone."

"We head back to the city on Monday," she said.

"I'll be there next week."

"And your wife?" She wasn't sure which designation she liked least, her name or her title.

"She flies back on Wednesday. On Saturday, Ashley's coming down from Poughkeepsie to join me in the city."

"Call me," Corrine said, not at all certain whether she wished to encourage or dismiss him, their conference punctuated by the arrival of a waiter looking for more ice.

As they stepped outside, she spotted her husband engaged in what looked like a heated discussion with a pale, chubby stranger, who seemed to be cowering.

She hurried over as the guests, increasingly, turned to observe the scene.

"It's my job to express an opinion," the man was saying.

"It's your job to attract attention to yourself by doing hatchet jobs on your betters, you fucking troll."

"Who's being ad hominem now?"

"Damn right I am. You just turn around on your Birkenstocks and get your fat ass off my lawn."

Steve Sanders, who looked like a young Trotsky and wrote for the *Times,* had been hovering at the edge of the battle. "Russell," he said, "let's be reasonable."

"Fuck you, Steve," he said. "There's nothing reasonable about his bitchy little tirades. I can't stop him from writing them, but I sure as hell don't have to put up with his company at my own party." The man in question was retreating with tattered dignity under the gaze of half the partygoers.

"I didn't know he'd attacked one of your authors, or I never would've brought him."

"I'm sure you wouldn't have," Russell said, his rage dissipating as its object retreated.

"What was all that about, my love?" she asked a few minutes later, drawing him away from the party, toward the potato barn.

"That was Toby Barnes."

"Who?"

"The little twat who wrote that nasty review of *Youth and Beauty* in *Details.*"

"For God's sake, Russell, that had to be fifteen years ago. It was another lifetime."

"I remember it like it was yesterday. The headline was 'Uncouth and Snooty.'"

She thought it was kind of magnificent that Russell was still defending Jeff after all these years, if not very politic. "Is it wise to humiliate him like that? Now you've made a real enemy."

"Fuck him, he was already my enemy."

"Well, don't forget that you publish a lot of authors who might not want to be on Barnes's shit list."

"They'd be glad to know that I'd fight for them just like I fought for Jeff."

"Well, let's see if we can salvage this party, slugger. Smile and laugh and show them that all's well," she said, taking his arm and leading him back into the crowd.

Russell's outburst, far from dampening spirits, seemed to give the party a new source of energy. He was congratulated by half a dozen of the guests, most of them artists or writers, all of them at one time or another the recipients of nasty reviews. The drama provided grist for dozens of conversations about art and criticism and hospitality, and was reported the following Tuesday in a gossip item on Page Six.

The party continued on for several hours, until finally the guests melted away and Corrine found herself sitting alone on the front porch, smelling the primal brine of the invisible ocean, listening to the waves rolling in beyond the dunes and the brittle song of the crickets, who seemed to be eulogizing the summer, the chill in the air a melancholy premonition of fall. Far away, from somewhere inside the house, she could intermittently hear Russell's muffled baritone as he regaled some straggler. Farther away, Luke was doing who knew what. Maybe she'd had too much to drink, but she suddenly felt terribly sad. Instead of being reassured by the familiarity of these sensations, she was depressed by them. The first time she'd felt the autumn approach across the dunes from this very spot, she'd been a young woman. Summer was over and she was fifty years old, her life going by so fast that the fog drifting in over the grass seemed like an omen.

14

―――――

NO LESS THAN THE FARM, the city is attuned to the rhythms of
the seasons, although here the autumn, rather than the spring, is the
season of rebirth and renewal—the start of a new year for Gentiles no
less than for those who celebrate Rosh Hashanah, the time to shake
off the torpor and idleness of August and send the children back to
school, where they will start fresh, make new and interesting friends
and perform even better than last year; a season of restaurant and gallery openings; the time when the fashions of the following year are
unveiled on the runways as the gingko leaves turn yellow, Fashion
Week giving way to the New York Film Festival, the opening of the Metropolitan Opera and the Philharmonic and City Ballet, the big charity
galas and later the art auctions at Christie's and Sotheby's and Phillips
de Pury, which will tell us how rich the rich are feeling this year. It's
also, less profitably, the season when publishers roll out their biggest
and most promising titles.

Before leaving for lunch, Russell stopped in to see Jonathan, who
was just across the hall. "When do we see the *Times*?"

"Any minute now."

Jonathan's office was sparsely decorated, the walls bare except for
the poster advertising Carson's book and another for Arcade Fire.

"You heard anything?"

"My source tells me we'll be happy."

They were waiting for their advance copy of the following Sunday's
New York Times Book Review, which reportedly featured a review of

Jack's book. The fact that they'd sent a photographer to take his picture in Tennessee two weeks ago was a positive sign, and Jonathan had been told the reviewer was a novelist of stature, which was also a good sign, although Russell wasn't entirely thrilled that he was a southerner; it was like the way the *Times* almost inevitably assigned women to review other women.

"In the meantime, he's missed his last two interviews."

"Did you call the hotel?"

Jonathan nodded. "Not picking up."

"I probably should've seen this coming."

"Maybe this could work for us," Jonathan said. "The whole bad-boy, *poète maudit* angle."

"We're trying to get people to write about the work," Russell said. "About what's on the page. We're trying to sell literature here." He realized even as he said it how pretentious this sounded, but he believed it. He just wasn't sure if he could convey the concept to this twenty-eight-year-old, who was wearing a vintage *Naked Lunch* T-shirt under an open flannel shirt. "I don't want Jack branded as some meth-addled cracker right out of the gate. He's already susceptible to the inevitable stereotyping: Southern writers are almost always relegated to their own ghetto of exotic decadence."

In a more general sense, Russell objected to the cult of personality, to the fake idea of *authenticity,* to the notion that the intensity of the life somehow certified the work, all the holy drunk/genius junkie bullshit that equated excess with wisdom, cirrhosis with genius. Blake had a lot to answer for, in his opinion. The road of excess leads to rehab, or the boneyard, more often than it leads to the palace of wisdom. He believed that literature was accomplished in spite of excessive behavior, not because of it.

"I'm fucking tired of this idea that getting drunk and/or doing smack turns an MFA candidate into a genius."

"But you've got to admit, chief, a lot of writers and artists are drunks and junkies."

"I don't admit that at all. I don't think the proportion of literary alcoholics runs any higher than that of alcoholic plumbers." Not for the first time he wondered where Jonathan found such tight jeans—were they sold like that, or did he have them taken in? And how did you get into the damn things?

"I don't know," Jonathan said. "Jesus, I could make you a list, starting with Christopher Marlowe. Most of the writers we both like were drunks or addicts or both. Just look at the modernists—Hemingway, Fitzgerald, Faulkner. Raving alkies. Not to mention the Beats. Most of the writers on *our list* are pretty fucked-up and emotionally unstable."

"They'd be better and more productive if they got their shit together. *Tender Is the Night* would've been a better book if its author hadn't been drunk half the time and wired on Dexedrine the other half."

"If you say so, Dad."

"Hey, I'm not moralizing. I'm just saying let's not confuse cause and effect."

"What about Burroughs?"

"His *subject* was drugs and derangement, so I guess we have to make an exception there. Ditto Hunter Thompson."

"So what do we do about the fuckup in question? About Jack?"

"Keep calling. If you can't reach him, I'll go over to the hotel room after lunch." He realized that if he sounded a little vehement on this topic, even overwrought, it probably had a lot to do with Jeff, who'd been slouching at the back of his mind all morning: His dead best friend, the genius junkie, was posthumously developing a cult all his own. Sales of his books were steadily climbing. It seemed like such a damn waste. Sometimes, still, it would hit Russell hard, how much he missed him. How angry he was at him still for not being around. No one had ever completely replaced him. Corrine said he should go to therapy. But then, she had Jeff issues of her own.

After lunch he searched his file cabinets and found the article that had so enraged him about *Youth and Beauty,* although, despite the fact that it had been his practice to make carbons of all his letters, he couldn't find the copy of his seething epistolary response. The clipping was from the April 1991 issue of *Details:*

Those who imagine that the guardians of high culture sit in the clouds, like gods, disinterestedly paring their fingernails while passing judgment on the literary offerings laid before them, should consider the canonization of Jeff Pierce as his posthumous novel, *Youth and Beauty*, slouches into bookstores. August voices from *The New York Times, The New York Review of Books* and *The Village Voice* have all breathlessly retailed a version of the archetypal tabloid narrative: young, talented, tortured artist, too sensitive for this world. Listen carefully to the faux-stentorian tones of critical consensus and you can hear, underneath, the screaming of teenage girls at a pop concert. (Of course, Pierce helped shape the narrative with his Keatsian title.) Nowhere in print, until now, will you find the opinion that he was a preppy junkie whose worldview was doubly circumscribed, by privilege and by addiction. . . .

"Can I talk to you about the party?" Jonathan asked, leaning in the doorway.

"How's it shaping up?" Russell asked, relieved to set this screed aside.

"Getting bigger by the minute."

Russell didn't really believe in publication parties, or at least he didn't believe in paying for them, because he didn't think they helped to sell books; basically, it was just a sop to the author's ego. But Jonathan had talked him into doing one for Jack after his reading at 192 Books, and now that the TBR promised to come in strong, it looked as if it was going to be the event du jour. The reading and party would take place on Monday, the day after most civilians would see the *Times*. All week, people had been begging to be added to the list, and Jonathan was now worried that both of their chosen venues might prove to be too small. The bookstore wasn't much bigger than the bathroom at Nobu, and the party room above the Fatted Calf, a kind of speakeasy for friends of the owners, which Russell had managed to book at an insider's price, was even smaller than the bookstore, but Russell thought it was perfect.

"It should be a fucking zoo," Jonathan said.

"That's fine," Russell said. "Far better than a half-empty room. Let's put on an extra bartender, though. Nobody minds being jammed up against a bunch of their peers or literary celebrities unless they can't get a drink."

"Richard Johnson from Page Six RSVP'd this morning."

"That's surprising."

"I think a lot of this is coming from the Web, Gothamist and Gawker and some of the bloggers. And then, strangely enough, there's a Web site called Tweakers.com that serves the speed-freak community, and they seem to have registered the fact that a couple of the stories deal with meth. They just posted the details of the reading."

"Methheads have their own Web site?"

"Several," Jonathan said, shaking his head as he walked to the door. "Jesus. Who knew?"

For twenty-five years, Russell had been trying to understand and channel that mysterious force alternately known as buzz or word of mouth, and now it seemed to have mutated into this new digital form.

It was always a little mysterious, what made some books pop and others evaporate. This week he'd sold rights in Spain, Germany and Italy, which basically meant that Jack's advance was covered and everything from here on was profit. Exactly how Russell liked to do it.

Jonathan rushed back into the office, waving several sheets of paper. "I've got it!"

"And?"

"It's a rave. ... I've only skimmed it, but it's basically a blow job. Here, listen to this: 'Jack Carson's characters are the demon spawn of Faulkner's Snopes family and Carver's lumpen proles, the descendants of Walker Evans's Depression-era subjects, trapped deep in the sunless hollers of Tennessee and Kentucky. Their American dream is a nightmare of cruelty and inbreeding compounded by privation; moonshine and meth their only escape, and yet Carson manages to invest their struggle to survive with a kind of stoic grandeur, and even, at times, to celebrate their inchoate yearning toward the light. ...'"

"Jesus, let me see that," said Russell, practically tearing the review from Jonathan's hands.

———

The afternoon before the party, Russell was looking over the reorders for the book, which were strong, when Corrine called, all worked up about a hard day with the bureaucrats at the New York City Housing Authority. She was trying to get permission to set up a food giveaway in the parking lot of a housing project in Brooklyn. "I don't know whether to be somewhat encouraged or thoroughly discouraged."

"Well, if you don't know, honey, I'm not sure how I would."

"Do you realize you call me *honey* when you're exasperated with me? I think you do it because you feel guilty that you're exasperated and it assuages your conscience."

"I can't say I'm aware of this alleged tic, nor do I believe it."

"All right, I'll stop bugging you. I'll see you at home."

"Not till late. Tonight's Jack's book party, remember?"

"Oh, right. Do you want me to come?"

"If I were you, I'd skip it. Looks like it's going to be a real hipster ratfuck. I won't be too late, I hope. If he wants to go out afterward, I'll send Jonathan."

In hopes of getting the guest of honor to the church on time, Russell decided to pick him up at the hotel himself. He arrived at the Chelsea just before six; when Jack didn't answer the call from the lobby phone, he asked at the desk, where they had no information on Mr. Carson's whereabouts. Why, Russell wondered, had he put him up in the same hotel where Sid Vicious had murdered Nancy Spungen? He turned and walked out the door and down the street to the Trailer Park Lounge, where he found the missing person huddled over a drink, looking exceedingly mournful sitting on his stool.

"I don't guess this was a real good hidin' spot," he said when Russell sat down beside him. His hair pointed in several directions and he had a greenish pallor. The kitschy bar and grill with its Elvis memorabilia had become Jack's home away from home in the city. It was his kind of joke: a real redneck in a fake redneck bar.

"You've done better, certainly."

"I don't think I can do this."

"Sure you can."

"I can't get up and read my stories to a bunch of smart-ass New Yorkers."

"Just look at it this way—most of the characters in your stories could kick their asses all the way to New Jersey."

"Most of my characters are dumb crackers."

"I wouldn't call them dumb. They actually seem very savvy to me. If they were competing on *Survivor*, these New Yorkers wouldn't stand a chance. They'd get kicked off the island in a heartbeat by your boys and girls. I'll tell you a secret about smart-ass New Yorkers; ninety percent of them are former hicks who landed here utterly clueless after being the least popular kids in their high schools. The popular ones stayed back home, where they were wanted."

"Just fuckin' shoot me now."

"Have another drink."

"Don't mind if I do."

After another vodka, he seemed slightly less terrified.

"What are you going to read?"

"I have no fuckin' idea."

"Well, let's think of something. Read the story you think is least likely to go over with this audience, and I bet you it'll bring the house down."

"I need some blow," he said.

"Well, sorry, but I used up my last gram about twenty years ago."

"Somebody's comin'," he said. "I have to wait."

"A dealer?"

"A friend," Jack said.

Russell pointed out that the reading started in ten minutes, but Jack wouldn't budge until his friend arrived—a petite, voluptuous brunette with a gold nose ring who introduced herself as Cara.

"You got the stuff?" Jack asked.

"Come on," she said, walking off toward the bathrooms.

Russell finally got them both into a taxi ten minutes after the reading was supposed to have started, somewhat fretful about Jack's condition. He seemed just as drunk as before, only now he was twitching and chewing his lower lip. As they approached the bookstore on Tenth Avenue, they could see a milling throng on the sidewalk. The chatter of the crowd subsided as Jack emerged from the cab and shuffled through the gauntlet, Russell guiding him with a hand on his shoulder, apologizing as they pushed forward into the mob. "Got the reader here. Sorry, coming through. Excuse us. . . ."

There probably weren't more than a hundred people, but the place was packed to capacity, half seated in the chairs that had been set out and the rest standing, crowding the floor as the stragglers from outside struggled to get in. Astrid Kladstrup, overdressed for the occasion in a tiny black cocktail dress, waved to him from the back. He couldn't believe it had been a year since he'd taken the keeper of Jeff's Web site to lunch, or that he'd managed to resist her.

It was as good a crowd as Russell had ever seen here, and the atmosphere was charged with anticipation. The audience seemed convinced that they were in on something special, pleased with themselves for being here and anxious to have their expectations fulfilled. Russell wished he could tell Jack that the crowd was with him—that they wanted him to be someone they could say later they'd seen at the very beginning, that they'd follow him almost anywhere tonight as long as it was novel—but Jack was enduring the pleasantries of the owner and the staff. He looked as if he'd just crawled out of bed after sleeping off a terrible bender—his hair an unruly mess, his face drawn and gaunt.

He was fucking perfect.

When he started to read, the crowd collectively leaned forward; Jack was mumbling, and speaking so fast that it was difficult at first to make out the words, even for Russell, but a helpful staffer adjusted the mike and a hush fell as he started again. He was still mumbling, and occasionally slurring, but it was just possible to make out most of what he was saying.

He read "Family First," a story about a young woman from a small Tennessee town who is sexually abused by her father and runs away to Memphis, where she eventually ends up working for an escort service. Years later she gets an outcall for a trick at a motel and arrives, only to find her father waiting there, and she shoots him with the pearl-handled revolver she stole from his truck the night she ran away.

We have already learned that this is a girl who knows how to hit what she shoots at, and though she wants to kill him, and we want her to, she shoots him through the thigh and walks away, leaving the pistol behind on the bedside table.

The climactic action all happened in less than a page—what had once been three pages describing her thoughts and feelings, until Russell had cut and pared much of it away, saving the essentials and exposing, as he saw it, the hard, adamantine core. It was all there, but Jack had told too much in his original draft, hadn't trusted his material, when, in fact, he'd already set it all up and provided everything the reader needed to know. And Russell, as he saw it, had shown him what was already there, and how to overcome his fear of not making his case explicit, and had cited the eternal cliché that less is more. He didn't want credit, but he knew he was right, and he was grateful that this incredible material had come to him so that he could help to make it what it wanted to be. Even the draft he'd first read, cluttered with exposition, had had that vertiginous liftoff that he always wished for at the end of a story, the simultaneous feeling of rising out of the mundane comprehension of our mortal experience and the sensation as we rise of looking down into the abyss, an intimation of redemption—or damnation—that was all the more powerful for being left almost unspoken, and now the audience felt it, too; the combination of the story itself and how clearly the crowd was validating his assessment of its worth made Russell's eyes well with tears, as did, perhaps, the knowledge of how hard-earned Jack's hard-boiled wisdom truly was: the absent father and abusive stepfather, juvenile detention, the fast-food jobs and bar fights. It was all there in the stories. It was all *his*.

The applause was prolonged and clamorous, and many who were sitting rose to their feet. Russell knew it was a great story—no one could have convinced him otherwise—but it was exhilarating to hear Jack read it and to see the response, almost unmediated by preconceptions. He was actually a powerful performer, his obvious reluctance lending weight to the reading. The audience knew they'd heard something special. The *Times* had prepared them to be impressed, but it hadn't necessarily prepared them to be physically moved.

As for Jack, he looked stunned, as if he didn't know what to make of all this. He nodded and blinked, waved once and then retreated to the signing table, where his new fans pressed in on him.

Russell chatted with the staff and examined the shelves while Jack signed books, finally extracting him after more than an hour. The young drug courier, Cara, followed him out to the street. Astrid Kladstrup, who'd been smoking on the sidewalk, sidled over to join their group. "That was amazing," she said to Jack, who merely grunted as a taxi pulled to a stop beside them. Clearly a city girl, Cara opened the cab door and thrust Jack into the backseat, sliding in beside him and pulling the door closed. But the maneuver failed to discourage Astrid, who slipped around the back to the opposite door of the cab and inserted herself on the other side of Jack, forcing Russell to claim the front seat.

He gave directions to the Fatted Calf while Cara explained to Jack that he really should have had his party at KGB in the East Village, before launching into a speech about her other favorite bars and clubs, babbling melodiously, filibustering her rival. She was still talking when they arrived at the restaurant. This battle for Jack's attention, and the youth of the crowd upstairs, made Russell feel suddenly old and weary. He stayed just long enough to introduce Jack to some of the other writers on hand, then struggled down the stairs against the incoming tide of bodies, leaving Jonathan to keep an eye on the star of the evening.

The publicist showed up at the office just before noon the next day and stepped into Russell's office to give his report. "You missed the whole second wave, which was pretty fucking crazy. Nancy Tanner got hammered and danced on the bar, and these two girls got in a catfight over Jack, and then sometime around one-thirty he disappeared with Dan Auerbach."

"Who's that?"

"Guitarist for the Black Keys. Anyway, I got a message from him at four-thirty this morning. Hard to understand, between the accent and the slurring and the music in the background, but I think he was looking for cash."

"Definitely time to send him home to Tennessee."

"Well, you might want to rethink that. The 92nd Street Y just had a last-minute cancellation and they wonder if he wants to share the bill with Richard Conklin on Monday night. Actually, it was Conklin himself who requested him."

"Jesus," Russell said. For all his belief in Jack, he was kind of amazed at the rapidity of his rise, and slightly worried about how the young author would handle it. He had a lot of issues to begin with, and Russell wasn't sure that his previous life on the ragged edge of American civilization had prepared him for the ordeal of literary celebrity. "Tell them if we can find him by Monday and he wants to do it, they can have him."

15

"WOW, I FEEL LIKE I JUST CLIMBED OUT of the Wayback Machine, this is, like, so eighties. Isn't that David Byrne over there? It's like any minute now we're going to see Keith Haring and Basquiat slouching around."

"I know, it's like my nose is twitching. I suddenly feel this overwhelming urge to tease up my hair and do some blow."

"It's not like cocaine ever went away."

"It did for some of us, honey."

"Is the man of the hour finally clean?"

"What, Tony? That's the whole point of this show. It ought to be subtitled *My Thirteenth Trip to Rehab Finally Did the Trick*."

"Actually, I was shocked to hear he was still alive."

"The way I heard it, Arkadian saw him staggering around the Lower East Side in rags one night, took him home and paid for a stint at Hazelden."

"That's the nicest thing I've ever heard about Gary."

"Not really. He's making fifty percent on every canvas Tony sells from here on out; plus, he bought masses of the old paintings for next to nothing while Tony was detoxing. And those are the ones everyone suddenly wants. Basically, it was totally in character for Gary."

"Oh, look, isn't that Dash Snow? He's so hot."

"So hairy, you mean."

"Speaking of the recrudescence of drugs."

"The what of drugs?"

"It just means drugs are back."

"I keep telling you, they never went away. Every twenty-two-year-old in this city has a dealer on speed dial."

The one with the too-blond hair and the Pee-Wee Herman shrunken suit, sensing that she was eavesdropping, turned and glared. "Can I *help* you?" he said.

"I don't think so," Corrine said, retreating into the crowd and trying to find Russell, who was supposed to meet her here.

The artist was hidden inside a distant scrum of bodies, a nimbus of LED light and clamoring, interrogative voices.

Eventually she spotted Washington, who was chatting up a pretty Asian girl in a neon green mod dress with intricate tattoos mimicking sleeves. He appeared momentarily discomfited when he saw Corrine, but quickly recovered his composure, kissing her cheek.

"This is my friend Corrine Calloway," he said, clearly at a loss for the girl's name.

"I'm Jenna," she said.

"I was just giving Jenna a little art historical context. Basquiat, Kenny Scharf, Futura 2000."

"That's very kind of you," Corrine said. "You have the real pedagogic instinct."

"I just love the eighties," Jenna said. "You guys are so lucky you were around then."

"Yes, they were . . . memorable," Corrine said. "Except that, they say, if you can remember them, then you probably weren't there."

Momentarily puzzled, Jenna forged on. "I mean, the whole club scene, Area and Danceteria, and the graffiti thing. That must've been so cool."

Corrine hadn't been to the clubs in question and hadn't been all that fond of the graffiti thing at the time. She remembered when every urban surface was covered with strange names and slogans, and how it had reflected the dread and menace that was the psychic weather of the city back then, the visual equivalent of boom boxes and car alarms, the backdrop for muggings and murders. Subway cars entirely obscured beneath the colorful malignancy, which in her mind seemed to have something to do with their thoroughly erratic schedules and tendency to break down mid-tunnel. And even the color was quickly swallowed up by the pervasive pre–catalytic converter filth in the air, an encompassing sootiness that turned chartreuse to mustard, pink to burgundy, white to gray. In time, this girl's tattoos would suffer the same fate.

"Remember those paintings on the sidewalk that were like crime scene outlines of bodies," Corrine said. "Like the ones police draw at murder scenes? And everybody assumed they were real, because it just seemed like, *of course*. There was so much fucking crime."

"Richard Hambleton," Washington said somewhat smugly.

She suddenly realized they'd had this same exchange just recently. "Yeah, well," she said, "I'll take your word for it. He knew what he was doing. That guy had the zeitgeist down cold. I remember coming across those and thinking, Yeah, this is how we live and die in New York. *That* was the eighties," she said, turning to the young woman in green. "Looking over your shoulder all the time, convinced that you'd get mugged or killed. Having your purse or gold necklace snatched on Fifth Avenue. Waking up in the middle of the night with some junkie trying to pry apart the bars on your bedroom window. Watching people you knew die of AIDS. But *otherwise*—fun."

"That was very eloquent," Washington said after Jenna fled.

"Just trying to provide some sociological context to go with your art history," she said. She wondered what Luke would have made of her commentary and wished he could have heard it.

"You lived on the Upper East Side, for Christ's sake."

"I got around," she said.

"Yeah, *right*. Between Park and Madison. Who did you know who died of AIDS?"

"Are you seriously asking me that?"

"Oh, shit, sorry," he said.

The subject of Jeff having been raised, if only obliquely, she said, "It might interest you to know that I once rescued Tony Duplex from a drug den on Avenue B."

"You're red-lining credulity here, honey. If you'd said a *poker game* on *Avenue A,* I might have almost believed you."

"It's true. Jeff called me one night. They were being held hostage by a drug dealer who they owed a lot of money. I had to deliver cash."

He looked at her as one might at a small child who persists in fibbing.

She shrugged, hoping to convey indifference to his opinion, although, in fact, she did want him to know she wasn't as straight and as predictable as he imagined. She could be bad—she *was* bad, and sometimes she felt like such a fucking impostor. She didn't want to be the perennial good girl, the doting mother and faithful wife. Washington would understand. She almost wanted to tell him about Luke, that she wasn't just some prude in a plaid skirt and penny loafers. She, too, had her secret desires and sins. Who better to confide a crime to than a serial criminal? But of course she couldn't.

"Where's Veronica?" she asked, seeing her husband slaloming awkwardly toward them through the crowd.

"At the office, I expect. And here's your husband. The phrase 'bull in a china shop' yet again comes to mind," Washington said as they watched Russell apologize to an art lover in a fedora whom he'd elbowed sideways.

"I prefer to think of him as puppyish," she said.

"It's getting a little late in the day for that fucking analogy," Washington said before gripping Russell's hand. "Don't see you at many art openings, Crash."

"A lot of Tony's art has captions," Corrine said. "Russell prefers his art with text." Actually, she knew, it was Duplex's connection with Jeff that had sparked Russell's interest. When he died, they were supposedly working on a project together.

Washington led them all into the second, slightly less crowded room of the gallery, where the older paintings—the ones that they'd seen and taken for granted in their youth—were hanging. The earliest had been rescued, or stolen, from the street—from lampposts and windows and the boarded walls of construction sites. Colorful figurative cartoons complete with captions.

"I used to see these fucking things plastered all over the subway stations," Russell said wistfully.

Corrine didn't herself remember any such thing, but she recognized some of the images, including the iconic EAT THE RICH painting, which featured a skeleton attacking a top-hatted pig in a tuxedo with a giant knife and fork. And three versions of the ENJOY COKE series, showing a young man with a Colt .45 jammed in his nostril. Duplex's iconography and his technique had become more subtle and refined as the eighties progressed and his work moved indoors to the walls of galleries and collectors' lofts without necessarily losing its exuberance. The captions became more enigmatic, at least for a while, the brushwork more nuanced, the palette more complex. And suddenly she came across a canvas depicting a man and a woman separated by the words YOU WERE RIGHT. SORRY. It was similar to the canvas Jeff had given her long ago, which was presumably still in the closet at her mother's house, and which, it seemed, might actually be worth something.

Standing in front of the painting, she registered a disturbance in the buzz of voices in the next gallery, a spike in volume and intensity, and turned to look just as a man with a bandanna covering his face like an outlaw in an old Western movie charged into the room and looked around before running toward them, holding some kind of cylinder in front of him, taking aim at the first ENJOY COKE painting, which suddenly exploded with a new color scheme—and seemed to bleed as he sprayed an unreadable cursive symbol on the painting. She realized that the cylinder was a can of spray paint and that the man was marking the canvas, appropriating it for himself, that the lightninglike mark was his signature, his tag, if not his name.

He dodged around Corrine when a beefy blazered man lunged for him, using Russell as a human shield, shoving him at the security guard and breaking for the exit. A second guard suddenly appeared in his path and wrestled him down below her sight line.

"Well, that seals it," Washington said. "Tony Duplex is back, baby."

"Was that part of the show?" asked a young woman behind them.

"It is now," Wash said as the two security guards hustled the spray painter into the main room.

"You don't think it was planned?" Corrine said.

"Well, far be it from me to be cynical, but whether it was or whether it wasn't, I'd guess that Arkadian's not at all unhappy about it."

"How much are Tony's paintings going for, anyway?"

"After this, probably twice what they were going for yesterday."

It soon became apparent that they'd shared front-row seats at the event of the season. Somehow Russell ended up getting interviewed by *Entertainment Tonight*. Facts and rumors were being traded like especially tasty canapés. The party had acquired a new energy, at once both festive and valedictory, but except for the artist himself, who appeared genuinely upset about the defacement of his painting, the former note seemed dominant, the crowd reacting in a manner that might have reminded an outside observer of hometown fans who'd just witnessed a great sporting victory, although a different observer might have guessed that the giddiness of those in the gallery resembled the relief of witnesses who had been passed over by a catastrophe, a tornado, say, that had wiped out several buildings without casualties, and the party certainly would have lasted well into the night if the Pinot Grigio and Prosecco hadn't run out after an hour. Eventually it flickered out, only to flare up again at Bottino, the art-world cantina on Tenth Avenue, and later just a few blocks away at Bungalow 8. Russell and Corrine returned home to the kids, but he got a call from Washington a few hours later, summoning him to the after-party, which he pretended to be reluctant to attend, before eventually deciding that his friend probably needed the company, then returning finally at two-thirty, smelling of booze and cigarettes, just like in the good old days.

16

WHEN THE PHONE RINGS HOURS AFTER Corrine fell asleep, she assumes it's Russell, calling from the Frankfurt Book Fair. But the voice on the other end is Jeff's, raspy and tense, telling her he really needs her help. She reminds him it's two in the morning.

"I'm in kind of a jam, here, Corrine. I need money like *yesterday*."

"How much money?"

"A thousand as fast as you can get here."

She doesn't ask him if it can wait till morning, knowing that, at least in his mind, it can't. It's a lot of money—a month's rent. She knows he's in trouble, or he wouldn't have called. She focuses on practicalities, reminding him of the two-hundred-dollar limit on ATM withdrawals and discovering, on searching her purse, that she has less cash than that on hand.

"Where are you?" she asks.

He gives her an address on the Lower East Side, a quadrant of Manhattan she's never set foot in during her three-year tenure in the city.

But she does have her rainy day fund, an emergency stash of twenty-dollar gold pieces her grandfather had given her for her eighteenth birthday. He'd told her not to tell anyone, to save them until the day she really needed them. She gets dressed, descends in the elevator, and nods at the startled doorman; it's a crisp October night adorned by a gibbous moon. At the Chase Manhattan on Second Avenue, she withdraws her limit. The first cab refuses to take her. "Ain't going down there this time of night," the driver says. "That's the fucking DMZ."

The second cabbie is skeptical, but he sets off without comment.

Eventually he asks, "What's that address? You going to that club, what's it called, Kill the Robots?"

She shrugs. "I don't think so." They finally find the number they're looking for on a block of burned-out, boarded-up tenements. At street level the boards and the bricks are festooned with colorful graffiti. The sidewalk is buckled, the street deserted. The address is painted on a piece of plywood covering the windows of a downstairs storefront, which, like the rest of the block, appears desolate and abandoned except for the anomaly of a shiny heavy steel door. The driver shakes his head and looks at her ruefully, as if giving her a chance to change her mind. She almost loses heart; it's the most frightening corner of the city she's ever seen and she can't imagine walking out of here unmolested. The cabbie tells her he'll wait while she tries the door.

She pushes a buzzer beside the door, sees a shadow cross the peephole from within. The door clicks open and she takes a last glance at the cab before stepping inside.

A wiry, twitchy young Hispanic guy wearing a red bandanna nudges her forward down a darkened hallway and raps on another door. The second door swings open, revealing a murky expanse, shrouded in smoke, illuminated by the glow of a television tuned to a Spanish-language station. Jeff and his friend Tony Duplex are sprawled on a ratty sofa, one of several that look as if they've been dragged in from the street. Sitting beside them in an armchair, watching the TV, is a middle-aged Hispanic man in a wife beater with multiple tattoos covering his neck and arms. He seems to be on easy terms with Jeff and Tony. A figure of indeterminate race and gender is passed out on another couch, covered by a quilt. The air is thick with cigarette smoke, infused with some kind of acrid chemical smell.

Jeff nods at her, though he seems reluctant or unable to move.

"So this is your friend?"

Jeff nods again. "Did you bring the money?"

This time, Corrine nods, not trusting her voice. But she realizes she has to explain. "I have a hundred fifty in cash," she says, seeing the man's eyes flash, the sense of stoned camaraderie suddenly evaporating. "And I have twelve hundred in gold."

She hands him the cash and three twenty-dollar Liberty gold coins.

"Gold closed today at four hundred and nine dollars an ounce. In case you're wondering how I know this, I'm a broker at Merrill Lynch. Each of those coins weighs just under point nine six ounces of gold, so you're looking at almost three ounces, which in bullion is worth about twelve hundred and thirty, although a collector would pay a lot more than that for the coins."

For a moment the man looks confused, and Corrine fears that she's blown it, but suddenly he laughs.

"What da fuck, dis one, she da fuckin' secretary da treasury," he says, hefting the coins in his palm.

Amazed at herself for having produced this speech, she coughs and rubs her eyes, which are burning from the acrid smoke; when she opens them, the tattooed man is fiddling with a triple-beam scale that has materialized on the table in front of him, placing the coins on the tray. She feels light-headed and nauseous and all of a sudden she can't stop coughing, and she isn't sure if any more is said, but the next thing she knows, Jeff's clapping her on the back as he leads her out of the room, and only as she's leaving does she see that the man at the door has a silver pistol in his belt.

The air outside is only slightly less funky and fetid, the street dark and deserted. Jeff takes her hand and walks her west, toward civilization.

"Pyramid," Tony mumbles.

"I should get her home."

"Think we all need a fucking drink." The last thing Tony needs is a drink, she feels certain, watching him stumble up the sidewalk, tacking like a leaky sailboat to port and starboard in his forward progress.

A few minutes later they're standing outside another tenement storefront, the door guarded by a hulk in a pink sequined halter. He does a complicated handshake with Jeff and waves them into the din: a smoky room with a stage at the far end, where a drag queen in a gold lamé jumpsuit is prancing and singing "Let Me Entertain You." Many in the audience are also cross-dressing men. She wonders how it is that Jeff, who looks so out of place in his Brooks Brothers shirt, seems so at home here, receiving and returning greetings as he tows her toward the bar. She's sort of furious at him for bringing her down here and exposing her to drug dealers and armed thugs, but also sort of mesmerized by these delicate pretty boys carrying lunch boxes and the broad-shouldered divas in poofy blond wigs, by the topless woman dancing virtually unnoticed beside the bar. For a moment she understands that impulse, feels the urge to experience that freedom. But it's fleeting; she could never do such a thing.

She wants to talk to Jeff, to demand an explanation, an account of the earlier proceedings, get an apology, perhaps, but the music's too loud to talk over, so instead she quickly drains the vodka tonic he places in her hand and asks for another. He introduces her to people with unlikely names and improbable hairstyles and they watch two more acts take the stage, the second culminating in several minutes of shrieking that's billed as an homage to Yoko Ono.

Finally, she walks out in a huff.

Jeff catches up with her on the sidewalk.

"Can you find me a cab?"

"Can we talk first?" He lights a cigarette, hands it to her, then lights one of his own.

She searches for a cab, but for a moment the street is empty.

"You've got to start taking care of yourself," she says.

"I like it when you take care of me," he says.

"I don't ever want to get a phone call like that again."

"Noted."

"Can you please get me a cab?"

"Come home with me."

"You know I can't. I'm married to your best friend."

"That hasn't stopped us before."

"I wasn't married then."

"It's not too late."

"What do you mean by that?"

"'Come live with me and be my love/and we will all the pleasures prove.'"

"I can't believe you'd say that."

"I was just quoting Christopher Marlowe."

"Jeff, I love Russell."

"I think you love me."

"I do, but that doesn't mean I need to be with you. It certainly doesn't mean I want to be married to you."

At that moment a dirty Checker cab rolls up to the entrance of the club, and several gaudily attired passengers clamber out.

"Don't go," Jeff says.

She kisses him before climbing into the taxi, waving to him as he stands there smoking on the curb.

The next afternoon, a Tony Duplex painting is delivered to her apartment with a note: *This painting reminds me of us. Tony says thanks. Love Jeff.*

She'd never spoken of the incident to Jeff or anyone else and had sent the painting off to her mother's house, asking her to stash it in the closet, where it had remained these many years. At least she hoped it was still there. It had occurred to her even at the time that the painting was worth far more than the coins she'd parted with, but she'd never considered selling it then, and later, Tony had more or less disappeared, along with the buyers once clamoring for his art.

She'd never told Russell about that night, feeling that it was part of her secret history with Jeff.

Every marriage, she convinced herself, can bear a few secrets.

17

RUSSELL HAD FINALLY MANAGED TO BOOK a reservation at Gaijin, the underground restaurant, after getting referred by his friend Carlo, having first heard about it from Washington, who had so far been unable to get them in. There was no listed number, no reviews and so far only a few cryptic references online.

When he called, Russell was asked, by a woman with a heavy Japanese accent, how he'd gotten the number. "From Carlo Russi, the chef."

"And what is his phone number?"

Russell gave her Carlo's cell number.

He'd almost concluded that he'd been disconnected when the woman came back on the line and asked him how large his party was, then told him they would be expected at seven o'clock on the following Thursday.

"Please to not be giving this number to anyone." Apparently if you were Carlo, you could refer someone, but not if you were Russell Calloway.

She gave him the address and told him the restaurant was behind an unmarked door beside a clothing boutique. He should ring the buzzer three times.

After hanging up, he'd immediately called Washington to gloat, and to invite him and Veronica to dinner. Washington pretended to be only mildly interested.

"How can it be a secret restaurant?" Corrine asked when they were en route in a cab. "What does that even mean?"

"Well, basically that they don't have a listed phone number or address or a sign or even a name on the door and in order to get in you need to be referred by somebody who's already been there."

"Do we know anything about it?" Corrine asked. "Such as what kind of food they serve?"

"I think it's kind of Japanese avant-garde."

"How can food be avant-garde?"

"If it's really, *really* fresh? Anyway, Carlo said it was brilliant."

"It all sounds deeply pretentious. And Carlo weighs three hundred pounds, for God's sake. He'd eat his own children if you dunked them in Bolognese sauce." Corrine could happily subsist on green salad and canned salmon and had limited patience for culinary adventurism.

"Actually, he's lost a ton of weight," Russell told her.

"Ah, the cocaine diet."

"No, he stopped that after his heart attack."

At the corner of Lafayette and Bond, they found the Lees, who'd been searching for the place. Russell had been less precise with his directions than the woman on the phone, but after locating the clothing boutique, he tried the buzzer one door to the west. Just as they were about to try the door on the other side, they were admitted by a slim young man in a tight red suit. After a brief interrogation, they were led through a long hallway into a small room furnished with a heterogeneous mix of tables and chairs—from a store on Fourth Avenue dedicated to fifties design—all of which were for sale here. The walls were adorned with framed book covers—Japanese manga featuring pop-eyed schoolgirls and ninjas, as well as the equally lurid and stylized covers of Avon paperbacks from the forties and fifties—*The Chastity of Gloria Boyd, I Married a Dead Man, Six Deadly Dames.*

It was blessedly free of the standard tchotchkes of the typical sushi joint. Only two very young couples were already seated, leaving four tables vacant.

"I hate it when I feel like I should whisper," Corrine whispered.

"We're just a little early," Washington said. "Apparently my man here couldn't get us a prime-time reservation."

"I could have gotten a later reservation for *two*," Russell said. "Maybe I should have."

"You boys sit across from each other so you can rhapsodize about the food," Corrine said. "Just don't start arguing about Clinton and Obama again, please."

"Yeah, let's definitely give that subject a rest," Veronica said. Their household, too, was divided on this issue, Veronica being a staunch backer of Hillary, Washington equally ardent for Obama.

The waiter, who didn't appear to be of legal drinking age, informed them that the house cocktail was called the Rudyard Kipling and combined umeshu, Japanese plum brandy, with a fifteen-year-old Kentucky small-batch bourbon and house-made blood-orange bitters.

"What the fuck's the difference between house-made and homemade?" Washington asked. "Everywhere I go lately, it's house-made fettuccini and every other goddamn thing."

"Homemade, technically, could refer to something made elsewhere, in some kind of artisanal environment," Russell explained. "House-made tells you it was made here, in-house."

"Hallelujah!" Veronica said. "My vocabulary is growing by the minute. But really, Russell, *artisanal environment*?"

He shrugged and ordered the house cocktail for all, declining to ask, given the existing level of skepticism around the table, why the miscegenated blend of Asian and American ingredients was named for the poet who wrote that "East is East and West is West, and never the twain shall meet." The bartender, he'd been told, was one of the new breed of scholar/mixologists who'd made a name for himself at a celebrated Lower East Side absinthe bar.

"Russell," Corrine said, "you know I hate it when you order for everybody. Maybe some of us don't want the damn Kipling."

"Forgive me, my love, but Carlo said it's not to be missed. And as for the food, there's no choice anyway. It's a tasting menu."

"Oh God, the dread *tasting menu*. Another night of endless plates. Death by a thousand bites."

"Seriously," Veronica said, "Washington took me to AKA last week and I thought I was going to puke, there was so much food."

"That wasn't the food; it was the four bottles of wine we drank while waiting for the food to come."

"God, I know, Russell took me there last month," Corrine said. "Thirteen courses spread over four hours. He definitely didn't get lucky that night."

"*Tasting menu,*" Veronica said. "Two of the scariest words in the English language."

"For you girls, maybe," Washington said. "For us, the two scariest words are *breast reduction.*"

"Hilarious," Veronica said.

He couldn't get away with that joke, Russell thought, if Veronica wasn't a C cup. "The portions here are very small," he noted.

"You've never even been here," Corrine said.

"I've read about it," Russell said.

"I thought you said it was totally under the radar."

"There've been a few blog posts."

"I feel like nobody has any primary aesthetic encounters anymore," Corrine said. "Every time we pick up a book or sit down to a movie, we've already read the commentary."

"I'm surprised to hear you admit that dining could be an aesthetic experience."

"Some of you certainly think so."

"Look at the waiter," Washington said. "That motherfucker's positively anorexic."

"That's a good sign, at least," said Veronica.

The cocktails arrived, along with tiny plates of minuscule crabs. Corrine and Veronica studiously ignored the tiny crabs and resumed their conversation.

"Not bad," Russell said, crunching on a crab pinched between his thumb and forefinger.

"Boring," Washington countered.

"The cocktail's good." Since Russell had gotten the reservation, he assumed a proprietary degree of responsibility.

The waiter arrived with the first course: "Chef would like you to begin with *O-dori ebi*," he said, placing in front of each of them a plate with a squirming deshelled prawn.

"It's alive," Corrine said with horror.

"This is known in English as dancing shrimp. After shell is removed, chef place a small piece of wasabi on spine of shrimp, which stimulate him to dance."

"That's so disgusting. And barbaric."

"Enjoy."

"I'll take yours," Russell said once the waiter had retreated.

"Take mine," Veronica said to Washington.

Russell downed his shrimp and then Corrine's.

"Tasty," Washington said. "Simple, but strong presentation."

"You two are appalling," Corrine said. "I'm going to call PETA."

"Let's just hope the vertebrates don't dance," Washington said. "So what's happening with the Kohout book?"

"He sent me some pages. They're good. We're publishing in the spring."

"You do know that Briskin called me to shop your offer?"

This revelation caught Russell entirely by surprise. "Well, thanks for not playing the game."

"I don't know how glad you should be. I always thought he was a slippery bastard. I heard Harcourt passed, too."

"That worked out for me, then," Russell said, trying to sound nonchalant.

"Yeah, but the question you should be asking yourself is, *Why?*"

"I couldn't agree more," Corrine said.

"I'll see you all at the National Book Awards," Russell said. He suddenly felt slightly queasy, and it wasn't the dancing shrimp. It hadn't occurred to him that others had decided against the book; he thought he'd preempted it.

As the plates were cleared, he changed the subject, asking Washington for his prognostications on Manhattan real estate. His friend had always been much savvier about financial matters, and since he'd ascended to the executive suite of the publishing house where Russell had once toiled, his income had taken a big jump, though he certainly made less than his wife, who worked for Lehman Brothers as in-house counsel. He and Veronica owned a three-bedroom loft in a former factory a few blocks from the Calloways, although, with its doorman, gym and spa, it seemed light-years away in space and time.

A rumor had reached Russell that his landlord was thinking of forming a condominium for the purpose of selling off the five apartments in the building, and while it was possible the Calloways could continue to rent, Russell wanted, not unreasonably, he felt, to become a home owner for the first time in his life.

"I'm fifty years old and I've never owned any real estate," Russell said. "How pathetic is that?"

"Up to this point you've had a pretty good deal," Washington said. "Rent control—now, those are two of the happiest words in the language."

"Unless you're a landlord," Veronica interjected.

"True, but I feel like it would be nice for once to own the roof over my head."

"Actually, in a condo, the association owns the roof."

"Stop being a wiseass, Wash. You know what I'm saying."

"You wish to be a man of property. A chatelain."

"What *I* want," Corrine said, "is to have more than one bathroom before my hair turns gray."

"We can do that if we own it," Russell said.

"Oh God, can't we just find a grown-up apartment? We have two children."

"We've got to get in the game first, and if there's a conversion, we'd get an insider price here. Plus, I want equity in an asset that's bound to appreciate. I feel like I've missed out on this incredible real estate boom, and if we wait much longer, we'll never be able to buy in."

"The whole point of booms," Corrine said, "is that they go bust."

The conversation was interrupted by the preparation of the next course, which consisted of big matsutake mushrooms grilled at the table over a small charcoal brazier and spritzed with fresh lime juice. These, the waiter explained, were a great delicacy in Japan, "like Japanese truffle." Even Corrine thought they were delicious, although she was highly skeptical of the following course, a deconstructed teriyaki chicken—teriyaki ice cream, over which the waiter ladled chicken demi-glace—and she completely rebelled against the fifth. "Chef calls this transgressive fusion," he announced, placing the square plates in front of them.

"Jesus, what the fuck," Washington said. "Is that like Chuck Palahniuk making sweetbread sushi?"

"This is lily paste dumpling wrap around foie gras. And this twenty-four-karat gold leaf," the waiter continued, dusting each of the dumplings as Russell watched his wife's expression grow incredulous. "And this," he said, sprinkling what looked like bacon bits over Corrine's plate, "crushed quail skull." She refused to try it even after the other three declared it delicious. Russell was the only defender of the next course, the uni soufflé, and the situation threatened to turn ugly with the arrival of a plate laden with what looked like creamy comma-shaped extrusions of semifreddo.

"This *shirako*," the waiter said proudly.

"I can't believe we were supposed to eat fish sperm," Corrine said in the cab. "Jesus, Russell."

"Not my favorite, I have to admit."

"But you *ate* it."

"Well, I tasted it. I certainly didn't finish it. But I think I owed it to myself and the establishment to at least try it."

"That's so disgusting. I don't even want to sit next to you."

"I'm not saying I'd do it a second time."

"Has it ever occurred to you that your obsessive gourmandism may have something to do with Storey's eating issues?"

"Whoa, hold on here. That's a reach."

In recent months, Storey had developed a passionate interest in food and had gained some ten or fifteen pounds. Russell wanted to point out that it didn't resemble his own passion—the word *obsession* was slander—in that it was fairly indiscriminate. They'd both been concerned, though reluctant to discuss it with her for fear of making it more of an issue. Corrine said it would be a huge mistake to make her feel self-conscious, even though she was horrified by corpulence and considered it a sign of moral weakness. It was one of her few prejudices.

"You have an unhealthy interest in food," she said to him, "and now she seems to be developing one, too. At breakfast she wants to know what's for lunch, and at lunch she asks about dinner. And she's started watching that damn Food Network."

"Look," Russell said, ready with his defense, "this all started right after Hilary decided to tell the kids she was their real mother. That has to have rocked her world, whether or not she's talked about it openly. The fact that she hasn't seems pretty strange to me. If there's been a sea change in her behavior, that might be a good place to start looking for an explanation."

"Maybe, but you don't have to make them both think food's so damn important."

"Do you have a problem with my weight?"

"No, you're looking pretty good, considering, but that's only because you're blessed with a high metabolism. And if you really want to know, you could lose a little around the middle."

"Is that why you don't want to make love anymore?"

"Don't be ridiculous. And anyway, we're talking about our *daughter.*"

"I'm not being ridiculous. Things were good last fall—I felt like we were sexually attuned again for the first time in years—and then it went to shit again."

"That's a little extreme."

"Think about it. When was the last time?"

"I don't know, a couple weeks?"

"Seven weeks. I practically had to beg for it."

"I didn't know you were keeping track."

"I am."

"There are cycles in a marriage; you know that."

"Yes, I do. But it's not like the fucking weather. It's not out of anyone's control. It's volitional."

"Complaint registered." She sighed theatrically and threw herself back against the seat. "Now can we finish talking about Storey?"

"We can. I think that her sudden bingeing might just as likely be a reaction to your food and weight phobias as to my issues. But honestly, I think it's just a phase. Like your lack of interest in sex."

He considered this a rather neat rhetorical maneuver, although it became clear, as the silence in the cab stretched several blocks and followed them into the elevator, that it was at best a Pyrrhic victory. They each greeted Jean, and separately said good night to the kids, who'd just turned out their lights. Ferdie was curled up with Jeremy, who asked, "How was the secret restaurant?"

"It was pretty fun."

"Mom didn't like it."

"No, she didn't."

"What was the secret?"

"The secret was that they have shrimp that dance."

"That's weird. Night, Dad."

"Good night, son."

After returning from the bathroom, she undressed behind the closet door and emerged in full pajamas, a red cotton top and bottom that had never once been removed in the heat of passion, and settled into her side of the bed with her book, Joan Didion's memoir about her husband's death—not necessarily a good sign. He could see from the tight set of her mouth that she was not likely to say anything, the silence settling around them like setting concrete. He picked up a manuscript, an addiction memoir he wouldn't even have glanced at if the agent, whom he respected, hadn't assured him of its literary quality. He just didn't think the world needed another one of these, except that they seemed to continue to sell, even after the scandal of *A Million Little Pieces,* as if there were a bottomless appetite for true-life tales of degradation and redemption. It was by this time formulaic, a genre as unvarying in its stations of the cross as an episode of *Law & Order,* although there were variables—coke instead of heroin or, in this particular case, meth.

"I might just read a little more," he said when she clicked off her light.

"That's fine," she said.

Fifteen minutes later he knew that she was still awake, could sense her consciousness from across the king-size bed. The tension was palpable; his continued reading was giving her an additional grievance to store up against him. He put down the manuscript and turned out his light, but while he was trying to come up with a conciliatory remark, he heard the rhythmic breathing of Corrine's sleep.

At one-thirty he went to the bathroom and took an Ambien. He heated a mug of milk in the microwave and stirred in some Ovaltine. Taking it to the couch, he surveyed his kingdom, such as it was—the bookshelves with their signed first editions, the Berenice Abbott portrait of Joyce, the almost abstract Russell Chatham landscape they'd bought from the artist himself on a trip to Montana, the Wiener Werkstätte side table they'd bought at a flea market in Pennsylvania for seventy-five bucks; these were among the few items of worldly value, and they didn't add up to all that much—certainly not enough to cover the down payment on the loft—but everything here had been gathered by the two of them together over the years and he felt a keen sense of conjugal proprietorship in the family portraits and bric-a-brac, the cracked leather club chair from his father's den, the *Those Calloways* poster, the kids' artwork framed on the walls or attached to the refrigerator with magnets—the backdrop they'd created over many years for the ongoing story of their lives.

He couldn't believe that after all this time, as hard as he'd worked, he wasn't sure he could even afford to buy this decrepit loft with its sub-code wiring and peeling paint, wavy floors and a single bathroom. Was this too much to ask? He'd known when he chose his profession that it wasn't terribly lucrative, but he hadn't anticipated then that someday he'd be fifty, with two school-age children. Nor had he realized that Corrine would abandon her job at Merrill Lynch early on, that she'd be working in the nonprofit sector. He was proud of her, but her paycheck left something to be desired.

He retreated to the bedroom, with the clock ticking on his Ambien; he needed to be lying down with all the lights out when it kicked in, or else he'd lose the moment and be awake all night.

He lay down at a little after two o'clock and woke up exactly five hours later with the jangly headache that inevitably resulted from taking Ambien after a night of drinking . . . first the house cocktail, then two bottles of Pol Roger, then who knows how many of those sneaky little carafes of sake. Had he actually eaten that disgusting sack of fucking fish sperm? He *must*'ve been drunk.

Something else was bothering him, lodged at the back of his mind like a tiny fishhook. It was like that dream song of Berryman's where Henry wakes up afraid he's killed someone, but "nobody is ever missing." What the hell was it? After he'd awakened the kids and turned on the news, the nagging question finally came to him: Why had Washington passed on Kohout's book?

18

SPRING WAS COMING TO the Hemel-en-Aarde valley even as the autumn deepened in New York. Just back from the Transvaal, Luke was restless; the vines and the grass were bright green once again, while the fossilized bones of ancient hominids and the animals they'd killed and the stone tools they'd carved continued their ancient slumber. Sometimes a fragment of a jawbone or a knife point would appear in the vineyard, exposed by plowing or erosion. Along with a handful of Civil War bullets and belt buckles from his childhood home in Tennessee—relics of the Battle of Franklin—three Acheulean hand axes graced Luke's desk: faceted stone lozenges with a pleasing heft in the palm, the oldest and longest-used implements made by human hands, unearthed in the vineyard.

He loved the valley, but he was also tired of it, and at this moment he missed New York, where nothing was ancient and a new crop of stores and bars and restaurants pushed up between the cracks of the sidewalks to flourish for a season or two, before they, in turn, were crowded out by newer ones. Though he'd spent three decades in the city, in recent years he associated it mostly with Corrine; he was nostalgic for interludes they'd never shared, constrained as they had been by the need to hide their affair—picnics in Central Park, shopping sprees on Madison Avenue, leisurely dinners at Italian restaurants recommended by the *Times*. In fact, he'd hardly ever had the leisure for these urban idylls he imagined now, working sixteen-hour days, shuttling by Town Car from apartment to office, office to airport, bound for Columbus or Little Rock, pausing occasionally to refuel at the Four

Seasons or celebrate a deal at '21' or accompany his wife to one of the charity balls that seemed to be her chief recreation, where he diddled his BlackBerry under the table as she flirted with his friends and the husbands of her friends. He cherished certain memories of urban rituals with his daughter, but in his heart he knew he'd been a part-time father at best. His real life had been lived on LCD screens, Manhattan as the backdrop for due-diligence drudgery and occasional heroic digital feats of high finance. Which is why he'd retired from the private equity firm he'd cofounded. Within days, the planes had crashed into the towers, and all his plans had gone sideways.

At the bar in the living room, he poured three fingers of scotch into a tumbler and retreated to his study, where he checked the closing numbers for the financial markets in New York—the Dow and S&P up again, the rand continuing its slide against the dollar—and tomorrow's weather forecast, sunny, with a high of seventeen degrees centigrade, which he had to convert in his head, non-Fahrenheit degrees still unreal to him after three years in the valley of heaven and earth, though the weather didn't matter so much now that the grapes were harvested, the new vintage mellowing in the cellar, beyond the reach of the elements, except, perhaps, the tidal pull of the moon. While he was not of the dancing-naked-among-the-vines school of viticulture, his midlife foray into farming had given him a new respect for the rhythms of the spheres and the unseen forces of the natural world, which were as inexorable as the operations of markets. He knew that the wine tasted unsettled in the barrel as the full moon approached, just as he knew that the price of bonds moved inversely to interest rates, and he now felt far more attuned to the cycle of the seasons than in the days when he'd lived in conference rooms and airports.

Checking his e-mail, he found invoices for materials for the new school in the township, a request for a water-catchment system from a nearby district and an unwelcome missive from his ex.

Luke

    I can never remember what time it is there and I don't want to risk waking your child bride, but need to talk to you about Ashley. She came down to the city last weekend and was a mess. You know I'm hardly one to think a girl can be too thin, but Ashley's beyond skinny. I tried to talk to her about it, but of course she's in total denial. I really don't know if it's drugs or not, but I think she may need to go somewhere and I think you really need to get involved here. You know she doesn't listen to me; you seem to have succeeded in turning her against me. She'll be out of school as of mid-May and I think you need to be on deck. She can stay here at the apartment with us the last two weeks of May, but after that we're going to London and then we've chartered the Lawlors' yacht for two weeks, cruising the Amalfi coast, and I don't think she should be here in the city alone. Sarah Bradley has invited her to stay at their place in Southampton, but I don't think she should be on her own all summer. I know there are lots of needy orphans and teenage brides in Africa, but your own daughter needs you right here in America. Charity begins at home, Dad.

Sasha

Luke immediately dialed his daughter, but his call went straight to voice mail. "Ash, it's Dad. Please call me."

He thought about calling Sasha but knew that he'd have a hard time keeping a lid on his emotions.

Sasha

Am deeply concerned about your report on Ashley's health. When I saw her last month, she seemed well, if thin, but if you think she's underweight, then the situation must indeed be dire. As you may recall, your sarcastic attitude when she was a little heavy as a teen helped to contribute to these body-image problems, and your diet pills certainly helped launch her drug problems. I'm going to talk to Ash and some of her friends, and you can be sure I will take whatever action is necessary.

Luke

The American obesity epidemic did not extend to wealthy Manhattan and its spheres of influence, its satellite prep schools and summer colonies, where females in particular seemed susceptible to anorexia and bulimia, at least the ones in his immediate orbit, his ex-wife, his daughter . . . possibly even Corrine. In the case of Sasha and her friends, it was a religion, practiced at Pilates studios and private gyms and restaurants' ladies' rooms. For all those bony Upper East Side women with their sharp elbows, slenderness was a virtue, standing in for all the others that had been discarded.

It occurred to him that the solution to at least two of his own problems might involve a quick trip back to New York.

All at once the lights went out and the computer screen faded. Luke reached for the flashlight on his desk and fished his key ring from his pocket, unlocking the top desk drawer, where he kept a loaded SIG Sauer. The power was somewhat intermittent in the valley—in most of the Cape, for that matter; Eskom, the power company, was notoriously unreliable. On the other hand, late-night farm invasions had become increasingly common to the north, armed gangs breaking in and murdering white families, with the tacit approval of the ANC, which advocated the redistribution of land and sent out periodic calls for "colonialists" to abandon their farms. Rape, torture and mutilation were common features of these attacks, which usually began with the intruders cutting phone and power lines, and Luke couldn't help tensing up whenever the lights went out, even as he felt paranoid for doing so.

He went to the window and looked out over the vineyards, but he could detect no movement; hurrying to the bedroom, he found Giselle asleep on her back, her arm draped across her face, her head in the crook of her elbow—her habitual pose in sleep. He was grateful that she was a heavy sleeper, since he was a restless one. He was about to check the phone, when he heard the generator kick in and saw the glow of the hall light in the bedroom doorway. He picked up the phone and was reassured by the dial tone. As soon as he put the receiver in its cradle, the phone rang.

"Hello?"

"Luke, Charles here. Just wanted to make sure all was well."

"We're fine here for now. The generator's gone on. You've got power there?"

"Same as you. Just another blackout, then."

"Thanks for checking in."

"Sleep well."

"Who was that?" asked Giselle, opening a single eye.

"It was Charles, just checking to see we were okay. The lights went out."

She sat up in bed. "Oh shit."

"They're on again now."

"Jesus. Now I'll be awake all night."

"It was nothing."

"No, but it could've been."

"Let's not dwell on that."

"How can I not dwell on that? That's absurd. You can't will yourself not to think of something. Did you hear what they did to those women and children up in the Transvaal?"

"It hasn't happened around here."

"No, but it's only a matter of time. It's not as if we're stuck here. Charles and Emma don't have much choice, but we can leave anytime we like."

Even as he was listening to her, he was admiring her, the swell of her breasts emerging from under the sheet, framed by her cascading strands of blond hair. He couldn't help desiring her and despising himself a little for it.

"Of course there are problems," he said, "but I think things are moving in the right direction." Even as he said this, he realized he was arguing a position in which he no longer believed. He'd lost much of his enthusiasm for his adoptive home, yet he felt it necessary to defend his former position, to maintain the old battle lines.

"Wanting that to be true doesn't make it true. It's only a matter of time before what's happening in Zimbabwe starts up down here. Mbeki thinks Mugabe's a great leader."

Luke couldn't help recalling a safari he'd taken in Zimbabwe not long after the civil war there finally ended, to Hwange and Victoria Falls, when it seemed that the transition would be successful, when Mugabe appeared to be responsible, even idealistic.

"Sometimes I think you're so afraid of being perceived as racist, with your southern American guilt; you can't admit what's actually happening in this country. This isn't the United States. I grew up here, I love this country, but it pains me to say that I don't really believe there's a future for me here. For us. I wish it were otherwise. But we have to at least *think* about the future. Luke, you know I want to start a family, but I don't want to raise my children in a country that doesn't want them, a country where they'll be blamed for the sins of their ancestors, always seen as colonialists and usurpers."

Luke could understand this part of her argument; if he'd had any interest in starting a family, then he would want to do so back in the States. But he was fifty-eight years old and already had a twenty-year-old daughter. "Sometimes I worry you married me for my passport," he said.

"God, Luke, that's a terrible thing to say." She turned away and buried her head in her pillow.

"I didn't mean it," he said, rubbing her shoulders. "I'm sorry." She remained obdurately burrowed into her pillow. "It's just that I can't walk away from the foundation."

"You don't need to be here day to day. I mean, fund-raising's your primary obligation, and you certainly aren't going to find any funds here. And the winery pretty much runs itself most of the time. As long as you're here for harvest and crush. Or you could probably sell the winery to Charles. It's not like you're making money at it."

He wasn't even sure why he was arguing the case for staying in the Cape, although certainly the foundation did have something to do with this. It made him feel needed and useful in a way that he hadn't felt before; he'd single-handedly brought fresh water, a new school and a clinic to the township down the road. On the other hand, he'd never felt the same enthusiasm for this place since the accident. He'd grown weary of his whole African adventure.

He knew he was being reflexively contrarian. If Giselle had been dead set on staying in her homeland, he might well have been arguing the other side. In fact, he was ready to go home, but not with her.

"I don't want to wait any longer," she said, turning to face him and putting her arms on his shoulders. "I want a family. I want a baby. I don't know what you're waiting for, but I know you haven't made love to me in almost two weeks." Her eyes suddenly welled with tears. "I'm not sure if it's because you don't find me attractive anymore, or if you're afraid I'll get pregnant. But I can't go on like this."

He climbed into the bed beside her. "I'm sorry," he said. "I got all caught up in the harvest. And then Ashley was having all that trouble at school."

"Aren't you attracted to me anymore?"

"Of course I am. You're one of the most beautiful women I've ever seen."

"Are you worried I'll get pregnant?"

"Maybe a little."

"Don't you want a family?"

"I just need to get used to the idea."

"That was what we always talked about." She was sobbing now, and he found it impossible to speak honestly with her. If he were truly honest with himself, he would have to say that he didn't want to be a father again, that he hoped the issue might be equivocated indefinitely, but she was determined to force his hand. Until he had finally resolved his feelings for Corrine, he couldn't possibly make her pregnant. Nor could he keep denying her forever, and his desire to postpone the reckoning, combined with genuine regret and even love, evolved almost imperceptibly from comforting her into gestures of stimulation, her sobbing transformed to moaning as she thrashed off his belt and trousers, his reservations and scruples melting away as he thrust himself inside her.

He woke shortly after dawn and left his wife sleeping, dressed and took his coffee out to the patio, looking out over the valley, the golden vineyards spilling down to the Onrust River and the rusty mountains rising up to the north. A small troop of baboons ambled up the service road before disappearing into the vines. There was a slight chill in the air, the coffee cup throwing a faint nimbus of steam. At this moment it was hard to credit any of last night's anxieties.

He went down to the chicken yard and picked up five eggs, two brown, two small white eggs from the bantams and one a faint, ghostly blue. In the kitchen he fried them and cooked sausages, then took a tray into Giselle, who stirred and smiled up at him, seeming to float on the feather bed as if on a cloud of postcoital serenity.

She sat up and settled the tray on her lap, delicately selected a sausage and lifted it to her lips, nibbling teasingly.

Having long since emerged from the spell of the bedroom, he felt the need to establish a more quotidian tone. "So what does your day look like?"

"I'm going down to the township to help the vet. We have dogs to dip and spay. And you? Will you come along?"

"Actually, I've got to wait here for that oenologist. He's coming down from Stellenbosch to help us with a stuck fermentation. That last lot of Pinot won't finish off. Seems our indigenous yeasts have gone on strike. They refuse to reproduce. We may have to play some Marvin Gaye and light some scented candles to get them in the mood."

"Let's eat in town tonight. I'm feeling a little cooped up."

"All right."

Later, he walked her to the door, kissed her good-bye.

"Will you think about what we talked about?" she said.

"Which part?"

"The part about starting a life away from here."

"Okay," he said, even as he wondered if he had the courage to ask her for a divorce. Suddenly it seemed the only honorable thing to do. He tried to dissociate this possible course of action from the thought of a possible future with Corrine. He certainly had no guarantee that she'd ever leave her own marriage, but he couldn't in good conscience ask her to until he was free of his own. Could he do it? He felt exhilarated by the prospect, the glimpse of freedom on the horizon. But whatever happened, he realized, this chapter of his life was over.

"And about us having . . . children?"

"I'm sorry," he said, sighing and looking away from her.

"What do you mean?"

"I can't do it," he said. "I just can't."

19

OFF-SEASON, THE TRAIN OUT TO MONTAUK was almost empty, the faint residue of sweat and stale beer the only reminder of summer hordes.

They'd changed trains in Jamaica, Queens, and racketed along past the brick apartment buildings and the duplexes, tactfully dodging south of the bedroom communities of Long Island, the golfing and horseback-riding enclaves of the wealthy along the North Shore, rolling through the aluminum-sided postwar suburbs housing homicidal teens, philandering plumbers, dandy mobsters, as well as presumably others who never featured in the New York tabloids, the vegetation taking over as they got farther from the city and the homes of commuters were replaced by summer homes, passing through the leafy utopia of Southampton, with its shingled mansions behind privet hedges, shimmying onward to Bridgehampton and East Hampton and then out along the narrow isthmus of scrubby sand dunes that barely connected Montauk to the Hamptons.

Montauk was the farthest extremity of Long Island, the end of the road. It had once been an island and still felt remote from the gilded summer communities to the west. Each fall as the ocean cooled, the striped bass followed the churning biomass of baitfish pouring down the coast from Maine and Cape Cod across Long Island Sound to Montauk Point. Not long after the summer tourists departed, the town was taken over by campers, recreational vehicles and Jeeps sporting huge toothy tires, with custom rod and cooler racks mounted on their front grilles, piloted by sportsmen from mid-island and upstate and Jersey who stood on the beach throwing vaguely fishlike plastic plugs with fearsome treble hooks into the surf, apex predators in pursuit of *Morone saxatilis*.

The locals tended to be more enthusiastic about visiting fishermen than about the summer people; especially unwelcome in this Irish community were the hipsters, scruffy chic invaders from the East Village and Williamsburg attracted by the working-class authenticity their presence was diluting. Overlapping with this group, if not quite coextensive, were the surfers, who swarmed the beach at Ditch Plains every year in increasing numbers. Class warfare was palpably simmering in the salty air. As a fly fisherman, Russell would be suspect, an elitist with a wandlike rod throwing dainty feathered hooks. For his part, Jack wanted no part of this hoity-toitiness. Where he came from, dynamite was part of the fisherman's arsenal, but in this case he would settle for a stout spinning rod.

Russell's friend Deke was waiting for them at the station, slouching against his rust-pitted 60-series Land Cruiser, a relic of the Reagan administration; inevitably when Russell saw this dilapidated vehicle, he uttered the phrase "It's morning in America."

"What the hell does that mean?" Jack asked.

"A vapid slogan from my youth. Come meet Deke."

Introductions and manly handshakes were exchanged. The inside of the Toyota Land Cruiser was even more depressing than the pockmarked exterior, littered with fast-food debris, newspapers, shotgun shells, fishing tackle and cigarette butts. It looked as if some tweaker had been living out of it for weeks.

Russell had known Deke since the eighties, when he was an A and R man for Atlantic Records. He'd flown too close to the sun on wings made of cocaine and had eventually crashed here on Long Island Sound, where he'd reinvented himself as a fishing guide. He already owned the boat, and fishing was, as he said, the only thing he was good at besides scoring dope.

"I used to have a good ear, too," he told Jack as they pulled out of the marina in his unnamed boat, a twenty-six-foot center-console Parker that had once boasted upholstery and working gauges. "But you know, once you hit your thirties, it's hard to keep on top of it. You gradually lose your feel for it, lose your grasp on the balls of the zeitgeist. The new bands are kids barely in their twenties and you're suddenly feeling nostalgic for the fucking Smiths and the Clash and Dinosaur Jr.; then before you know it, *you're* the fucking dinosaur. There were the great ones, like Mo Ostin and Seymour Stein, who go on and on, but basically it's a young man's game."

"The drugs must've been good, though," Jack said.

"Oh yeah, the drugs were amazing. That was the air we breathed. All access pass."

"So, my man, what was, uh, your drug of choice?"

"Hell, I liked 'em all, though I have to say that it was crack that finally kicked my ass. I'll tell you what was probably the greatest experience of my life, before it wasn't, was chasing the dragon. Line it up, a little rock of crack, two pellets of smack. Oh my God, that was the fucking ultimate."

Jack nodded, as if this were a perfectly reasonable assertion. "Gotta love the speedball."

"I don't think anything ever made me so happy in my life," Deke said. "And you—what's your poison, man?"

"Well, you gotta understand where I come from, crystal meth's like mother's milk. It's practically the family business. I mean, hell, cookin' speed and makin' shine were the only jobs some people in Fairview ever had. So meth was in my veins, so to speak. But the kind of nastiness I've seen down in those hollers would have turned a weaker man to the Lord. In my case, I just moved my business upmarket to coca products and opiates."

"Jesus," Russell said. "I'm trapped on a boat with the fucking Glimmer Twins."

It was a perfect day, bright and cool, with wisps of cirrus drifting through a steely blue firmament, nudged by a western breeze. They bounced up the north side of the point over Shagwong Reef and rounded the eastern tip of the island, turning south. On one side the lighthouse, a relic of George Washington's administration, was perched on the cliff above the waves, two hundred yards closer to the encroaching surf than it had been when it was built; on the other, three thousand miles of ocean stretching all the way to Ireland.

Five or six boats were clustered a couple hundred yards off the point. Deke gave them a wide berth and cruised down along the south beach, where the surf casters were spread out along the shoreline, some of them casting, most just standing on the beach with their rods at the ready, waiting for signs of life.

"When the blitz is on, they suddenly multiply," Deke said. "Line up shoulder-to-shoulder along the shore, casting into this seething cauldron of bait and bass. The surf casters are like the birds—they suddenly show up, swarming where the bass come up, like they're summoned by some mysterious instinct, or maybe by cell phone. For six weeks these fucking guys abandon their lives and sleep out here in campers and shitty motels. And they hate us—the guys in the boats."

Deke cruised past the huge radar dish, the lighthouse's ugly modern twin, built during World War II, Deke said, when German submarines regularly popped up here. Deke followed the shoreline all the way down to Ditch Plains, the surfing beach, where a few stalwarts in wet suits were bobbing on their boards. Russell pointed out the old Warhol estate.

All at once the birds materialized over the tide line off their bow, dozens of them diving and rising over the swells like flags flapping on a battlefield. Deke gunned the boat and raced toward the feeding frenzy, slowing as they pulled in close and maneuvering for position as the other boats aimed for the same two acres of disturbed water, where thousands of fins slashed the surface, the gannets plunging into the water for the bait and the gulls skimming the surface for the scraps, the oily smell of the anchovy slaughter mixing with gasoline exhaust.

"Holy shit," Jack said. Deke got him set up in the stern while Russell took the bow, casting into the maelstrom and hooking up on his second retrieve. The fish took eighty yards of line before he was able to turn it. Looking back, he saw that Jack was also into a fish. It was another ten minutes before Russell got it to the boat. Deke came around to help him bring it in and unhook it, a fat, shiny fifteen-pound striper that he lifted by its tail and dropped into the water.

"What the fuck," said Jack, who by this time had lost his fish. "You're lettin' him go?"

"Catch and release," Russell said. "The code of the fly fisherman."

"Shit, man, that's like gettin' all the way into a girl's bedroom and then just tuckin' her in and kissin' her good night. I just don't get that at all."

"There'll be more," Russell said. "What happened to yours?"

"He tried to wrestle it in, broke the line," Deke said. "That's all right; we'll get the next one."

The bait had moved with the current up the shore. Deke followed the birds and the boats to the next blitz, finding an opening and planting Jack in the prime spot, instructing him on his cast. Russell decided to wait until his friend got one on before he started in again. The water was seething with boats and fish and birds, all of them frenzied in their own ways. Jack flubbed his first two casts and caught Deke's shirt with the third.

"Slow down," Russell said. "Take your time."

He kept casting and reeling as fast as he could, failing to connect with anything. "What the fuck?"

"Slow down your retrieve a little," Russell said.

"You know I'm gettin' fuckin' tired of you always tellin' me what to do."

"All right," Russell said, retreating to the front of the boat to fend for himself, hooking up on his first cast and brooding as he played the fish, his feelings mutating from stunned to hurt to angry. Ungrateful prick. He wasn't so obtuse as to think this was about fishing. But he'd plucked this kid from obscurity, and his judgment had been vindicated, for Christ's sake. He hadn't gotten any credit for the sentences he'd sharpened, the paragraphs he'd trimmed of fat, and he didn't want any, but neither did he expect this kind of resentment. He landed the fish on his own and unhooked it without bothering to look back to the stern.

Eventually, Jack hooked another one, after they'd moved the boat again, and Russell abandoned his post in the bow to watch the end of the fight, resisting the urge to tell him to stop bulldogging the goddamn fish, letting Deke carry that weight. And when the fish was finally in the boat, it turned out to be a whopper, at least twenty pounds, bigger than the two Russell had caught.

"Of course I want to fuckin' keep it," Jack said, in answer to Deke's question. His exhilaration seemed to clear the air.

"Nice work," Russell told him.

"Thanks, man. Look, I'm sorry for snappin' at you like that. I was just gettin' frustrated."

"That's okay," Russell said, although a certain formality set in between them, Jack at several points soliciting his advice, Russell congratulating him on each fish he brought to the boat. At the end of the day, at the dock, they both asked Deke to join them for dinner at their hotel, a former crash pad for commercial fishermen and hookers that had been renovated, and redecorated with a surfing theme. Russell convinced the chef to cook Jack's bass, and Deke held forth on rock-and-roll excess, all the compliant beauties and tequila sunrises on Mustique and mountains of glistening blue-flake Colombian cocaine. He became rhapsodic on this last subject. "It was the color of topaz, as iridescent as a fresh-caught false albacore," he said. "It was the color of the eyes of the first girl I ever slept with, a Swedish exchange student who appeared like an angel in my high school and, for some reason I will never understand, chose to bestow her gloriousness upon me. It was the color of munificence."

This rhapsody reminded Russell of a passage from Sheilah Graham's book about Scott Fitzgerald, in which everything about the author, from his eyes to his lips, was described as being blue.

"Don't you miss it?" Jack asked, sipping his fifth vodka and soda.

"Miss what?"

"You know. The drugs. The life."

"Only every fucking day," he said, looking mournfully at his Diet Coke, his own blue eyes glazed and shiny like ponds in the desert landscape of his ruddy face. "You never lose the desire, the compulsion, the yearning. Instead, I go to a meeting every day."

As if to compensate for Deke's sobriety, Russell and Jack drank far too much, and passed out almost simultaneously in the room with twin beds, beneath vintage black-and-white photos of surfers in Maui.

The next morning, at breakfast, they eventually found a subject of conversation in their guide.

"Fuckin' guy's like the bard of cocaine," Jack said. "If the Medellín cartel ever needs an ad campaign, I got the man for the job."

"I'm still trying to decide what made him harder, the coke or the Swedish girl."

"Oh, I can tell you that. It was for sure the coke."

On the train back to Manhattan, Jack broke a long silence to tell Russell that he'd signed on with Martin Briskin. Up until this point, Jack hadn't felt the need for an agent, letting Russell handle rights on the first book. While it was inevitable that Jack would sign up with someone, Russell couldn't help feeling a little put out, not least because Jack had picked the great white shark of literary agents, the man who treated publishers as mortal enemies.

"Briskin's one of the top guys, for sure," he said.

"I just got a lot comin' at me," Jack said.

"I understand." Perfectly reasonable—but still it felt like the end of something. For almost two years, Russell had been Jack's advocate, his liaison to publishing and New York and the wider world beyond.

"He got *The New Yorker* to take a story. It's coming out next month."

"What story?"

"A new one. You haven't seen it."

Russell sat back, absorbing this information. "Congratulations."

"Thanks."

"Next month?"

"Yup."

"Do you want me to take a look at it?"

"I'll for sure send you an advance copy."

Up to this point, Russell had placed most of Jack's stories in literary magazines; *The New Yorker* had rejected two of them. And, more significantly, he'd edited all of them before they were submitted.

"Great fishin'," Jack said, as they parted on the platform at Penn Station.

"It's something special," Russell said.

"So I hope you're okay with the Briskin thing."

"I can't say he's my favorite agent. But I'm happy for you about *The New Yorker*. I just would have loved to have seen the story before he sent it out."

"I needed to do it myself," Jack said. "I needed it to be mine."

"Well, of course. All the stories have been yours."

"But I needed it to be really mine, to sound like me. Sometimes I feel like you're manicurin' my prose. Makin' it yours."

"I want it to sound like you. You've got a voice—not that many people do. The last thing I want to do is stifle it. I'm just trying to make sure the voice comes through. Clear away the clutter."

"If you ever saw the trailer I grew up in, you'd know that clutter's part of my deal. I'm just sayin' when you cut three sentences out of a paragraph—"

"It's just a suggestion. You can always ignore it."

"It's not that easy. You're this big-deal New York fuckin' editor. I'm a hick from the sticks. And I have fuckin' issues with authority figures, in case you haven't noticed."

"I'm sorry. I guess I didn't know you felt that way."

"Don't get me wrong, Russell. I'm grateful as hell for everything you've done."

"That sounds like the prelude to a kiss-off."

"No. I just need you to let me be myself."

"I thought I had."

"You've been great, man. You believed in me when nobody else did."

"I still do."

They hugged awkwardly.

"Okay," Jack said. "We good?"

Russell nodded. He felt mournful; it was the end of something. But there was nothing to be done. He had often imagined that someday his children would make him feel this way—that all his efforts to launch them into the world would be appreciated but, in the end, unwanted.

"Share a cab downtown?" Jack asked.

"Sure," Russell said, realizing that for perhaps the first time in their association he had no idea where Jack was staying or with whom.

———

The next day he got a call from Steve Israel, a rare book dealer who'd been a class ahead of him at Brown. Steve had turned his English lit degree into a lucrative business. It amazed and occasionally irritated Russell that selling first editions of Hemingway and Joyce had enabled Steve to buy a brownstone on the Upper West Side.

"Yesterday I got a call I thought would interest you," he said. "Bookseller in Nashville says he has the original manuscript of Jack Carson's short story collection, heavily annotated with your notes."

"Where the hell did he get it?" Russell asked.

"I was a little suspicious, but he claims he bought it directly from your boy. Apparently, he needed some quick cash."

"Oh Jesus. What do you think the guy paid?"

"I can tell you what he wants—five thousand."

"That sounds a little high."

"Not if Jack wins the National Book Award, which I hear is possible. Plus, the extent of your annotation makes it a historically interesting document."

"Well, I don't need the fucking thing."

"I just thought I'd tell you it was out there. And I wanted to offer you first crack. Let me just say, as a friend, that he faxed me some pages and I found them fascinating. You have a reputation as a real blue pencil guy, but some people might find the extent of your work . . . well, almost a form of coauthorship."

"What are you saying, Steve?"

"I'm just wondering if you want this floating around out there. Or if *he* does. Carson is on his way to becoming an important American author and skeptics might say this calls his achievement somewhat into question."

"That's bullshit."

"Just trying to give you a heads-up here, Russell."

"If I hadn't known you all these years, I'd say it sounds like you're trying to blackmail me."

"I can't even believe you'd use that word, Russell. I could sell this thing for a handsome profit with just one phone call. I called you first because I thought we were friends. And because I'm telling you I think you should consider getting this off the market."

"I'm sorry, I'm just a little upset. It's nobody's fucking business how I edit, but obviously I'd rather not have this in circulation."

"Well, if you're lucky, it will find a private buyer who just sits on it until Carson's really famous."

"Steve, let me think about this and ring you back. I've got to take this call."

"Suit yourself," he said.

20

CORRINE WAS MEETING Veronica and Nancy at Declan's, the midtown cafeteria of the big publishing houses, literary agencies and TV networks—the kind of place where, if you read *Vanity Fair* and watched *Charlie Rose,* you'd recognize many of the faces in the room, and if you were yourself one of those bold-name faces, you'd know everyone at the surrounding tables. Clean and well lighted, with a bleached minimalist decor, the better to show off its complicated patrons, accented with a few mainly abstract canvases on loan from artists who were regulars. The venue was Nancy's choice; having recently come out of seclusion in Sag Harbor, where she'd been working on a novel, she didn't want to risk not seeing or being seen.

Walking to the table, Corrine passed a network anchor, a network owner, a movie star and three or four assorted journalists she'd run into with Russell.

As the maître d' had informed her, Nancy and Veronica were already seated.

"Hello, hi, sorry I'm late."

"No, that's okay. We got here early."

They both seemed nervous, as if they'd been caught talking about her.

"This is such a nice idea," Corrine said. "We hardly ever do this."

The other two exchanged a guilty look.

"At least I don't," she added.

"It's true," Veronica said, "we really should do this more often."

"But actually, this isn't necessarily just a casual girls' lunch," Nancy said, sounding a little stilted.

"No? What is it?"

The waiter chose this moment to ask what kind of water they would like—all three simultaneously calling for tap.

"Was it the nineties," Veronica said, "when we discovered bottled water? And how it was so cool to order your name-brand water?"

"Whereas now it's just pretentious and environmentally unsound," Nancy noted.

"So what kind of lunch *is* this?" Corrine asked.

"It's kind of an intervention," Nancy said.

"'An intervention'?"

The waiter returned. "May I get you ladies anything to drink?"

Corrine and Veronica ordered iced tea, Nancy a Bloody Mary.

"It can't be my drinking," Corrine said after the waiter left.

"It's more of a relationship intervention."

"Someone you love reached out to us," Nancy said.

Corrine felt a tingle of fear at the back of her neck. Her first guilty thought was that this had something to do with Luke, about whom she'd dreamed last night.

"Who are we talking about?"

"Your sister."

"My *sister*?"

"We think she deserves a hearing. It's been a year, Corrine."

"She's very hurt and very sorry for what she said that night. Isn't it time to forgive?"

"I can't believe she's using you guys to get to me. And I can't believe you're falling for it."

"She is your sister," Nancy said.

Corrine could imagine her staging this, like a scene from one of her books. If she was really unlucky, it might *become* a scene in one of Nancy's books.

"And she's . . ." Veronica let the predicate hang, unspoken.

"Let me guess: *the mother of my children*."

"I wasn't going to say it like that. But she did a wonderful thing for you twelve years ago, and surely that counts for something."

"She wants to know the kids. She misses them. Shouldn't she have that right?"

"I kind of like the status quo. Honestly, it's been much less stressful not having her around."

"Corrine, let's be honest," Nancy said. "You're a little insecure about the whole biological mother thing."

"I resent that."

"I know you do. That's because it's true. I'm sorry, I love you, but I think you're almost grateful to have an excuse to keep Hilary away from the kids."

"I am. She's a train wreck."

"Yes, but that's not what I mean. You're afraid of what kind of relationship might develop."

"That's ridiculous."

"Is it? Come on, Corrine, this is me you're talking to. I know you."

Veronica seemed content to sit on the sidelines for the moment.

"Even if you're right about me, there's Russell to consider. He's told me many times he'll be happy if he never lays eyes on her again."

"Well, I'm sure you could change his mind."

"I'm not so sure."

Nancy's phone, which was on the table in front of her, buzzed and vibrated.

"She's here," she said.

"You *didn't*."

"Just hear her out."

"I can't believe you set me up like this," she said, seeing Hilary coming toward them on the arm of the maître d'. When Corrine saw how sheepish and cowed she looked, she lost her steely resolve, and by the time Hilary got to the table, her face was quivering with the attempt to contain her emotion. Corrine stood and hugged her sister, irritated at her own soppy reaction.

"I knew if you just saw each other—" Nancy said.

"Oh, shut up," Corrine said, sitting back down.

"Hey, sis," Hilary said. "I like your jacket."

"It's an old hand-me-down from Casey and I'm sure you've seen it before."

"Chanel is Chanel is Chanel," Nancy said.

"Is that Shakespeare?" Veronica asked.

"I think it's Gertrude Stein," Nancy said. "Well, anyway, Hilary, you look good."

"I've been on a juice fast the last three days, but the sad truth is, I still look at least a year older than I did when you last saw me."

She did look older to Corrine. Although still annoyingly pretty and shapely, she seemed to have finally entered middle age—if just barely—having belatedly lost her teenaged aspect, although this perception might have been abetted by her outfit, a white blouse buttoned to the neck under a gray suit with a knee-length pencil skirt, the most sensible and sober ensemble Corrine had seen her sister wear since their Nana's funeral. She was definitely playing the penitent.

"So," Hilary said. "How's Russell?"

"Nothing changes chez Calloway. You haven't missed much."

Hilary asked for a Bloody Mary and examined her menu. "What should I order?"

"The Cobb salad is the thing to get," Nancy said. "They have this huge menu, but for some reason nobody ever orders anything else. If you want to feel like a regular, order the Cobb salad and ask them to hold the bacon, the blue cheese, the egg and the dressing."

"What's left besides lettuce?"

"Not much. Water and fiber and the sweet smell of self-denial."

"Actually, that doesn't sound bad," said Corrine. It was just the sort of thing that drove Russell crazy; she could hear him saying, *Cheese and bacon is what makes it a Cobb salad, goddamn it,* but unlike most humans, she wasn't all that crazy about either, and she hated heavy lunches. She didn't like walking around feeling like a stuffed sausage in the afternoon. When the waiter returned, Corrine ordered the Cobb without the cheese and bacon. She retained the egg, though, and asked for the dressing on the side.

The waiter listened stoically as each of them subtracted ingredients from their salads. "Anything to start?" he asked wistfully.

"Let's get a bottle of wine," said Nancy.

Hilary seconded the motion; Corrine found herself distracted by the sight of her husband, who was being escorted into the room by Declan, the eponymous host.

"Of all the gin joints in town," Russell said.

"I hope you're not having lunch with your girlfriend," Declan said, mugging and winking.

Russell was maneuvering into position to kiss Nancy when he spotted Hilary and blanched.

"Hello, bro."

"*Hilary.*" An acknowledgment, almost an exclamation, but less than a greeting. He looked stunned.

"You can blame me," Nancy said. "I engineered this little reunion without your wife's knowledge."

Russell nodded contemplatively. Polite as he was, he was not ready to pretend he was okay with this.

"I could have sworn you said you didn't come here anymore," Corrine said, hoping to alleviate the tension. "I know I heard *someone* say he was tired of these uptown power lunch spots and he was going to make the world come downtown."

"My dining companion specifically requested this venue."

"Is your lunch date a superficial narcissist?" Nancy asked.

"Wait a minute, what does that make us?" Corrine asked.

"I'm meeting Phillip Kohout," Russell said.

"Oh my God," Hilary said. "Introduce me, please."

"Me first," Nancy countered.

"I'm sure he'll be delighted to sign a few autographs," Russell said. "In the meantime, I'll leave you ladies to it."

"Well, that seemed . . . fine," Nancy said, clueless.

"If you mean there wasn't any profanity or violence," Corrine said, "then yes, it was a huge success."

"Russell's a gentleman," said Veronica.

Corrine was tempted to take off her jacket—it was like a sauna in here—but she felt self-conscious about her arms, the flab under her biceps. "God, is anybody else hot?" she asked, fanning herself with the menu.

Veronica exchanged knowing looks with Nancy.

"What?" Corrine said.

"It's not actually hot," Nancy said.

"I'm practically freezing," Hilary said.

"Well, I'm hot."

"It's . . . the change," Nancy said.

"What change?"

"Hot flashes?"

"What? No way," Corrine said, even as she wondered. She *had* been getting hot recently, especially at night, waking up in a sweat, and her period was two weeks overdue.

"Are you having trouble lubricating?"

"Lubricating?"

"You know, sexually."

"For God's sake," Corrine said. "I'm just a little warm." It seemed as if there was a pause, a dialing down of the volume in the room, as heads turned toward the entryway, where Phillip Kohout was shaking hands with Brian Williams. Escorted by the solicitous Declan, he stopped at several tables to shake hands and kiss cheeks.

"I wouldn't mind sharing a cell with him," Nancy said.

"He's shorter than I expected."

"Aren't they always."

As he was passing, he caught sight of Corrine and said, "My God, it's true, *everyone's* here. Corrine, you're a vision." He dipped in to squeeze her shoulder, and then, when this move wasn't rebutted, he kissed her cheek.

"And you, Phillip, are a flatterer and a clichémonger."

"Please, Corrine," Nancy said. "Is that any way to talk to a war hero?"

"Ms. Tanner, I don't believe I've had the pleasure," he said. "But of course I'm a big fan of your work."

"Well, likewise," she said. "And I admire your courage."

"It doesn't take much courage to get captured, I'm afraid."

Much as she was remembering how much she disliked him and his smarmy charm, Corrine didn't forget her manners. "Phillip, this is my friend Veronica Lee and my sister, Hilary." Only belatedly did she realize she hadn't afforded Hilary the courtesy of a surname, but Phillip's reaction made it clear he didn't require one.

After politely shaking Veronica's hand, he clutched Hilary's as if she were in imminent danger of falling out of her chair.

"How is it that Corrine never told me she had a sister?"

"When it comes to her intellectual friends, she's basically ashamed of me."

"Perhaps there's another reason she's kept you hidden."

"It's true," Corrine said. "I'm quite protective of my little sister's innocence." She couldn't quite believe that no one laughed at this.

"Well, if I promise to get her home early, perhaps you'd allow me to take her out for a drink. Only if she's of legal drinking age, of course."

Corrine was afraid she was going to vomit right here at the table before this grotesque insipidity was terminated with Hilary's giving him her phone number.

"Farewell, fair ladies," Phillip said before sliming off to Russell's table.

"Isn't he the charmer," said Nancy. "He actually looks cuter in person."

"How is it that he's single?" Hilary asked.

"I think he was married, briefly," Corrine said.

"What's happened to Dan?" asked Veronica.

"Well, actually we're not together anymore," Hilary said. "I loved Dan—I mean, he's a great guy and all—but ultimately it just couldn't work. Our backgrounds were just too different. Look, we try to pretend we're a classless society, but we're not, and his guilt over his divorce really dragged our relationship down. Last I heard, he was about to move back in with his ex-wife, which is fine with me. Though it makes me kind of wonder, you know, what was the point of our whole relationship."

"From his point of view," Nancy said, "I'd guess he probably got some excellent sex."

"I've already gotten two drunken late-night booty calls," Hilary said. "But it's over. I've moved on, and he will, too."

Corrine already knew about the split but wanted to hear Hilary's take. She found her little sister's snobbery kind of amusing, this idea of some great class divide between them. If anything, Dan, with his Queens College degree, was far better educated than Hilary, who dropped out of horsey Hollins after freshman year, though it was true she'd attended some of the country's more prestigious boarding schools—all of which eventually requested that she leave. Corrine had always believed Dan was a decent man, not to mention a steadying influence, and she was sorry he was gone. He was also the breadwinner, which raised the question of how Hilary was supporting herself—the answer to which was usually synonymous with whomever she was sleeping with.

"I'm working on a pilot for a TV show—kind of a *Sex and the City*, but grittier," Hilary said after Veronica broached the subject of employment. "And I had a part in *Law & Order* last month."

"Is that still shooting?" Veronica asked.

"I love *Law & Order*," Nancy said.

"And that pays the rent?" Corrine asked skeptically.

Nancy gave her a look.

"I'm actually staying at a friend's place on 57th right now. It's pretty nice. You should come see it."

Ah yes, a friend.

The denuded Cobbs arrived, large white bowls of naked lettuce, along with a bottle of Pinot Grigio. Everything was either white or green.

"Maybe I could get you a part in my movie," Nancy said.

"Is it happening?"

"We start shooting this summer in New York."

"That's great."

"Well, it's ninety percent," Nancy said. The adaptation of her second novel had been on the verge of getting made for the last five or six years, not actually that long, when you considered the history of *Youth and Beauty*.

"Who's playing you?"

"Well, it's not really me," Nancy said. "I mean, it *is* fiction."

"Of course," Veronica said. "The plucky blond protagonist bears no resemblance to her creator."

"I think Jennifer Aniston would be perfect," Hilary said.

"Too goody-goody," Nancy said. This subject of who should play Nancy's alter ego had been a recurring theme for years. So far as Corrine knew, no one had ever proposed an actress whom Nancy hadn't found fault with.

"What about *your* movie?" Hilary asked. "The one based on Jeff's book."

"I'm not holding my breath. I haven't heard anything since I turned in the last draft in September."

"I saw a kid reading the novel on the subway last week," Veronica said.

Corrine nodded. "Russell says the sales are rising steadily. It's become a bit of a cult novel on campuses."

Nancy said, "Did I mention I'm speaking at Vassar next month?"

After lunch, Corrine went to the office, where she regretted that glass of Pinot Grigio when she started to doze off in front of her computer. She needed to make sure there were enough volunteers for this week's Greenmarket food rescue; right now, she was three short. Four days a week, their volunteers scoured the Union Square Greenmarket at closing time for unsold produce. She should have hit up her lunch partners, the salad strippers; she was still irritated at being ambushed like that, but the idea of Hilary or Nancy volunteering was laughable. Yet she'd been moved, in spite of herself, to see her sister, although she didn't want to do it too often, and she still didn't think she was a great influence on the kids.

At five-fifteen she left to pick up Jeremy at his karate class. He'd resisted most of their attempts to interest him in athletics, but Russell had watched a few samurai movies with him, and most of the weird cartoons and video games he liked seemed to be inspired by Japanese martial arts; karate had dovetailed neatly with the aesthetic of Pokémon and Digimon and Dragon Ball Z. As it turned out, the Japanese hadn't conquered the United States, as it was feared they might in the mid-eighties when they bought Sony and Rockefeller Center; back then, every best-selling business book was, more or less, some *Way of the Samurai* knockoff. But they'd definitely achieved a lock on the fantasy life of young American boys.

"The sensei gave me an excellent for my Heian Nidan kata," he told her, emerging from the dojo with his backpack.

"That sounds very good."

"It has twenty-six moves and it's really difficult to master."

"Way to go, Jeremy."

"Probably, if somebody tried to mug us on the street, I could take him."

"Well that's good to know, but I don't think there are that many muggers out there." It used to be a rite of passage; all of her friends had been mugged in the eighties and she'd had a purse snatched on the number 6 train in '81; Russell had outrun a pair of thugs in the West Village not long after, or so he claimed, but lately you didn't hear about these things happening in Manhattan.

"Dylan Lefkowitz's sister got mugged last week," he said. "Some Hispanic dudes stole her cell phone."

"Well, I hope you're not planning on using karate on the street."

When they arrived home, Storey and Jean were just returning from French club. "Did Russell say anything about dinner tonight?" Corrine asked Jean.

"He say the kids get takeout from Bubby's. It's Monday."

"Oh, damn." Corrine had forgotten it was date night, a tradition they observed as frequently as they could. She so didn't feel like it, having already had a big lunch; plus, all of a sudden she felt as if she was finally going to get her period any minute now—having gotten strangely irregular lately after years of twenty-eight-day cycles. She wondered if the girls were right about her being perimenopausal. It's not that she would miss her period, God knows, but she was afraid of losing some vital aspect of femininity.

After feeding the kids and supervising homework, she and Russell had walked up the street to Odeon, which had been around as long as they had, surviving relentless new trends in cuisine and restaurant design, its retro neon diner facade resembling some lost Edward Hopper painting from the forties, though in fact it had opened its doors in the Reagan era. For Russell, it had the melancholy patina of several fondly remembered meals in the company of Jeff Pierce; there wasn't that much left of the New York he'd inhabited. For Corrine, who hadn't been present on most of those boys' night out occasions, it had the virtues of being a block from their loft and serving a classic chèvre and frisée salad.

There was also the bonus, for him, of being greeted by name by the young woman at the front podium, and escorted to their regular table. Russell was no different from any other denizen of the city in his need to be recognized and coddled in his own corner of the metropolis.

While he and the hostess chatted, her mind drifted to Luke, at his faraway winery. Or maybe he was at the game farm? He'd called a few days ago to say he was coming to town next week. They hadn't made specific plans, but he'd made it clear he wanted to see her. And while she hadn't been quite as explicit, she wanted to see him, too, though she couldn't really justify this sentiment.

Suddenly the hostess was gone and Russell said, "Please don't tell me Hilary is back in our life."

"Well, I didn't make any dates, obviously. And just so you know, I had no idea she was going to be there."

"Dare I ask what she's been doing?"

"I told you she broke up with Dan six or seven months ago and now she claims she's writing a TV pilot."

"Jesus, that'll be must-see TV. What, exactly, are her qualifications?"

"Don't forget, she appeared on two episodes of *Law & Order*."

"So has everybody else we know."

Desperate to change the subject, she said, "Kohout was quite the conquering hero at Declan's. He must've enjoyed that."

"Well, why not. He's earned his moment in the spotlight, I'd say."

"And he's soaking it up big-time."

"What have you got against him, anyway?"

"I don't know, I've always thought he's very full of himself. I just don't think he's a good guy. Plus, I don't like the idea of your risking all this money on his book."

"You've got to risk it to make it."

"Your whole business model is based on finding books that the big publishers aren't chasing. You're niche, remember?"

"So maybe I want to broaden the niche."

"What's that, a paradox? A niche is by definition—"

"Yes, Corrine, I'm aware of the definition."

"Shall we hear the specials?" he asked, turning to beam at the waitress, who'd appeared beside the table.

Corrine excused herself, feeling her period arrive all at once, and walked gingerly to the ladies' room. For better, and worse, she was still in the game, despite her dear friends' eagerness to perform last rites on her womanhood.

21

"ONE DAY I WAS A TEACHING ASSISTANT in Iowa City," Phillip said, "and then suddenly my picture was in the *Times Book Review* and I'm on the *Today* show."

They were at KGB, an East Village bar known for its literary readings and authentically rude, Russian-style service. Russell had invited him to hear Jack Carson read, and afterward, as the rising star disappeared into the throng of admirers, Phillip was garrulously apologizing to Russell for his long-ago breach of contract while revisiting the days when he, too, had been a celebrated new fiction writer.

"As soon as the semester ended, I moved to Manhattan, flew to Hollywood on a first-class ticket and hung out with River Phoenix at the Viper Room three nights before he croaked out on the sidewalk. On the one hand, it all seemed perfectly natural, my just deserts, a slightly belated recognition of my innate talent and hard work. Of course, I'd always believed I was an unappreciated genius. On the other hand, I felt like a complete fraud, overpraised and unprepared for the role I'd been thrust into: a wunderkind, the voice of a new generation. And I wondered why it wasn't me who'd OD'd outside the Viper Room, given the amount of coke I'd snorted that night. I'd dabbled in coke before, but now that I had money and a modicum of celebrity, I was hitting it way hard. The first time I ever did coke, I knew I'd found my drug, my own best self. I felt *normal*, like I could walk into a room and imagine that I belonged among other humans without any degree of self-consciousness. So it seemed in the beginning, and for years to come. Eventually you figure out it makes you more self-conscious and cleaves you entirely from the great majority of your fellow humans, who are not doing coke all the time, and forces you to lie reflexively and incessantly, calling your agent at ten in the morning to cancel a lunch-time reading in Philadelphia because, you claim, you have a sudden attack of diverticulitis, not because you've been awake all night doing blow with a waitress from Bar Tabac. Eventually you're lying before the fact, bailing on any event that isn't likely to involve coke, and lying after the fact, apologizing for the missed dinner, the missed birthday, the missed deadline."

Russell could see a group of young women registering Kohout's presence; they were too cool to fuss about it, though he could sense they were annotating the sighting among themselves.

"Still, I was maintaining, in a way. You tell your agent and your putative editor the second book's going great. Pages soon, any day now, really good stuff. It's amazing how many people are willing to be lied to. It takes a village, right? It almost makes you believe in the innate good-ness of humanity, experiencing the credulity of the species. The more famous you are, the more your mendacity will be indulged. Women—you hate to say it; it sounds sexist, but fuck it—seem to be particularly afflicted with the will to believe, with the capacity for gratuitous hope, particularly with regard to promises of reform."

Glancing over at the other side of the room, beneath the Soviet-era posters, Russell could see a ripple of hilarity passing through the scrum of bodies around Jack.

"Meantime, the screenplay's gone through three drafts and a dozen script conferences and your Hollywood agent is taking longer and lon-ger to return your calls. Eventually, of course, there's the intervention. You remember that, I guess?"

Russell nodded. How could he forget? Ambushing Phillip at ten in the morning at his apartment. For Russell, it was an eerie and unwel-come reminder of his first such operation, though the paraphernalia was different, rolled-up bills and razor blades instead of needles and spoons, heroin having been Jeff's poison. In the end they'd failed to save Jeff, but only because he was already infected with HIV, and the thought that he could have acted earlier tormented Russell through the years, which was one of the reasons he consented to take part when Phillip's brother had called him. Russell, Marty Briskin, Phillip's former girlfriend, Amy, who had the key to let them in, the brother and his roommate from Amherst, plus the drug counselor, an earnest bearded empath in Birkenstocks and hemp trousers. Russell could imagine the horror, through Phillip's eyes, of being awakened after just a few hours of ragged sleep, to find this jury of his peers ensconced in the wreckage of his apartment, which still reeked of cigarettes and spilled vodka, the coffee table cloudy and streaked with coke residue. A waking nightmare for sure. The brother was the point man, shaking him awake, first gently and then more vigorously. When he realized that they weren't going away, he staggered into the bathroom and spent fifteen minutes in the shower. The Hollywood agent weighed in for precisely nine minutes on speakerphone, talking about doing coke with various movie stars before clicking off to get on a call with another movie star. Phillip denied everything, of course. He didn't have a problem. A little recreational use. The assembled company shared terrible stories of perfidy and malfeasance; carrots and sticks were deployed, and eventually he agreed to the two-month stay at Silver Meadows.

"It was actually a relief," Phillip said, "when it all came crashing down, and all my undeserved success had been punished. Once I detoxed, I saw the experience as the subject of my next book. And even though you had the right of first refusal, we all knew I could get more money elsewhere, and honestly, I knew you were too much of a gentleman to hold me to my contract."

"Is that supposed to be flattering?"

"I'm just trying to explain—no, I'm trying to *apologize*. In the end, you were lucky you didn't have to publish that piece of shit, although I have no doubt you would've made it a better book. As it was, my so-called editor at HarperCollins didn't edit at all. The problem was, I didn't believe in the redemption I was selling. My commitment to sobriety was more tactical than spiritual. And I'd failed to notice the rise of the memoir as the preeminent literary form of the nineties."

"If you'd called it a memoir," Russell said, "it might have done better."

"It would have. Look at James Frey. People wanted to think the degradation was real, never mind that memory's totally unreliable—an addict's memory most of all—that addicts are liars first and foremost, the fact that most novels are memoirs and most memoirs are actually novels."

A young woman crashed into their table, spilling most of her drink on Phillip. She gaped at him and said, "I know who you are."

"If only I could say the same," he said.

Jack Carson sat down at the table, having divested himself of his fans, and after a few minutes, Phillip got up and disappeared with the young woman.

"Be right back," he said.

"That guy's so full of shit," Jack said.

Russell was beginning to fear that this was indeed the case. There was no sign of Kohout when he bailed twenty minutes later.

22

TURNING EAST ON SPRING STREET, Corrine marveled anew
at the upscale boutiques that had infested SoHo ever since Prada
invaded—Chanel and Longchamp and Burberry—wondering when,
exactly, Manhattan had become a collection of luxury brands and fran-
chise outlets: Dubai on the Hudson. She stopped briefly to look in the
window of Evolution—an exception to this depressing trend—Russell's
practically favorite store, which sold fossils and bear skulls and mete-
orites and other twelve-year-old schoolboy desiderata. On a stucco wall
a few doors up the street was a drippy graffito: FIGHT TERROR WITH
GLAMOUR.

The late-autumn chill, the turning season, reminded her of all she
wanted to accomplish, and of all those past vows of seasonal renewal,
awakening a vague but powerful sense of yearning exacerbated by a
new note of desperation at the thought that she had fewer Novembers
ahead of her than behind. And now, as if to provide an object to that
inchoate sense of longing, Luke had reappeared.

If she didn't tell Casey about it, she felt that her date with Luke that
night might seem less real, or at least less of a betrayal. As much as she
loved confiding in her friend, this seemed like an even greater violation
of Russell's trust; and she had vowed not to sleep with Luke, which
Casey would find hard to believe. Since it was Casey's turn to come
downtown they were meeting at Balthazar, which her friend liked
because it reminded her of Paris, although she could never refrain
from saying that it *wasn't* La Coupole.

Casey was waiting up front, wearing her version of downtown attire, a black velvet biker jacket with epaulets and silver chains over a white T-shirt and skintight black leather jeans, along with some kind of quilted black leather boots. She was visibly unhappy to be jostled by the walk-ins and out-of-towners crowded around the door. After she gave Corrine a full complement of three kisses on the cheek, Corrine managed to get to the maître d', a tall, svelte Eurasian beauty, and claim her reservation.

They followed the woman's spectacularly long legs past the row of booths reserved for VIPs—although Corrine didn't actually recognize any of them today, just a bunch of very self-satisfied downtown potentates—and sat down at a nice little table.

"All the times you come here," Casey said, "you'd think they'd give you a booth."

"Russell always gets one, but it never occurs to me to ask."

"It's just that they're more comfortable," Casey said, which might have been true, although Corrine suspected that comfort had little to do with her desire to be seated conspicuously in a booth. "I could get Washington to make the reservation next time if you don't want to bother Russell."

It took Corrine a moment to process this. "Oh my God, don't tell me . . ."

Casey couldn't help smirking. "I ran into him last week at the Literacy Partners benefit, I'm on the board, actually, and Tom was out of town, as usual, and I guess Veronica was home with the kids."

"So you decided you might as well get a room?"

"Well, come on, it's not like there isn't a lot of history there."

"You used to say it was chemistry."

"Whatever it is, we found out we still have it."

"How did this *happen*?" Corrine asked, though she knew their affair had begun back in the eighties.

"One cocktail at a time. Then one, um, button at a time. Do you really need me to spell it out?"

"So you just suddenly decide to jump into bed?" Strangely, she wanted to know all the preliminary details. Even after engaging in an affair of her own, it still seemed amazing to her that married adults could end up in bed with people who weren't their spouses.

"We flirted and then later we went to a bar around the corner. And then we got a room."

"Where?"

"Some hotel on the West Side."

"How am I supposed to feel about this? You know that Washington and Veronica are almost our closest friends."

Casey's skin looked great; Corrine wondered what exotic new peel or process had burnished it.

"You've always known about, well, our little infatuation."

"I thought it was over."

"It was, but I guess the embers were still smoldering. And it's not like you and Veronica are all that close."

"We're having dinner with them tomorrow night. How am I supposed to act?"

"Don't pretend you don't have any experience here."

"You're implying that I'm a hypocrite?"

"Well, now that we've alluded to the topic, what's going on with Luke?"

Corrine had been hesitant to bring this up with Casey, since she wasn't quite certain how she felt about Luke's marital dissolution and she was fairly certain what her friend's reaction would be. Even so, she couldn't help wanting to share the news. Plus, she needed an alibi for tonight, and Casey was the only friend she had who was complicit. "He's back. I'm seeing him tonight."

"That's great. Where are you meeting?" she asked eagerly—an aficionado of the discreet Manhattan rendezvous. If you didn't know better, it might be easy to imagine that there would be countless refuges in the teeming city where lovers could meet, anonymous in the crowd, but anyone who had lived in Manhattan for long knew that it was essentially a village, and that your roommate from prep school or your husband's business partner was always accosting you on the sidewalk in Chelsea, or from the next table at the little out-of-the-way trattoria in the East Eighties.

"I couldn't really think of a place. He's staying at the Carlyle, so we'll just order room service."

"That's brilliant. It certainly saves a step."

"There's something else." She paused and lowered her voice: "He's getting a divorce."

"Oh my God."

"Well, yes."

"That's huge."

"I know. But I don't know what to think about it."

Casey, uncharacteristically at a loss for words, reached over and clutched her friend's hand.

Corrine was relieved when the waitress turned up to ask, "Have you had a chance to look at the menu?"

"No, but we'll have the Balthazar salads and split an omelette," Corrine told her, reverting to custom.

"Actually, I'm on this new diet," Casey said. "Could I just get some maple syrup and lemon juice with hot water?"

"I don't know if we have maple syrup."

"Well, can you ask? And also some cayenne pepper."

Corrine studied her. "Is that what's making your skin look so good?"

"You have to try it. I've lost five pounds in three days. I can't believe you didn't notice." Once the waitress walked away, she said. "I can't believe Luke's getting divorced. Are you completely freaked-out?"

Corrine nodded.

"What happened? Was it his idea? Do you think it had anything to do with you?"

"We've only talked briefly, but he said it had to do with his not wanting any more kids. She really wanted them."

"That's something these guys should take into account before they marry young bimbos."

"He sounded really sad," Corrine said.

"Well, of course he's sad. But that doesn't mean that part of him isn't happy."

"I don't want it to be about me," Corrine said. "It can't be about me."

"If you say so," Casey said.

The waitress returned to report that maple syrup was available.

"The hell with it, I'm absolutely starving," Casey said, "so we'll just have the Balthazar salads and the omelette."

"Just one omelette?"

"That's correct. And *two* glasses of Chardonnay."

"Is the Mâcon all right? Or would you rather the Chablis? They're both made from Chardonnay."

"Fine, whichever, the Mâcon," Casey said, and after the waitress left with the menus, she muttered, "I hate it when they act like not ordering two courses per person is some kind of fucking faux pas."

"I always feel like I should get the steak frites," Corrine said, eyeing a plate at the next table with a shiny, charred lozenge of beef and paper cones of french fries. "But I also think it's kind of gross. I mean, who could eat that in the middle of the day?"

"Speaking of eating issues, how's Storey doing?"

Corrine wished she'd never brought up the issue of her daughter's weight gain. She should have realized it would give Casey another chance to compare Storey unfavorably to her own perfect daughter, who, on top of everything else, spoke Mandarin.

"I'm hoping it's a phase. Russell thinks it might have something to do with the whole Hilary mess. He thinks she started gaining right after that incident, which is true. She was always a skinny little chicken, and then it's like she started eating at Thanksgiving dinner and hasn't stopped. You won't believe her favorite TV show. *Barefoot Contessa*."

"That fat-ass who used to have the pricey food store in the Hamptons?"

"That's the one. Now she's on TV, demonstrating how to inject butter directly into your thighs, and for some reason my daughter finds it fascinating."

"I told you, you should take her to my nutritionist."

"I don't want to call attention to it. She's self-conscious enough already."

"Believe me, even if you don't, her peers will. This is no town for fatties."

"You've got to be careful what you say, or next thing you know you're dealing with bulimia." Much as Corrine hated to see Storey overweight, she was terrified that she might transmit her own issues to her daughter. She knew, in moments of clarity, that she had to be careful. When she was at Miss Porter's, she'd been hospitalized with bulimia, and she still struggled against the occasional purging impulse. Or rather, still succumbed, occasionally. Hardly ever, though. It had been months.

As if reading her mind, Casey said, "There are worse things than the occasional voluntary puke. It's just one of those basic feminine specialties, like faking an orgasm."

One of Corrine's biggest fears was that she would start to judge her daughter, that she would hate in Storey what she hated in others. Every bit as troubling was that Storey seemed to be getting very judgmental of Corrine, criticizing her tics, her dress, her habits at every turn. They'd always been so close, but suddenly Storey seemed to be pulling away. Whenever she let herself remotely fantasize about a future with Luke, she had only to imagine Storey's reaction in order to squelch it.

Leaning over to pick up her napkin, she was surprised, as she righted herself, to see her face in the smoky mirror behind Casey, as if for a nanosecond she didn't quite recognize the middle-aged woman, so like her, only slightly older. In her heart she was still twenty-seven, or thirty-three. At most forty-two. She'd always resisted the idea of getting work done, but maybe it was time to start thinking about it. There was a lag, a long delay between the calendar and her image of herself. Every few years her age consciousness lurched forward, propelled by some event or encounter, without ever necessarily catching up to the present.

"Have you been having sex with Russell?" Casey asked.

She leaned forward and whispered, "I can't even remember the last time. A few months ago he was complaining that I didn't put out, and now he seems to have lost interest. Maybe I've let myself go a little." A busboy arrived with bread, but they both waved him away as if he were Satan himself.

"Have you thought about getting your eyes done?"

"Do I look that bad?"

"Not yet, but it's time to start thinking about these things. You don't want to wait until you really need it. Preventive maintenance is the thing."

The waitress brought their wine and returned almost immediately with their salads. "Would you like fresh pepper?"

They declined in unison.

"I can't believe they still go through that ridiculous pepper ritual," Corrine said. "They were doing that when I first arrived in the city, except the pepper mills were gigantic then."

"It was the big eighties. Big hair, big shoulder pads, big-ass pouf dresses. Big Rubirosas."

"According to *Vogue,* the eighties are coming back."

"They've been coming back for years," Casey said. "I love this salad."

"Russell says truffle oil is just olive oil flavored with a synthetic chemical compound that mimics the taste of truffles."

"What a killjoy. Someone was trying to tell me yesterday that Splenda isn't actually made from sugar and I said don't tell me what it's made from. It can be made out of camel shit as long as it's zero calories and tastes good."

"*Love* Splenda."

"Now if we could just get somebody to invent a zero-calorie Chardonnay, life would be just about perfect."

That night, Russell was making a risotto for the kids, instructing a rapt Storey, who stood beside him at the stove on a step stool, the two of them taking turns stirring the rice, while Jeremy sat at the table doing homework with Ferdie in his lap—a domestic tableau that seemed specifically designed to dissuade her from her illicit plans. She could join them, sit and talk with her husband and the kids about their day, but instead she was leaving them to meet her former lover, under the guise of a girls' night out. Her day seemed to have a French theme—she might as well light up a fucking Gauloises, right here.

She would have felt better if Russell hadn't taken this occasion to compliment her appearance. "Looking good, honey. It must be true—girls dress for other girls."

Storey glanced up from her stirring. "I've never seen you wear so much makeup." Her tone seemed slightly waspish. Was it her imagination, or was there also a touch of suspicion? They really needed to spend some mother-daughter time soon—tomorrow, or at least this weekend.

Corrine was wearing a baby blue A-line halter dress that stopped just above the knee, which she'd bought after lunch today at Century 21, and a pair of Gucci pumps with a four-inch heel that Casey had passed down to her last month after deciding they pinched her toes. Under the scrutiny of her husband and daughter, she was conscious of how much time she'd spent primping for the evening.

She was a terrible person.

"Why do you look so sad?" Jeremy asked.

"Just sad to be leaving you."

"Then stay."

"Can we watch *Survivor*?" Storey asked, sensing an opening.

"You know the rules. It's a school night." Not to mention that she thought it was a ridiculous show, despite the fact that some of her friends were obsessed with it.

"But we've done our homework and you let us watch last week and now we need to see if Gillian gets voted off the island."

"I'll leave that up to your dad," she said, not wanting to give in, but knowing that Russell would take the path of least resistance.

The elevator shuddered to a stop on the ground floor, where she encountered her neighbor Bill Sugerman, who was clutching a laundry bag with one arm and a squirming toddler with the other. "Hey, Bill, how's it going?"

He sighed and grimaced. "This isn't exactly what I pictured, you know, when I thought about my life."

Unprepared for this burst of candor, she stood slack-jawed as he walked past her into the elevator.

She arrived at the Carlyle a nervous wreck, feeling short of breath as she rode up in the old-fashioned elevator with the polite, petite operator in his braided uniform and cap, who looked exactly like an elevator man in one of those New York films from the thirties, delivering Carole Lombard or Norma Shearer to an assignation with Cary Grant or Ronald Colman.

Her sense of self-possession was further eroded at the sight of Luke, framed in the doorway of his room, his rueful grin made more poignant by the scar and the slightly cloudy, out-of-focus eye. Whether sensing her reserve, or out of shyness, he didn't embrace her, but merely leaned forward and kissed her cheek. "It's so great to see you. Please, come in."

"It's nice to see you, too."

She surveyed the large formal living room with its view of Central Park and the strident towers of the West Side through the windows to the east, its well-worn, almost shabby Louis Quinze decor. Wildly expensive, no doubt, but not stupidly ostentatious.

"I love your dress."

"Thanks. You don't know how badly I want to say I found it in the back of my closet, but actually I bought it this afternoon."

"Well, why do you sound so unhappy about it?"

"I'm mad at myself because, well, I bought it for you, because I wanted to look good for you."

"I'm flattered and honored."

"So why am I mad at myself? I should be mad at you."

"I'm not aware of having done anything to incur your wrath."

"You came back. You called. You constitute a moral dilemma."

He turned and walked to the little bar alcove, where a bottle of Dom Pérignon was chilling in a sweating silver bucket, and poured out two flutes. Jesus, that stuff, room service, cost as much as her dress—probably more. Was it appropriate to be celebrating a divorce? Without having resolved this question in her mind, she accepted one of the flutes and sipped.

"I understand. But I hope you'll still have dinner with me."

She walked over to the window and looked out over Central Park. "Have you ever noticed how much more interesting and flamboyant the Upper West Side skyline is than the Upper East, all these great whimsical buildings along Central Park West, the Majestic and the Beresford and the Dakota with their towers and turrets and their mansard roofs. The buildings over here are much more monolithic and uniform."

"Kind of like the people who live in them," he said.

"As you did not so long ago."

"That's how I know. I'm a recovering Upper East Sider."

"What does that mean?"

"It means, I guess, I left my job, and my circumscribed world here, because I wanted to broaden my vision. Does that sound pretentious?"

"Absolutely."

"Well, my first attempt to escape has ended in failure."

"Just because your marriage ended, it doesn't mean you failed. I'm sure you learned a lot. The foundation is a wonderful accomplishment."

"Yes and no. I imagined myself as a hands-on philanthropist, working with the people I was trying to help, but now I see myself sort of gradually fading away. I mean, yes, I'm going to endow the foundation, sure, but if I'm honest with myself, I've kind of lost interest in running the thing day to day. It was all part of the African adventure, which started to lose its allure after my accident."

If he hadn't accused himself of fickleness, she might have thought as much herself, but she appreciated the self-awareness implied in this account. "Some people are good at starting things, but not necessarily at running them."

"I think Giselle was part of that whole African fantasy. Safari girl, athletic and outdoorsy."

They were standing at the window. He gestured at the seating area; she sat on the couch, while he took a seat on a facing club chair, drumming his fingers on the arm.

"Where is she now?"

"In London, but she wants to move to New York. She's a citizen by marriage, so she might as well."

"Great. Maybe we can all have lunch."

He looked at her blankly.

"That was a joke. Why doesn't anyone ever know when I'm joking?"

"Sorry."

"And what about you? What are you going to do?"

"Actually, I've gotten pretty involved in the Obama campaign. Fund-raising from my old cronies." He stood up, walked over to the bar and leaned against it.

"That's very cool."

"I was suddenly worried you might be a Hillary person."

"Why, because I'm a woman?"

"No, just because I've always imagined that we have similar views and tastes, and I would have been slightly disappointed if we hadn't picked the same candidate."

"That was a good answer. And yes, I'm actually an Obama person."

"Great minds think alike."

He was pacing around the room; she wondered if he was nervous, or merely restless. "Does this mean you're moving back?" she asked warily. She wanted him back in the city, even though she knew it would complicate her life tremendously.

He nodded. "I thought I might look for an apartment downtown."

Why is everyone moving downtown? she wondered. "At least you can afford it," she said.

"Is that a jab?" He sat down on the couch now.

"No, I'm just saying we've so outgrown our place and we can't afford anything bigger in the neighborhood, since we're competing with movie stars and hedge funders."

"Maybe I could help."

"Luke, you know I can't accept that kind of help from you."

"I don't see why not." He tapped his foot soundlessly on the rug. "I'd like to think you wouldn't categorically rule out the possibility in advance."

He went to the bar and refilled her glass with champagne.

"I don't want to feel like this divorce is about you and me," she said.

"It's not about you and me. But it's not *not* about you and me."

"Just to be clear—she's not leaving you; you're leaving her?"

He nodded, sat down again.

"I feel terrible."

"Me too. But I also feel relieved. And hopeful. Is that a terrible thing to say?"

"I don't know."

Sitting beside her on the couch, he was close enough that she could smell him.

"I can't pretend I don't want you," he said, looking pained.

"Just to be clear, do you mean you want to sleep with me?"

"I think I actually meant more than that. But, yes, of course."

"Maybe if you did, you'd get me out of your system," she said. She was remembering how much she'd always wanted him, and feeling a resurgence of that desire. It was involuntary—but there it was.

"I don't think so," he said. "But I'd love to try."

He leaned over and kissed her; she liked it as much as she'd remembered.

She recoiled at the rasp of the buzzer, startled.

Luke got up and opened the door, ushered the man with the cart inside, assuring him that they could remove the chafing dishes and set the table themselves, shoving a bill into his hand and firmly guiding him out. After closing the door, he walked over to the couch and lifted her in his arms and carried her into the bedroom. At last, she thought, disloyally, a man who's not obsessed with eating, although this turned out to be not entirely the case. He eased her down on the bed and removed her dress and her panty hose before going down on her.

What followed validated the fantasies of the years in between this and the last time they'd made love; afterward, as she lay panting on the bed, she said, "Goddamn it!"

"What's the matter?"

"I was hoping it wouldn't be as good as I remembered."

"I'm sorry I haven't been a disappointment to you."

"Well, anyway, now we can just go on with our lives."

"I'm not so sure about that," he said.

23

THE SHADOWS GREW LONGER in the windy canyons of TriBeCa, and soon it was time to throw away the shrunken, collapsed pumpkins and bring the winter coats out of storage. Although they'd been eager to go trick-or-treating again this year, Jeremy and Storey announced over Thanksgiving dinner that they were too old now for *The Nutcracker*—a family tradition since they were toddlers.

December was the swiftest month, the days growing shorter as the invitations and the obligations mounted, hats and coats and gloves laboriously donned and doffed, Christmas cards signed and addressed, presents chosen and purchased. And the parties, which by the middle of the month came to seem like work, waking to the alarm parched and headachy and chilly in the dark, too soon after the last cocktail, the last farewell; frost veining the windows, chilled air leaking through the gaps in the warped, paint-layered frames, burrowing deeper in the covers and moving closer to the hot lump of your husband.

All the new restaurants that year seemed to be hangar-size Asian fusion spots decorated with giant Buddhas and aquariums stocked with predatory fish, but tonight the boys had chosen a faux-rustic place in the Village, the interior of which resembled a Provençal farmhouse. Cylinders of brown paper bound in twine turned out to be their menus, which faithfully listed the source of all the ingredients, most of them organic. Corrine's duck hailed from Bucks County, Pennsylvania.

"Are you done with Christmas shopping?" Veronica asked her as their husbands dissected the bill of fare.

"Almost. Storey, naturally, picked her own, a princess bed from Pottery Barn that's supposed to be delivered tomorrow, and assorted slutty accessories from Juicy Couture. Jeremy's getting a cell phone—I forget what kind; Russell did that—plus some horrible video games. On the other hand, I haven't finished the Christmas cards."

"I can't believe you still do cards."

"Russell insists. You know how he is about Christmas."

"We do it all online—shopping, e-cards."

"I wish we could visit my mother online and dispense with the actual trip to Stockbridge."

"That's still on?"

"Afraid so. I go up a day or two early to spend a little extra time fighting with Mom, then Russell and the kids come Christmas Eve and we leave as early as possible on the twenty-sixth for five days skiing at Killington—a package we bought at the school auction." The Lee clan, she knew, was going to Saint Barth's, their own destination last year.

After dinner, the four of them retrieved their coats and wraps from the coat check and bundled themselves against the cold, their misty exhalations like empty speech balloons as they walked past the Greek Revival town houses on Downing Street and waited for a cab on Varick. The chilly air revived her and reminded her of other wintry city nights—the sidewalk debates about the next stop, the farewells to friends, the last cigarettes, and, suddenly very specifically, of a cold night long ago not far from here when, leaving a long-since-shuttered bistro, they'd passed a young boy huddled, shivering, in a shadowed doorway and she'd stopped to ask him if he was okay, Russell palpably irritated by what he called her "missionary impulse," suspicious of all sidewalk mendicants, the boy so young, barely a teenager, saying, finally, "I'm cold," and she'd unfurled her scarf and stooped to wrap it around his neck, turning to look at Russell, and to his credit he'd understood, taking several bills from his wallet and handing them to the boy, the memory warming her even as it made her unbearably sad for the lost boy and for the years that had disappeared between that moment and this.

"What's the matter?" he said now, pulling her close. "Are you *crying*?"

"It's just the cold," she said.

———

"I'm glad you've patched things up with your sister," Jessie said, pouring her first vodka of the day, four fingers in the same heavy juice glass she'd been using since Corrine was a kid. It was four in the afternoon, the commencement of cocktail hour, apparently. Once upon a time, it had kicked off at 6:00 p.m., but at least there was still some boundary. Before pouring her first drink, Jessie had watched the clock over the kitchen stove while the minute hand clicked toward its apex, although there was no numeral to mark the twelve o'clock spot—the numbers were piled in a jumble at the bottom of the clock face, which bore the legend *Who Cares? I'm Retired.* It was one of the few furnishings that had changed since Corrine was in high school. And in fact, Jessie wasn't quite retired, still putting in a day or two at the antiques store she ran in Stockbridge, or so she claimed, though more and more she left the management of it to the lesbian couple who'd worked there since graduating from Bennington a decade before.

"Actually, I haven't entirely made up with her," Corrine said. "I just sort of humored her and made a vague threat about getting together."

"None of us is perfect. Although sometimes we thought you were. Don't forget it wasn't so easy for her, following you, with your straight A's, and Miss Porter's and captain of the lacrosse team. Ivy League, summa cum laude, and then marrying Russell right out of college. I think the only role left for Hilary was the bad girl."

Corrine was sort of amazed at this idealized portrait of herself. "Well, she must feel better now that I've failed to live up to my early promise."

"Your life looks pretty great from where I sit, kiddo. A good husband, two great kids. Not that I've seen them recently."

"They'll be here tomorrow, Mom."

"One big happy family," Jessie said. "Enjoy it, because you never know when your husband will run off with your best friend."

"I don't think Russell's rich enough to tempt Casey."

Sooner or later, Jessie inevitably steered the conversation back to her own sense of loss and betrayal, the husband who'd indeed run off thirty years ago with her best friend, although usually this came later in the evening. It had become the defining event of Jessie's existence, the original sin. Corrine was determined to steer clear of this miasma as long as possible and excused herself, saying she wanted to unpack.

Visitors never failed to be surprised at the gloomy ambience of Corrine's room, which Russell characterized as "preppy Goth"; aside from a few athletic trophies and a lacrosse stick, the predominant decorative element consisted of grave rubbings from nearby Colonial graveyards. Like many adolescents, Corrine had exhibited a strong morbid streak, along with an interest in local history. She'd spent hours wandering the cemeteries in search of tragic stories, taping newsprint to the stones and rubbing charcoal over it, the ghostly letters as they appeared seeming like nothing so much as spirit writing, like terse communiqués from the dead. A few were selected for the crude beauty of the stonework, skulls with angel wings being her favorite motif. But most she chose for the poignance of their inscriptions. Here was little Hattie Speare, who died in 1717: *An Aged Soule Who had seene but 7 Wynters in this World.* As a teenager, Corrine was haunted by this one and spent many hours imagining the life that might have inspired it. These grim haiku helped her to survive adolescence. She found them comforting, much as others took solace in songs of heartbreak.

She opened the door to the closet and dug back into the depths, parting the phalanx of musty dresses and blouses, stepping over the rows of embarrassing shoes and boots, pushing aside the boxes behind them until she uncovered a big flat package wrapped in cardboard and sealed with duct tape. She wrestled it out into the room and cut the tape with a box cutter, pulling away the layers of cardboard to reveal an oil painting she hadn't looked at in over twenty years, a canvas by Tony Duplex.

She propped it up against the bed and stood back for a closer look. It was a single canvas divided into three panels. The center panel was a map of Manhattan pasted on the canvas; he had painted the bust of a man on one side and on the other a woman. The painter had managed to imply a relationship between the two, though they were not looking at each other; the images were less stylized, more realistic and lyrical than most of Duplex's figures. Painted neatly across the bottom of the map were the words OH SHIT, I GUESS I SHOULD HAVE KNOWN IT WOULD BE LIKE THIS.

She had always thought the two figures in the painting were, in Jeff's mind, himself and Corrine. She needed to decide what to do with the painting, whether to sell it now or to hang on to it in the hope that its value might appreciate. For the moment it seemed safe enough here, along with the other artifacts of her past that she couldn't yet bear to part with, including the very few surviving mementos from Jeff. He'd been careful in what he committed to writing; she was sad now that, out of a sense of discretion, he'd never sent her an actual letter. Instead, he'd sent her books with underlined passages, pointed and poignant texts. She took a small box from the closet and pulled out one that Jeff had sent her after Russell had returned from Oxford; they'd been married a few months later. She'd been working as a broker downtown and Jeff had mailed this slim volume, *The Poems of Sir Thomas Wyatt,* to her office, and, as a kind of quiet rebuke and lament, included a bookmark marking the poem "They Flee from Me."

> They flee from me that sometime did me seek
> With naked foot, stalking in my chamber.
> I have seen them gentle, tame, and meek,
> That now are wild and do not remember
> That sometime they put themself in danger
> To take bread at my hand; and now they range,
> Busily seeking with a continual change.

> Thanked be fortune it hath been otherwise
> Twenty times better; but once in special,
> In thin array after a pleasant guise,
> When her loose gown from her shoulders did fall,
> And she me caught in her arms long and small;
> Therewithall sweetly did me kiss
> And softly said, "Dear heart, how like you this?"

It was no dream: I lay broad waking.
But all is turned thorough my gentleness
Into a strange fashion of forsaking;
And I have leave to go of her goodness,
And she also, to use newfangleness.
But since that I so kindly am served
I would fain know what she hath deserved.

The second book was a battered old hardcover without dust jacket, a 1959 edition of a medieval text, *The Art of Courtly Love,* by Andreas Capellanus, wherein a letter addressed "To the illustrious and wise woman M, Countess of Champagne" was underlined. She didn't need to reread the letter, having done so many times. Two nobles, a man and woman, supposedly wrote it in order to pose a question: whether true love can exist between husband and wife, and whether lovers have any right to be jealous of spouses. To which the countess answered, at some length, that love by definition cannot obtain between man and wife, who are duty-bound to each other, but only between lovers, who choose each other freely, and whose jealousy is a concomitant of their love. Jeff had thought this very clever, and apposite, at the time, a few months after Corrine married Russell. It seemed almost ridiculous, given the situation, the friendship between the two men, and their mutual desire for Corrine, that Jeff's major was Elizabethan literature, his senior thesis about the conventions of courtly love. As events unfolded later, it seemed incredibly touching that he'd chosen to write about the antique notion of a love both illicit and spiritually elevating, a love that existed outside the legal sphere of marriage. Did he see himself even then as her vassal, her knight?

Back in her school days, she would not have believed it was possible to love two people, but she had learned that it was. And the sadder truth was that possession blunted desire, while the unattainable lover shimmered at the edge of the mind like a brilliant star, festered in the heart like a shard of crystal.

24

IT HAD ALMOST BEEN PERFECT, Washington thought, this thing with Casey. They were both happily married—or at least he was, and certainly she was *conveniently* married, with no desire to alter her domestic arrangements, or to abandon her rarefied social and economic spheres.

He had experienced less convenient situations—the single girls who started out seeming carefree but gradually started whining about spending Valentine's Day on their own and eventually threatening to call his wife. The tears in restaurants, the tantrums on street corners, the unannounced appearances at the office. The eventual phone calls to his apartment, *his home,* where he lived with his family. Yes, Washington could honestly say he'd paid for his sins. He liked to believe he had pretty good radar for crazy, but the equipment sometimes malfunctioned due to libidinal interference. Generally speaking, the crazier the babe, the better the sex. Crazy was freaky. Crazy was hot. And it was hard to walk away from that, or to rule it out in advance.

Casey, though eminently sensible and conventional in many regards, was a fucking demon in the sack, a lioness of desire. Any prejudicial stereotypes he might have entertained about the frigidity of rich WASP women went right out the window the first time Casey hauled him into a bathroom stall at the Surf Club back in the eighties. He was drunk and high, but she was voracious, and wasn't about to admit that failure was an option, and after a few minutes he had the illusion that he was going to be swallowed whole, which wouldn't have been a bad way to go, really, crotch-first into eternity. They'd been on and off ever since, sometimes going years between intimate encounters, but the sexual chemistry remained so potent that they kept coming back, and over the last few months, after five years of abstinence, they were making up for lost time, fucking like teenagers; the illicit nature of their affair, the enforced separations, and the need for secrecy stoking their desire. There was nothing like strange, after all. He'd heard some men express a preference for home cooking, but Washington loved dining out.

And yet, lately, he'd found himself wondering if he wasn't getting too old for this shit. The last time he found himself undressing in her presence, he'd actually felt a brief twinge of conscience, a kind of yearning to do the right thing, although Casey had quickly obliterated these thoughts with action. Her latest plan was positively freaky. When she found out that they were both attending the Nourish New York benefit at the Waldorf, she'd decided to take a room there. "We arrange a time, during cocktails. You excuse yourself, I excuse myself, we meet upstairs, fuck our brains out and return to our respective spouses," she said a week before the benefit, when they were lying in a midday postcoital tangle of sheets at the Lowell, a small, expensive hotel they'd been using like a private club for a while now. He'd felt like a trespasser, a criminal, the first time he stopped at the front desk and said he was meeting Casey Reynes. He thought it was crazy for her to book under her own name, but she said Tom never looked at the Visa bill. He'd been lying in bed, wondering idly how much the room cost, when she launched her proposal to spice up Corrine's benefit.

"Damn, you're sick," Washington said.

"And you love it," she said, slapping his thigh beneath the sheets.

He knew her well enough to know that the idea of the spouses downstairs was part of the thrill. It was completely perverse if you thought about it, but he was not immune to the buzz; betrayal was an aphrodisiac unto itself and, as with all rushes, the dose of the drug had to be raised, continually, in order to maintain the high. The near presence of her husband and his wife, downstairs in the ballroom, oblivious, was the Spanish fly in this particular scenario.

"It is outrageous," she said, "but at the same time it's foolproof. I sometimes worry about private detectives—I mean, I don't really have any reason to think Tom suspects anything, but practically everybody uses them sooner or later. The beauty of this is, there's no chance of his having me followed when I'm actually *with* him."

"Hold on a fucking minute," Washington said. "Rewind. You suspect you're being followed by detectives? And you're just telling me now?" In the midst of his panic, he was hearing Elvis Costello's "Watching the Detectives," part of the sound track of his early days in Manhattan.

"It's not that I suspect it so much as I want to be totally careful. Amanda Giles was carrying on with her yoga instructor—"

"'Carrying on'? What kind of euphemism is that?" It amazed him that a girl who had been screaming "Fuck my hungry pussy" ten minutes before could suddenly resort to such a genteel locution.

"All right, she was fucking her yoga instructor. And the next thing she knows, her husband's showing her pictures of herself and Swami Tommy in some supertantric positions that the authors of the *Kama Sutra* hadn't even thought of."

"'Swami Tommy'?"

"Are you going to nitpick my language or listen to my story?"

"Actually, I liked it; I was just curious if that was really his name or your clever coinage."

"Who knows what his name is? He's the fucking yoga instructor."

"Okay, good one. Proceed."

"Thank you. But that's basically the story. Blah blah blah, photographic evidence, notice of marital discord, divorce court, activate prenup infidelity clause with only one year to go before the five-year escalator clause kicks in. I'm just saying it's foolish not to be careful. To watch one's back, as it were."

"Do you think there's even a chance that he's having you followed?"

"I'm just saying you can't be too careful."

"And would you call what you're proposing *careful*?"

"That's exactly what I'm saying. It's genius."

"It's utterly twisted."

"I thought you liked twisted." She lowered her head and inserted her tongue into his ear.

"There's freaky. And then there's crazy."

But he had to admit crazy was hot; it was the hottest. But *twisted* was the perfect signal to stop. To end it for good. Not that he relished telling her that.

She called him twice at work that week to try to talk him into changing his mind, but up in his office on the thirty-first floor, under the sickish fluorescent light, the idea did not seem any more sensible than it had wrapped in Frette sheets at the Lowell.

The night of the benefit, he felt incredibly nervous, suddenly uncertain of his composure in the event of an encounter between Veronica and Casey. He was hoping she'd given up on her plan by now; at any rate, he had no intention of participating.

His son, Mingus, in whose face he inevitably saw the lineaments of his mother at her most beautiful, protested their departure: "This is the third night you've been out this week."

His sister said, "Caroline Cartwright says her parents go out every night." Zora was enamored of this new friend, whose father ran a hedge fund. Next week she was flying to Palm Beach on the Cartwrights' G5 for a sleepover birthday party.

"I'll bet Caroline's mom has a new dress every night," Veronica said.

"I expect so," Zora said haughtily, basking in the reflected glory, even her diction elevated by this grand association.

When Veronica had confessed to feeling self-conscious about wearing a dress that she'd already worn earlier this month, Washington put his foot in it by saying that no one would notice, which prompted her to give him a dirty look. All he meant was that it wasn't as if either one of them appeared all that often in the party pages among the socialites and celebrities. She was especially skittish, he figured, because her firm was being honored with the Corporate Leadership Award tonight, Veronica herself having had a hand in directing some of the corporate tax write-off largesse to Corrine's charity, and her boss of bosses would be in the room.

"Don't give Rosalita a hard time," she told the kids.

"And don't call to complain if she doesn't let you play Halo," he added.

"Wash, I can't find my phone. Will you call it?"

"You don't need it; I've got mine."

"You know I hate not having my phone."

It's true, he thought as he pressed her number. She had that maternal fear of being unreachable to an excessive degree, at least it seemed excessive to him, though as far as he could tell, nobody—man, woman or child—felt secure going anywhere without a phone these days. As he heard the ring tone on his end, her phone chirped from the couch, where they'd been watching the news.

"We won't be late," she said after recovering her precious phone and wedging it into the tiny crystal-studded Judith Leiber clutch that she'd bought at a silent auction at an earlier charity benefit, a bibelot shaped like a butterfly and just big enough for the phone and a lipstick, though not long enough for her reading glasses, which she asked Washington to carry.

Surveying his kingdom, which he was fond of saying looked like heaven as designed by a feminine disciple of Le Corbusier—a vast hardwood plain with rounded outcroppings of beige, black, and white furniture, and two beautiful beige children—he wondered why he didn't stay home more often. He was feeling particularly vulnerable and nostalgic tonight. The prospect of encountering Casey had him rattled and made him more susceptible to domestic sentimentality. He wanted to be a good guy, really he did. He was committed to future reform. He felt, much as Saint Augustine had in the years of debauchery and lechery before his conversion, theoretically willing but, practically, unready. *Lord, save me, but not yet.*

When they got to the Waldorf, he was in a quiet panic and immediately threw back two martinis, at which point his nerves started to settle. Veronica had just drifted off toward the auction tables to talk to a friend when he spotted Casey bearing down on him.

"Hello, lover." She was looking pretty delicious in a very formfitting shiny turquoise satin gown. It was automatic, or perhaps autonomic, the stirring in the groin, the surge of warmth that suffused him at the sight of her. Damned if he wasn't getting a hard-on.

"Good evening," he said, trying to maintain his cool as he thrust his right hand into his pocket to cover the erection. "I like your dress."

"Why, thank you," she said. "Given the way it fits, there wasn't any room for undergarments, I'm afraid."

"Yes, I can see that."

"Enjoying yourself?"

"It's a wonderful cause," he said, playing hard to get.

"What is?"

"Feeding the hungry. Isn't that why we're here?"

"I'm feeling a certain hunger myself." She leaned forward, coming in close to his shoulder. "Actually, I'm here to fuck you. Room 308. I'll be there in three minutes."

She seemed confident of his complicity, which sort of bugged him, but she looked so fucking good, and she was so utterly, sluttishly shameless, that he realized at that moment he would follow her, even as he vowed that this would be the last time. It felt as if he had no choice in the matter. The die had been cast millions of years ago. Evolution. The instinctive drive to spread genes as widely as possible, no matter that reproduction was not part of his conscious program tonight. As Casey shimmied toward the elevators, he felt biologically programmed to follow. He clocked Veronica moving down the auction table with her friend Becky Fiers, admiring the wares, the donated handbags and jewelry and furs, before following his mistress.

Upstairs, the door was ajar; he tapped on it, and, getting no response, entered cautiously. Casey leapt on him from behind the door, scaring the shit out of him.

"Jesus!"

She shoved her tongue in his mouth before he could say more and groped his crotch, squeezing his cell phone in his pocket before moving on to her intended target. After what might have been seconds or minutes of mutual kneading, he carried her over to the bed and dropped her on it.

"Unzip my dress and put that big cock inside of me," she demanded, rolling over on her side to facilitate the process and then sliding out of her dress; pushing up his cummerbund and unzipping his trousers, reaching in and finding the item in question, which emerged briefly before disappearing into her mouth.

Rising eventually from her knees, she pushed him down on the bed and jumped on top of him. "Fuck me deep and hard!"

He barely managed to fulfill her command before the whole thing was over, Casey shouting "Fuck me, fuck me, fuck me" as he exploded inside of her, his ardor heightened by fear. Quick as he'd been, he'd been worried even before he finished about the time, and whether his absence would be noticed.

Rolling off of her, he said, "Sorry, that was some kind of speed record."

"Don't apologize. I take it as a compliment that you were so excited."

He waited a beat, two beats. "I hate to say it, but I think we should probably get back."

"Wouldn't you love just to stay here and see how long it takes for them to notice?"

"I think I'd rather live to fuck another day."

He helped her with her dress and then tended to his own outfit. Although they hadn't, in their haste, bothered to remove his shirt, he discovered that two of his studs had popped out.

"Shit," he said, groping the bedspread. "We've got to find my studs. I can't walk down there with my shirt open."

"Relax, stud. They have to be here."

Eventually they found both, though he was acutely conscious of the seconds and minutes ticking by, one having fallen to the floor during the struggle. Putting them in was a pain in the ass at the best of times, working one hand up under the shirt while the other poked them in from the other side, trying not to pop out the ones that were already in place, and tonight he was particularly maladroit. Standing in front of the full-length closet mirror, he finally succeeded in fastening one, but the second one fell to the carpet.

"Fuck fuck fuck. This is why the English had valets."

"And why men on Park Avenue have wives," she said. "Let me help."

In fact, she was clearly experienced in the procedure, and finally he looked presentable, but when he looked down at his watch, he saw that despite his Quick Draw McGraw impersonation, almost twenty minutes had elapsed since he'd left the ballroom.

"We should definitely leave separately," he said, adding reluctantly, "Ladies first."

"I'll be feeling you inside of me during the speeches," she said, kissing him at the door.

"I like that idea," he said, almost pushing her out the door. He was grateful that Casey and Tom had their own table, that he wouldn't have to sit with her through dinner. He didn't think he could handle that.

He looked again at his watch, waited thirty seconds, and poked his head out the door. Finding the hallway empty, he bounded out and waited at the elevators, pressing the button repeatedly, reflexively checking his pockets for wallet, cell phone and keys.

Withdrawing his phone from his pocket, he looked at the screen and saw Veronica's name. It took him a moment to register the time code, to see that it was advancing, to realize that the line had been open fourteen minutes and counting.

Horrified, he punched the red button to disconnect and considered the options. There was certainly a chance that in the din of the party she might not have heard her phone, ensconced inside that ridiculous clutch. And even if she had answered, what were the chances she would have heard anything comprehensible, given that his phone was in his pocket, muffled by all that fabric? On the other hand, Casey had been even more vocal than usual.

The elevator finally arrived, though he was no longer quite so eager to get downstairs. He kept running through the possibilities as the car descended, and walked back through the lobby dreading his encounter with Veronica and trying to anticipate her reaction, wondering if he would be able to read her at first sight. She had a pretty good poker face and had lots of experience with being disappointed by her husband's behavior. If she seemed to be ignorant of his transgression, he would find a way to get hold of her phone and erase those fourteen minutes.

The reception gallery was almost empty, the stragglers disappearing into the ballroom as the lights flashed on and off, signaling the start of dinner. Despite feeling that his knees might buckle beneath him, he somehow made his way through the tables, eventually discovering his own in the middle of the room. Veronica was already sitting next to Russell. At least she has a good seat, he thought, dreading the moment of eye contact, and indeed her expression was neither warm nor welcoming when she looked up at him, although it might have merely indicated her impatience with his prolonged absence, as opposed to knowledge of his activities. Then, with a sinking feeling, he saw her phone next to her place setting, though she might have removed it from her purse after he'd broken the connection.

A stranger took the chair beside her then and she was distracted by introductions as Washington moved around the other side of the table to his own seat and threw himself into conversation with Corrine, who seemed almost as skittish as he was. Having pretty much organized the event, she was telling him about all the last-minute glitches and about the competition among the gala committee women for time at the podium.

"They all want to speak," she was saying. "Personally, I'd rather shoot myself than get up there, but every one of them seems to feel that her husband's fifty grand entitles her to take the stage. And half of them haven't even sent the check yet. Actually, the only exception is Karen Fontana, and her husband donated a million bucks! Only don't say I told you that, because he genuinely wants to remain anonymous. If only the others could act like that."

When Washington finally looked over at Veronica, she seemed to be engrossed with the stranger on her left, and he began to allow himself to believe he might have escaped, that he might have been given another chance—a chance to get his shit together and appreciate the life they had together, to stop taking her for granted and stop fucking around, to love his kids and come home early at night to the bosom of his family. He promised himself that if he were somehow spared exposure tonight, he would never stray again.

At first her failure to make eye contact was a welcome reprieve, but after the speeches started and she failed to so much as glance his way, it started to seem pointed and deliberate.

Washington's attention was diverted by a short speech from a tiny woman in a purple dashiki and matching headdress, who said she was an immigrant from Ghana, ineligible for food stamps or welfare, and unable to feed her family until she'd learned about Nourish New York, and who concluded her speech with a shout-out to "Miss Corrine," who had taken a special interest in her case. Mortified, the object of her approbation blushed as heads turned toward their table and the applause mounted.

As the speeches dragged on, he began to think he couldn't bear the suspense any longer, and he texted her—testing the waters.

Hey you.

Across the table, she looked down, picked up her phone and glanced up at him inquisitively.

Boring, he texted.

She lowered the phone to her lap, typing a response. *Haven't had enough excitement for 1 nite?*

He looked up from his phone, but she'd turned away and was watching the podium.

Hopelessly, he texted back: *????*

Without looking over at him, she eventually picked up the phone and took it in her lap, biting her lip as she laboriously tapped out the answer on the keypad. He was almost afraid to check when his phone finally buzzed.

Wonder if she's feeling you inside her during the speeches?

He glanced up, meeting her gaze, a look he was all too familiar with but had hoped never to see again in this life. And for the first time in a long career of attending benefits, he wished the speeches would never end.

25

REPORTERS ON CNN WERE DISCUSSING the upcoming Wisconsin primary and predicting a win for Obama when they left the kids with Jean and walked down the block to Odeon. As soon as they were seated, he spotted Washington at a nearby table with a young woman in a sleek black dress who looked more Condé Nast than Corbin, Dern—an unwelcome sight insofar as he felt it might provoke Corrine. As Washington's best friend, and a male of the species, he was afraid he'd somehow be implicated; in fact, he felt guilty already, as if Corrine, seeing this, might intuit his own sins of thought, if not of deed.

"Oh God, there's Wash," Corrine said as she unfurled her napkin.

"You'd think he'd at least have the decency to take it out of the neighborhood," Russell said. Veronica had thrown him out of their apartment the night of Corrine's benefit some two weeks before.

"Well, it's not like he hasn't begged her to take him back. Actually, it might be good for them both if she saw him here with a bimbo."

"I guess you're right," he said, careful not to cast his lot too openly with the straying husband.

"It could just be a business thing," she suggested.

"Yeah, I suppose."

"I'm not saying Washington's a saint."

"That would indeed stretch credulity."

"But it takes two to derail a marriage."

"I'm not sure I believe that," Russell said. "I wouldn't say I blame Charles Bovary for his wife's behavior."

"I don't see why not. He was kind of a pathetic doofus."

All at once he wondered if it was possible *she* was having an affair. Was she building a case for herself, a defense brief? But he couldn't conjure any suspicious memories, and the hypothesis didn't stand up to scrutiny—just a flash of paranoia.

"I'm just saying I think she changed the rules on him. For years she turned a blind eye, then suddenly she drops the boom."

Actually, this wasn't uncharacteristic of Corrine, this tendency to take the man's side, to see the male point of view. It was one of the things he loved about her, although it put them on opposite sides in the Democratic primaries. She'd become an early supporter of Obama, whereas Russell believed fervently in Hillary, feeling that the freshman senator from Illinois had come out of nowhere, and that he was the beneficiary of a kind of psychological affirmative action; backing him made white Democrats proud of their liberal open-mindedness. Maybe Hillary wasn't all that lovable, but she had the experience and the battle scars and the policies. Yet even here in New York, where racism was as unfashionable as herpes, casual sexism was like smoking: unfashionable in theory, but not without a certain retro appeal—a thesis that seemed to Russell to be confirmed by the buzz around *Mad Men,* which everyone had been watching. Even downtown, where Republicans were scarcer than unicorns, nostalgia for the age when a woman's place was in the home or the typing pool still bubbled under the surface.

The waitress came by. "Negroni and a glass of champagne?"

"Absolutely," Russell said.

"You love it that she knows what we drink," Corrine said.

"Why wouldn't I?"

When the waitress returned with their drinks, they ordered their food. Washington, having spotted them, waved from his table.

"I hate frisée," Russell said. "It's barely food; it has the texture of excelsior—those weird wood shavings they used to use for stuffing taxidermied animal corpses and packing fragile goods before the advent of Styrofoam peanuts." He was stalling, trying to postpone the agenda. The landlord was officially converting their building to condos, so now they had to come up with a plan. They'd barely be able to afford the place, but he was determined to try.

"Yes, your views on frisée are well known, Russell. It's a good thing we didn't move to France, where it's a staple, back in '04."

They'd told their friends back then that they were moving to France if Bush won the election—or rather, Russell had.

"Although maybe we should have," she added.

"How so?"

"I just thought somehow we'd be *somewhere* else by now. I can't believe we're still sharing one bathroom among four people. I want to live like grown-ups, Russell."

"Living in the city involves certain sacrifices. We could probably have four bathrooms in White Plains, but would we want to?"

"Do we still want to live here? Look around you. When we moved here, it was funky and cheap; now it's a suburb of Wall Street. The artists have been replaced by bankers and trust fund brats. When I take the kids to school, I'm practically stampeded by guys in suits with briefcases."

"Lou Reed and James Rosenquist still live here."

"And they're both rich as hell. Look, if the kids get into Hunter, we really need to think about moving uptown, and if they don't, we need to go somewhere where they can get a great public education. We agreed Hudson River Middle was just an interim move. I won't sacrifice their prospects for some romantic notion of a bohemia that's extinct. It's gone, Russell. It moved to Williamsburg, or Red Hook, or maybe it just died. There aren't any starving poets left around here. Instead of trying to buy our apartment, I think we need to move to a less expensive part of the world, with better schools."

"Like where?"

"I don't know. Brooklyn? New Jersey?"

"I can't believe you said New Jersey." Russell suddenly felt like a losing contestant on that terrible show his kids watched, about to be kicked off the island. *His* island.

"There are beautiful places in New Jersey. Steve Colbert lives in New Jersey. So does Richard Gere."

"Fuck Richard Gere. I lost two hours of my life watching *Bee Season,* and I'll never get them back."

"Even the Upper East Side is cheaper than this neighborhood. And it's where, fingers crossed, they'll soon be attending school."

"The Upper East Side? Do I look like a—"

"Like a middle-aged preppy? Yes, as a matter of fact, you do. Do you realize we live in the most expensive zip code in the city? Even if we had two million, I wouldn't want to spend it on our shitty old loft. We lived happily uptown for years, and you used to say you hated lofts."

"It's our home. And it won't cost anything like two million."

"I bet it does. We could get a house in, say, Park Slope for much less."

"I hate Park Slope. The People's Republic of. Strollers and food co-ops and self-righteous Manhattan bashers."

"For a liberal, you can be incredibly bigoted and narrow-minded. Anyway, there are lots of other neighborhoods in Brooklyn. Most of your staff live in Brooklyn, and so do a lot of writers."

"One less since we lost Mailer," Russell said wistfully. She was right that the city was changing, even shrinking, but he wasn't about to abandon ship. "Good old Norman. You remember his place in Brooklyn Heights?"

"Brooklyn Heights is crazy expensive," Corrine said. "It's virtually Manhattan."

"If we bought the loft, we could renovate it, add another bathroom."

"Where would we put it? On the fucking fire escape?"

Russell was getting agitated, desperate to score another drink.

"Russell, I want you to be honest with yourself and with me. We're living like grad students and our kids are getting a crappy education. Here's something else I don't understand. Why is it necessary to eat at restaurants two or three times a week? That's what, a few thousand dollars a month? We can't afford to live here anymore."

"We can't afford *not* to live here," Russell said peevishly.

"That's just childish and nonsensical. I don't even know what that means."

"It means I'm one of those people, as Updike put it, who believes that anyone who lives anywhere other than New York must, in some sense, be kidding."

"Do you realize we could get a town house in Harlem for what we'd end up paying for a stupid loft we outgrew ten years ago? Seriously, more and more people like us are moving up there, but it's still affordable. And it's on the way up."

Harlem? Jesus Christ—though Bill Clinton had his office there, didn't he? Honorary black man, though lately he'd lost some of that cred campaigning against Obama. "At least it's Manhattan," Russell conceded. "Barely."

"What does Manhattan even signify anymore?" she said. "Certainly not what it did twenty-five years ago. Now it's an island of wealthy people shopping in the same stores you can find in San Francisco and London and Dubai. Look around you, Russell. Look at the shiny condos going up all around us, crowding out the middle class and your old bohemians, blocking out the sunlight. I want you to grow up and get serious about this. We need to start looking for another place to live, and if you can't face up to that, I'll start looking on my own."

What he wanted to say was that being a resident not only of Manhattan but of *downtown* was an irreducible core of his identity. He was as much—if not more—a New Yorker as those who found themselves here through the accident of birth, through no inclination or effort of their own, he and his tribe of restless striving immigrants from the provinces and the farthest corners of the earth, who'd been inexorably drawn here and had made the city their own, who'd shaped it and been shaped by it. And for Russell, New York was downtown Manhattan: Greenwich Village, SoHo, TriBeCa. He could even imagine a case being made for Chelsea or the Flatiron District. He refused to believe that the city no longer had room for people like themselves, refused to concede New York to the Power and Money team. It needed the Art and Love team, goddamn it: actors who were not yet famous; used bookstores and the people who worked in them, and professional waiters and dog walkers and piano tuners. It needed bassoon players and chorus line dancers as well as the corps de ballet, watchmakers and furniture restorers and cobblers and dealers in rare coins and stamps. It needed underpaid blue bloods with degrees from Brown who fed the undernourished, and midwestern refugees who published literary fiction. It needed *them*. This was the city he'd chosen of all the places in the world; to live anywhere else would feel like exile.

26

"I'M DESPERATE TO SEE YOU," Luke said.

Dying to see you was a cliché, but *desperate* gave her pause. That sounded sincere. She must be desperate herself to be taking Luke's call in the bedroom, with Russell and the kids only a few yards away, but it was Valentine's Day, after all. Luke was visiting his daughter up at Vassar; he was calling to tell Corrine he wanted to take her away the following weekend.

"Can you at least tell me our destination? I can't just run off without saying where I'm going."

"Let's say winter wonderland. Pack some warm clothes. And your birthday suit."

"What are you—twelve years old? I mean, who even says 'birthday suit'?"

"Deeply smitten middle-aged men, apparently."

"I can't just disappear for a whole weekend."

"Why not?"

"Because I have a family." Even as she said it, she was thinking more about logistics than about morality, wondering if she could pull it off.

After they hung up, she called Casey, who had a house in Connecticut, where, theoretically, they might spend a girls' weekend.

"I can't believe you lecture me about Washington and now you want me to be your alibi for a dirty weekend with Luke."

"First off, I didn't lecture you. I just told you I didn't want to get in the middle of it."

"Well, if you get Washington to call me, I'll cover for you."

"Are you blackmailing me?"

"*Please*, Corrine. You, of all people, should know how it feels."

Corrine hated having her situation conflated with Casey's. But she did need her help.

That night they had dinner at Bouley, their traditional destination on February 14, only a few short blocks from the apartment, although their transit was complicated by the residual ice and snow of Tuesday's storm.

After they'd settled into their usual table, the sommelier handed Russell the wine list while she examined the menu, looking for greenery and simplicity amid the elaborate compositions, oblivious to the inevitable and incessant wine talk, which to her was like the chatter of starlings. She was stirred from her reverie when Russell said, "I had lunch with Washington."

"How is he?"

"Not great. But I'm assuming you already know that."

"Well, yes, I guess so."

"So you knew about this thing he was having with Casey?"

"At some point, yes, she confided in me."

"I can't believe you never told me about this."

"It was in strictest confidence."

"I'm your husband. We're not supposed to have secrets."

"Oh, come on. You don't have any secrets from me?"

"I can't think of any."

"I doubt that."

"And this involves my best friend."

"All the more reason not to tell you. I'm sorry, but I was in a terrible position."

"I felt like an idiot. He just assumed I knew."

"Well why didn't *he* tell you if he's your best friend? You speak to him practically every day. What the hell do you two talk about, anyway? Sports? Recipes? Indie rock bands? This is what never ceases to amaze me about men, this masculine code forbidding any discussion of emotions, or anything that's actually important."

She'd delivered some variation of this speech a hundred times, but at this point she could see it was effective.

"We wait until it's important," Russell said, though his indignation seemed largely rhetorical at this point—the argument driven more by inertia than conviction. "And maybe he assumed that I'd be judgmental, that I wouldn't approve."

"So how is he?"

"He's chastened."

"He should be."

"He's staying at the Mercer while she mulls things over. You know, I honestly thought he was over this kind of shit. I mean, there comes a time where you settle into the life you've chosen and accept its boundaries and limitations."

As sensible as this sounded, it also seemed sad and defeatist—as if long-term monogamy was ultimately a function of exhaustion.

"I take it Tom doesn't know," he said.

She shook her head.

"Poor bastard," he said. Then, after a moment of silence: "I'm famished. Let's order."

Russell ordered a marc after dinner and spread his arms out across the top of the booth in a posture of intoxicated satiation. He was just slightly slurring his words. "So how's Casey holding up?" he asked, returning to the earlier subject.

"She's pretty freaked-out," Corrine said. "Actually, I was thinking about going with her up to Litchfield next weekend, if it's okay with you." She hadn't known she was going to say this until the opportunity had presented itself. It was almost scary how accustomed one could become to deception.

"What am I going to do with the kids all weekend? I've got a lot of work."

She'd hoped this wasn't going to be hard; at the same time she could feel a kind of imminent relief in the prospect of Russell's resistance, a sense of the decision being taken out of her hands, of being saved from herself.

"Well, I suspect Washington will have the kids for at least one day that weekend and he probably needs to entertain them somehow. You two could team up."

He swirled his glass, examining the amber liquid before taking a swig. "Okay, I guess," he said. He was seldom happier than when savoring a digestif after a good meal.

"How goes the Kohout book?" she asked, suddenly feeling generous, trying to change the subject before he changed his mind, to be curious and open-minded about a matter over which they'd previously clashed.

"It's good, so far. Very compelling. I'm still waiting for the final pages."

"Aren't you publishing in, what, three months?"

"God and Phillip willing."

"You sound worried."

"There's a lot riding on this. A hell of a lot."

She reached across the table and took his hand. "It's going to be fine," she said, hoping this was true. "You'll make it work."

She felt tense and anxious after they put the kids down, wondering about Russell's intentions and her own desires. Sex was practically mandatory on Valentine's night; even when they'd been in a winter drought, they'd almost always rallied for the occasion. It had been many long weeks since they'd consummated a sloppy coupling on New Year's Eve, and while she didn't feel like initiating proceedings tonight, she was open to suggestion, to a reinvigoration of their dormant romance. She told herself she was willing to give him a chance to change her mind about going off with Luke next weekend. When, after reading a manuscript for half an hour and turning out the light, he kissed her chastely on the cheek and said good night, he unwittingly sealed his fate.

As the date of her rendezvous approached, Corrine grew increasingly concerned about the weather; a snowstorm was forecast to move in the night before her departure. "Don't worry," Luke said. "A little snow won't hurt us. Even if commercial flights are canceled, we'll be able to take off from Teterboro."

"What if I can't get there?"

"I'll send Brendan. He's an ex-cop and he's got a Suburban that can climb Everest."

A few days later, after taking the kids to school, she returned to the loft to wake Russell and finish packing. Having slept badly, he was in a lousy mood, cranky about everything in the newspaper, including Obama's surging prospects against Hillary. "I mean, what do we really know about this guy?"

"We know he opposes this disastrous war, which Hillary voted for."

"Based on faulty intelligence," Russell said.

"We all operate from faulty intelligence," Corrine said, not entirely certain what she meant at first, but suddenly convinced it was a good description of the human condition.

"I still don't understand why you're driving into a snowstorm."

"Casey's driver says we'll be fine. He's an ex-cop." This was actually true; the Reynes, like many of their peers, including Luke, employed retired cops as chauffeurs, in no small part to avail themselves of the privileges and perks those gentlemen enjoyed. But now it occurred to her that Russell might be tempted to call Casey or Tom to check on her. In a panic, she called Casey from the bedroom. "Don't worry," she said. "Tom's in Dubai, and he doesn't know or particularly care where I am. As for Russell calling me, if it happens, I'll dodge the call and let you know he's looking for you."

"I'm suddenly imagining every way I could get caught. Not to mention I'm flying off in a blizzard."

"Live dangerously," Casey said. "If I sit next to one more dinner partner who asks me where my kids go to school, like I did last night, I'm going to jump out the window."

Corrine called Luke and asked, "Are we really doing this?"

"Absolutely. I just talked to the pilot. He says we're good to go. And Brendan's waiting for you downstairs."

Russell grudgingly accepted a kiss on the cheek. "I think you're crazy."

"I'm doing it for Casey," she said. Could she really be someone who lied this easily? "She's going through a rough time."

Luke's driver was indeed waiting on the street, brushing the snow from the hood of his Suburban.

"Do you really think we'll be okay getting to Teterboro?" she asked.

"No problemo. You just leave that to me, miss," he said, closing the door behind her.

Brendan might have been fearless, but other drivers were creeping and sliding and fishtailing in the snow, slowing their progress toward the tunnel. When they finally reached the Jersey side, they got caught in a long line of cars backed up behind a jackknifed tractor-trailer. By the time they arrived at Teterboro, the snow was falling with a vengeance—the wipers snapping back and forth like twin swords fighting off the barrage—and she couldn't see how they could take off, her disappointment tempered by relief. Maybe it was for the best after all. Maybe it was a sign.

At the entrance, the driver intoned the magic tail number into the intercom and the gate rose slowly to admit them. She'd been here a couple of times with Casey and Tom, but the idea of flying on a private jet still seemed unreal to her. She remembered some stupid joke of Tom's, to the effect that if you had a tail number, you'd never be lacking for tail. At any rate, she wasn't likely to run into anyone she knew out here.

Luke was waiting inside the terminal, looking winter weekend-ready in a navy turtleneck and a leonine shearling coat. As they kissed, he nearly squeezed the breath out of her, and she felt her scruples thawing.

"Are you ready?" he asked.

"Surely we're not actually going to fly?"

"Nothing to worry about. Just a few inches of snow."

At that point a pilot walked over, introduced himself and asked if they were ready.

"Do you really think it's safe?" Corrine said.

"We're fine," he said, "but I think we'd better get moving." It seemed to her that he sounded less confident than Luke.

"Let's do it," Luke said, taking her hand.

They followed the pilot out across the snowy tarmac to the plane, the luggage following along behind on a cart.

The interior smelled of new leather and aerosol. The cabin was just tall enough for her to stand in the narrow aisle, though Luke had to stoop. She settled into a beige leather seat.

"Was there ever a point," she asked, "at which you woke up and said, 'Holy shit, I can't believe how much money I have'? Or is it just a gradual acclimatization? Do you just get used to it?"

"Both," he said. "You do get used to it, but sometimes, some days, you look around and can't believe this is how you're living. Today, right now, would qualify as one of those moments."

Instead of taking the compliment, she brooded on the implications. "Do you think the pleasure one takes in material well-being is like passion, that it eventually fades?"

"Who says passion has to fade?"

Before she could point out the inevitability of its fading, the pilot came back to instruct her on the safety features of the jet.

"Hope you don't mind—I'm going to be flying the plane," Luke said after the briefing. "But it's a short flight, and we've got a great copilot."

This revelation only served to reawaken her fears. "Luke, are you sure we're not being reckless? Besides, I don't even know where we're going."

"I wouldn't risk your safety for the world. And you'll like our destination." He kissed her and followed the copilot to the cockpit.

It was strange, Corrine thought as they lifted off, being the only passenger on a plane. She wasn't sure she was the kind of person who could learn to be comfortable with wealth. Or was it just that she'd never had the chance to? She'd spent most of her life on the Art and Love team.

Less than an hour later they descended through the clouds over a landscape of downy white hills, the serenity of the view providing a stark contrast to the violent bucking of the plane as they approached a small New England town, Corrine clutching the armrests, wondering if this might, in fact, be the end, the final reckoning for her dishonesty and disloyalty, for sins past and those not yet committed. PRIVATE JET CRASH: LOVERS KILLED EN ROUTE TO TRYST.

The bumpy touchdown came as a blessed relief.

"Welcome to Vermont," Luke said, emerging from the cockpit.

"I thought we were going to die."

"What, that little patch of turbulence?"

"Were you always this—"

"*Unflappable?*"

"I was going to say *reckless*. Or maybe *heedless*. I was going to say 'Were you always such a reckless asshole?'" Even as she said this, she remembered that he'd run toward the towers that day while others were running away.

"If I were risk-averse, I'm sure my life would be very different," he said with evident relish.

An SUV was waiting for them just beyond the ramp. Luke signed for it, shook hands with the pilot and tipped the man who loaded their bags into the back.

"Are you ever going to tell me exactly where the hell we're going?" she said as they drove out through the gate.

"Wouldn't you rather be surprised?"

"I guess I'm not really an adventurer at heart. I like to know what's coming around the corner."

"Well, I'm grateful that you were adventurous enough to come along with me."

"It's totally out of character, I assure you."

"Good."

"Can you at least tell me what that big obelisk was that I saw while I was praying for my life to be spared? Or was that a hallucination?"

"That was a monument built to commemorate the Battle of Bennington during the Revolutionary War."

"I got into Bennington," she said, "but I decided it was a little too far-out for me."

"I dated a Bennington girl once," Luke said. "She was a real wildcat."

"I want to hear about all the other girls in your life."

"It's not like this huge list."

"Then it'll be easy for you to tell me."

"I don't pretend to be an expert, but in my experience when women say they want to hear about their romantic predecessors, they don't really mean it."

"I'm not like those other bitches," she said.

"Indeed you're not."

After driving south through the valley for ten minutes, they got off the highway and followed a road up into the hills, turning into a long driveway that culminated in a rambling white farmhouse with green shutters that crowned a snowy hilltop. A decrepit red gambrel-roofed barn came into view behind the house as they shimmied up the driveway, the tires spinning and spitting snow.

"I can only assume you have a golden retriever waiting to complete the picture."

"I don't even know if you're a dog person."

"I'm a ferret person, actually. Though I grew up with terriers."

"I didn't know there *were* ferret people."

"We like to root around, uncovering things and bringing them to light."

He pulled up in front of the house and said, "Shall I carry you over the threshold?"

"That might be premature. Where are we, anyway?"

"Pownal, Vermont. A friend's house."

"It looks as if we'll have plenty of privacy."

The interior had a shambolic, layered quality that suggested decades of slow accretion, faded and frayed carpets, surfaces covered with books and magazines and journals, shelves sagging with the weight of more books, treasures and oddities, split logs and newspapers stacked beside the brick fireplace. Off the living room was a small overstuffed library. The master bedroom had a fireplace, wallpaper in a trellis and vine pattern, a telescope and a four-poster bed that almost touched the low, sagging ceiling.

"I love this place," Corrine said.

"It belongs to my favorite history professor. I've been visiting for years. He's in an assisted-living facility in Williamstown now, about ten miles down the road."

"I forgot you went to Williams."

"But I remember your telling me about a weekend you spent there your sophomore year."

"God, yes. Tod Baker, homecoming weekend, 1977. Did I really tell you about that?"

"You did."

"And you thought it would be romantic for me to revisit the scene of my humiliation?"

He suddenly looked worried. "As I recall, it sounded idyllic."

"Well, yes, except for the part where I puked in his lap."

"You neglected to mention that detail."

"But otherwise, yes, idyllic."

Luke had packed two coolers of food, and that night, while she sneaked off to the library to call home, he laid out a spread of caviar and foie gras and cheese, along with an array of premade salads. "I don't actually cook," he said when she came into the kitchen and found this feast laid out on the table.

"Thank God for that," she said, kissing him.

Sex with Luke had been thrilling from the beginning, but she'd never felt so adventurous or voracious as she did over the next forty-eight hours. Her ardor was informed by a sense of transience, an awareness not only of the hours ticking away on the hilltop but of the gradually unwinding spring of her own vitality. She would probably never feel this kind of desire again; with Russell she had far too much history to ever again experience the thrill of discovery. She had a fervent desire to do everything with Luke, to have a store of memories to draw on in the cold nights to come.

That night, she lay back on the bed as he started to play with her, and gently guided his hand. She was amazed how quickly she came under the gentle thrum of his finger. As the tremors subsided, she released her grip on his forearm and moved her hand down his body.

Finding him thoroughly hard, she was seized with a sudden inspiration. "I want you to put it in my ass."

This was not a sentence she'd ever uttered before, and she was only slightly less surprised than he was, although he didn't object or try to debate the point. She reached over to the bedside table for the bottle of Kiehl's body lotion.

She tried to imagine it from his point of view as he slowly advanced, the deferral of gratification as he paused and gently pressed again, pausing at her sudden intakes of breath.

"Are you okay?"

"Yes," she said.

It must have been difficult for him to go so slowly when his instinct was to thrust ahead. There was a last spasm of painful resistance and then suddenly she yielded and he was inside of her and the pain metamorphosed into something that increasingly resembled pleasure. She hadn't even been sure that she would enjoy this, her initial desire more symbolic than physical. It had been years, a few times long ago when she and Russell were new, but she wanted to do this with him, to have this intimacy, and now she felt more connected to him than ever and wanted to always remember this feeling.

"I want to remember what you smell like," she said, lying on his chest afterward.

"I'm right here," he said. "No remembering required."

But perversely, she felt the night and the weekend slipping away. She couldn't help it—she was already thinking ahead to missing him later.

That morning, she woke to the smell of bacon frying, the bed beside her empty. Please God—not another man who wants to feed me breakfast, she thought, although on second thought she realized she was actually hungry. She put on the silk robe she'd packed, peed, brushed her teeth and hair, dabbed on some lip gloss. Seeing his Dopp kit open on the sink, she couldn't resist glancing at its contents, particularly the prescription bottles: Lipitor, Ambien, Cialis and Adderall. She couldn't help being slightly disappointed about the Cialis, preferring to imagine that his sexual stamina was a tribute to her, but the Adderall was more surprising. Half the kids in Manhattan were taking it for attention deficit disorder, real or alleged, the other half for weight loss or the sheer speedy buzz of it. Was he taking it to treat himself or to fuel himself? Did it matter? ADD would certainly explain some of his tics, his sometimes manic demeanor.

When she went downstairs to the kitchen, he put down his spatula, embraced and kissed her, his day-old beard rasping her face, then returned to his cooking, humming what sounded like "Rehab." Was it just her imagination, her new knowledge, or was he way too alert and energetic at this early hour? "I thought you didn't cook?"

"Only breakfast."

"Do we have plans today?" she asked, taking a seat at the kitchen table.

"We do. After breakfast we're getting in the car."

"To go where?"

"That's a surprise."

After polishing off a poached egg on toast, Corrine went upstairs to dress.

They drove down Route 7 to Williamstown, a place she hadn't laid eyes on in three decades, the campus an attractive architectural mélange of Federal, Gothic, Romanesque and various flavors of modernism.

"Did you love it?" she asked as they turned up the driveway of what appeared to be a white marble Doric temple.

"Mostly," he said. "Do you know where we are?"

"Not exactly," she said.

"The Clark Art Institute. I've arranged for a private tour."

A young man was waiting at the main entrance, and he led them inside. She remembered now—she'd spent a hungover morning here, hiding from her date among the Renoirs and Monets. The guide was explaining that the Clarks had been wealthy New York collectors who, fearing that nuclear apocalypse might wipe out Manhattan, had built this museum in the Berkshires to house their collection, thereby greatly disappointing the trustees of the Metropolitan Museum of Art.

"Hard to believe that they could have accumulated a collection of this magnitude in a single generation," Luke said.

"You sound jealous," Corrine said.

He shrugged.

"Is there anything in particular you'd like to see?" their guide asked.

"Could you show us *Interior at Arcachon*?" Luke said.

"Oh, certainly. That's one of my favorites."

Luke looked at Corrine expectantly.

"The Manet," she said after a pause, remembering.

"You told me it was your favorite painting," he said, looking disappointed, as they followed their guide across the marble corridor.

"I can't believe you remembered that." More to the point, she couldn't believe she'd almost forgotten it. She *had* said that, and it was true, or at least it probably was true when she told him that it was, though she'd forgotten in the interim. Had it really been her favorite painting in the long years between first viewing it as a college student and talking to Luke about art in the days after 9/11? It seemed more likely that the turmoil of that time had, like an earthquake or a volcanic eruption, thrust up buried memories and emotions, that this particular memory had been reawakened in the aftermath. What was most significant to her, at this moment, was the fact that Luke had remembered. This whole trip, she saw, had been organized around the impulse to reunite her with her putative favorite painting.

And here it was: a small gray-brown canvas, an intimate interior, a young man smoking a cigarette while an older woman across the table, his mother, looks up from her writing to take in the view of the sea through the open French windows. At the time, decades ago, she'd been hard-pressed to understand why the painting made such an impression on her, having none of the heroic eroticism of his *Olympia,* or the tragic grandeur of *The Execution of Emperor Maximilian.* But the sense of calm—and restfulness—was mesmerizing; the gray of the walls and the sea was the color of afternoon, of contemplation.

"I know it's just a small domestic scene," she said, feeling obliged to explain her esteem for the painting. "But back then it made me incredibly wistful and nostalgic, I think because my own family was in such a state of perpetual conflict."

"Manet had just returned from the Franco-Prussian War," the guide said, "and you can feel how deeply he relished this peaceful family vignette. The ease and serenity are palpable."

"Why don't you meet us in about ten minutes in front of the Piero della Francesca," Luke told him.

"I can't get over your remembering this," Corrine said as the young man slunk off. "Or that you brought me here. It's very . . . I'm impressed. And touched." She kissed his stubbly cheek.

"It is a lovely Manet," he said.

"Had you noticed it before? You were probably disappointed when I told you that this little canvas was my favorite painting."

"I don't remember noticing it when I was at Williams, but I came up here after you told me that to see it."

They contemplated it together until he said, "Of course, my favorite Manet would have to be *Le Déjeuner sur l'Herbe*."

"But of course. Heroic scale, clothed men, nude women—what's not for an alpha male to love?"

He chose to ignore her taunt. "When I was growing up in Tennessee, I had these godparents, not actual godparents but kind of spiritual godparents, the Cheathams. They were friends of my parents and I used to fantasize that they were my real parents. They were very sophisticated and collected modern art, this in a place where everyone hung hunting prints and family portraits. Joleen Cheatham took me to museums and taught me about art. They had this drawing or maybe a print, a late Picasso called *Le Déjeuner sur L'Herbe*, which entranced me. I didn't know at the time it was a riff on Manet's painting, but I was fascinated by the composition, two nude women among clothed men. I also had a serious crush on Joleen—we're talking erotic dreams and fantasies, and it all got mixed up together, my feelings for Joleen and art and my early interest in sex. Then later, as a student, when I saw Manet's *Déjeuner sur l'Herbe*, it was like stumbling on the key to the tortured mysteries of my adolescent sexual development."

"You don't seem all that tortured to me," she said.

"I sublimate like hell."

"Perhaps," she said, "I owe this Joleen a debt of gratitude."

They strolled through the galleries, browsing, grazing on the treasures—the gemlike Piero, the seascapes by Turner and Homer.

Afterward he showed her scenes of former triumphs and failures—the freshman dorm on the quad, where he'd lost his virginity; the stately Federalist classroom building, where he'd defended his thesis on income distribution; the Gothic chapel, where he'd married Sasha. He left her at the library while he went to visit his old professor at the nursing home, and afterward he took her to lunch at a restaurant on a hillside south of town.

Touched by the extravagant gesture of the private tour and the fact that he'd remembered her story about the Manet, she tried to explain to him the insecurity she'd felt at the time, the tension and psychic violence, the shouting matches and ruined holidays. She was in the middle of a story about a Thanksgiving shoving match when he opened his menu and began to peruse it.

"Are you reading the *menu*?"

He lowered it and looked up, startled by her tone.

"I was just—"

"I was in the middle of telling you about the traumatic events of my childhood and you start reading the goddamn *menu*?"

"I'm sorry."

"Was it that boring?"

"No, I promise, I really was listening."

"Go ahead. Focus on the menu. I wouldn't want to distract you from planning your meal."

"I'm sorry. Sometimes I just have difficulty focusing."

"Is that why you take Adderall?"

"Well, yes, actually."

"I just happened to see it in your Dopp kit."

"It must be nice to have X-ray vision."

"All right, I'm sorry, I looked."

"No, you're right. It's a problem. I'm easily distracted. Sometimes, I have the attention span of a gnat. I'm surprised it took you this long to complain." He reached over and put his hand on hers. "I didn't *mean* to hurt your feelings."

———

Snow was falling again as they drove back up the valley to the house.

Their desire and their attempts to sate it reached a kind of crescendo pitch that night; they woke in the middle of the night to try it again, and then once more just before dawn. They rose afterward to watch the sky turn silver and pink across the meadow, which had a fresh layer of snow. After breakfast they strapped on cross-country skis and explored the countryside for an hour, briefly staving off the regret of imminent departure, though Corrine became increasingly melancholy as the sun rose higher in the sky, wondering if this might be the last time she would be alone with Luke like this, realizing that her real life lay elsewhere.

"I hate Sundays," Luke said as he helped her unbuckle her bindings, as if reading her thoughts.

"Me, too," she said, brushing the snow from her jeans as he unlaced his boots.

"Why don't we stay an extra day?"

"I can't," she said.

"Why don't we just stay, period?"

"What do you mean by that?"

"I mean let's be together," he said, stepping out of his jeans and dumping them in the foyer.

"That's crazy."

"Why? What's crazy is that I let you get away once, and I don't want to make the same mistake again."

"I love that you feel that way, but trust me, it will pass."

"It's been six years and the feeling hasn't passed yet."

"That's because you didn't have me. If you had, you would have gotten sick of me years ago." And yet, even though she believed this, she found herself marveling that he actually wanted her still.

"You know, I'm used to getting what I want," he said.

"Does that arrogant rich-guy line work on other girls?"

"I'm sorry," he said. "Sometimes I forget you're not like anyone else."

"*That* might work," she said, stepping out of her jeans.

———

They landed smoothly at Teterboro, Luke emerging from the cockpit after the plane braked to a stop. As they walked across the tarmac to the terminal, she took his hand and held it. Inside, she was trying to steel herself for their parting, when they were accosted by Kip Taylor, sitting in the waiting area, who rose to greet them. "Corrine, Luke, what a . . ."

He seemed unable to finish the sentence, his surprise spawning confusion.

"Kip, I've been meaning to call you," Luke said. "Got a company you might be interested in."

Kip nodded skeptically. Corrine, too, was at a loss for words.

Luke said, "Headed someplace glamorous, I hope?"

"A little bonefishing down in the islands," Kip said.

"Russell still talks about that trip with you last winter," Corrine said, her voice sounding off-key, even slightly hysterical.

Before she could cobble together some plausible explanation, Kip said, "Give him my best," then turned away and walked over to the counter, leaving her to wonder if it was only her own guilt that made this sound so much like a reproach.

"Oh my God," she said as they walked to the front door. "What must he be thinking?"

"He's going to think what he's going to think," Luke said tautologically. "But he has no reason to *say* anything."

Even if this were true, she felt the weekend had been tarnished, if not ruined, with this abrupt reminder of her obligations and her place in an intricate web of social and familial and even commercial relations. Whatever had made her think she could just run away?

27

THE CITY GREW TALLER TO THE NORTH, the lowlands of SoHo and Greenwich Village giving way to the towers of midtown. In the foreground: Chessie Steyl, the actress, in a shiny purple dress with a plunging neckline, whom Russell was complimenting on her performance, hating himself a little for the inevitable clichés, the obsequiousness of the fan, even as he felt warmed by her proximity, and her acknowledgment of his existence. Their acquaintance, casual though it might be, was based on a few encounters at gatherings like this, a party following the screening of her latest film in the penthouse of the Soho Grand Hotel. Close up, he felt she had as much iconic presence as the Empire State or the Chrysler buildings glittering behind her. Russell occasionally sent her books he thought she would like, and she would inevitably send him a thank-you note, an actual handwritten missive on a monogrammed Crane notecard—she was a product of Greenwich, Connecticut, after all—and sometimes mention these titles in her interviews. Knowing Russell gave her a little shot of lit cred, helped her feel she was smarter than she looked, which, in fact, she was. For his part, he'd been thinking for a while that she might be perfect for the lead in the film adaptation of Jeff's novel. She looked to him quite a bit like the younger Corrine Calloway. It would be an elegant sublimation of his desire for this sexy young actress to see her play the fictional version of his wife.

"I just got the galleys for Toni Morrison's new novel," she said, offering him a cigarette from her pack of American Spirits, which he accepted, although he hadn't smoked in years. She produced a Zippo from her purse.

"May I?" he said, taking the lighter. He cupped his hand around the flame as she leaned over, offering a thrilling view of her breasts.

"What else should I be reading?"

It was flattering that she seemed to be devoting all of her attention to him, putting her hand on his arm and drawing him into a conspiracy that excluded all of the noisy and populous party in her honor. "Have I sent you Jack Carson's short stories? No? Really amazing. He's like a latter-day Raymond Carver, a smart hillbilly Hemingway. Incredibly powerful stuff. And I'm just publishing this memoir by Phillip Kohout—you know, the guy who got captured by the Taliban? He was going to come with me tonight, but he has a stomach thing. I don't know if you got the invitation, but we're having a launch party next week."

"I can't wait," she said, letting go of his arm to attend to the publicist who was whispering in her ear, the spell broken as she nodded and turned back to Russell, flicking her cigarette away and kissing his cheek in parting.

Russell watched her waft away, her serene self-containment unpunctured by the spiky anxiety of her handler, and Russell found himself alone on the terrace, which seemed terribly cold now, high above the icy, sparkling city. The metropolis was uncharacteristically silent against the din of the gathering inside the penthouse, a ridiculous circus from this vantage: the babble, the postures and gestures, the ambition and striving and yearning coiled therein . . . the way the energy in the room shifted and realigned as the actress entered from the terrace. For a moment, he recognized how artificial it all was, but he, too, was part of it.

Back inside, he was heading for the bar when he was accosted by Steve Sanders, a cultural reporter for the *Times*. Decent guy, bit of a nerd, he somehow managed to get everything just slightly wrong when he wrote about publishing. Not malicious, just slightly clueless and humorless. Russell hadn't seen him since the Labor Day party, when he'd brought that fat-ass hit man Toby Barnes along.

"I called your office earlier," he said, "but you'd already left."

"And here I am in the flesh."

"I also tried Phillip Kohout several times."

"Actually, he was supposed to be here tonight," Russell said, "but he canceled on me."

"Maybe we should, uh . . . " He motioned to an unoccupied corner, to which Russell followed him. His manner seemed ominous.

"What's up?"

"I wanted you to have a chance to answer these accusations before I—"

"What accusations?"

"Basically, my sources are saying that during the time Kohout was supposedly in captivity in the North-West Frontier Province, he was hiding out in an opium den in Lahore."

Russell laughed. "You're talking about the stuff on that Islamist Web site last week? I mean, come on, we saw that. It's a forum for crazy jihadist ranting. What evidence is there?"

"Dated photographs. Video. E-mails. All from the time Kohout claimed to be a captive in Waziristan. In fact, it seems he was briefly held, and roughed up, by some drug dealers he owed money to."

"Where's this coming from?"

"Obviously, I can't divulge my sources, but this is coming from people who saw him in Lahore."

"The fact that he spent some party time in Lahore doesn't mean he wasn't in captivity in Waziristan. He writes about it in the book." Russell's mind was racing, his sense of indignation undercut by a creeping sense of dread. The Internet was awash in conspiracy theories and unfounded innuendo, as Kohout had reminded him when the first post questioning his claim to have been captured was brought to his attention. But, like stopped clocks, cranks and lunatics sometimes told the truth.

"The evidence we've gathered suggests he was in Lahore the entire time. And according to our Washington desk, the State Department had doubts from the beginning. They're working the story on that end, and we'd clearly like to talk to Kohout and get his response. But in the meantime, I'm curious to get your reaction. Were you aware that Kohout was perpetrating a hoax?"

"Of course not. I'm still not aware of any such thing."

"I'd be interested to know what kind of vetting and fact-checking you've done to verify his story."

Russell felt dizzy and slightly nauseous. In fact, he'd done very little—the story of Kohout's abduction had been reported all over the world, including the pages of *The New York Times,* and the book itself was vivid, rich in detail and texture.

Suddenly, he saw a glimmer of light, a chance of reprieve. "If you want to talk about vetting," Russell said, "*The New Yorker*'s running their excerpt next week, and they've got the toughest fact-checking department in the world."

"What I hear—they've dropped the excerpt they were publishing precisely because of concerns about veracity. You didn't know about this?"

Could that possibly be true? If so, it was a very bad sign. Of course, he'd had his moments of doubt about Kohout's story, certain details in his narrative that didn't quite jibe with others, but Kohout's explanations had seemed convincing enough, though in retrospect Russell had been perhaps *too* willing to accept them, too facile in suppressing his concerns. And Kohout's last-minute cancellation tonight, just before the screening, suddenly seemed suspicious, and telling. Thinking back on it, he realized Phillip had seemed a little flustered and out of sorts this past week, hadn't he?

Suddenly, Sanders was holding a small digital recorder in front of his nose. "Would you care to comment on the allegations?"

"No, I fucking wouldn't." He couldn't print that in the *Times.* He glanced at his watch: ten-forty, too late for tomorrow's paper. Assuming Sanders felt he had enough to go with, Russell had less than twenty-four hours to get this figured out. In the meantime, he shouldn't be pissing the guy off. "Obviously, I've got to look into this," he said. "I'll call you first thing in the morning."

"This isn't going to go away, Russell," Sanders said, looking uncharacteristically fierce behind his round steel glasses, seeming less clueless and nerdy than at any time in their acquaintance.

Sanders followed Russell as he pushed through the crowd toward the elevator. In his haste to escape, Russell almost collided with Chessie Steyl, who was being interviewed by a video crew.

"Oh here's my friend Russell Calloway," she blurted. "He's a brilliant editor. We were just talking about books. He's, like, my literary mentor. Mostly he publishes fiction, but he was just telling me about this memoir by that guy who was captured by the Taliban. I'm so bad with names—what was it, Russell?"

"Um, Phillip Kohout."

"I can't wait to read it," she said.

The interviewer seemed not to know what to make of this exchange; Sanders, though, appeared to find it fascinating, hunched over his notebook, scribbling away, his head bobbing up and down like a hungry crow pecking at carrion.

The mailbox of the subscriber you are trying to reach is full and cannot accept new messages at this time.

Russell wasn't the only person looking for Phillip, apparently—that lying bastard. He decided to try cornering him in his apartment, only a few blocks away at Spring and Sullivan—a breach of Manhattan etiquette necessitated by the urgency of the search. He had to tread carefully, the frozen SoHo sidewalk slick as a water slide against the leather soles of his new cordovan loafers.

There was no answer to his repeated ringing of Phillip's buzzer. He would have called Briskin, Phillip's agent, who would at least, presumably, know if *The New Yorker* had backed out of the deal, but he didn't have his home or cell number.

Almost more than anything else, he dreaded telling Corrine. She'd been against his acquisition of the Kohout book from the start, and while she hadn't exactly questioned its authenticity, she'd certainly questioned the author's character, which was really the ultimate point at issue. She didn't trust him, and now he felt it in his gut: She was right, and he was screwed. He'd printed 75,000 copies of the book, more than half of which were already in transit to bookstores at this moment; advanced copies had been in the hands of reviewers and journalists for weeks. Just two days ago he'd written Kohout a check for $250,000; Briskin had asked for an early payment of the amount due on publication—a request that now looked highly suspicious. The book was, for all intents and purposes, already published.

Standing on the sidewalk outside Phillip's building after fruitlessly ringing his buzzer, he realized that one of the few people he knew at *The New Yorker* lived only a few blocks away, and on an impulse he set off for Thompson Street, even as he wondered whether she might still be living there after all these years. As he approached the doorway, he felt a tingling of recognition that seemed to suffuse his bloodstream, heating the surface of his skin; for years he'd visited this apartment for late-night assignations with a woman with whom he'd never shared a meal or accompanied to a social gathering, arriving in the middle of the night after a drunken business dinner or a book party. He hadn't hit that buzzer in many years—9/11 had served to break the spell—and he'd seen her only once in the aftermath, though he still called upon the store of memories of their past encounters when he was in need of erotic stimulus, and now, involuntarily, he felt a stirring in his groin as he found himself standing in front of the familiar door. Checking the names on the row of buzzers, he found hers and pressed it, jumping when the intercom crackled with her voice.

"Who is it?"

He could hardly bring himself to answer, ashamed as he was of his neglect of her for the past six years. But then, he'd always felt a measure of shame standing in front of this door. "It's Russell," he finally managed to croak.

The intercom went silent, and after what seemed like an eternity he was about to turn away, when he was startled by the harsh metallic jangle. He reached for the door handle and pulled it open.

"I don't believe it," she said after letting him in. She was wearing a faded black T-shirt and white panties. There was a blue bruise with yellow highlights on her left thigh and her legs had a faint dusting of black stubble. It was the smell that was most familiar at first, a potent alloy of pot, dry rot, decaying food, dirty laundry and Japanese incense, which failed to mask the other smells. Behind her, on the floor next to the bed, was a pile of unwashed clothing; in the little kitchen, a half-eaten egg roll sat on plate beside a tangle of sesame noodles.

He stood in the doorway while she slouched against the door frame of the kitchen, just a few feet away.

"After all these years you just barge in here like nothing's changed."

"I know. I'm sorry."

"Are you at least going to come in?"

He stepped just inside the apartment and closed the door behind him.

"Why did you want to see me?"

"Because I'm in trouble and I need your help."

"I think you wanted to see me because you wanted me to suck your cock. Isn't that why you wanted to see me?"

"Don't say that."

"Why shouldn't I say it? It's not true?"

"That's not why I came." He suddenly realized that telling her the real purpose of his visit—that he hadn't come for her at all, but merely for information that she might, by virtue of her employment, possess—seemed worse than saying he'd come for sex.

"Are you sure? Because that used to be why you came. You couldn't stay away, could you? Do you remember how you'd come here in the middle of the night and ring my buzzer because you just knew that no matter what time it was I'd suck your cock for you?"

"Yes, I remember," he said, his voice quavering.

"Would you like me to suck your cock now?"

She moved toward him, approaching within inches, the top of her head coming just up to his chin, and cupped her hand on his crotch. "I bet you'd like that, wouldn't you?"

"That's not why I came. I need to know if *The New Yorker* has canceled the Phillip Kohout piece."

She grabbed at his crotch. Pushing her away, he almost knocked her over.

He turned, wrenched the door open and ran down the stairs. Halfway up the block, he heard footsteps, turned to see her loping after him, her panties showing beneath a quilted parka.

Before he could quite decide what to do, he found himself running;

it was absurd, running from a hundred-pound girl. It was a reflex, an instinctive response; he'd just started running; he wanted to be rid of her, to put this entire sordid portion of his life out of mind forever, and she seemed determined not to let him escape. But he was risking his life in these new loafers and it soon became clear she could keep up with him.

He stopped at the corner of Spring and Thompson and turned to confront her.

"This is ridiculous," he said, trying to read her expression as she stood a few feet away, panting. "What do you want?"

"What do *you* want? You were the one who came to *my* door."

"Look, I'm sorry. I don't know what I was thinking. It was a bad idea. Can we just say I made a stupid mistake and I'm sorry?"

"You think you can just make me disappear? That's what you always thought, wasn't it? That I just ceased to exist when you weren't using me."

"If I made you feel that way, then I'm truly sorry."

A festive couple reeled toward them, their laughter chiming in the empty canyon of Spring Street, then dying as they approached Russell and Trish. Russell looked at the girl, with her messy straw curls, wrapped in a flowing black and white kaffiyeh, rolling his eyes in the hope of communicating the fact that he had no connection to this wild waif on the street, that he had nothing to do with the bruise on her thigh, trying to communicate his status as a hostage to the semi-naked woman in Uggs and a parka, but the young woman showed no flicker of sympathy, turning up her pierced nose, mildly suspicious, disdainful of the tableau and its players, leaning into her boyfriend's argyle sweater to mutter "Freak show" as they rolled past, laughing as they receded to the west.

"What do you want?" Russell demanded.

"What do *you* want?"

"I just want to go home, okay?"

"Home to your perfect wife, Corrine."

"Just home."

"How do you think Corrine would react if she knew you'd come round to see me tonight?"

"Come on, Trish."

"Oh, what, I'm just supposed to melt when you say my name?"

"I'm going now—okay?"

He turned and stepped down from the curb, crossing Spring, heading downtown. When he looked back over his shoulder, he saw that she was following some ten paces behind. He turned and faced her again.

"What are you going to do, follow me home?"

"That sounds like an interesting plan."

He turned again and broke into a run, but he was hampered by the slickness of his soles, which gave him minimal traction and kept him perpetually struggling for balance. When he turned to look back, she was in pursuit, half a block behind him.

He spotted a cab heading west on Broome Street and waved it down, nearly slamming into it as he slid on the street, jumping in and slamming the door just as Trish reached the curb.

"Just get me out of here," he said to the cabbie, a Sikh. "And lock the doors."

She was yanking on the handle of his door, but he held it shut until the man had activated the locks.

"Go, please."

While the cabbie seemed to be assessing the situation, Trish walked to the front of the cab and threw herself across the windshield. The driver leaned on his horn, with no effect. She remained sprawled on the windshield, her white panties pressed against the glass in front of the driver's face, looking in at Russell with an expression that was uncanny and serene, which seemed to say, You see what I'm capable of?

"Hey, I do not need this shit. Go. Get out of my cab."

"She's crazy," Russell said.

"Get out!"

"Come on, man."

"I call the cops."

"Okay, call the cops."

He disappeared below the seat back and reappeared brandishing a large curved knife—a *kirpan*. The name popped into his head, something he'd read; all baptized Sikhs were required to carry one.

"Okay, okay."

He threw open the door and launched himself toward the Hudson, getting a good lead on her this time, dodging south on Sixth Avenue. He couldn't believe he was fleeing this wisp of a girl, and yet he couldn't see any alternative, as he was afraid she would follow him all the way to his loft. A girl who would throw herself on the windshield of a cab wasn't going to stand on ceremony. He considered the subway station as he approached Canal Street but thought better of it.

She was still close behind him when he got to Canal Street, dodging through the late-night tunnel traffic.

Once he took off his shoes, he was able to put some distance between them, but he realized that he had to stop leading her to his home. Did she know his address? He veered east on Lispenard and ran all the way to Broadway before turning back downtown; looking back from the corner of Walker Street, he didn't see her behind him, and he thought he might finally have ditched her, though he continued to move obliquely, down Church and east again on Walker, only gradually slowing his pace and registering the numbness of his feet.

He approached his building from downtown, via Chambers Street, scanning the street, which was, thankfully, deserted.

The apartment was dark. He pulled off the shredded remains of his socks and deposited them in the kitchen trash bin, then tended to the soles of his numbed feet with damp paper towels.

In the bedroom, he moved stealthily as he undressed.

"How was it?" Corrine asked when he'd settled in beside her.

"Oh, baby, I'm in so much trouble," he said, rolling over and burrowing into the warm, fragrant refuge between her arm and breast, his heart still pounding with panic.

28

"CORRINE, WE HAVEN'T SEEN YOU IN AGES."

"Hello, Sara. Athena."

"We've been thinking of you."

"That's good to know."

"If there's absolutely anything we can do . . ."

"I'll *absolutely* be sure to let you know."

No matter how early Corrine arrived to pick up the kids, Sara Birkhardt and Athena Goldstein always seemed to be waiting outside the school, inseparable and inevitable as the gargoyles adorning the Gothic Revival building across the street. In fact, she often chose to delegate picking up the kids to Jean, which seemed to constitute a form of malign neglect to these Battery Park harpies in their pastel Lululemon tops and black leggings. Even worse than their disapproval, she realized this afternoon, was their faux sympathy and sugar-coated schadenfreude. But Jean was taking a sick day and she'd had no choice but to make the pickup—Russell could sometimes buzz down from work, but she hadn't even bothered to ask him today. God knows he had enough to worry about—a few days earlier he'd been bushwhacked by a TV news crew outside his office.

Some of the sixth-grade parents let their kids find their own way home, but Corrine wasn't ready for that. She'd arrived in New York just a few months after Etan Patz had disappeared between his parents' SoHo apartment and the bus stop on his very first unescorted morning expedition, and while the city was far safer now than in 1979, she saw absolutely no reason to tempt fate.

"We all love Russell," Athena said.

"He's a terrific father," Sara said.

"He really is," Corrine said.

The other mothers were acting studiously ignorant, quietly conferring or staring at their BlackBerries while the Caribbean nannies formed a separate cadre a little farther up the block.

"Please give him our love."

"I certainly will."

Taking out her own cell phone and staring at it blindly, she hoped to ignore her ostensible support group. She was dying to tell them that her kids weren't long for this shitty school, having gotten into Hunter, but if they hadn't heard already, they'd find out soon enough.

"He must feel terribly betrayed."

She decided this observation didn't require an answer.

"I mean, they were friends, weren't they?"

"Not really," Corrine said. "Associates, obviously, but it wasn't as if they were close—more a question of circumstances throwing them together, like when you find yourself socializing with people just because your kids go to school together."

It was hard to tell whether this was overkill, or too subtle by half; both women were still absorbing and evaluating the insult when the doors swung open and the kids started pouring out, a trickle of older boys at first, pushing and testing out their voices in the open air, then successive waves of liberated children, her own emerging separately, Jeremy first, his friend Nicholas tugging on his arm and shrieking about some unfinished business, then Storey in her little gang of four—Taylor, Hannah and Madison, three new friends so precious that she kept them as far away from her family, or at least her mother, as possible.

"Hey, Mom, it's you," Jeremy said, sounding pleasantly surprised. "Can Nick come home with us?"

"Not today, honey. You have karate, remember?"

"Oh, right."

Storey huddled with her crew up the sidewalk.

"Are you taking me to the dojo?"

She nodded.

"In a taxi?"

"If we see one."

"Nick says the subway is for poor people."

She hated that sort of thing—it was precisely the kind of attitude they'd hoped to avoid by keeping their kids downtown, not that they'd had much choice, of course, until the kids had been old enough to take the test for the gifted program at Hunter. But these distinctions were losing their relevance in an era when hedge funders were colonizing SoHo and TriBeCa.

Storey finally tore herself away from her friends and slouched over.

"How was school, honey?"

"Same old, same old." As they started walking north, she said, "Taylor says Dad's a criminal."

Corrine stopped in her tracks, half-tempted to troop back and find the little bitch's mother, whom she'd seen among the waiting parents. "Tell me exactly what she said."

"Is it true?"

"Of course it's not true. What did she say?"

"She said that it was in the news that Dad published a book that was full of lies."

She squatted on the sidewalk in front of them, allowing a curious mother and son to pass by before saying, "Listen, you guys, your dad made an honest mistake. He trusted someone he shouldn't have trusted."

"That guy Phillip," Jeremy said.

"That's right. Your dad published his book, having every reason to believe that it was true."

"Wait a minute," Jeremy said. "I thought Dad published fiction."

"Dad usually does. That's probably what he's best at. But this was supposed to be a memoir, a true story—except now it looks like it wasn't. Your dad got fooled, along with a lot of other people. But he didn't do anything criminal. Stupid, possibly, but not criminal."

"Whoa, Mom," Storey said. "I can't believe you just said that."

"I'm trying to be honest with you guys."

"But Dad's incredibly smart." This was a point of faith with the kids, a tenet of the family creed. Dad the brilliant, Dad the Oxford scholar.

"Smart people sometimes do dumb things. And the guy who wrote the book is pretty smart, too. But besides being smart, your dad is generous and honest and he believes other people are honest, too. Which, of course, isn't always true."

"I knew that guy was a jerk," Jeremy said.

"You thought that?"

"Yeah. He just seemed kind of phony. He had this way of trying to talk to kids, trying to seem cool. It was just totally fake."

Corrine was impressed. "Actually, I thought so, too," she said. "Your dad can be a little too trusting."

"Are you mad at him?" Storey asked.

She sighed, wondering how nuanced you can be with your own children. "No, I feel bad for him." Of course she'd been supportive and sympathetic in the three days since the scandal had broken, but her sympathy had indeed sometimes given way to anger. She'd always had a bad feeling about the book, not only the dizzying and unprecedented advance he'd laid out, but also about the project itself, both author and publisher having abandoned their proven métier for reasons of fashion and commerce. And now they were all four going to suffer for the mistake. And she was upset with Russell for defending Kohout that crucial first day after the news broke, giving that halfhearted statement of support to the *Times* instead of instantly acknowledging his mistake. She could hardly bear to look at her husband the next night as they watched Kohout, who appeared to be sedated, try to defend himself on the *Charlie Rose* show. But she felt guilty, too, that she'd never told Russell about the time Phillip had hit on her not long after his first novel had come out. Maybe that would have helped tip the scales against him.

While Jeremy practiced his high kicks and his kata at the dojo on Lower Broadway, Corrine took his sister shopping at Necessary Clothing and All Saints, browsing with her amid the endless racks of jeans and cheap sundresses. Anything that Corrine picked out elicited either a shrug or a sneer, and the items Storey picked seemed chosen to provoke.

"What's wrong with it?" Storey said, holding up a tiny sequined halter.

"I think it's a little . . . trashy."

"You think anything cool's slutty."

"I did not use that word."

Why was her daughter so irritated with her? she wondered. It was possible that Storey's mood reflected her distress about her father and the recent scandal. In the end, Corrine swallowed her reservations about the skimpiness of a two-piece bathing suit and about the price of a pair of True Religion jeans, in hopes of scoring a few points.

Back home, while the kids settled down to homework, she went to the bedroom and gave in to a long-simmering impulse.

"How are you?" Luke asked.

"I'm fine." She tried to sound light and casual; she'd thought about calling him several times over the last few days, but now that she heard his voice, she wasn't at all certain about confiding in him. On reflection she saw that her troubles were joint, marital property, that sharing them with Luke would be disloyal to Russell, a principle she clung to even though it was rendered somewhat absurd by the fact of her serial betrayals.

"I was a little worried. I heard—well, about that book."

Luke was in London, and for a moment she was surprised to learn this news had traveled across the Atlantic. On the other hand, it seemed to be everywhere right now. She was afraid to pick up a paper or turn on the TV.

She sighed. At least she wouldn't have to pretend everything was fine.

"Well, I've had better weeks. As has Russell." It seemed important at this point to mention his name, something she very rarely did in conversation with Luke.

"Should I ask how he's holding up?"

"Probably not, but I'm sure you can imagine."

"I suppose so. I'm so sorry."

She was beginning to wish she hadn't called.

"Is there anything I can do?"

"I can't really think of anything. Unless you have access to a time machine, so I could go back and somehow prevent this mess."

"Sorry."

"Just checking. As a person of limited means, I find it strangely comforting to know there are apparently still things that money can't buy." She knew this sounded vaguely antagonistic, maybe even specifically so, but she couldn't help it.

"I can assure you there are many of them, Corrine."

"I'm afraid I wouldn't know about that."

She had a feeling that the sooner she got off the phone, the better. She knew Luke was trying to be sympathetic, and she wasn't really mad at him, but neither did she think he was the right person to comfort her on this occasion. That was her mistake. Even though she loved him, she couldn't muster any sweetness toward him at the moment.

"I just want you to know—"

"Let's talk later, okay? This just isn't a good time right now. I'll call you soon." Every phrase sounded more perfunctory than the last, but she couldn't seem to help herself. She could feel the hurt and confusion in his silence. If she hung up now, she was afraid they might not recover, and perhaps that was all for the best; perhaps this was the moment to end it, however unexpectedly. But she wasn't necessarily ready for that, and knew this feeling would probably pass, that she'd wake up in the morning yearning for him, as she so often had since seeing him walking up West Broadway covered in ashes, so she said, "I love you" before hanging up on him.

"Who was that?"

Corrine gasped for breath as she turned to see her daughter framed in the doorway. "Just a friend."

"Who?"

"No one you know."

"Why do you look so guilty?"

"You startled me."

"Does Dad know this friend?"

"As a matter of fact, he does. Are you through with your homework already?"

"Why are you changing the subject?"

"Because the subject is finished. There's nothing more to say about it."

Storey kept staring at her, and Corrine found it hard to meet her judgmental gaze. When had she become so hostile? And why? Was the question of biological motherhood finally resonating? Or was this just a function of her age?

"Is there some reason you've become so critical of me recently?"

"I've just become more observant," Storey said. "Plus, you and Dad taught me to have high standards."

"I hope we also taught you a little about the value of compassion and empathy."

"Whatever," she said, turning and disappearing from view.

29

RUSSELL ARRIVED TEN MINUTES EARLY and took a seat at the bar. He'd read about the restaurant, Bacchus—the two-hundred-dollar prix fixe; the hundred-thousand-bottle cellar; the four Lehman bankers who'd run up a $72,000 tab, which got the senior partner at the table fired after an exposé in the *New York Post*—but hadn't ventured inside until Tom Reynes suggested meeting there. The cocktail lounge was all shiny lacquered wood and tender matte leather, the bar itself a single piece of luminous patinated Cuban mahogany, which had once, so the bartender informed him, graced the original, long-vanished Waldorf-Astoria on lower Fifth Avenue.

In the interest of starting slowly, Russell ordered a Pellegrino and, out of curiosity, asked to see the wine list, only to be informed that there were two, one for the reds and one for the whites. Ah, yes, he'd read about that. He asked to see both and was presented with matching brown leather volumes, each weighing several pounds, which thoroughly engrossed him until Tom arrived, fifteen minutes late, greeting the bartender with a hearty handshake before turning to Russell.

"Sorry, meeting ran late," he said. "Shall we go to the table?" The maître d', a slender African-American in a tight black suit, had appeared beside him, and bowed them into the dining room.

On the way to the table, Tom paused to exchange greetings with diners and staff. Impeccable in a blue-gray birdseye suit, he bantered with the waiter and requested the sommelier, an improbably young man with an elfin face and a tattoo of grapes on his neck.

"Good evening, Mr. Reynes," he intoned.

"Evening, Don. Let's crack a bottle of white. How's the '89 Ramonet Montrachet showing?"

"Sick juice. You'll love it. I just opened a bottle for Mr. Trousdale last night."

"Trousdale, that fucking poseur. He wouldn't know a good wine if he licked it from Scarlett Johansson's coochie." He turned to Russell. "You know Larry Trousdale? Dumb-ass, but he made a big score shorting the telecoms back in the day."

Russell shrugged. "I've heard the name."

As they glanced at the menus, Tom said, "So, you've really got your tit in the wringer."

Russell nodded. "That's one way to describe the situation."

"At least you've been smart enough to stay off the airwaves. I saw that so-called author of yours on CNN the other day when I was at the gym. He just dug himself a deeper hole. We're supposed to feel sorry for him because his novels didn't sell and he was addled on drugs? Fucking idiot. I mean, what was he thinking when he decided to write this book? For that matter, what were *you* thinking when you decided to publish it?"

Russell was relieved when the sommelier showed up with the bottle of white, depositing two large gossamer-thin glasses in front of each of them, opening the bottle, and pouring a dollop for Tom, who swirled the glass, sniffed it, swirled again and finally tilted it toward his lips.

Russell realized he was holding his breath while awaiting the verdict. Tom smacked his lips as he lowered the glass back to the table and nodded curtly.

The sommelier poured half an inch into Russell's glass and returned to give Tom a few more milliliters. It tasted like honey, except that it wasn't actually sweet. "Wowsah!"

"Yeah," said Tom. He took another sip before leaning back in his chair and cracking his knuckles. "So tell me, weren't you even a little bit suspicious about that son of a bitch's story? I mean, the name alone's a red flag. Like, who's he in cahoots *with*?"

"Eventually, yes, I became suspicious. But I have to say he was very convincing, and I was hardly the only one drawn in. *The New Yorker* was within a day or two of publishing an excerpt, and all the networks were fighting for an interview."

Tom shook his head and swallowed the rest of the wine. "Don't you have some kind of due-diligence process? You didn't ever ask yourself, 'How come the big corporate publishers aren't outbidding me on this?'"

Again, Russell shrugged. "There was plenty of interest."

"But not bids?"

"I preempted."

Tom sighed.

Even before the appetizers, Russell was going to have to eat some humble pie. He was on Tom's turf, in the role of supplicant, hoping that Corrine's best friend's husband could help him out of the financial sinkhole into which he was being sucked. Already struggling before the Kohout debacle, he was now desperate. Kip Taylor, citing liquidity issues, refused to invest another nickel in McCane, Slade. Right now, Russell had about three weeks' worth of cash on hand.

Much as he wanted to despise Tom's easy air of privilege, Russell always felt a little beta in Tom's distinctly alpha presence, as he had at Brown with the New York and Boston preppies, the boys with BMWs and ancestral summer homes in Nantucket, the Vineyard or the Hamptons. Tom had gone to Princeton, but it was the same hierarchy. Guys like him set the tone at the Ivy League campuses, arriving with hereditary knowledge that the midwesterners and the scholarship students like Russell yearned to acquire. They had the worn, faded rugby shirts, the Bean boots, the Barbour jackets and the phone numbers of girls at Smith and Holyoke. They knew which professors and which courses to avoid, knowledge passed down by their siblings and upperclassmen at Andover or St. Paul's. Even though you wanted to hate them, you couldn't help envying their careless ease, their sense of belonging and dominance. Corrine had been one of them, sort of, which was part of her appeal, but she'd been more than that, too; she'd had a kind of nerdy earnestness, which made her more approachable than the others, especially for someone like Russell, who'd been supremely confident in his intellect, if not in his wardrobe.

Born on Park Avenue, schooled at St. Bernard's and Groton, Tom had pulled himself up by his grandfather's suspenders. That august gentleman had been a cofounder of the investment bank Reynes, McCabe and Simms, and Tom was the beneficiary of the income of one-third of his fortune, held in trust, which would have allowed him the leisure to do nothing at all, but Tom had gone to work for a rival firm and added many millions more to the ancestral bounty. An übermensch in a bespoke suit, he was current court tennis champion at the Racquet Club, four-time doubles grass-court tennis champion at the Meadow Club in Southampton and three-time club champion at Shinnecock Hills.

A waiter approached, holding a bulbous wineglass with a long, delicate stem—wherein a shallow pool of crimson shimmered—reverently setting it on the table in front of Tom. "Your friends wanted you to taste this," he said, nodding toward a table at the other side of the room where four suits hoisted their goblets in salute.

Tom lifted the glass and swirled it, the ruby liquid surging up the sides of the bowl, sniffed and then tilted the huge bowl toward his lips, inhaling a sip and seeming to chew on it before setting the glass back down. "You guys are a bunch of pedophiles," he called out. "This wine's a baby."

Howls of indignation rose from the other table. "No way, man. This wine has tits," one of them shouted.

"T and A in liquid form!" another testified

"I didn't say I didn't like it," Tom bellowed. "I just said it was barely legal."

"It's a '94 Harlan," the tit man shouted.

"I rest my case—an eighth grader!" Tom raised his glass toward the group before resuming his study of the wine list. "Fucking guys, they're from Goldman. They do some trading for us. They're young, and still into the Napa cult Cabernets; it's the gateway drug. They're players, though, I'll give them that. That bottle is like twenty-eight hundred dollars on the list."

"Jesus Christ," Russell said.

"Lacryma Christi, indeed," Tom said. "Taste it. It's actually pretty damn good, but I can't tell them that."

Russell raised the glass gingerly and took a small sip. Maybe it was just the power of suggestion, but he was inclined to agree with the guy who said the wine had tits. It was mouth-filling and round, like a breast that was too big for your mouth but nevertheless inspired you to try to inhale it.

Although there were several couples spread around the room, it had the air of a men's club; instead of squash, the sport here was competitive oenophilia.

Tom waved impatiently at the sommelier. "Don, bring those guys a taste of the Montrachet and let's start thinking about a red wine. How do we feel about the '82 Cheval Blanc?"

"Tasted it last week, in fact, and it was singing."

"Yes, but what the fuck was it singing, exactly?"

"I'd say it was singing Kanye's 'Good Life.'"

"Well, let's crack it open, and give those Goldman boys a little taste."

"Right away, Mr. Reynes."

"That's a serious bottle of wine," Russell said, as the sommelier hurried away.

"Life's too short to drink badly," Tom said. "I mean, I don't even touch the wine at those benefits the girls are always dragging us to. They always have top-shelf vodka and bat-piss wine. You're a bit of a buff, aren't you?"

"I'm an enthusiast. But I can't honestly say I often get to drink First Growth Bordeaux." Russell stated this fact as a disclaimer, partly in the hope of absolving himself of responsibility for the bill.

"Well, brace yourself. Because here comes a fucking brilliant example."

As the sommelier cut the foil on the bottle, Tom said, "So what's your number, Russell?"

Although they'd known each other for more than twenty years, this was only the second time they'd dined à deux. Russell had initiated this meeting more or less out of desperation.

"Honestly, I need five *hundred* K to make it through the year. Of course I'd give you some of my equity. But in the long run, I'd like to buy out my partner."

"I take it the feeling is mutual."

"Well, I think he's lost some of his enthusiasm for literary publishing."

"I bet. Although literature isn't exactly what got you into this predicament. Your specialty is fiction, right?"

"I suppose so. That's what we're known for."

"You're an expert in that field—in that market."

"Well, I don't know that I'd say that. I do trust my judgment about what literature is, and my ability to recognize it, and we've got two editors I trust, as well, but I doubt anybody can predict with certainty what's going to work with the public." As soon as he said this, he wanted to retract it, not because it wasn't true, but because he was asking Tom for money.

"But you know better than most."

"Yes, I suppose so."

"That makes you a market specialist. My point is, stick to the market you know."

Like a dutiful student, Russell nodded.

Satisfied that his lesson had been absorbed, or else bored with the topic, Tom said, "I'll send my guy over to look at the books tomorrow. Meantime, let's order something to soak up the wine."

The sommelier was still standing by, waiting for a judgment.

After tasting it, Tom pronounced the wine sound, if not *quite* as good as the last bottle he'd had from his own cellar, and asked that four glasses be sent to the Goldman table. "Show them how it's done in Bordeaux," Tom said.

"So how's Corrine?" he asked after they'd ordered. Russell had found the menu a polyglot document that blithely mixed French, Italian and Asian terms under the banner of New American cuisine. The raw seafood was listed under the banner of "crudo" rather than sashimi, drizzled in olive oil rather than ponzu or soy sauce, whereas a fried seafood medley was billed as "tempura" rather than fritto misto; and at least half of the main courses were cooked sous-vide, a high-tech method of slow boiling in plastic bags pioneered by the Troisgros brothers in Roanne, France, which all the ambitious New York chefs had recently adopted for their own purposes.

"Corrine's fine," he said. "I don't know. Busy. Distracted."

"Busy and distracted can be good," Tom said.

"Not necessarily." He paused, uncertain of how honest he wanted to be. Russell was generally reluctant to discuss his marriage with anyone; with Washington and his other friends, he always felt the need to put on a good front, to live up to the notion that he and Corrine were an iconic couple. Somehow it meant a great deal to him to imagine that people still believed that. But his guilty knowledge of Tom's marital difficulties made him more comfortable about opening up.

"I can't remember the last time we had sex." Disloyal as he felt saying this, it was a relief, and strangely exhilarating.

"Well, of course you can't. You've been married, what, twenty-five years? Your wedding was a few months before ours, right? Hell, I was there. I remember doing lines in Corrine's bedroom with your friend Jeff. I mean, fuck, we all just celebrated our twenty-fifth anniversary. What do you expect?"

"I expect to get laid once in a while," Russell said.

"Well, of course you do, but what does that have to do with your wife?"

"Don't you and Casey—"

"Sure we do. At least three times a year. Valentine's Day, her birthday and on my birthday, I get a blow job."

The somm reappeared, bearing yet another glass, which he placed atop a cocktail napkin in front of Tom. "From the gentlemen at the other table," he said.

After swirling, sniffing and sipping, Tom offered Russell a taste.

"It's amazing," he said.

"It is," Tom said, lifting the cocktail napkin from the table and dabbing his lips with it.

One of the Goldman boys detached himself from the group and sauntered over to the table, glass in hand. Tom made the introductions and then they sorted out the weekend's golf plans.

"So what do you think it is?" the man asked, nodding toward Tom's glass.

"I was almost tempted to say Masseto," Tom said, teasing out the conclusion, "but on second thought I think it's '82 Pétrus."

The other man was crestfallen. "Shit, you saw the bottle."

"Not easily done, that, when you had Don wrap a napkin around it." Indeed, Russell observed that the bottle on the table across the way was swathed in white linen.

"Impressive, Reynes."

"How did you guess?" Russell asked after the banker rejoined his friends.

"I know these guys. After my wine, I knew they'd have to try to top me. They don't know Burgundy, so that means a First Growth Bordeaux from a great year. There are eight first growths, if you count the unofficial three on the Right Bank, and Pétrus is the only one that's a hundred percent Merlot."

"Still, I'm impressed."

"As a matter of fact, I probably *would*'ve nailed it," Tom said. "But I didn't leave it to chance." After glancing over at the Goldman table, he lifted up the cocktail napkin that the sommelier had placed under his glass, on which *82 Pet* was scribbled. "I tip him much better than they do. Plus, I'm an investor in this place." He seemed very pleased with himself. "In life, in business, you need an edge. Information is power, Russell. You try not to leave anything to chance. I never make a trade unless I think I know more than the other guy does. That's what I was saying to you earlier."

"I'm not sure whom I could bribe to find the next best-seller."

"If you're confident in your ability to spot literary talent, if you have an edge in that area, then use it."

Over the course of the next two hours, the exigencies of his professional life faded away as they progressed through a seven-course tasting menu and several bottles of exceptional wine, his anxieties anesthetized until, near the end of dinner, he wondered whether he'd be expected to split the bill, which undoubtedly would be larger than any he'd ever seen in his life.

Men in blue and gray suits stopped by the table from time to time to chat with Tom, to inquire after his golf game and his wife, to share their wine. It was a nice club to belong to, if only for the night. They were all brothers in the big-ticket buzz. Expensive winos. Wait, Russell thought, what was that from? It came to him: Keith Richards's side project.

After yet another of these well-tailored acolytes of Mammon and Bacchus returned to his table, Russell asked, "So where *do* you go for sex, if not home?"

"Usually to a town house on East 73rd."

"You have a girlfriend there?"

"I do. In fact, I was just thinking I might stop by tonight. You should join me."

"We're talking about . . . a whorehouse?"

"Well, that's a rather inelegant term. I prefer to think of it as a gentlemen's club."

Russell realized that he was serious, and couldn't help being fascinated by the idea of such places. Of course he knew they existed—every year or two you read about another busted bordello in the *Post*—but he'd never known anyone with firsthand experience, or at least he didn't think he had, until now.

"Seriously, you should try it."

"Even if I put aside all other considerations, I'm sure I couldn't afford it."

"Tonight's on me. Dinner and a hooker. If we're going into business together, we need to trust each other."

Russell couldn't imagine himself crossing that line, paying for sex, which was precisely what made the prospect so intriguing. It wasn't as if he'd never been unfaithful to Corrine, and the ongoing sexual drought at home seemed like an ameliorating circumstance. Under the influence of at least a liter of insanely expensive wine, the prospect seemed not entirely unappealing—even without the suggestion that Tom's investment in his company was contingent on his participation.

"Russell, you're killing me here. Don't tell me you've been perfectly behaved all these years?"

He shook his head.

"This is a guilt-free zone, dude. An exchange of cash for services. On the emotional level, you remain entirely faithful, which is what women really care about."

The notion that Tom imagined he knew what women really wanted was so comical that Russell couldn't help snickering, choking on his water in a fit of intoxicated hilarity.

"What's so funny?"

"Nothing," Russell said. He didn't want to offend his host and couldn't help wondering if it wouldn't be ungrateful, not to mention impolitic, to turn down Tom's generous offer. And wouldn't he be cheating himself, in a sense, out of an archetypal adventure? What man hasn't fantasized about that experience, even those, like Russell, who'd grown up in the era of feminism and considered themselves fellow travelers—which made the potential guilt metaphysical as well as personal.

The more he thought about it, the more he found the prospect frightening, and thrilling.

Reappearing after a short absence, Tom said, "It's all arranged." He reached across the table and put a yellow pill down in front of Russell.

"What's this?"

"Cialis," he said. "Let's face it, we've had a lot to drink and we're not twenty anymore."

Even as he swallowed the pill, Russell wasn't certain if he could go through with this.

When the bill arrived, Tom waved off his tentative hand and slapped down his black American Express Centurion card, the one reserved for cardholders who spent more than a million a year, which clanked like real currency against the silver metal tray cradling the innocent-looking slip of paper that itemized the staggering tab.

A black Lincoln Town Car was waiting for them outside. Tom gave the driver an address on East 73rd. Russell couldn't quite believe he was doing this. He kept thinking that he should ask the driver to stop, tell Tom that he'd changed his mind. It was crazy. He couldn't do this. But the car wafted uptown on Madison, and Tom kept talking about how hot the girls were.

"Don't you worry about the place getting busted?"

"The madam's married to a cop in the Tenth precinct and she has everybody paid off all the way up the line."

They pulled to the curb in front of a somewhat drab brownstone in the middle of the block. Two Town Cars, identical to their own, were idling there already. And it occurred to Russell that just as he'd begun to question his own faith in the inexhaustible mystery of the city, he was being initiated into a new corner of it. For as long as he'd lived here, apparently there were parts of it he still wasn't aware of—unknown universes behind closed doors, new republics around the corner and up the block, all awaiting discovery.

They ascended the steps and Tom rang the buzzer, which was presently answered by a slim middle-aged blonde in a maroon kaftan, whom he introduced to Russell. Gretchen had the lined, leathery face of a heavy smoker and looked very much like the chatelaine of an Upper East Side town house, accepting a kiss on the cheek from Tom and leading them into a front parlor that was redolent of cigarette and cigar smoke, which failed to mask the tang of mildew. It was furnished haphazardly with sofas and chairs upholstered in disparate fabrics, like the living room of a second-rate sorority house. Framed etchings of scenes from mythology hung on either side of the fireplace, the busiest of which appeared to depict the rape of the Sabine women, but most of the walls were bare, showing veins of cracked plaster and peeling paint. Russell had been expecting something more tasteful and expensive, or far tackier, whereas this was merely drab.

A slender redheaded beauty appeared in the doorway, draped in a blue silk robe. Tom lit up as she glided across the room and embraced him; obviously they were well acquainted.

"I'm afraid I don't know anything about your friend's tastes," Gretchen said as she turned from Tom to Russell, who felt his heart pounding in his chest, "But I think you'll be very pleased with your date," she said, taking his right hand and rubbing it between her palms. "In fact, here's Tanya now."

Russell turned and saw, framed in the arched doorway, wearing a leopard print robe, his sister-in-law, Hilary.

30

CORRINE WAS ALREADY LATE when she arrived at the Grand Concourse and 149th Street, having just missed her subway after dropping the kids at school, shouting for someone to hold the door and watching as the train pulled away, the man with the stupid hat with earflaps staring at her moronically with his arms pinned to his sides. After waiting fifteen minutes for the next train, she found herself fighting a headwind on 149th Street, and she was half an hour late by the time she turned onto Morris Avenue.

The line of clients—so they called them—stretched from the parking lot back around the corner some fifty deep up the avenue, supplicants in parkas and fleeces, ski caps and babushkas and African head wraps—tropical splashes of color against the drab pregreen cityscape, the scene reminding her of the view outside her mother's kitchen window on a winter morning, blue jays and cardinals and towhees clustered around the bird feeder. One man wore a bright orange vest and cap, as if he'd just come from an early-morning deer hunt; another was in full army camo, skulking near the back of the line.

The orientation meeting was just breaking up, the volunteers scattering to their stations, Luke McGavock among them, so out of context that for a moment she didn't even register the surprise. She hadn't spoken to him for a week, and it had been two months since she'd laid eyes on him. She was taken aback, after these long intervals, by her reaction to his presence, by the quickening of her metabolism, a kind of mental flush that made her feel simultaneously light-headed and keenly focused. She could go for days without thinking of him, and after a time she could imagine that seeing him wouldn't affect her. He was dressed down in jeans and fleece. Catching sight of her, he stopped in the middle of the parking lot, shrugging his shoulders and flashing a rueful, boyish grin. Sometimes the things we love most in our adored ones can become, like that grin, the things we hold against them. She kissed him as she would a friend—on the cheek. He was freshly shaven, and her resolve to be businesslike was eroded by the scent of his skin.

"I was afraid you might not show up," he said.

"In other words, you didn't come here out of the goodness of your heart to help distribute food to the needy."

"My motives weren't entirely pure. *Mixed* would be the charitable way to describe them. But I think motives are usually mixed, don't you?"

"I'm not sure if you thought this was a good time to catch up, but I have three hours of work ahead of me here."

"I understand and I'm here to help. I'm on carrots today."

"An important station. If anyone asks, tell them that beta-carotene is partly metabolized into vitamin A, which can improve vision, though it won't enable you to see in the dark. That was a rumor started by the RAF during World War I, disinformation to disguise why their pilots were shooting down so many German planes at night. The cover story was that it was due to high carrot consumption among the gunners, when in fact it had to do with the development of radar."

She realized she was babbling out of nervousness, which must have been painfully obvious.

He was looking at her fondly, as if she were a familiar, harmless lunatic.

"When did you get back?" she asked.

"A few days ago. I thought maybe we could have lunch after we finish up here."

"It's possible. Let's see how the morning goes."

"Well, you know where to find me," he said, jogging off to his station.

For once, their supplies held out till the end and the morning passed without incident. Corrine was painfully aware of Luke's presence, even as she tried to pretend she wasn't; if anything, she visited the carrot tent less often than the others. Luke seemed to be performing his duties cheerfully and efficiently, getting along well with the women working alongside him, at least one of whom was annoyingly attractive.

"So, I assume you have a car?" she asked him after she'd finished her duties.

He shook his head.

"You took the subway?"

"No, but I let the car go. It seemed sort of, I don't know, it just didn't seem quite right having a Town Car standing by for three or four hours while I handed out carrots at a housing project."

On the one hand, she gave him credit for his decency; on the other, she'd been looking forward to a ride downtown. She was getting a little weary of trying to live within her means. "I guess we're taking the subway. It's a kind of underground train."

"Genius idea."

They could, of course, have had lunch in Manhattan, but wanting to see how he reacted, she took him instead to a Salvadoran restaurant on 149th that Doreen, one of the clients, had introduced her to last year.

"You come here often?" he asked after she led him to a Formica table for two.

"Occasionally," she said.

"I'm not sure I buy that," he said, taking a seat across from her. "What do you order?"

"They do a chicken dish I like," she said. At least that's what Doreen ordered, although for the life of her she couldn't remember what it might be called.

"You're sure you want to eat here?"

"Absolutely," she said, despite having second thoughts about the venue and not feeling particularly hungry. Only two other tables were occupied—a Hispanic couple with a toddler and a pretty, solitary young African-American woman in light blue medical scrubs, reading *Us* magazine.

An obese waitress waddled over and tossed two plastic-coated menus between them, sending Luke's empty water glass spinning like a top toward the edge of the table, but he grabbed it and prevented it from sailing to the floor. The waitress's lack of concern, before she turned and swayed back toward the counter, seemed to indicate this sequence of events was strictly routine.

"Kind of ironic, those poor girls I was working with today from the Bear Stearns back office team—they'll be needing handouts themselves."

"How so?"

"Bear Stearns went under last month. The shorts were in a feeding frenzy and the New York Fed reneged on a line of credit. They were out of business in days."

She'd read something about it; for a moment she thought of Veronica, but, no, she was at Lehman Brothers. "Should the rest of us be worried?" she asked.

"I am. The subprime mortgage market's melting down," he said. "I'm basically bearish."

"Have you told your friend Obama about this?"

"He's got more immediate problems right now—this Reverend Wright thing is dogging him."

Before Corrine could respond to this, the waitress heaved back up and leaned over to fill the water glasses, overfilling Corrine's, water flowing over the Formica and soaking her napkin. "You ready to order?" she asked.

"What do you recommend?" Luke asked.

She shrugged. "For your skinny ass, maybe *chicharrón de pollo con tostones.*"

"Sounds delicious. Shall we get two of those?"

"Just a *café con leche* for me," Corrine said.

The waitress rolled her eyes.

"One *café con leche* and one *chicharrón de pollo.*"

After she walked off, Luke said, "If you have doubts about the food, please warn me now."

"No, it's not that. I'm just not hungry."

"I find it a little odd that someone with—how to put this delicately?—an ambivalent attitude toward food would become involved in feeding the masses."

"You're not the first person to say that. But you should know better than anyone that it all started when we were working at the soup kitchen. The cops and the rescue workers weren't starving, but it was still gratifying to feed them, and I started thinking about how many people in the city actually had trouble feeding themselves and their families. And I also saw how *badly* those people were eating, the kind of crap that they were putting in their bodies. And the more I looked into it, the more I learned about how difficult it is for lower-income people to get basic nutritional information, not to mention access to fresh, healthy food."

"I didn't mean to sound critical, Corrine."

"And besides, I resent that remark about food issues. I have issues with gluttony and gourmandism. It's like chefs have become gods and restaurants have become the new nightclubs. Our friends talk about truffles the way they used to talk about cocaine. My daughter watches the Food Network, for Christ's sake. That there *is* a Food Network is a little hard for me to fathom. When did that happen? Foodie culture has become the newest cult of conspicuous consumption, and I find it annoying as hell. The pursuit of *bottarga* is just as superficial as the pursuit of the latest Kelly bag. Neither one fills a basic need."

She paused, realizing she needed to get hold of herself. "Sorry, I'm ranting."

"Maybe you're just avoiding the other subject."

"What other subject?"

"Us."

"Are we a subject?"

"Imagine if instead of just handing out vegetables you could be handing out millions of dollars."

"What are you talking about?"

"We could have our own foundation. You could really make a difference in the world."

"Are you proposing to me?"

"I just want you to think about what life could be like."

"You already have a foundation." It seemed like a peculiar objection, but she was flummoxed.

"We'd subsume it under the umbrella of the Corrine and Luke McGavock Foundation."

"Wow," she said, stunned. "I'm not sure I've ever heard a statement that so thoroughly intermixed noble and selfish intentions."

"They're always intermixed, Corrine."

"I don't believe that. What about the hopes we have for our kids?"

"An interesting example, that. You could say that in caring for our kids we're promoting our own genes. But if you really care about the welfare of your children—and I know you do—maybe you should consider what I could provide for them. The opportunities they don't have now."

"That's so not fair," she said, although she'd sometimes allowed herself to wonder what it would be like—not to run a foundation or to indulge fantasies of wild consumption, but to be freed from the hard choices of allocating scarce resources. Even if money couldn't buy happiness, it could redeem a great many sources of unhappiness. She saw now that for a long time she'd underestimated the importance of financial security and that in doing so she had circumscribed her prospects and those of her children. And yet she still subscribed to the values on which she'd based her life, still believed that the acquisitive instinct was one of the lower impulses on the scale of human values. Was it just some residual cultural snobbery that made her feel that Mammon worship was boorish? And would her children thank her when she explained that she'd left Russell in order to improve their material well-being?

All at once she spotted a flaw in his argument. "I thought the big reason you split up with Giselle was that you didn't want children."

"I didn't want to start a new family with *her*."

"But I don't understand why you want to take on a broken family with me. What the hell's wrong with you?"

"You're right," he said, just before his lunch was slapped in front of him, chicken parts drowning in an orange swamp beside a mesa of yellow rice. "It doesn't make sense. It must be love, I guess."

31

JACK LANDED AT LA GUARDIA a few minutes early and called the dealer from the cab on the way into the city. By the time he arrived at the Chelsea, a little after 6:00 p.m., Kyle was waiting in the lobby. "I was having breakfast down the street," he explained. He was wearing the full Williamsburg: Peterbilt trucker's cap, red flannel shirt over a Pabst Blue Ribbon T-shirt.

They went up to the room, where Kyle unloaded his backpack and laid out his wares—coke, smack, Xanax and several grades of weed. "How's the H?" Jack asked.

"Better than last time. Really clean. Try it."

Jack pulled a framed hunting scene from the wall and laid it on the coffee table, ripped open a bindle and laid out a third of it in a thin line, then rolled up a twenty and hoovered the smack. It burned a little before it began to warm him from the inside out. Very soon he felt as if the world around him were slowing to a manageable speed. Everything was going to be all right.

"Ummm," he said. In a moment he'd summon the energy to buy more of this before he forgot.

"Good, huh?"

"Oh yeah."

"Seventy for a bundle. Ten bindles."

Jack nodded. "Uh-huh."

"How much do you want?"

"Better make it two."

"Okay, just take it slow. This shit's strong."

"Long as I don't shoot it, I figure I'm fine."

"How about the coke?"

"Show me." It was possible he was pausing a long time before answering; he wasn't sure.

"I've got the regular. And then I've got the Bolivian blue."

"Blue flake?"

"Like the scales of a bluefish, baby."

"Oh, man. Let me see that." The mythical blue flake. It was like the white whale. You heard about it, but he'd never actually seen it.

After what seemed like a long time, Kyle pulled a folded packet from his backpack and opened it up, nudging the layered fragments with an X-Acto knife, moving them back and forth to catch the light. "See the blue?"

"I think so." Jack was pretty sure he did. It was a beautiful flake, for sure, like shards of white mica with blue-gray highlights.

"How much?"

"Two fifty."

"Holy shit."

"That's because I don't cut it and my supplier doesn't, either. If you want the regular, it's a hundred—fine with me."

"No. I want this," Jack said. "Do me a favor and chop me a line."

It hit his sinuses clean, without the acidic bite of a bad wash or a bad cut, and when it dripped down the back of his throat, he felt the prickly tingle in his scalp and knew he'd made the right choice.

In the end he bought two grams of the blue and two bundles of the H with cash he'd withdrawn over the last two days in Nashville.

He was supposed to go to Russell and Corrine's for dinner, which was kind of the last thing he felt like doing. It was six-forty-five and dinner was supposedly at eight. He did two more lines of the smack and suddenly it was eight-fucking-twenty. At some point he'd set up his iPod dock, and the Black Keys were playing.

He thought about blowing off the dinner but instead did two lines of coke, which set him right up, put some fuel in his tank. His current outfit of jeans and a black Kid Rock T-shirt would have to do. If he even thought about changing, he'd never make it.

Downstairs, he hailed a cab and made it to their door a few minutes before nine. Corrine was sweet and welcoming; as uptight as she could sometimes be, she seemed to have this almost maternal affection for him and to forgive him his sins, but Russell was a little pissy, messing around with the pots on the stove. It was a mystery to Jack how any dude could give a shit about cooking. But then, he wasn't that much into eating, either.

"Glad you could make it," Russell said, sounding more peevish than glad.

"Sorry. That flight always gets delayed."

He retreated as Russell hacked away at some greenery splayed on the cutting board.

Given Russell's mood, he was especially happy to see Washington. Here was a guy who didn't judge lest he be judged, always good for some laughs. Sharp as hell tonight in a trim black suit and a white shirt that looked as crisp as a potato chip, his skull shaved clean and shiny, like it was buffed. They bumped fists and hugged.

"Whaddup, cracker?"

"Just soakin' up the sights in the big city, blood."

"New York, New York, just like you pitchered it."

"Skyscrapers and everything."

"Maybe I can show you some other sights later on, after the grown-ups have gone to bed."

"Sounds cool, man. I'm in the mood. Where's the missus?"

"She's taking a little time off from the matrimonial state. I'm in the penalty box."

"Damn, sorry about that. But I guess you're used to it by now."

Washington shrugged, as if to suggest that it was a force majeure kind of deal.

"You know Nancy Tanner?" he asked.

"Yeah, for sure," Jack said as she leaned toward him—at first he was baffled, but then he realized he was supposed to kiss her cheek.

"We're old pals," Nancy said. He'd met her the first time he'd come here, maybe, and they'd gone out together to some glitzy lounge. She wrote chick lit or something. She was pretty hot, actually, for somebody who had to be pushing fifty, looking very fine in a tight little gold minidress. She had a mole on the left side of her face, above her lip, like Cindy Crawford.

Russell came over with a vodka for Jack, having regained his perfect hostly demeanor, and introduced him to a middle-aged painter named Rob and his much younger boyfriend, Tab.

"Tab? As in acid?" Jack asked.

"As in Hunter," the kid said. "The actor. It's my stage name. Tab Granger."

The painter looked pained by this revelation. Jack could tell from the way he held himself, how he shook hands—like it was a distasteful obligation—that he was a very big deal, at least in his own mind, like Jack was supposed to recognize his name and be pissing his pants to meet him. Another fucking famous New Yorker. Everyone in New York was sort of famous. Every time you went into a restaurant, some dude was arguing with the hostess, doing some version of the "Don't You Know Who I Am?" dance. The painter's hands and fingernails were all crusted with paint, which seemed sort of like an affectation.

"Rob's got a retrospective at the Whitney," Russell said.

"Second-youngest painter ever to get one," Tab chipped in.

"And who exactly is Whitney?" Jack said. He knew he shouldn't, but he couldn't help himself.

"Very funny," Russell said.

The other two looked confused.

As late as he was, Jack wasn't as late as the actress they were setting him up with; at least that was the impression he got when Russell told him that Madison Dall wanted to meet him. Madison was some indie film darling who behaved badly enough to make the tabloids on a regular basis, or so he was told. And apparently a great fan of Jack's, especially now that the screenplay loosely based on his book was making the rounds. Madison came from some hollow in Kentucky and supposedly felt like she knew all the characters in Jack's book. She arrived a few minutes after he did, wearing a tiny red dress with spaghetti straps, and immediately started taking up a lot of space. Skinny but with fairly major tits, and while he couldn't be certain, they moved as if they were real.

"Wow, I'm, like, so incredibly honored to meet you," she said, a little bit of Kentucky coming through on her vowels. *Honored to might you.*

"Great to meet you, too," he said.

"I'd say I'm a big fan of your work, except that's like fucking saying 'Hello' in Hollywood speak; it's what you automatically say whenever you meet an actor or director. It activates my gag reflex. And I never want to say it when I actually mean it, if you see my point."

"Let's just say you think I'm a genius."

"Yeah, that's better." Milky complexion, lightly dusted with freckles, and a wild mane of unruly copper hair. She was looking at him with a directness that seemed to charge the night with possibility. If this were an acting class and she'd been told to look seductive and available, then she'd definitely be getting an A plus right now. She was going to be trouble, in a good way.

The two Calloway children appeared, Jeremy and Storey, politely introducing themselves and shaking hands. Old beyond their years, these New York City kids. Taller than he remembered. The girl was shorter but looked older, thirteen going on thirty.

"You remember Mr. Carson," Corrine said, her arm around Jeremy's shoulder.

"My dad's looking forward to reading your new book," Jeremy said.

"How old are you now?" Nancy asked. She enunciated as if she were speaking to an idiot or a deaf person, obviously not too used to kids.

"Twelve and a half," Jeremy said.

"Wow, that's amazing," Nancy said.

"Well, it's not like an accomplishment or anything," Storey said.

"Dinner is served," Russell announced from the kitchen. Corrine instructed them to find their place cards at the table and bring their plates over to the counter, where the food was laid out. At some point, Russell had changed into a burgundy velvet smoking jacket, which looked a little ridiculous by Jack's lights, though he couldn't help being impressed yet again with the scene; he'd never encountered this kind of sophisticated domesticity until his first dinner party at the Calloways' on his first trip to New York. His mother had never entertained, and holiday dinners with his relatives had been dutiful and depressing, generally concluding with tears and fisticuffs. He couldn't then have imagined a world where children with military posture politely retired to their rooms while artists and writers got elegantly shit-faced on fine wine, talking politics instead of sports, talking shit about other artists and writers.

Jack found himself seated next to Madison, who smelled really good and liked to emphasize her points by squeezing his knee.

She was now explaining how much she liked his story about the moonshining brothers. "What was that one called?" Every time she leaned forward, he was treated to a glimpse of her nipples.

"It's called 'Shine,'" Jack said.

"Oh God, of course. Duh!"

Russell overheard this and said, "That's one of the greatest stories of the last quarter century. Although I did have to persuade Jack not to spell out what happens to the older brother in the end."

"Yeah, I don't know what I was thinking," Jack said. "I'd be nothing without my editor. Everything I am today, I owe it all to Russell."

"That was very tacky of you, Russell," Corrine said.

"I didn't mean to take credit for anything major," Russell said, taken aback by the reaction to his remark. "I mean, I knew it was a great story the first time I read it."

"Then that's what you should've said the first time," Corrine said.

"You're lucky, Jack," Nancy said. "My editor's barely literate. Last week she told me my protagonist wasn't likable enough and not to use so many big words."

The conversation subdivided again. Madison told Jack about the first time she'd gotten drunk on shine when she was twelve, and then Nancy joined in from the other side, telling a story about her first drunk, when she'd vomited in her purse during a high school football game. Russell orbited the table, filling wineglasses, slapping Jack on the back as he passed.

"Hey, sorry, buddy. Didn't mean to be a douche bag."

"No big thing," Jack said.

At the other end of the table, they were talking about September 11.

"It's like it never happened," Washington was saying. "We were all going to change our lives, and in the end we're the same shallow, grasping hedonists we used to be."

"Some people changed," Corrine said, all of a sudden seeming very sad.

"Like the poor bastards who got sent to Iraq," Russell said.

"I, like, barely remember it," said the child actor.

"That's because you were eight when it happened," said the painter.

"Nuh-uh. I was . . . twelve."

Corrine said, "I think for anyone who was here, it's a wound that's just barely scabbed over. When you hear a low-flying plane, you tense up in a way you never did before. And let's not forget we lost a friend, Jim Crespi."

"Poor fucking Jim," Washington said.

"If you weren't here, you have no idea," the artist said. "But I don't think anyone who was here then will ever get over it."

"Give me a fucking break," Washington said. "New Yorkers aren't capable of dwelling on the past. When was the last time we talked about Jim? I can't even remember what I did last night."

Russell said, "Not everyone drinks as much as you do, Wash."

"God, I just remembered the weirdest thing," Nancy said. "I think I slept with two firemen that week. They'd been working at Ground Zero for like three days and they came up to Evelyn's, all sooty and exhausted, and everyone was buying them drinks, and I ended up taking them home."

"You slept with both of them at the same time?" Corrine asked.

"It was a weird time," Nancy said. "We were all fucked-up."

Jack didn't have much to contribute to this, having been at home in Fairview. He'd been cranking the night before in a friend's hunting cabin, then slept through the next day and hadn't even heard about it till late that night. Since everybody at the table was still yammering about September 11, he decided to take the opportunity to go the bathroom and do some more drugs.

He wiped the top of the toilet tank to make sure it was dry and laid out a bag of the H, cutting and snorting two rails. He was planning to do the coke afterward, but he found his legs getting a little rubbery, so he sat down on the toilet seat, and when the door opened, he was afraid he'd been in there a long time.

Madison was in the doorway, and instead of retreating, she came in and closed the door behind her. "Got anything for me?" she said.

"I got some blow," he said, not wanting to mention the other. "Just give me a minute to get my shit together here."

If he could just focus a little and remember how to use his limbs, he'd be fine, but he needed the coke in order to get volitional. It was a vicious circle. Before he could make any progress, Madison got down on her knees and unzipped his jeans and took his cock in her mouth, which made focusing even more difficult. He closed his eyes and tried to enjoy it even as he worried about whether he could get hard or not, but it turned out he could.

When he heard what sounded like someone rattling the door handle, he opened his eyes again. Young Jeremy was standing there staring in wonder at the sight of Madison's mane bouncing up and down in Jack's crotch. It might have been five or fifteen seconds before he closed the door.

Jack knew he was in deep shit, but he felt the reckoning could wait; right now he just really wanted to finish what Madison had started.

He realized once he stepped into the hall that the bathroom door was visible from the dining table, where his own seat and Madison's were conspicuously vacant. After cleaning himself off and giving her some of the coke, he'd suggested she wait for a few minutes after he returned to the table, though at this point he wasn't sure why he'd bothered.

No one seemed to take any notice as he sat down, until Nancy looked at him and said, "Did you two have fun in there?"

Jack shrugged and filled his mouth with some of whatever it was Russell had cooked, some kind of fucking meat in a sauce. From her side of the table, Corrine looked resigned.

A few minutes later, after Madison had returned to her seat, twitching like a madwoman and chewing on her lower lip, Storey appeared and tugged on Corrine's shoulder. "Jeremy saw two people having oral sex in the bathroom," she announced.

Glaring at Jack, Corrine stood up and walked with her daughter back to the bedrooms, presumably to check up on her emotionally scarred son.

"Well," Nancy said, "I guess now we know what you guys were doing."

Russell didn't seem to know how to react. He shook his head and poured half a bottle of red wine into his glass. Jack flashed what he hoped was a rueful grin, insofar as he was able to control the muscles of his own face.

Jack felt something rubbing against his ankle just before Madison screamed.

"Fuck—a rat!" She pushed her chair back from the table and jumped to her feet. Jack stomped the furry creature with the heel of his boot.

"That's Ferdie," Russell said, leaping to his feet and circling to their side of the table.

"That *was* Ferdie," Nancy said.

"What the fuck's a ferdie?" Madison said.

Whatever it had been, it was now a bloody mess on the floor.

"Jesus, Jack. Fuck! That was our fucking pet ferret," Russell said, crouching down to examine the carnage. The creature gave one last quiver.

"I'm sorry, man, I thought it was a rat."

"Rats don't have furry tails," Russell said, gingerly touching the thing with his finger. "Poor little Ferdie. Oh Jesus." He sounded as if he were about to cry.

Corrine reappeared. Taking in the scene, she turned pale and asked, "What happened?"

"It's Ferdie," Russell said, still kneeling there.

Approaching closer, she put her hand to her mouth when she saw the squashed pet. "Oh my God, is he—"

"He's dead," Russell said, standing up and heading her off, throwing his arms around her shoulders.

"What happened?" she asked.

"Damn, I'm really sorry, you guys," Jack said. "It was an accident."

Storey, who had crept over to see, started howling.

"Oh my God," Corrine said, looking at him with horror.

"I think you should go," Russell said.

"Oh my . . . Jesus," Corrine said, her voice breaking, barely audible over Storey's wails. "You killed him? You killed Ferdie? What the fuck is wrong with you?"

"He thought it was a rat," Madison explained.

"You're right, I'll go," Jack said, retreating to the elevator door and standing to wait as the car rattled upward from the first floor, listening to Corrine sobbing on Russell's shoulder while the other guests sat helplessly at the table.

Madison glanced back and forth between the Calloways and Jack before joining him just as the elevator arrived.

"That party's definitely over," she said as the doors finally closed.

"I can't believe I killed their ferret."

"I can't believe they *had* a ferret."

"This is bad."

"Well, you probably won't get invited back for the Memorial Day party."

"Jesus."

"He'll have to forgive you. You're too good a writer."

"You don't understand. I was going to fire him."

"What?"

"I was gonna tell him this week."

"Why are you firing him?"

"Because he treats me like a baby. Because he thinks he knows how to write my stuff better than I do. Because he thinks he made me. You heard him tonight, talking about how he changed the ending of 'Shine.'"

"So what're you going to do?"

"The thing is, I like the guy. And I sure can't fire him now."

The elevator stopped at the ground floor.

"Where to?" she said.

"I don't care. Anywhere—just so long as we can do more drugs. I don't know if there are enough goddamn drugs in the world to make me forget that fucking dinner party, but I'm sure as shit gonna try."

32

THE FIRST FRIDAY OF EVERY MONTH was the food giveaway at the Grant Housing Project in Harlem. Carol, the realtor, was among those who showed up for the volunteer orientation.

"I was going to call you," she said, her unruly salt-and-pepper hair pulled back in a ponytail with a scrunchie. "I don't know if you're still looking, but there's been a price reduction at that town house on West 121st. The bank's threatening foreclosure and the owner's desperate. It looks like they're going to do a short sale."

Much as this announcement piqued Corrine's interest, she couldn't help feeling this wasn't the time or place for that conversation, though she had loved the house Carol had showed her two months earlier. Most of the families in the crumbling housing project were on some sort of public assistance, and the median income for a family of four, of which there were very few, was around twenty thousand.

"Let's talk afterward," Corrine said before setting up the separate stations for turnips, carrots and acorn squash.

They'd met here after Carol first volunteered a year ago, and within minutes Corrine had heard the whole story: "We were the perfect couple, Upper West Side liberal Jewish intelligentsia version. He taught political science at Columbia. Culturally we were Jewish—we did the bar mitzvah and the bat mitzvah—but basically we were nonobservant. We were secular humanists, and proud of it. We thought that religion was divisive; superstition, the opiate of the masses. Fast forward to 9/11: Howard's brother worked for Cantor Fitzgerald; he's on the one hundred and fifth floor when the first plane hits. They were close, so Howard's on the phone with him when the tower collapses. And he goes into a funk. We all go into a funk, right? But Howard doesn't come out of his, and he turns to religion. He starts going to synagogue and then he joins this Orthodox shul, and I try it a few times, but my heart's not in it. I tell him, 'Hey, honey, it's your thing.' He becomes ultra-Zionist and insists we keep kosher, and he wants to send the kids to Hebrew school, and eventually he quits his job and moves out of the house and joins this Hasidic sect in Brooklyn. Suddenly I've got no husband and no income. So that's how I got into real estate."

When she heard that Corrine was thinking about moving, Carol had talked up the virtues of the far Upper West Side, the high eighties and nineties, where they looked at several three-bedroom apartments in a nice prewar building. But Corrine's price range kept driving them north, till Carol said, "For about the same money you could get a town house in Harlem. The housing stock is incredible—block after block of late-nineteenth-century town houses. As recently as five years ago, I wouldn't have advised someone like you to consider it. I mean, I wouldn't want that on my conscience. Now, I'd say jump before it's too late. Sure, it's still rough around the edges, but you're already seeing features in *New York* magazine. You don't want to be the last white people through the door."

"I'd hate to think we were displacing the . . . local residents."

"It's not you; it's the economy. Market forces. The neighborhood has already been ravaged. It was heroin in the sixties and seventies; then the crack wars in the eighties and nineties wiped out what was left of the middle class. A lot of these properties—the best values, really—are abandoned foreclosures. Boarded-up town houses used as drug dens for the last couple of decades. And the others are already renovated. Those are getting pricey. I'm not sure you could swing that. It's funny, though, the kind of white people who consider moving to Harlem—I don't count the speculators, of course—are precisely the kind most prone to liberal guilt."

"What about, you know, crime?"

"Oh God, SoHa, it's totally safe."

"SoHa?"

"South Harlem. Get it? It's SoHo for the aughts. I'm not saying it's the Upper East Side, but it's safer than the Upper West Side was when I was growing up. We lived on Riverside, and my mother wouldn't let me walk to Central Park because Amsterdam and Broadway and Columbus were so dangerous. You've heard of Needle Park, right? They made that film with Al Pacino. That was Broadway and 72nd. You had these well-to-do Jewish upper-middle-class families on the river and on the park, but everything in between was the freakin' Wild West. Junkies, muggers, perverts in raincoats. Broadway was lined with SROs full of released mental patients. The good old days. Hah! Compared to that, Harlem, today, it's gotten to the point where it's hard to score drugs, so they tell me. The trade's mostly moved uptown to Inwood."

Harlem. It was a heady concept. Russell had a completely irrational dislike of the Upper West Side, but Harlem, upper as it was, might just appeal to his sense of urban romance. She hadn't even told him she was looking yet. She wanted to find something and present him with the whole package. *A town house in Harlem* was an evocative phrase, charged with tension, contradiction, vibrating between poles of domesticity and urban menace. Corrine had a tenuous ancestral tie to the neighborhood, her grandfather having fallen under its spell after being taken to a jazz club by his friend Carl Van Vechten, and he'd told her many stories about those visits.

The idea had grown on Corrine after she took a tour with Carol two months ago. They'd focused their search south of 125th, as close as possible to the kids' new school on East 94th, looking at duplexes and town houses, whole and divided, including a few that were boarded up and derelict, fetid, the walls covered in graffiti, crack vials underfoot, some of them mere shells and others with century-old decorative flourishes intact: elaborate moldings and fireplaces, magnificent staircases and monumental arches.

She'd been completely and utterly smitten by the last house of the day, an Italianate brownstone on West 121st Street that had been partially renovated by the owner, who'd bought it in 2006 and quickly run out of money. This was the house that Carol wanted to talk about now. The parlor floor was composed of two theatrical rooms with fourteen-foot ceilings and egg and dart molding, joined by a soaring arch. The front room had been restored to its former glory, with Carrara marble fireplaces flanked by Ionic columns. "This kitchen wasn't even here; it used to be downstairs. Look at this," Carol said, on the day of the tour, beckoning her to the back room, a huge kitchen and dining area. "Sub-Zero, Miele dishwasher, granite countertops, the works." Corrine could see Russell getting excited about this. "Plus the boiler and the roof are new," Carol had added. "After that, well, it gets a little rough." The rooms on the upper floors were in various states of disrepair, but by no means unrecoverable. Many of the windows were boarded up or bricked over, and the top floor was a junkyard, but Corrine was absolutely giddy, given the space, the sheer number of rooms, and the fenced-in backyard. "If she'd finished the job, this place could easily go for one five, one seven, but that's the beauty of it. You can finish it yourself, and you've got a motivated seller."

"It's still a stretch," Corrine had said wistfully.

"It would be easy to seal the lower stairs and rent out the basement apartment for income to defray the mortgage."

She pictured herself here, in a house, with her family: Russell reading in front of the fireplace, the children playing with their friends in the backyard. It seemed almost attainable, and yet she knew that it was more than their present circumstances would allow. And then—she couldn't help it—just for a moment, she wondered what Luke would think of the place.

"I'm pretty sure we can get it for one point one," Carol said to Corrine now, after the last cabbage had been distributed.

She'd never been one to yearn beyond her means, but she desperately wanted this house and told herself if she could only find a way to get her family there, she would be happy with her lot, and with the man she'd married, and never wish for more.

33

ARRIVING HOME SHORTLY BEFORE SEVEN, Russell collected the mail, finding among the bills and cards from realtors a slim envelope addressed to him in Jack's loopy, backward-leaning hand. This aroused his curiosity, an actual physical letter from one of his authors, as if they were Perkins and Hemingway in 1927. Why the hell would Jack be writing him a letter?

Jean was standing at the elevator door to present her grievances. "The kids is hungry, and Miss Corrine, she stay late at the office, and I got my choir practice tonight I'm gonna be late for."

Jeremy looked up from his laptop. "What's for dinner?"

"Good question."

"Don't forget it's meatless Monday," Storey called from the couch. She'd recently become a vegetarian, out of ethical concerns, and while she couldn't convert the family entirely, they'd agreed to forgo animal products once a week. Even Mario Batali was doing it, she pointed out. Although Corrine worried about Storey getting the right kind of nutrients, she was thrilled that she'd lost ten pounds in the past six months, even as she'd grown two inches. Now, like her mother, she worried about calories and assiduously studied the ingredients labels of all packaged foods.

Reading the back label on the jar of Rao's marinara sauce, which Russell was heating while waiting for the pasta water to boil, she announced, "It's gluten-free and cholesterol-free. But the pasta has tons of gluten. I mean, pasta is like pure gluten. We should think about getting brown rice pasta."

"I can assure you," Russell said, "it will be a cold day in hell before you see brown rice pasta in this kitchen. Besides, it's meatless Monday, not gluten-free Monday."

"Dad, you said *hell*." At one time, Jeremy had said things like this with a genuine sense of reproach, but it was now ironic, a kind of joke between them, based on their mutual recognition of Jeremy's new twelve-year-old sophistication, with him poking fun at his younger self.

"Call me when dinner's ready," he said. "I'm going to finish my geometry."

"Aunt Hilary phoned me," Storey said after he'd drifted off to his room.

"What? She called you? Why?"

"She does sometimes."

"What do you talk about?"

"Not much. Girl stuff. I think she's kind of lonely."

"Have you told your mother?"

Storey shook her head. "No way. I don't think Mom would approve."

"You're probably right."

"Don't tell her, promise?"

"I promise."

"You don't like her very much, do you?"

"Hilary? I don't know. Let's just say I'm grateful to her when I see how beautiful you've become."

He turned up the volume on *All Things Considered*: *"A defiant Hillary Clinton heralded her campaign victories and boasted of her millions of supporters last night—conceding nothing to Barack Obama even as her rival crossed the critical delegate-number threshold to secure the Democratic nomination. . . ."*

He couldn't help noticing that Storey ignored her mother when she got home a few minutes later, in contrast to her brother, who bounced around her like a puppy while describing his day.

"And what about you?" Corrine asked Storey, who was sitting on the couch with a schoolbook. "How was your day?"

"Same old."

Corrine was taking a week off from drinking, so over dinner Russell finished a bottle of Gigondas by himself, pouring the last glass at the table while Corrine helped Jeremy with his math. He was about to reach for a manuscript, when he remembered Jack's letter, which he retrieved from the kitchen counter.

Russell,

Damn, man, this is about the hardest letter Ive ever had to write and Ive got halfway into a bottle of vodka to work up the balls to do it. I hoped we could work this out so I wouldnt have to, but its got to the point where I got to say what Ive got to say. Nobody knows better than me how much I owe you and I will always be grateful for that. (Or maybe Im supposed to say "No one knows better than *I*," you could tell me, I know, so just ignore the fucking grammar for once OK.) You discovered me and put me on the map. You put your reputation on the line for me. And I won't forget it. But at the risk of sounding like some fucking new age twat I have to be myself and I feel like you want me to be some idea of me that you want to put out there, you want me to be the redneck version of you. I'm not saying my sentences are always perfect or even always grammatical but sometimes when you get finished with them I dont even hear myself in them anymore. I have my sound and I like to think some kind of music in the prose but when you start rebuilding my sentances I feel like the tune and the rhythm gets lost. Maybe its just a tin whistle but its my tin whistle. I think you look at a story and think its a machine that can be improved but I think a story is more like an animal. Its like your performing taxadermy on a living thing. You might make it look better by your lights but youve done kilt it in the meantime. And why is shorter always better? Its like sure you can save five words but whose fucking counting. It's not like I'm charging you by the word but sometimes that's what it feels like. I tried to tell you all this maybe I didnt try hard enough but its hard for a high school dropout cracker like me to stand up to his hotshot New York Ivy League editor you know. Youre Russell fucking Calloway. Which is good and bad. I let you push me to much and if I don't push back really hard than it will be true. Its just time for me to move on you know. Its like life or death for me. I know youll think its about me signing with Briskin but its not. Ive been thinking about this for a good long while and its what I need to do for myself. And Im way fucking greatful for everything. I love you, man. And I value your friendship. And I hope we can still be friends but I know youll hate me after this and I wouldn't half blame you.

Jack

PS. Really really sorry about your feret

34

WHEN SHE LEFT HER OFFICE THAT NIGHT, a fierce rain was
falling—slanting, in fact—angling at the behest of heavy gusts of wind,
which lifted Corrine's umbrella and turned it inside out. She was
soaked through long before she escaped into the subway.

Riding home on the number 1 train, reading *The Reluctant Fun-
damentalist,* she looked up and spotted Russell way down the car,
drenched and bedraggled in his old Burberry. On second glance she
almost thought it wasn't Russell, but someone who looked like him—an
older, worn-out version of her husband. But it *was* Russell, and she was
shocked by his slumped comportment, his slack demeanor, even by the
gray in his hair. Did he actually have that much gray? When had that
happened, and why hadn't she noticed it? He looked like one of those
exhausted souls she saw every day on the subway, men she imagined
stuck in jobs they hated, going home to wives they didn't love, or perhaps to an empty room somewhere out near the end of the subway line,
to heat a can of soup on the hot plate and watch TV. What was most
surprising was that he wasn't reading—Russell was always reading. But
now he was standing, staring at the empty window, holding the over-
head rail, swaying with the motion of the car. She was so unsettled by
his appearance that she slipped out the door at the Houston Street stop
and waited for the next train before continuing on to Canal Street.

When she got home, he was sitting on the couch with Jeremy, watching *Lost,* a flagrant violation of house rules on a school night. Neither
of them even glanced up until she stepped between them and the TV,
at which point Jeremy yowled, "Mom!"

Russell looked up at her with mild interest. He didn't seem quite so haggard and affectless as he had on the subway, but neither did he seem like his normal self. It was as if he'd aged while she wasn't paying attention, becoming thoroughly middle-aged. Unnerved all over again, she walked away without speaking to either one of them, retreating to their bedroom, where she promptly burst into tears.

That night, while she was helping Jeremy with his homework, he asked, "What's the matter with Dad?"

"Why do you think anything's wrong with Dad?" she asked.

"He doesn't seem happy. He doesn't tell jokes and funny stories at dinner."

"I think maybe he's working too hard."

"Is he still depressed about that fake memoir?"

"Well, probably."

It was 3:32 a.m. when she woke up suddenly, alone in their bed. She found him in the living room, watching an infomercial for an exercise machine.

"Are you all right?"

"I couldn't sleep. I didn't want to disturb you."

She *was* disturbed, though, that he was watching an infomercial, but it seemed too embarrassing to allude to, almost as awkward as if she'd caught him watching porn. She remembered at least a dozen times when he'd flipped around the channels at night or on the weekends, saying, "What kind of losers actually watch these things?" Now he was actually watching a bunch of aging athletes demonstrating some stupid machine. Russell played tennis and skied but hated exercise for its own sake. The only possible excuse she could think of was the cute blonde in the blue leotard with the spectacular bod who was providing the narration.

"Why don't you come to bed?

"I'll be in soon."

"Russell, what's wrong? Is something worrying you?"

"Just the usual."

He continued to stare at the screen. The chick in the blue leotard was chatting with some washed-up boxer.

"Would you tell me if something were really wrong?"

He nodded without looking away from the screen.

"Have I done anything to make you unhappy?" This was as close as she could come to asking him if he suspected anything.

He shook his head.

After a few minutes, when it became clear he wasn't going to move, she said good night and waited for him in the bedroom.

She wondered if her own absorption in her romance with Luke had prevented her from noticing her husband's decline. Was it possible he'd discovered something, overheard some conversation between them? Could he have gotten into her e-mails and found one from Luke? But no, few as they were, she scrupulously, unsentimentally erased them as soon as she'd read them and discouraged that form of communication. She'd heard of too many others discovering affairs that way. It was possible that Kip had told Russell about running into her with Luke at Teterboro. On reflection, though, she thought it more likely that he was still suffering from the fallout of the Kohout scandal. It had been a terrible blow both to his pride and the balance sheet of the business, although he hadn't been very forthcoming about the latter, and she hadn't pressed him very hard on this. She knew he'd rather not tell her if he didn't have to.

When he finally came back to bed, she pretended to be asleep, though she remained awake beside him, sensing that he, too, was awake but incapable of breaking the silence between them.

35

ONCE UPON A TIME, Washington's kids had been thrilled to go
to the Museum of Natural History—the dinosaurs, the dioramas of
cavemen and American Indians and African wildlife, the giant blue
whale floating like a zeppelin over the great hall, the planetarium—but
they'd complained bitterly when he'd proposed it this Saturday morning, and he'd been forced to improvise, ending up at the Calloways'.
While it would be an exaggeration to say that Jeremy and Mingus were
close friends, they were brothers in arms when playing Halo 3, trading roles between the Master Chief and the Arbiter, nuances of personality disappearing in the pursuit of their roles within this alternate
universe. The situation with the girls was more complicated; Zora
was a year older than Storey and several rungs above her in the intricate social hierarchy of junior high, a fact somehow understood and
acknowledged by both, despite the fact that they attended different
schools. Although it was a warm, sunny spring day, the air cleansed
and refreshed by yesterday's downpour, outdoor activities weren't up
for consideration—they'd reached the age where their habits began
to resemble those of the vampires who were becoming so popular in
television shows and young adult fiction. Both girls were deliriously
excited about the first *Twilight* movie, hitting theaters in the fall, and
had instructed their parents, who were sometimes invited to screen-
ings and premieres, to be on the lookout. In the meantime, they were
willing to settle for *Forgetting Sarah Marshall*.

Russell, who seemed deeply out of sorts, begged off, citing a pile of unread manuscripts, so Washington took the girls up to the multiplex at Union Square.

In the popcorn-redolent theater he sat next to Zora, who poked him awake twice during the movie, hissing that he was snoring. As he was dozing off again, he was roused by his text message signal. Furtively checking his phone, he saw it was from Casey Reynes: *Suite at Lowell. Under name of Lily Bart. Come ASAP.*

He met Russell and Corrine for an early dinner with the kids at Bubby's—ignoring several texts from Casey—before returning his own kids to his former home. The loft looked particularly appealing, so vast and opulent in comparison to his sublet studio in West Chelsea and yet so homey and familiar—the old family seat. There was his favorite reading perch, the Arne Jacobsen egg chair with its soft cinnamon leather in the corner by the southeast windows, and his vintage McIntosh sound system with its luminescent blue-green dials nestled in its zebrawood console with all his old vinyl, the Miles and the Coltrane, the Dizzy and Bird LPs. Somewhere among them was a copy of Charles Mingus's *Pithecanthropus Erectus,* the only possession of his father's that had passed down to Washington, left behind when he abandoned him and his mother in Trinidad. For years he'd thought if he could decode the title, he would discover his father, or at least his essence, titillated by what the priapic *Erectus* suggested.

Veronica appeared, greeting the children, falsely cheerful and haggard of mien, listening as they narrated the day's adventures, while Washington waited just inside the door.

"How are you?" she asked after the children had melted away to their rooms.

He shrugged. "You?"

"Things have been pretty scary at work. Rumors flying and the stock's taken a beating. I hate to be the bearer of bad news, but our college fund is half what it was last month."

"It'll come back," he said, though he had no information about the situation at Lehman Brothers; he was just trying to reassure her.

"Let's hope."

Watching for a cab on Greenwich Street, he got another text: *Where the hell r u? About to call concierge for Rent-a-Hunk.* He told himself that if he didn't see a cab in the next three minutes, he'd text back that he'd been unavoidably detained, but just then one of those new cabs that looked like a tiny school bus pulled over.

He wondered if he was up for this—still under the spell of nostalgia for a lost domesticity brought on by his visit to the loft, feeling the old protective instinct in response to Veronica's distress—even as the driver hurtled uptown, braking and accelerating, leaving Washington vaguely nauseous by journey's end. Debating whether to stop at the desk or stride boldly to the elevator, he could already detect that extra level of scrutiny from the little pink-faced twerp behind the counter and the bellman poised by the elevator, both of them white. He still found it hard to believe that people were giving the brother better than even odds of winning the election. He didn't see that happening.

"I'm here to see Lily Bart," he said, wondering if the man behind the desk was a Wharton fan. "I believe she's expecting me."

"Ah, yes, Miss Bart mentioned she might have a visitor and asked me to tell you that she's just gone across the street to—oh, I believe that's Miss Bart now."

He turned around to see Casey coming through the door, looking very slinky in a black leather jacket over a silver shirt.

"I'd almost given up on you," she said, taking his arm and leading him to the elevator. "I went to Bilboquet for a cocktail."

"I had the kids," he said.

"Can't you just hardly wait to ship them off to boarding school?"

"First I'd have to convince their mother," he said, though in fact he had no intention, or desire, to send his kids away to school. As a weekend dad, he missed them already.

She attacked him even before the elevator doors swooshed closed, grabbing his collar, smashing her lips against his and thrusting her tongue in his mouth, her breath hot with alcohol, tinged faintly with juniper.

"I've been so waiting for you," she said, panting and pushing her hair back from her face as the doors slid open.

She took his hand and led him down the corridor, their progress abruptly checked by someone emerging from a room in front of them, a man in a Barbour jacket and red wide-wale cords, who looked as if he was en route to his hobby farm in Millbrook.

"Oh my God," she said.

"Casey?"

The man—Casey's husband, Washington was by now pretty certain—seemed puzzled, whereas she was clearly dumbfounded.

"What are you doing here?" she demanded.

"I just had a meeting," he said, although the real answer to the question became apparent as the door from which he'd emerged opened, revealing a peppermint ice-cream cone of a girl in a white terry-cloth bathrobe: long pink legs and red locks.

"That's your fucking meeting?"

"Well, yes, as a matter of fact. And what, might I ask, are you doing here?"

Casey emitted several short exhalations before finally finding speech. "Who is this bitch? Your new secretary?"

"Actually," Tom said, "she's my girlfriend. Laura, this is Casey, my wife. Casey, Laura."

Washington had to hand it to Tom, who seemed very much in control of the situation, the least flustered person in the corridor. The girl was flabbergasted, her face, already pink, flushing even deeper as the seconds ticked past.

"As long as we're on the subject, perhaps you'd introduce me to your friend."

"You know Washington."

"Apparently not nearly as well as you do."

"We were just . . ." Casey couldn't seem to conjure a suitable predicate to complete the sentence.

Looking at Washington, Tom said, "Better you than me."

Washington shrugged; mortified, of course, but also impressed by his ostensible rival's command of the situation.

"If you could get it up," Casey hissed, "maybe I wouldn't be here with him."

"I've never known Tom to have any difficulty in that area," Laura said.

"Don't you dare speak to me, you slut."

"You don't need to hear this," Tom said to the girl, nudging her back in the room with a little pat on the ass. "I'll call you later," he said, easing the door shut. "Now if you'll excuse me," he said to his wife.

"I certainly will not excuse you. You can't just walk away."

"I really don't see the point in staying. You're clearly occupied."

"You bastard. I'll ruin you."

"Oh, please."

"You won't be welcome anywhere in this town after I tell people how you treated me. You think your little tramp friend's going to be welcome at the Deepdaleses' or the von Muefflings'?"

Washington was pretty certain that the Deepdales and the von Muefflings, whoever the fuck they were, would be happy enough to welcome the new Mrs. Reynes to their fetes in due course, after the divorce went through. So far as he could tell, second wives were the backbone and gatekeepers of haute New York society. All those secretaries, shopgirls, yoga teachers, models and escorts who were waiting with open arms and legs for the tired, muddled moguls of Manhattan, whose first wives didn't understand them, didn't fuck and suck them the way they wanted to be fucked or sucked, or who just bored them silly—these were the women who usually inherited the earth, or at least the Upper East Side, Southampton, Palm Beach, and other select private-jet destinations. The other wives would be sympathetic to Casey, and indignant at Tom, but in the long run Tom and Laura would be fine, and in time Laura could, if she were socially ambitious enough and Tom's fortune robust enough, become one of those wives who guarded the kingdom against interlopers like her younger self. Casey's future was harder to predict, although he'd once heard her express her horror at the fates of former friends who, after divorce, found themselves obliged to sell real estate or art to their former peers.

He was grateful this wasn't his world. And all at once, he knew where his place was, where his heart tended.

Casey watched as Tom disappeared into the elevator, and then turned to Washington, her features still puffed with rage. "I guess you think this is all pretty amusing."

"Yes and no."

"So what should we do?"

"I know what I'm going to do."

Twenty minutes later, he was standing outside the door of the loft in TriBeCa, practicing his speech as he waited for Veronica to open the door.

36

RUSSELL WAS SNORING BESIDE HER when the bedside phone woke her up Sunday morning just after eight. For some reason, she was afraid it was Luke, until she saw Casey's name on caller ID.

"I've left you like a million messages and texts."

"Casey?"

"Tom's run off with some bimbo."

"What?"

"Can you meet me at Balthazar in thirty minutes?"

"I'll try. Make it forty-five. Let's say nine."

Russell and the kids were still asleep when she left; she taped a note to the medicine cabinet, saying she'd be home before eleven.

Her friend was waiting for her at one of the banquettes along the back wall, overdressed in a formfitting black leather jacket with epaulets over a shiny silver shirt. It looked like last night's outfit.

"I can't believe it," Corrine said as she sat down.

"*You* can't believe it?"

"Who is she?"

"Nobody. Miss Nobody from Nowhere."

"Do you think it's serious?"

"He called her his girlfriend. To my face."

"I don't know what to say."

"I know."

"Are you . . . You must be devastated."

"I'm furious, is what I am."

"What happened? How did you find out?"

"I caught him in the act."

"In flagrante delicto?"

"Not quite. I ran into him in the hallway of the Lowell last night, coming out of a room. Rumpled hair and clothes, shit-eating postco-ital grin. And this little redhead hottie in a terry-cloth bathrobe with her boobs hanging out, sending him off with a kiss."

"What were you doing in the Lowell?"

"The point is, I caught him coming out of the room, and he was so busted, he didn't even try to make it sound plausible. He just sputtered something about having a meeting in the hotel."

"So what did you do?" Corrine couldn't help imagining this scene from Tom's point of view, imagining herself as Tom—caught in the act.

"I turned on my heels and stormed off."

"Didn't he try to stop you?"

"Of course he did."

"So he's sorry."

"Not nearly as sorry as he will be."

"I know, it's devastating, Casey. But given what's at stake . . . you don't want to act rashly."

"What am I supposed to do? *Forgive* him?"

"Not now, okay, not tomorrow, but don't you think that some-day you'll want to? Given the alternative? Granted, it's a terrible betrayal—but in the context of all those years together? And let's face it, it's not as if you haven't strayed." Suddenly pondering the prospect of getting caught herself, Corrine was wondering if Tom was relieved, if part of her would feel relieved.

"You sound like you're on his side."

"Not at all. I just want you to think hard before you decide to leave your marriage. People make mistakes. Marriages have different chap-ters, and some of them are dark. I don't mean to excuse what he did, but maybe, just for a while, after all these years you started to take each other for granted and he felt neglected and he felt his own mortality and at a low moment someone came along who made him feel young and special and invincible again. I'm just saying."

"He won't feel invincible after my lawyers carve him a new one."

"I still don't understand what you were doing in the Lowell. It's such a weird coincidence. Were you following him?"

"I had no idea."

"You just happened to be at the Lowell?"

"I was meeting someone," she snapped.

"At what point did he call her his girlfriend?"

"What do you mean?"

"Well, it sounds like he was flustered and then you stormed off before he could explain."

"I'm sorry, I'm traumatized and it's all a bit of a blur."

"So what happened after that? Did he come home last night?"

Casey shook her head.

"He was probably just too ashamed to face you. But I'm sure he'll come back."

She snorted derisively. "Good luck to him."

"Give it time."

Even as she was sympathizing with her friend, she couldn't help being deeply conscious of the fact that Casey had been blissfully unfaithful to Tom over the years, so the moral high ground was real estate to which she couldn't plausibly aspire. Or rather, she might, but that co-op board was never going to let her in the building.

Corrine couldn't help extrapolating about her own life; what if, while she'd been obsessed with Luke, Russell had been carving out a life of his own? Was it possible that his malaise reflected some romantic impasse? That he was tortured by having to decide between two lives or depressed—as she'd once been, after Luke left New York—by a hopeless love affair, a passion he'd renounced but couldn't forget? She'd been so absorbed by her own secret life, she hadn't stopped to consider the possibility that he might have one, as well.

"I'll take him for everything he's worth," Casey said.

"Do you have a prenup?"

She shook her head, smiling savagely. "That's the beauty part."

"That's . . . *wow.*" For people in their circle, of their means, it seemed to Corrine, there had always been a codicil to marriage vows.

"We were young and in love."

"Well, try to remember those days before you make any big decisions."

"I guess the timing isn't great for Russell," Casey said. "I know Tom was going to invest in his company."

"Really? I had no idea."

"I'm sorry, I just assumed you knew. I've actually been going through a whole moral dilemma about that anyway. Ever since Washington told me about Russell losing Jack Carson, I was in this really weird position where I didn't feel like I could tell Tom, but at the same time it did seem relevant to McCane, Slade's fiscal health. Oh shit," she said, seeing Corrine's face. "You didn't know about that, either?"

"When did this happen?"

"I don't know, but Washington told me about ten days ago. I don't think he realized Tom and Russell were going into business together. Which put me in this totally awkward position. Anyway, I gather Carson wrote Russell a letter. Basically, thanks but sayonara. You honestly didn't know?"

That night, they lingered at the dinner table, Russell nursing a last glass of Pinot Noir that he hadn't even bothered to comment upon. Corrine waited until the kids had retreated to their rooms to do homework before relating the saga of Tom and Casey.

"I still can't believe it," she concluded.

"You said this girl was a redhead?"

"Why, do you know her?"

He seemed to pause before he shook his head.

"I mean, it certainly wasn't a perfect marriage, but after all these years I'd just assumed they'd always be together."

"The phrase *perfect marriage* ought to be abolished," he said. "It's a pernicious oxymoron."

"Do you really believe that?" she said. "People used to say that about us. We were that couple once."

"Please don't make me feel bad about stating the obvious."

"But we *do* have a good marriage?"

"Let's not play this game."

"Humor me, Russell. I'm worried about you. And about us."

"We'll be fine."

"But why aren't we fine right now? It doesn't feel fine. What's wrong? You've been virtually catatonic the past two months."

Corrine reminded herself to tread lightly, conscious of her own role in the estrangement. At the same time, she was weary of their lack of intimacy. Part of her just wanted a decision to be made for her.

"It's not you."

"Well, then, tell me what it is. I'm your wife. Not telling me what's wrong is a form of dishonesty. If you're in trouble, I need to know. Is there someone else?"

He looked up, startled. "Of course not," he said.

So that was off the table. "Is it about Jack?"

"Jack?"

"Why didn't you tell me he left you? How could you not tell me something that important? And how could you not tell me about soliciting an investment from Tom?"

He looked at her helplessly, pleadingly. Before he turned away, she saw that his eyes were welling with tears.

She leaned into him, kissed his neck and hugged him close, feeling his resistance fade as he exhaled and wrapped his arms around hers. At some point she realized he was crying, his torso convulsing rhythmically against her shoulder. She held him tighter, until the sobbing subsided.

Afterward, he showed her Jack's letter.

"I can't believe he'd do this to you after all you did for him."

"The news hasn't broken yet, but it will any day."

She stroked the hair away from his damp forehead. "I'm so sorry, honey."

"And then I'm well and truly fucked."

"Writers change publishers all the time."

"Jack isn't just another writer. He's a game changer. And I'm not just any editor—I'm the guy who published the infamous bogus memoir a few months back."

"I've hated the bastard ever since he killed Ferdie. Face it, Russell, the guy's a train wreck. You have other books, other writers."

"Not as many as I used to. And submissions have been way down this spring. I can't even get agents to send me books."

"We'll be all right," she said. As worried as she was about Russell, and about his business, in a possibly perverse way she was grateful for this crisis, for the opportunity to weather it with him. If she'd been waiting for a sign, this might well be it.

37

SPRING ARRIVED LATE, fitful and grudging, and then refused to make way for summer, which was fine with Russell. Even if he'd been eager to display himself on the lawns and beaches of the Hamptons that summer, which he wasn't, their straitened finances pretty much ruled it out, as did the sale of the Sagaponack farmhouse—for six million dollars—in March, a few days before Bear Stearns collapsed.

But with the economy sagging under the weight of the subprime mortgage crisis, the buyer's financing was delayed, and in mid-June the Polanskis offered the house to the Calloways, without charge, on the condition that they'd vacate on a week's notice. Corrine, who'd always handled communications with the Polanskis, was delighted by their generosity, and Russell couldn't think of a reason to decline the offer. So it looked as if he had no choice but to spend his summer among the voyeurs and exhibitionists who were his friends and peers, on the only spit of land in America where his business was remotely a matter of public interest.

Real estate was a hot topic in the Calloway household that summer. When their TriBeCa landlord opened with an offer of $1.5 million for the loft, Russell was forced to admit they couldn't swing it, not when he was struggling to keep his company afloat. While he fervently searched for financing in a tightening credit market, Corrine, he felt certain, was scouting real estate in the upper reaches of the metropolis.

The Calloways spent the last two rainy weekends in June cocooned beside the steely, too-cold-to-swim-in ocean, juggling playdates and sleepovers for the kids. Finally, in July, the sun returned from wherever it had been hiding, tennis was reinvented and Corrine moved out to the beach full-time with the kids, her summer sabbatical being one of the few perks of the nonprofit sector.

On Thursday nights, Russell rode out to Sagaponack on the jitney, returning to the city early Monday morning. Far from resenting his schedule, he cherished the solitude of these bachelor weekdays, working late and dining with a book at the bar at Soho House or the Fatted Calf, loved walking home through the clamorous, sweaty youth brigades of the Meatpacking District. He was bewitched by the vistas of feminine flesh, the exposed limbs and shoulders and the upper slopes of breasts swelling above halter tops, the flimsy summer dresses clinging at the top and fluttering up above the knees. He wanted them all, these girls of summer, but he didn't want any of them enough to act on his desire. Sometimes he found himself haunted by the regret that he'd never been a single man in the city, never walked these streets free and open to romantic adventure, to the spontaneous pursuit of erotic impulse, having moved in with Corrine as soon as he returned from Oxford and then marrying her soon after, although those early days had their own burnished halo of romance, when New York seemed to be a frontier teeming with infinite opportunities. Even now, despite their seasonal recurrence over the decades, the blasts of heat from the subway grates, the tarry smell of the melting streets like a bass note beneath the acrid tang of urban compost, the animal, vegetable and human waste decomposing and fermenting in the heat, invariably carried him back to his earliest, happiest years here, before they had enough money or vacation days to escape the summer heat, when the city, having been abandoned by the geezers, belonged to them and their kind. The days before they could afford an air conditioner, sprawling, stunned, on damp sheets, naked and slick with sweat and each other's secretions.

On these weekday evenings, Russell had dinner with Washington or Carlo Rossi, or caught up with friends he'd been too busy to see during the school year, flagging a cab or wobbling home in the humid fug, buzzed on cheap rosé, catching a last blast of heat from the subway

vent in the sidewalk just outside the door, arriving home around midnight to pass out in front of *Frasier* and *Seinfeld* reruns. Television was
a consolation for being alone, a solitary, guilty pleasure. He inevitably woke up with the TV on, a few hours after he'd fallen asleep, the
pressure of his bladder as insistent as the alarm. He hardly ever slept
through the night anymore. This was the only time he felt lonely and
missed his family, the hour or two before dawn, when he lay awake
racked by thoughts of bankruptcy and mortality. Like Fitzgerald at
Asheville, trembling in the 3:00 a.m. darkness—except that, unlike
Fitzgerald, he had no *Great Gatsby* to show when he met his Maker,
only a thin portfolio of clerical accomplishments in the service of literature. And several gaudy failures—his failed takeover of Corbin, Dern;
the Kohout debacle. In fact, after a long struggle with his Catholic
upbringing, he no longer believed he would meet anyone on his departure from this existence, and the notion of oblivion filled him with
despair. He'd always been an optimist, able to convince himself that the
best was still ahead, that every day held the promise of new adventure,
but now he seemed increasingly conscious of his failures and anxious
about the future. It was impossible to be optimistic at three-forty-five
in the morning, at the age of fifty-one, and there were times when he
was absolutely terrified at the prospect of his own extinction. Finally,
he took half an Ambien or a Xanax and waited for the panic to subside.

In the daylight, despite the dull ache at the back of his skull from
the Ambien—the feeling that his skull had been trepanned by dental
drills—and the parched prickle in his throat, he felt grateful that he'd
survived the terrors of the night.

That month, the contract holder on the Sagaponack house, a
thirty-four-year-old banker from Lehman Brothers, was poised to close
on the property and came twice to inspect the house before concluding that he would tear it down. When Corrine reported this to Russell,
she was indignant. "This goddamn zillionaire philistine in a pink golf
shirt with a giant polo-player logo and his wife with her fake tits and
her John Barrett Salon blond hair planning their McMansion."

While it looked as if they could probably stay on through Labor Day,
it was now clear this would be their last summer there, and that the

house itself, after surviving a hundred and fifty years of hurricanes and nor'easters, would succumb to the wrecking ball, a fact that further eroded Russell's self-esteem, and added to his sense that the world as he knew it was crumbling around him. How was it that after working so hard and by many measures succeeding and even excelling in his chosen field, he couldn't afford to save this house that meant so much to his family? Their neighbors seemed to manage, thousands of people no smarter than he was—less so, most of them—except perhaps in their understanding of the mechanics of acquisition. Partly, he knew, it was his lack of the mercenary instinct. Never caring enough about getting and keeping and compounding, he'd felt himself above such considerations and stayed true to the ideals he'd formed in college, at the expense of his future. If he'd been savvy and resourceful, he could have bought this house years ago, or, more important, a place to live in the city, but as things stood, he owned nothing; he'd missed the biggest real estate boom of his lifetime and even now that the bubble was bursting, his own finances were more precarious than ever. It was increasingly difficult to avoid the conclusion that he was, by the conventional measures of familial and professional achievement, a failure.

Russell stayed at the beach throughout August, working mornings at the rickety wicker desk in the den overlooking the potato fields. For the first time in many years, he declined an invitation to play in the artists' and writers' softball game—an event that had its origins in a pickup game back in the fifties with the likes of de Kooning and Pollock and Franz Kline nursing their hangovers on a scrubby lawn in the unfashionable town of Springs; the game had later been infiltrated by art critics and other writers, eventually becoming an annual spectacle in which movie stars and politicians vied for spots in the lineup, the painters claiming the actors as fellow artists; the politicians usually played with the writers—an acknowledgment, as one novelist suggested, of their accomplishments in the field of fiction. By virtue of his occasional essays and book reviews, Russell had qualified as a writer and had played for years, and while the mode of the event was more comic than epic, he'd prided himself on his accomplishments on the field, dependable and, occasionally, distinguished. This year, he just didn't have it in him.

After moving out to the beach, he found time for simpler pleasures—cooking for the family, seeking out the best tomatoes and corn and fresh fish; fishing, playing tennis and bodysurfing with Jeremy. He watched John Edwards admitting his extramarital affair on ABC; he watched hours of the summer Olympics with the kids. He liked to think he was comporting himself as a model father and husband, largely avoiding the big social events, the benefits under the big white tents, the clambakes on the beach and the movie premieres in South-ampton and East Hampton. He told Corrine he was sick of all that, that he wanted to cherish, with her and the kids, these final days in this house where they'd spent their summers for twenty years. Corrine was too smart to buy it but too loving to call him on it, except once. They were curled up together in bed on a night when they'd skipped a party he'd enjoyed for years. "It's been so nice," she said, "these past few weeks, I could happily skip the next hundred cocktail parties, but I know it's like a punishment for you. I've waited for years for you to get a little weary of the endless social treadmill, but I hate to see you crawl away and hide like a criminal."

"I *have* gotten a little weary of it," he said. "Suddenly the whole thing seems empty and exhausting. August in the Hamptons—it's not relax-ing; it's work. It's like climbing Everest."

"It's been like that for a long time, but you never complained before."

"We all have our tipping point."

"Have you given any more thought to whether we're going to have the party?"

Russell had previously had the excuse that they might be thrown out of the house on a week's notice, but now their residency was secured through Labor Day. "It's a lot of work," he muttered.

"Come on, Russell, it's only three weeks till Labor Day. I can't believe I'm having to talk you into this party, but people have been calling to ask me about it. You've created a tradition."

"Corrine's right, actually," Washington said the next night as they stood amid the throng at the bar of the American Hotel in Sag Harbor.

They'd just finished two sets of tennis at the public courts down the road and Washington had insisted on buying the loser a gin and tonic. "You've kept your head down for a while now, but it's time to get back out there. Not having the party's like some admission of guilt. I mean, how many books have you published in your career? Two hundred? Three? You made a bad call, and it's too bad, Crash, but you've got to get back on the goddamn horse. You've done your time in the wilderness and we're all ready to forgive, forget and party on."

"There's also a question of funds. Kohout wasn't just a PR disaster. I lost more than half a million bucks."

"How much do you need? For the party, I mean."

"I can't take your money."

"Call it a loan, then. I need this fucking party."

That same night, Steve Goldberg, the coach of the writers' softball team, called to appeal to him to play the next day. An old friend or at least acquaintance of Russell's, Steve was a sportswriter for the *Times*. "We need you out there, Russell. The fucking artists have a couple of ringers this year; they've got this guy Junior Gonzales who played in the minors for the Yankee organization. Apparently, he made a ceramic frog in sixth grade and that qualifies him as an artist."

"I'd love to, but I've got a lunch," Russell said.

"What fucking lunch? This is the game, Russell. Lunch happens every day. The writers need your help." It was supposed to be a fun, even frivolous, event, a fund-raiser for local charities, but Steve took it very seriously.

In the end, Russell allowed himself to be bullied into it. Applying Washington's rationale for the party, he told himself this was as good a way as any of showing that he wasn't down-and-out; the game was virtually the only public event of the season out here, most functions taking place behind tall hedges, at the end of gated driveways manned by security guards with guest lists on clipboards.

"I'm glad you're playing," Corrine said. "I'll be over after I drop the kids off at the Toomeys'."

By the time the first ball was thrown out by an Iraq vet with prosthetic legs, some five hundred spectators had gathered along the first and third baselines. Color commentary was provided by Tim Watkins, the NBC correspondent, who introduced Russell as "editor extraordinaire and Most Valuable Player in 2004."

He started as catcher and hit a hard grounder for a single in the second inning. Corrine arrived as he was donning his mask for the third inning. Three plays later, with the bases loaded, Tom Jarrow, the artist, whacked a high fly into center field. Russell ripped off his mask and took a wide stance over home plate. The runners held their bases until the center fielder made the catch and threw the ball to the second baseman, who spun and threw it to Russell as the runner on third charged in. It wasn't a great throw and Russell had to reach high for it as he kept his foot on the plate. Though he was confident the ball was within reach, it somehow tipped the top edge of his glove and bounced off, hitting the backstop as the runner scored home. Russell couldn't believe he'd blown the catch, and the shock of it paralyzed him even as he registered the runner from second base approaching at full speed; he felt as if he were swimming through mud as he launched himself toward the backstop and finally snatched the ball just as the second guy sailed over home plate for another run.

The hubbub from the artists' side of the field underscored the terrible silence on his own side. No one said a word as Russell threw the ball back to the pitcher.

The writers were stoic as the next batter drove in the last man on base, giving the artists a two-run lead. When the inning finally ended with the next batter popping up, Russell had no choice but to remove his catcher's mask and join his teammates on the third baseline, standing among them like an invisible man, a pariah, as they encouraged one another with formulaic exhortations. But after four innings of steady hits, his side went down in quick succession—three batters and three outs—as if his error had disheartened and deflated them.

"I'm putting Riley in as catcher," Steve told him as the writers took the field. Benched for the rest of the game and thus denied an opportunity for redemption, Russell felt himself excluded from the camaraderie of the dugout, the backslaps and the high fives. He found himself wishing the artists would widen their lead beyond two runs, the margin of his error, but in the end that's what the writers lost by, and while no one expressed the sentiment, he knew they all thought he'd lost the game.

"You have to let the artists win once in a while," Corrine said, taking his arm as they retreated to the parking lot. "I mean, haven't you guys won the last three years?"

"Please don't try to cheer me up," Russell snapped. "That was possibly the most mortifying moment of my adult life," he added.

"Oh, come on, it's just a game."

"No, it's not. It's never just a game."

Two weeks later, their friends came out in force, including Steve Goldberg, who made no reference to the game. What he could not have predicted was the number of strangers who showed up, some in the company of invitees and some simply drawn by the buzz, like fish responding to chum in the water. A rock star with a home down the street arrived with a brand-new girlfriend on his arm—a debut that dominated the coverage of the party in the gossip press, which identified the mystery woman as a celebrity spinning instructor who'd previously been involved with the former wife of a hedge fund manager.

More significant to Russell were the graying literary lions who paid their respects. As the night progressed, the new arrivals became younger and less familiar, a fistfight broke out between romantic rivals, and the booze ran out just as the cops arrived in response to complaints from the neighbors.

The success of the party briefly revived Russell's spirits, although the hangover the next morning and the eventual bill for damage and cleanup quickly dampened them, as did, later, after they'd returned to the city, the description of him in *New York* magazine's paragraph on the party as "the editor behind the recent faux hostage scandal."

38

WHERE? WHAT?

She woke feeling anxious, as if she'd left some mundane but important task unfinished the day before, and it wasn't until she turned on the news that she was reminded of the date. Outside, according to the local Eyewitness News team, it was once again sunny and clear, as it had been that brilliant, balmy day seven years ago, with its cleansing breeze from the west, which bent the plumes of smoke from the towers east toward Brooklyn and beyond, as if pointing toward the ultimate source of the destruction. Russell had already fed the children and taken them up to their new school.

She carried her coffee to the front of the loft, looking out the windows, which needed washing, past the fire escape at the brilliant slot of blue sky where the twin towers had once loomed. Her phone chirped as she sipped her coffee. The caller ID showed Luke's number.

"Are you back in the city?"

"Indeed," Luke said. "Would it be disrespectful to say 'Happy Anniversary'?"

"Actually, we met on the twelfth," she said.

This summer he'd been traveling in Europe with his daughter and winding things down at the winery in South Africa, which he was in the process of selling. They'd spoken frequently, but she hadn't seen him since just before she'd moved out to the Hamptons, and he hadn't bombarded her with proposals.

"Can we meet for a drink?"

"Is that a euphemism?"

"If you want it to be, it is."

"Where?"

"You could come here, see my new place. I've sublet a loft in SoHo."

"Well, that's certainly convenient," she said. "I can't tonight, we've got a screening."

"Tomorrow night, then."

It would have been simpler, less nerve-racking, less fatal to her sense of the innocence of her intentions, to go to Luke directly from the office. She'd already told Russell that morning that she was having drinks with her colleague Sandy, preparing her excuse in advance. Yet here she was again in front of the vanity, having left work early, touching up her makeup and her hair. As she waited for Russell to get home, she gave herself a final check in the mirror and was startled when she saw Storey framed in the glass, behind her.

"Gosh, you scared me."

"Where are you going?"

"I'm having a drink with Sandy, from work. She's getting married."

Storey seemed on the verge of delivering some sort of challenge, but then she turned and disappeared.

When Corrine emerged from the bedroom, Russell was at the kitchen counter, pouring Maker's Mark into a glass. It was not a festive cocktail, but a palliative one—such was clear from his drawn mouth and drooping posture.

"Are you going out?"

"Meeting Sandy for drinks. Remember?"

"Oh, right."

"You're awfully dressed up for just Sandy," Storey said.

"I've had this dress for ages," Corrine said, trying to control the timbre of her voice.

"Why are you wearing your black lace bra?" Storey said.

"What? How could you possibly know what bra I'm wearing?"

"I saw it laid out on your bed."

She froze, trying to decide whether to deny the charge, but Russell seemed indifferent.

"You only wear that bra on date nights with Dad."

"Sometimes it makes me feel better to wear something nice underneath. Especially when I don't feel like going out. It's a way of psyching myself up."

That Storey's suspicions were essentially correct only served to exasperate Corrine. Why was she so mistrustful and hostile to her own mother? So bitchy? She clearly sensed something was not as it should be. Corrine had always worried about Russell finding out, imagined the scenes and the possible outcomes, but the idea that one of her children might discover her secret had somehow never occurred to her. And had Russell just now turned and walked to the couch, plunking himself down in front of the news, because he was suspicious, or angry? Or was he utterly oblivious? The latter, she decided, when she walked over to check, ostensibly to bid him farewell. He was watching something on CNBC about Lehman Brothers—the company logo plastered at the top of the screen above a bunch of talking heads. Jeremy plopped down beside his father. She kissed them both on the top of the head.

Storey allowed herself to be kissed on the cheek. Corrine couldn't think of anything to say to her; instead, she tried out an indulgent smile that was meant to indicate tolerant bemusement. If she thought she was going to shame Corrine into changing her course of action, she was entirely mistaken.

Decanted from the cab into the glistening street, contemplating the entrance of the building, she felt a weird frisson of recognition. She was almost certain she'd been here many years ago, visiting Jeff—thought she recognized the elaborately ornamented cast-iron facade and Corinthian columns framing the tall, arched windows, although the building she remembered had had a filthy, sooty facade, with rust showing through the peeling paint. But, of course, the neighborhood had been transformed, like the rest of the city. It sort of made her sad, how polished and prosperous and tasteful it had become, like the streets of

SoHo, the real art galleries long ago replaced by shopping mall versions selling mass editions of Erté and Dalí and Chagall to the tourists—as if gentrification were a disservice to Jeff's memory, as if everything should have stayed dirty and dangerous forever.

Beside the door, in place of the series of assorted buzzers and doorbells mounted on plywood that she thought she remembered was a sleek stainless-steel panel with five identical buttons, each with an apartment number engraved beside it. Pressing 5, as instructed, she remembered Jeff leaning out of a window four or five stories up, throwing down a piece of wood with a key attached by a chain.

Luke's metallic voice on the intercom: "Come in. I'll send the elevator down for you."

There hadn't been an elevator then, had there? Or if there had been, it was broken, like practically everything else in the city back then. She recalled a long, ramshackle staircase, rising and receding toward the back of the building.

Luke was waiting at the elevator door, which opened directly into the loft. "Welcome."

She wasn't sure how it would feel to see him, but once she kissed him, everything came back to her.

He beckoned her inside with a broad sweep with his left arm to encompass the wide-open space, the high ceilings supported by a central colonnade of Corinthian columns with tall, arched windows on either end. Unlikely as it was, it might have been the same apartment, but she couldn't be certain. The furniture was haute loft—two chrome and leather Corbusier sofas, Marcel Breuer chairs. Big colorful Frank Stella geometric prints on the far wall, along with an Andy Warhol flower series litho and a big abstract color-field painting she couldn't identify. This could be any loft in SoHo, she thought, or, for that matter, in any city in the country.

"It came furnished," he said, observing her scrutiny. "Though the owner removed the expensive artwork and put it in storage. Apparently, he had a Bacon. All in all, not particularly original, I admit."

"No, it's nice," she said. "It's just, for a minute I thought I'd been here before."

"It does have what the realtor called a 'state-of-the art kitchen,' complete with a cappuccino machine and a wine cooler. Could I offer you a glass of champagne?"

"Yes, please." It was something to do, a way of postponing serious conversation or action. She didn't really know what she wanted and yet felt drawn to him, if only, perhaps, out of a long-standing habit, a Pavlovian reflex, whereby opportunity, rarely as it came, was inevitably seized. Given so little time together, they could hardly afford to waste any.

She followed him into the kitchen area and watched him unwrap the foil and untwist the wire.

"Don't you have a friend who works at Lehman Brothers?" he asked, grabbing the bottle with one hand and the cork with the other.

"Veronica Lee."

"Has she said anything? You know they're on the verge of going under." The pop of the cork seemed inappropriately festive.

"Oh God, I heard something about that, but I haven't had a chance to talk to her lately."

"The stock's cratering and they can't find a buyer. Unless they get a bailout, I'd say she's about to be unemployed—along with thousands of other people." He poured two glasses of bubbly and carried them over to a nearly invisible coffee table in front of one of the sofas, motioning for her to sit. "Do you own any stock?"

"Not Lehman, but I own some others."

She did have a secret little portfolio, a rainy day fund she'd never told Russell about, at first because it didn't seem worth mentioning, and, later, because it had grown just enough that she felt guilty about it, though not quite substantial enough for the down payment on the house in Harlem.

"I'm liquidating a lot of my portfolio, and you should, too. Financials especially. This will be the biggest man-made disaster since 9/11."

"That sounds alarmist."

"Let's hope." He sat down beside her on the couch.

She felt her pulse picking up, a flush rising on her face. "So what's happened with the foundation?" she asked. "Will you keep it going?"

"I've hired a new exec director. And I'll stay involved."

As he was pouring her another glass of champagne, he leaned over and kissed her, catching her by surprise, hooking his arm behind her on the couch and pulling her shoulder toward him, kissing her gently as she gradually eased into the kiss. She wasn't quite prepared for this and yet her body was responding without reference to her scruples, reacting to his familiar earthy scent as much as to the pressure of his hands and his lips. As he parted her lips with his tongue, she felt herself surrendering, leaning into him and pressing her breast into his hand, kissing him back, her body moving heedlessly forward along the rails of habit, unbuckling his belt and undoing the little clip in the front of his chinos, unzipping him without breaking her lock on his lips, while he, in turn, undressed her.

"That was amazing," Luke said, afterward.

"It was. I keep hoping it will go away."

"What?"

"This . . . desire bordering on compulsion."

"Why would you want it to go away?"

"Because it's complicating my life."

"So uncomplicate it. Move in with me."

"Yeah, that would simplify everything. But where, exactly, would I put the kids?"

He looked around. "It's only a sublet. I don't plan to stay here long."

"That would be a real aphrodisiac—you and me and my two children."

"You've got to make a choice sooner or later."

"Why? Isn't this enough?"

"You were the one who said it was complicated."

She sat up and started to gather her clothing. "If you'd stayed married, it would've been much simpler."

"Let's go back to the Berkshires next weekend," he said.

"We just got back from the Hamptons," she said, pulling on her dress.

"Then the weekend after."

She kissed his forehead. Suddenly, she realized, she couldn't wait to get home to her husband and children.

She hoofed it down Mercer Street, regretting her choice of heels, dodging her way through the drunken Friday night malingerers, pausing for breath at Kate Spade and setting off again before landing a clueless cabbie, who took her east on Canal toward Broadway, as opposed to West Broadway.

She half-expected to be greeted at home by an accusatory daughter and husband, but in fact, the household was asleep: Storey in her bed, wheezing softly; Jeremy silent in the boy-funky dark of his own room; and Russell snoring in bed, manuscript pages splayed on his chest— a sight that struck her as almost unbearably poignant and blessedly familiar.

39

A THREE-BOOK CONTRACT DESERVED to be celebrated with a three-night bender—that was Jack's feeling. Whether he'd ever complete three more books was a mystery he chose not to plumb too deeply. Highly unlikely at this rate. For the third night running, he found himself at the Beatrice Inn, sitting at the bar drinking vodka and watching the pretty club kids dance and snort and smoke. Cara had brought him here a few months ago and it had become a habit. Crazy fucking Cara, who found him any kind of drug he wanted and let him fuck her any way he wanted. Just last night, she'd gone down on him in the bathroom here while he was bumping up. But after two nights, he needed a break and had told her he was busy. He'd picked up this groupie girl at KGB and had had sex with her back at her apartment, but afterward he was still wide awake, and he'd ended up at the Beatrice. He was still trying to decide if he liked the place or not, but the fact that they let him in and let him do pretty much anything once there gave him incentive to approach the question with an open mind. Certainly low-down enough to suit his tastes, it looked and smelled like a dive. A smoky basement full of pretty, skinny skanks and hipster boys with clunky glasses and Chuck Taylor low-tops. Everybody smoking like it was 1948 and snorting coke off their keys, off the backs of their hands, off the top of the toilet tank in the bathroom, like it was 1984. X-heads with pinwheel eyes sucking lollipops after dropping disco biscuits. It was pretty much anything goes. Some celebrities, who seemed to behave themselves better than the party monsters. And old friends he'd made last night or the night before, including that painter Tony Duplex, who seemed to be on a tear after several years of—or so Jack had been told—yakking about his struggle against addiction. Here he was again, all dressed up in some kind of tight red suit with white winklepicker shoes that almost disguised how ragged and strung out he was—sunken eyes, dilated pupils.

"Hey, Jack, whassup?"

"Same old."

"You wouldn't be holding, would you?"

"Barely. I was thinkin' about calling my man Kyle."

"That'd be cool."

"You got a place we could meet him?" To score the drugs and do them here, he decided, was just too fucking complicated.

"Send him to my loft."

"Cool."

Twenty minutes later, they were at Tony's so-called loft, an entire building on West 27th, where he lived and worked. A bleary-eyed assistant opened the door for them, clad in a paint-stained chef's coat. Several unfinished paintings hung on the wall, dozens more stacked in racks. Another assistant was sleeping on a futon in a corner, curled under a dirty quilted duvet. A yellow Lamborghini Gallardo was parked in the middle of the space.

"Used to be a truck depot," Tony said.

"I should bring my truck here," Jack said.

"You got a truck?"

"Back in Tennessee. Black Chevy Silverado 1500 Double Cab."

"You can park it here anytime."

A metal staircase led up to the living area, a kind of a mezzanine loft within the loft, furnished with antiques, Chinese porcelain and Persian carpets, except for the kitchen area, which was stridently industrial. Jack had called the dealer from the Beatrice, and while they waited for him, they snorted the last of his stash. Jack laid out the lines while Tony put New Order's *Substance* in the CD player.

Tony found a bottle of Ketel One and filled two faceted crystal goblets with vodka. "You ever mainlined?"

"A guy's got to have some boundaries," Jack said. "I figure you're safe as long as you just snort. You?"

How does it feel to treat me like you do.

"A little. Just chipping. Rock was my downfall. I discovered freebasing round about '85 and that was my heaven and my hell. Me and Richard Pryor. Did it with him, too. The ritual of making it was part of the cult—it was a fucking ceremony. Dissolving the coke in water, adding the ammonia, stirring, precipitating out the impurities and finally the coke itself. That was the real deal. Nothing like it. Then crack came along, which was a kind of mass-market knockoff, an inexpensive shortcut, the Kmart version. But it was easy, it was cheap, it was insanely addictive. Making freebase became a lost art, like *affresco* painting."

"Whatever the fuck that is."

"It's like wet plaster fresco painting. Giotto perfected it. Freebase—that's like his Cappella degli Scrovegni."

"Whatever."

"Then crack came along and fucked everything up."

Jack checked his phone for texts and messages. "Maybe I should call him again."

"Good idea."

But the call went straight to voice mail. "Waitin' on the man, part five hundred."

"I hate dealers," Tony said.

"Scum of the earth."

"Are you sure this guy's coming?"

"He said he was."

"How long did he say?"

"He said twenty minutes. But that was thirty minutes ago."

"Dealer time. It's like dog years."

"Don't I fuckin' know it."

"Did he say where he was?"

"He said he was uptown."

"Shit, that could be anywhere. Did he say where uptown? Like Harlem uptown?"

"Just said he was on his way downtown."

"You can't believe any fucking thing a dealer says."

"Yeah, but what choice do we have, really?"

"We could just say no to drugs. You're probably too young to remember that whole fucking campaign. That was Nancy Reagan's big slogan in the eighties. 'Just say no.'"

"How'd that work out?"

"The drugs wouldn't take no for an answer."

"Maybe I should call him again."

"Definitely."

Jack dialed again, listened to the voice-mail prompt. "Fucker won't pick up."

"I know a guy," Tony said. "But he's up in Harlem, and we have to go to him."

"Man, that's a logistical nightmare."

Tony pointed to the car on the main floor. "This time of night, it's ten minutes in the Lambo up the West Side Highway, tops."

This sounded like a bad idea, but Jack was getting desperate, and he'd never let the fact of being impaired keep him from going somewhere to get more impaired.

Tony's assistant tried to stop them, but Tony insisted he was fine to drive and told him to crank the garage door open. Jack folded himself into the snug embrace of the cockpit as the engine roared to life.

40

STOREY HAD BEEN BEHAVING strangely all morning; she seemed agitated, on edge. Russell had roused Corrine, flexing that sense of superiority that accrued to the partner who'd gone to bed early, and requested her presence at the table, though he knew she didn't eat in the morning. Storey was rude to her mother at breakfast, which seemed to be the norm of late. She was feeling kind of insecure about the new school, granted, but this had been going on for months. Russell had called her on it. "Don't talk to your mother that way," he said, prompting her to flee the table in tears.

Later, after Corrine went out for a run, Storey marched out to the kitchen, where Russell was finishing the dishes, her lips drawn into a frown.

"What's up, honey?"

"It's about Mom."

"Yeah?"

"She's having an affair."

"What? That's crazy." Yet, somehow, he suddenly felt sick to his stomach.

"I found an e-mail."

"What were you doing in your mom's e-mail?"

"I was looking for a scrunchie for my hair. Her laptop was open on her desk. I'll show you."

Feeling light-headed, he followed her to the master bedroom. Corrine's AOL window was open, and the most recent e-mail, sent twenty minutes ago, was from someone called Luke, with the subject line *Last night was amazing.*

"I *knew* she wasn't going to see Sandy. And I've heard them talking on the phone." Her lower lip quivered with the effort she was making to contain her emotions, but finally she started sobbing violently.

He took her in his arms, trying not to cry himself.

"What are you going to do?" she eventually managed to say.

"It's going to be all right," Russell said with paternal insincerity. He had no idea what he was going to do. "You say you've heard her talking on the phone to this . . . guy."

She nodded. "Luke."

He didn't think he knew any Lukes. Stupid name. Was it better that it was a stranger? "When did you hear them talking?"

"A couple times."

"Starting when?"

"Maybe, like, six months ago."

"Have you ever seen him?"

"I don't think so."

"You really shouldn't be spying on your mother."

He could see immediately that he'd disappointed her, but he was still living in a prelapsarian universe in which the old rules applied.

Jeremy barreled in to announce that Washington and his kids had arrived. "What's wrong?" he asked, picking up on the gloom.

"Nothing's wrong," Russell told him. "Did you buzz them up?"

"Uh-huh. I better go out and wait for them," he said, running out of the room.

"Let's just keep this to ourselves for now," Russell said, giving Storey a hug.

"Okay."

"Go wash your face and then come join us."

As long as Storey had been in the room, he'd been able to treat this new knowledge as theoretical, but now it became physical. Finding it difficult to breathe, feeling nauseous, he sat down on the bed, hyperventilating. She'd betrayed him with a man named Luke. Was she really capable of treating him this way? Sleeping beside him while fucking a man named Luke. Lying to Russell, lying beneath a man named Luke. It was intolerable. Luke who—Skywalker? The apostle? *Bastard*. He didn't think he could bear it. He looked at the e-mail again: *Last night was amazing.* Just four words had changed the course of his life, cast doubt on his most fundamental beliefs.

Being married to Corrine was the central fact of his existence. After all these years, he'd imagined they were inseparable, their union inviolable. He went to the hamper in her closet and rooted through the dirty clothes, lifting a pair of panties and examining them for evidence before moving on to her lingerie drawer, finding the bra that had aroused Storey's suspicions on top. He pulled it out and held it up by its straps. Did *he* take it off her last night, or did she take it off while he watched? In fact, he noticed that some of the lace at the top of the cup was frayed, as if it had been torn off in haste. He held it to his nostrils, inhaling the unmistakable scent of Corrine, then tugged at the lace, ripping half the cup open before regaining control of his emotions. The bra was not so damaged as to suggest vandalism unequivocally. He needed time to think, to consider his response.

He heard Washington and the boys outside the door, chattering in a language he was no longer certain he spoke, or comprehended. How could he possibly go out there and pretend that he did? That he was the same man he'd been ten minutes before?

On a sudden, malicious impulse, he hung the bra over the screen of the laptop and walked out into the hall, pulling the door closed behind him.

"Sorry to crash in on you, chief, but I have the kids for the day, Veronica's at a meeting at the office, and I've flat run out of ideas."

Russell nodded, not trusting himself to speak.

"You okay? I guess you heard about Jack."

"What? Jack Carson?"

"Yeah, he ... I assumed you'd heard. Jack and Tony Duplex. High-speed crash on the West Side Highway early this morning."

"Is he okay?"

Washington shook his head.

"He's dead?"

Washington nodded. "Both dead."

"Tony Duplex? How do they even know each other?" Russell was shocked, though, as the news sunk in, he realized he'd always, in the back of his mind, feared something like this would happen.

"I thought you knew, man," Wash said, presumably referring to Russell's shell-shocked demeanor, for which, now at least, he had a plausible explanation.

For a moment he considered confiding in Washington, but quickly discarded the idea. He wasn't ready to share his humiliation. He couldn't bear the idea of anyone else knowing, at least not yet. Perhaps, especially, his best friend.

"Jesus Christ—Jack's really dead?"

"I wish I could say I was totally shocked," Washington said.

"Yeah, but still."

"I know."

"It was an accident?"

"They were in Tony's Lamborghini."

"Fucking lunatics."

Washington stepped forward and hugged Russell, slapping his shoulders blades gruffly. "I'm really sorry, man."

If he only knew.

"So it looks like the girls want to go to a movie and the boys want to stay here and play video games. Big surprise. Anyway, your choice, coach. I have to warn you, though, the movie is *Nights in Rodanthe*. I've got an invite to a screening at the TriBeCa Grand. On the plus side, you have Diane Lane, but weighing heavily against it—the fact that it's based on a Nicholas fucking Sparks novel."

Much as he wanted to get out of the house, Russell didn't think he could possibly sit through a romantic tearjerker. Neither could he imagine seeing Corrine right now. He couldn't honestly think of any activity or any known conscious state that would make this pain bearable, as the knowledge of all that had happened before Washington arrived came rushing back over him. Sad as he was about Jack, he felt he could bear that. "In that case, why don't you go with the girls," he said.

"Thanks a bunch. You're sure you're okay?"

"I'm okay. I'll watch the boys."

He felt unsteady, his legs weak. He tested them, walking down the hall to the living area, where the boys were sitting on the couch, staring at the TV screen, each thumbing his own video game controller.

Just then, the elevator door slid open and Corrine emerged in her running gear. In the light of his new knowledge, he half-expected her to look different, but she looked much as she had when she went out forty minutes ago, only sweaty and flushed. With her hair pulled back in a ratty bun, chest flattened in a running bra, she certainly didn't look like anyone's mistress.

He didn't know if he could face her, until he did.

"It's so humid out there," she said.

So, there was still weather.

"Wash came over with the kids," he said.

"That would explain why he's standing there next to you. Don't hug me," she said to Washington. "I'm all gross and sweaty."

"Sweaty's good," Washington said.

Sweaty was not good. Sweaty was a word that summoned images of Corrine engaged in carnal congress. It was a horrible word. Before he could turn his mind around, he couldn't help picturing Corrine in several lurid tableaux.

"What's wrong?" she asked, examining his expression.

"Jack's dead," Washington said helpfully.

"He got killed in a crash on the West Side Highway early this morning," Russell added.

"Oh, honey, that's terrible. I'm so sorry," she said, embracing him. He found himself flinching from her touch, and it had nothing to do with the sweat. "You must be devastated."

"I'm not sure what I feel."

"Poor baby," she said. "What can I do?"

Washington said, "Any chance you want to take the girls to see *Nights in Rodanthe,* starring Mr. Richard Gere?"

"Thanks, but I have to go to Union Square to supervise the Greenmarket rescue."

"What," he asked, "or should I say *whom*, is the Greenmarket being rescued *from*?"

"We rescue, so to speak, unsold produce and food products from the farmers' stalls at the end of the sales day, before it gets dumped in the garbage. How's Veronica holding up?"

Washington shrugged. "She's freaking out."

"Surely they can't let Lehman go under."

"We'll know soon," Wash said.

"Russ, I hope you're good to watch the boys," Corrine said.

He nodded reflexively as she walked past him on her way to the bedroom, realizing suddenly that he had no idea if this was the truth—if she was really going to the market. How many times had she lied to him? How many times had she gone out under some pretext to see Luke? Fucking *Luke*. He couldn't decide whether to be relieved that he wouldn't have to spend time with her right now, or outraged by the possibility that she was embarking on another rendezvous with this Luke. Would she be wearing her bra? The goddamn bra.

Waiting for the elevator with the two girls, Washington said, "I'll give your love to Diane."

Russell wondered how long it would take Corrine to notice the bra on the laptop. Would she see the e-mail? He realized it had probably come in after she'd gone out for her run, since she wouldn't have left it there on the screen. Would she put the two ostensibly disparate pieces of evidence together? Ripped bra, incriminating e-mail? This prospect brought, if not exactly pleasure, at least a brief cessation of pain. Did he want her to suffer? Yes, he decided, he did, just as he was suffering.

He managed to avoid her for much of the next hour, before she finally left for wherever she was going, and apparently she was just as eager to avoid him. Jeremy and Mingus, meanwhile, were lost in a make-believe world that he found himself envying.

He poured himself a glass of vodka and sat at the kitchen counter, where he was still sitting when Washington and the girls came home.

"How was the movie?"

"It was pretty good, but she was kind of old," Storey said, opening the refrigerator.

"They were both old," Zora said.

"Hey, Diane Lane is nine years younger than your distinguished dads," Washington said.

Zora cocked her head and regarded him with mild curiosity, as if waiting for the rest of his rebuttal, then followed Storey back to her bedroom, the boys following in their wake.

"You want a drink?" Russell asked.

"I'm good," said Washington. "Are you really okay? You looked all fucked-up."

"I found an e-mail. I think Corrine's having an affair."

"*Corrine?*"

"I don't know what to do."

"You're sure about this?"

"Pretty sure."

Suddenly the boys burst out of their room and charged back into the room, brandishing plastic swords.

"I've gotta get them home. Let me know if you want to catch a drink later."

Russell nodded.

"Damn," Washington said. "I can't say I saw this one coming." He hugged Russell, slapping him on the back, before herding his kids into the elevator.

"Why did Washington hug you?" Jeremy asked as the doors closed.

"We do that sometimes," Russell said.

For the rest of the afternoon, Jeremy acted as if he sensed something amiss, while his sister seemed eager to preserve the illusion of normalcy, although later, when the two of them were alone, she asked her father what he was going to do.

"I don't know yet."

"Are you going to get divorced?"

The word, uttered aloud, was shocking. As he tried to formulate an answer, he saw the tears welling in his daughter's eyes. He took her in his arms and held her. "I wonder if Diane Lane is single?" he said.

41

STILL STUNNED BY THE NEWS about Jack Carson, Corrine was peeling off her jogging clothes in the bedroom when she noticed her bra hanging from the laptop, which seemed odd. She remembered putting it away last night. Lifting it up, she saw that the cup was torn. Hasty as it had been, her disrobing at Luke's hadn't been violent, and she recalled it was intact when she'd taken it off again, later, at home.

She glanced at the computer screen and saw a new message from Luke: *Last night was amazing.* When had *that* come in? It hadn't been there when she'd logged on. And how could she have forgotten to log off? She erased Luke's e-mail, even as she realized that it was probably too late. How else to explain the bra on the laptop?

Had Russell seen that message? Oh God, please don't let him have.

She'd attributed his dazed aspect to Jack's death, but now she saw, to her horror, another explanation—but it was too terrible to consider. What was she supposed to do? How could she possibly face him? She couldn't. It seemed preferable to throw herself out the window.

She tried to think of an innocent explanation for the e-mail. Could she just deny? She'd been lying for so long, why not just keep on? And yet she knew she couldn't. It was over. The only way she could possibly even *start* to redeem herself was to begin telling the truth. Or at least stop lying, which was significantly different. If she told him the whole truth, she was afraid their marriage wouldn't stand a chance.

But what to do right now, at this moment? She couldn't imagine walking out there and facing him now that Washington was gone. Or was he? If Wash was still here, she could at least get out the door without a confrontation, and then consider her options.

She slunk across the hall to the bathroom, not seeing anyone, hearing only the beeps and chirps of a video game. In the shower, she wept, and curled into a ball on the tiles, wishing she could dissolve and disappear down the drain, to be spared the shame and the mortification, the horror of facing Russell and seeing the accusation and the hurt in his eyes. She prayed for a brief respite, a postponement of the inevitable. She hoped to escape the loft without incident, so that she could have time to formulate a response while going about her business at the Greenmarket, though she wondered how she could possibly concentrate on the simplest of tasks, much less present a socially viable front.

Ten minutes later, she thought her knees would buckle as she came upon him in the living room, sitting motionless in the armchair beside the couch, watching a football game, which was strange, since he seldom watched sports. Seeing the look on his face when he glanced at her, she realized it wasn't so much his expression as the sense that he was clearly trying to suppress his feelings, that his contemptuous smirk was a mask that barely concealed more frightening emotions.

"I'll be back in a few hours," she said.

He turned back to the television without answering.

Arriving at Union Square in a daze after missing her subway stop, she tried to immerse herself in the simple tasks of schmoozing the farmers and herding the volunteers, but throughout the afternoon she felt almost paralyzed with remorse and dread. Though she tried to convince herself that Russell knew nothing, she couldn't help believing the opposite. Not knowing was agony. At one moment she wanted to plead illness and rush home and the next she wanted to postpone her return for as long as possible.

Finally unable to bear it another second, she deputized one of the volunteers to finish the rescue and grabbed a cab downtown.

When she arrived home, Russell was sitting alone at the kitchen counter. As soon as she saw his face, she knew she was busted.

"The kids are with Washington and Veronica. I didn't want them around for this."

She didn't even have the heart to ask what *this* meant? She stood with her head bowed, waiting.

"Are you having an affair?"

Even though she knew this was coming, Corrine thought her knees would buckle beneath her.

"I was."

"You *were*."

"Russell, I can't even begin to tell you how sorry I am, and ashamed."

"Who's Luke?"

"Does it matter?"

"Of course it fucking matters."

"You met him at the benefit for his charity at the Waldorf. Luke McGavock. He started the Good Hope Foundation."

"Jesus Christ, that was, like, two years ago. Has it been going on all that time?"

"He was living in South Africa. I only saw him a few times."

"*Saw him.* It sounds like you did a hell of a lot more than see him."

"Russell, I'm so so sorry."

"I want you to leave."

"Can't we talk about this?"

"We just did. I want you out. Pack a bag. I don't want you under this roof."

"Russell . . ."

"I mean it. Get out."

She hardly remembered packing the small bag she was carrying when she arrived at Luke's building. It hadn't occurred to her to wonder what she'd do if he wasn't there.

"Oh, Luke," she said, starting to sob when she saw his face.

"What's happened?" he asked, taking her in his arms.

When she finally gathered the composure to blurt out her story, he seemed nonplussed. "I suppose it was inevitable," he said.

Holding her arm as if she were an invalid, he walked her over to the couch. The financial news channel was blaring from the big TV on the wall. A crawling banner at the bottom of the screen read: LEHMAN STOCK IN FREE FALL, MARKETS IN TURMOIL. He picked up the remote from the coffee table and muted the volume.

"Tell me exactly what happened, my love," he said, taking a seat beside her.

As she started talking, he glanced up at the television screen. And later, she would realize that was the moment he lost her. Not that he'd actually possessed her up until then, or that she even for a moment had considered what the recent crisis meant for her relationship with Luke, but as they spoke, it became clear that he had, that in his eyes the exposure of the affair was an opportunity rather than a calamity. Later, she could think of a fistful of reasons why she couldn't be with Luke; he was a man who was used to having his way, a man who moved from conquest to conquest. She believed he loved her, but she didn't necessarily believe in the durability of that love. He was *Déjeuner sur l'Herbe* and she was *Interior at Arcachon*. Ultimately, she would understand and enumerate her reasons for giving him up—the most elementary one being that he wasn't Russell, but also because at that crucial moment he'd turned away from her and was looking instead at the television screen.

She would stay for another hour, and Luke would try to convince her that, painful as it might be for Corrine and her family, Russell's discovery was as the lancing of a boil, a slicing of the Gordian knot, a fortuitous resolution of a lingering quandary. Now, he suggested, the primary obstacle between them had been cleared away, and while, yes, it wouldn't be an effortless transition, he was here to make it as painless as possible. He spoke words of solace and comfort, holding her and expanding on their future, and through her agony she heard him distantly, his voice fading in and out of her consciousness, as if he were speaking to her across a body of water buffeted by intermittent gusts of wind.

42

RUSSELL TOOK A SORT OF perverse satisfaction from the economic crisis, feeling that his own personal misfortunes mirrored those of the nation, glancing at the banner headline of *The Wall Street Journal:* CRISIS ON WALL STREET AS LEHMAN TOTTERS, MERRILL IS SOLD, AIG SEEKS TO RAISE CASH. And flipping through the *Post,* a headline closer to home: DRIVE FAST, DIE YOUNG: BAD BOY ARTIST & AUTHOR IN FIERY CRASH. The night before, after Corrine had left with her suitcase, weeping, and the kids, whom Washington had brought back home, had gone to sleep, Russell sprawled on the couch, watching the controlled hysteria of the commentators on CNBC. He raised a tumbler of Maker's Mark to the screen and toasted: "Let it all come down, baby."

In the morning, he woke up on the couch with a dry mouth and a piercing, almost unbearable awareness of Corrine's betrayal. He lay there, paralyzed with self-pity, until Jeremy came out to roust him and interrogate him about his mother's absence.

"Will she come home tonight?"

"We'll see. Now get dressed, or we'll be late for school." Russell wasn't emotionally prepared to discuss the situation this morning.

After taking the kids uptown to school in a taxi, he took the subway back down to the office. He didn't expect to accomplish much, but neither could he bear the thought of being alone in the loft all day. His staff, sensing his misery, attributed it to Jack's death, and after expressing their sympathy, they gave him a wide berth. He tried to imagine what he was supposed to do. He wanted to call Corrine and berate her, demand that she explain herself. He also wanted to punish her with silence, to make her suffer the agonies of wondering what he was thinking. In the meantime, the company's accountant called to tell him he needed cash by the end of the month, that their line of credit was tapped out. His best and perhaps only hope was Tom Reynes, with whom he had a meeting that afternoon.

As he hung up, Jonathan Tashjian appeared in the doorway. "Is this a bad time?" he asked, prompting Russell to laugh mirthlessly.

"Yes, it is," he said, "but come in anyway."

"I'm sorry about Jack."

"Not like we couldn't see it coming."

"You've got a lot of requests for comments and interviews."

"I'm really not in the mood today. Tell them to call Knopf. They're the official publisher now."

"We're the publisher of his first and so far only book and you're the guy who discovered him. Not to mention the fact we got more than three thousand orders this morning."

The effect of Jack's death on sales hadn't occurred to Russell until this moment. The inevitable spike might, if nothing else, buy the company some time. And talking to the press could raise McCane, Slade's profile and bolster the illusion that it was solvent, and relevant.

"Let's go through the requests," he said as Gita buzzed and announced that Phillip Kohout was on the line.

Jonathan's expression reflected his own feelings: distaste and disbelief. He hadn't spoken to Kohout once since the day the *Times* broke the story, though there had been many conversations with his agent, and his lawyers.

"Tell him to fuck off," Russell said.

He kept thinking Corrine would call at some point, but at the end of the day he was still waiting. Not that, if he were in her position, he'd know what to say. But it was her role to try, to beg for understanding and forgiveness.

A beautiful woman on the sidewalk, her shapeliness nicely defined by tight-fitting black yoga togs and a tank top in honor of Indian summer, turned out to be Hilary, lying in wait for him as he left the office. Russell paused in mid-step, mouth agape, unable to mask his surprise.

"You haven't returned my calls."

"I've got a lot going on, Hilary, in case you haven't heard."

"Yes, I'm sure you do."

"And I'm about to be late for an appointment."

"We need to talk."

"I think I said everything I wanted to say the last time we talked. I thought we agreed that it was a one-off. I gave you a month's rent. I thought you were going to get a job."

"I've been trying. That's one of the things I wanted to talk to you about. I'm applying for a job in PR at HBO and I need a recommendation. I know you know people there."

"I suppose I could do that."

"But I really need a loan in the meantime."

"Is that what you call it—a loan?"

"I'm desperate," she said, catching his wrist. "I'm going to be evicted."

"I'm desperate, too," he said. "You have no idea, Hilary. I'm at the end of my fucking rope. My friend Jack Carson just died and my wife's been fucking another guy for I don't know how long. I kicked her out of the loft, and the kids are a mess. My business is about to go under. And in case you've had your head up your ass and haven't heard, the whole global economy's headed into a meltdown."

The pedestrians were giving them a wide berth, glancing briefly at the shouting, gesticulating man in the blue blazer before veering away.

"Oh my God. Corrine's having an affair?"

"You didn't know?"

"I had no idea."

"So I don't really care if you tell her about my little peccadillo or not."

"Please. I'm just asking for a little help to see me through."

Russell reached for his wallet and removed two one-hundred-dollar bills, leaving only a twenty and some ones. "Here, that's it. That's most of my remaining net worth. Now piss off. I've had enough of the Make-peace girls to last a lifetime."

She seemed genuinely hurt, and as she turned away, he felt a twinge of guilt. Even now, as he watched her walk away, he was astonished, and mortified, that he still found her alluring. He'd always been attracted to her, but the fact that he could feel anything resembling lust in the wake of his crushing humiliation was practically miraculous, if not perverse.

Russell took the subway to 51st Street, just a short walk from the vener-able Brook Club, on 54th between Park and Lex. He'd been there only a few times—very blue-blood, old New York. George Plimpton had taken him there for lunch a few years ago, when they'd been working on an anthology of travel writing together that was unlikely to break even, much less cover the $35,000 advance. But it was an affordable gamble that he felt brought honor to his imprint as well as an opportunity to collaborate with one of the last American men of letters. When Plimp-ton failed to wake up one morning not long afterward, Russell was almost envious of the grace with which he'd departed, out with friends to a couple of cocktail parties, followed by dinner at Elaine's, slipping away in his sleep like a guest ducking out of the party without bother-ing anyone. A gentleman to the end, not wanting to make a fuss, or put anyone out, though several thousand souls took time out of their workday to attend his memorial at Saint John the Divine. And how many would come for me? Russell wondered. What Raymond Carver said in that poem of his—*to be beloved.* "And what did you want? To call myself beloved, to feel myself beloved on the earth."

Russell did not feel beloved on the earth.

Inside the lobby of the Brook, he presented himself to the liveried gent at the front desk, who told him that Mr. Reynes would meet him on the third floor. He took the circular staircase, noting an air of geri-atric decorum—or was it gloom?—among the members on the second floor. On the third floor, making his way to the front parlor, he detected a distinct undercurrent of melancholy in the murmuring convocation, several groups of two and three scattered around the room, sunken deeply into the sofas and club chairs, a faint honking akin to a flock of geese in the distance across a cornfield, the unmistakable whine of privileged white men with the blues. Russell suspected that most of them had lost a lot of money today, and that few of them were going to vote for Obama in November. Tom waved to him from a small table in the corner.

"Thanks for coming," he said. "Hell of a day. I'm going right back to the office after this, but I figured I needed a break. The fallout from this Lehman situation is brutal. Dow's down five hundred plus. Would you like a drink?" He looked tired, though by no means dispirited; indeed, he seemed cheery, as if invigorated by crisis.

He waved to the ancient server framed in the doorway.

"Hell of a weekend all round. All the big swinging dicks of banking huddled down at the Fed all weekend, trying to save Lehman and themselves. I lived through the crash of '87 and the dot-com bust, but I've never seen anything like this. Gonna get much much worse before it gets better."

The waiter hovered. Tom ordered a Bloody Mary and Russell decided it was probably a mistake to order a Negroni here. "I'll have a bullshot," he said—a manly, Waspy club drink to steel the nerves in the face of this onrushing bear market.

"I'm sorry about your, uh, situation," Tom said. "I ran into Corrine when I was picking up Amber. It seems she's staying with Casey."

"I asked her to leave," Russell said.

Tom leaned forward, nodding, uncharacteristically sympathetic and engaged. Or perhaps he was just curious to know what had happened.

"She's been having an affair. I just found out about it."

"God, I'm sorry."

Russell felt a sudden welling of emotion, a tightening of his facial muscles.

"What are you going to do?" Tom asked.

Russell shook his head. "Don't know yet. So what about you? Are you still getting divorced?"

Tom nodded. "Trying like hell to. It was a long time coming. But in the end, it just happened. Boom! Walk out a door straight into your future. You know as well as anyone that I wasn't so well behaved. But the really weird thing, the thing I wasn't expecting, I actually fell in love. It didn't even occur to me it was possible. And I can't tell you how great it feels. It was a huge relief, really, to find out Casey had been cheating on me. I mean, we have a lot of history together, and kids, and she's not a bad person, really, but I don't think anyone would accuse her of being deeply sentimental. That was part of the problem. I felt like our marriage was a business arrangement. Our parents grew up going to the same schools and belonging to the same clubs; we didn't have to bother to get to know each other, because we already did. I'm not sure I ever felt for Casey what I feel for Laura. In fact, I'm pretty sure I was never in love. Who knew you could discover love in your forties? Well, fifty-two, whatever."

Russell raised his glass, which the waiter had just placed in front of him. "Cheers, then. I'm happy for you."

"Thanks. She's an amazing woman. You should meet her sometime."

"Is it possible we already met? Or rather, that I saw her across a room?"

"It's possible," he said. "Though if you had, I trust I could count on your discretion not to say anything."

"Absolutely."

So Tom had fallen in love with a hooker.

"The thing is, this divorce could get messy, since we don't have a prenup. Can you believe it? Very old-fashioned. Or dumb. But Casey has money of her own and I'm hoping I can get her to be reasonable, though I have a feeling she's not going to make it easy. Anyway, long story short, my assets are pretty much frozen for the foreseeable future, not to mention the fact the economy has just turned to shit. Lehman's just the start of it. Money is going to get incredibly tight after this long binge of credit. The hangover is going to be heinous. I guess you see where I'm going with this. Sorry to say I can't make any kind of personal investments at this point. Anyway, I wish you every success and I wish I could be along for the ride."

Up until the last couple of sentences, his monologue had been surprisingly heartfelt and revealing. Only at the end, as the subject turned from love to money, had it become cliché-ridden and stilted. *Along for the ride?* Until a few moments ago, the collapse of a major investment bank had seemed somewhat remote, but now he felt a sinking, sickening feeling in his gut as he understood that he was collateral damage. He'd often told himself that he inhabited a world apart, that the machinations and fluctuations of the financial markets had nothing to do with him, and he was shocked to realize that he was deeply entangled in the current crisis. He'd always been a little scornful of that other world, the world of suits and money, but it turned out that devoting your career to letters didn't give you immunity.

"I always liked Corrine," Tom said before draining his drink and setting the glass down on the table. "I used to wonder how she put up with Casey."

"Now she's got no choice," Russell said bitterly.

As he was walking back to the subway Corrine called, her name on the screen of the cell phone surprising him, as if it were unfamiliar. He debated whether to answer.

"Yeah," he barked.

"It's me."

"I know. No surprises anymore." Did he have to explain mobile phone technology to her?

After a long pause, she said, "I just wanted to arrange to see the kids."

"When?"

"Maybe I could get them from school tomorrow, take them out for a bite."

"Fine," he said. "I'll tell Jean."

He thought about hanging up then, but he couldn't quite bring himself to do so.

"Russell?" she said, finally.

"Yeah?"

"I'm so sorry."

"Me too," he said, before closing his phone.

———

"I don't understand why Mom's staying with Casey," Jeremy said, brandishing a nubbly golden chicken finger. Russell had cooked his favorite childhood meal in the vague hope of normalizing a painfully abnormal domestic situation.

"They're having issues," Storey said.

"What issues?"

"We just decided that we needed to spend some time apart while we worked on some aspects of our relationship." God, that was stilted, he realized.

"Are you guys getting divorced?"

"No, we're not. We're just taking a breather."

Jeremy chewed moodily. "How come Storey seems to know what's going on?"

"I'm a girl. I notice things. I observe the people around me. You're a guy. You don't."

"Do we get to see Mom, at least?"

"Tomorrow afternoon," Russell said, "she's picking you up from school and taking you out."

"Out where?"

"I'm not sure; that's up to her."

"Why is everything happening at once?"

"What do you mean?"

"A bunch of kids' dads lost their jobs and everyone seems freaked-out about everything."

"It's a pretty scary time, son."

"Could you lose your job?"

"Well, publishing doesn't have that much to do with what happens on Wall Street," Russell said, wishing that this were actually the case. If the credit markets froze up, as seemed likely, his chances of survival were negligible. He had a strong premonition that everyone was going to get soaked and battered in the coming storm.

After saying good night to the kids, he lay down on the bed to watch the Giants play the Cowboys and fell asleep almost immediately, waking in the middle of the eleven o'clock news—just as a photo of a young Tony Duplex with his arm around Andy Warhol flashed on the screen, and then, to his astonishment, a shot of Jack Carson, looking uncomfortable in a tuxedo, standing next to Russell, that had been taken at the PEN/Faulkner Awards in D.C. the year before; this was soon replaced by scenes of anxious Lehman Brothers employees entering and exiting their midtown office building.

He slept intermittently that night, and woke up exhausted, enervated at the prospect of the day ahead and all the days beyond. The children, picking up on his mood, were frightened and solicitous.

He called Washington from the office and asked if he could meet for lunch. He arrived at the Fatted Calf half an hour early and ordered a Bloody Mary. He was halfway through his second when his friend arrived.

"You look like shit," Washington said, taking a seat across from Russell.

"That's good, because I *feel* like shit," Russell said.

"I guess you're entitled."

"How's Veronica?"

"Shell-shocked. Clearing out her office as we speak. Any word from Corrine?"

He shook his head. "We talked briefly about child-care logistics. She told me she was sorry." He shook his head derisively.

"She probably doesn't *know* what to say."

"It's hopeless," Russell said. "I don't even want to talk about it. Actually, I wanted to talk to you about something else."

"Whatever you want, coach."

"I want Corbin, Dern to buy McCane, Slade. I think it would be a win-win situation for both sides."

"It might make sense," Washington said after a long pause. "We'd have to look at the books. I promise to take it under advisement if you promise never to use the phrase *win-win* again."

As he was walking back to the office, he took a call from Hilary.

"I just wanted to tell you how sorry I am."

"Thanks. I'm sorry I was . . . unkind when I saw you yesterday."

"No, I understand. Look, I just wanted to say, if you ever need me to babysit, or anything, just call, okay?"

"Okay, thanks. I will."

"You promise?"

"Promise."

"All right, then."

"Thanks for calling."

43

Silver Meadows, New Canaan, CT.
10/27/08

Dear Russell:

I wanted to say how sorry I was about Jack, but really, that's the least of it. I'm not sure how to apologize for what I did to you, but I have to if I'm going to move on. Step 9. I'm up here at Silver Meadows, once again. Clearly I didn't learn much the last time. I thought if I tried to explain what happened, you might understand, though I don't expect you to forgive me. But I want at least to try to make amends. Where to begin? With the failure of my third novel? Returning from my sad little six-city book tour, I still had a kind of residual celebrity, which kept my social life interesting, and I turned to journalism. Because even if there'd been a demand for my fiction, I was utterly without inspiration.

And then the planes hit the towers. Ian McEwan summed it up the next day in *The Guardian:* "American reality always outstrips the imagination." Hard as it had been earlier, it was even harder now to imagine the role of fiction in this changed world. I wanted to be involved in the response to the most shocking event of my lifetime. But my various employers had their specialists: real journalists, foreign correspondents, policy experts. I tried to land an assignment in Afghanistan and then, later, Iraq. Even though I thought that war, the WMD war, was utterly fraudulent, I wanted to cover it, to swim the currents of history.

And suddenly, out of the blue, I got invited to a wedding in Lahore. The groom was from a wealthy Pakistani family, attended NYU and then became a fixture of the downtown party scene in the nineties, which is how I knew him. Always throwing parties, entertaining squads of models, sharing his drugs. He went home after 9/11 and settled down with a girl from his social class, though when I called him about the invitation, he said that the wedding festivities would resemble the New York bacchanals of his youth. "Lahore's insane, man. It's a party town. Come for the week. You won't regret it." This sounded attractive, and it occurred to me that I could turn the occasion to advantage. This could be my side-door entry into the great struggle.

I pulled together a list of contacts in Pakistan, journalists and government officials. My roommate from Amherst was an undersecretary of state, and after advising me not to go, he gave me phone numbers and briefings and deep background. I hoped to talk my way into some serious journalism about the Taliban and Pakistani politics; in the meantime, I had a single assignment for a travel piece about the city. So I embarked for Lahore, where the wedding was everything the groom had promised and more. Drugs were abundant and the festivities moved around town, from gated compounds to sprawling lofts. It's a majestic city with a patina of elegant decay, though I quickly gravitated toward its squalor. I met an English girl, a cousin of the groom's, and a week after the wedding the two of us were holed up in an apartment in the Gulberg neighborhood, where I discovered opium. Two weeks turned into four.

Marty Briskin eventually reported me missing. And the next thing I knew, the story was in the *Herald Tribune:* "American novelist missing, believed kidnapped, in Pakistan." When I'd failed to show up for an interview with a Pakistani intelligence operative, he'd called my friend at the State Department, and when Marty called the consulate, the search was on. Meanwhile, I got a text from the groom, asking if I was okay, telling me about the *Herald Trib.* A day later, there was a message on a jihadist Web site from a group that claimed it was holding me.

At first, it just seemed embarrassing. But then I sensed an opportunity. I'd already done my homework on the various jihadist factions, and in several Internet cafés I researched the stories of recent hostages. I thought, at the very least, it was good for an article, so I decided to hide out for a while and see where it went. Then, oddly enough, three weeks later I actually did get kidnapped, held against my will in a squalid room in Heera Mandi, the red-light district, after trying to buy drugs. I got robbed and pistol-whipped by two thugs and locked in a room, which I escaped from through a window after twenty-four hours.

Nine weeks after arriving for the wedding, I turned up at the consulate in Lahore, disheveled, skinny and seemingly disoriented, with cuts and bruises from the beating in Heera Mandi that validated the kidnapping narrative, so I stuck to it. The debriefing at the consulate was relatively easy, the one in Washington much tougher.

It was strange, undergoing a real-life interrogation by my countrymen in a windowless conference room in Washington, D.C., about imaginary interrogations in a windowless mud-and-wattle hut in Waziristan. I was scared of these government boys, but I stuck to my story, and when this tough little CIA geek in an oversized suit really had me up against the ropes, I said, "Weren't you the guys who claimed there were weapons of mass destruction in Iraq?" Finally it became clear that whatever the truth, I didn't have any actionable intelligence, so they cut me loose. I got the feeling that in their eyes, the propaganda value of a story about an American journalist faking his own kidnapping was strictly negative. And in the context of the official post-9/11 narrative—the war on terror—the lie was more useful than the truth, to them as well as to me.

Back in New York, Marty carefully managed and rationed press access, the idea being not to overdo it, to give me just enough exposure to drive up the price of the memoir without letting the public and the press get tired of me. He played the *Today* show against *Good Morning America*, Larry King against Anderson Cooper. I couldn't help wondering if Briskin had suspicions about my story, but like a good defense lawyer, he never asked me any questions, although he eventually told me that Random House had some concerns that seemed to derive from sources in the State Department, and I think that's why he decided to go with you for less money than he might have gotten from the big boys. As for me, you have to believe I somehow imagined that I was doing you a favor, making up for my shitty behavior the last time around. It's hard to explain, but by that time I almost believed my own story, with the help of a steady diet of drugs and alcohol. I was genuinely indignant when the reporter from the *Times* started dogging me after that ridiculous jihadist Web site questioned my account. As the evidence mounted, I became angry, and bitter, feelings that culminated in my disastrous appearance on *Charlie Rose*. That was the peak of my delusion—and, as many suggested, I was indeed drunk and high. The next morning, I knew it was all over and I felt strangely relieved. This is something you hear about over and over in AA and NA meetings, actually. Exposure of a great secret, of a pattern of lying, can be curiously liberating. But I realized, eventually, that my catharsis was your crisis, and I'm terribly, terribly sorry for the position I put you in. And I hope to find ways to make amends to you in the future.

Sincerely,

Phillip

44

THAT NIGHT IT WAS POSSIBLE, for once, to walk into almost any Manhattan restaurant at prime time—including those with secret phone numbers and those with phone numbers that always rang busy—and find a table for two or an empty seat at the bar. Traffic flowed smoothly up and down the broad avenues, and despite the mild weather, there were fewer pedestrians than usual, although here and there, in Times Square and at the intersection of Adam Clayton Powell Boulevard and 125th Street, crowds began forming not long after the polls closed, in anticipation of the celebration to come, although the mood remained subdued, the jubilation kept in check by the knowledge that the future of the republic would be decided elsewhere, far to the south and the west, where people were still driving to the polls in pickup trucks with gun racks in rear windows, or in burgundy Dodge minivans with MY KID'S AN HONOR STUDENT bumper stickers, or in rusted-out 700-series Volvos with faded GIVE PEACE A CHANCE and Grateful Dead STEAL YOUR TERRAPIN bumper stickers.

Meanwhile, in TriBeCa, five floors above West Broadway, in an old-school loft with warped hardwood floors and a tin ceiling veined with wires and pipes, the children had been granted a special dispensation to stay up until the decision was in, the high-pitched din of their play competing with the steady drone of Brian Williams on the television set. Election-night coverage had just begun, but it was far too early to pay attention. Three of their four parents were drinking Sancerre as they prepared for what they hoped would be a historic night, although the incipient euphoria was kept in check by the memory of disap-

pointment four years before, and by the suspicion that the rest of the
country, in the end, despite the tentative evidence of the polls, was not
ready to elect an African-American president, and, in this particular
eighteen-hundred-square-foot sector of lower Manhattan, the mood
was also tinged with a melancholy undercurrent, an unspoken sadness
due to the conspicuous absence of the fourth parent.

Russell topped off the wineglasses and tasted his Bolognese sauce,
which needed salt. Keeping it simple tonight—salad and spaghetti with
a choice of two sauces, Bolognese and marinara, the latter for the two
teenage girls, who were both vegetarians, although Storey ate so little lately, it was hard to tell; she seemed to have suddenly adopted her
mother's slightly hostile attitude toward food since the separation.

"They just called Kentucky for McCain," Washington said, looking
at his BlackBerry.

"Pennsylvania's going to be key."

"And Ohio."

"I'm so nervous," Veronica said.

"Remember how we all thought Kerry was going to win?"

"Come to think of it," Washington said, "weren't you supposed to
move to France if Kerry lost? Whatever happened with that?"

"We knew you'd miss us," Russell said reflexively.

"We miss you now," Veronica said.

After an awkward silence, Washington said, "At least we're drinking
French wine."

"Actually, I'm opening a Chianti with the pasta."

"You're so geographically correct, Russell."

Jeremy rushed over to the adult side of the loft to inform them that
Obama had won Vermont.

"We're on the board," Washington said, holding his palm out toward
Jeremy. "High five, my man."

"Are we pretty sure Obama's going to win?" Jeremy asked.

"It's not a done deal," Russell said. "I think there's a lot of white
voters who won't admit to a pollster that they'd never vote for a black
man."

Washington said, "No shit, Sherlock."

"But I'm cautiously optimistic."

"I think you were right the first time," Washington said. "No fucking way this country's going to elect a blood president."

"Washington, please," Veronica said. "The kids."

He was getting a little strident; Russell wondered if he'd had a few drinks before coming over.

"Can I have wine?" Jeremy asked after they were all seated at the dinner table. Russell had lately taken to giving him a small glass on special occasions.

"You can have a sip of mine afterward. Now clink glasses—lightly, no smashing—with the person next to you."

The kids managed not to break any stemware, though a fair amount of water was spilled.

"Are we going to win?" Storey asked.

"You haven't touched your spaghetti," Russell said.

"I had some salad."

Mingus was looking down at his phone. "Obama just won Pennsylvania."

"That's huge," Russell said.

"Does that mean we win?"

"It means the odds have just improved considerably."

Veronica said, "Hope you put that bottle of Dom we brought on ice."

After the dinner plates were cleared, the TV was again turned up. The kids watched briefly, cheering further Obama wins before disappearing into the bedrooms.

A perfunctory hometown cheer went up when New York was placed in the blue column, though there'd never been any suspense about that.

"Anybody else see that interview Brian Williams did with McCain and Palin?" Veronica asked. "Where he said New York and Washington, D.C., were the headquarters of the elitists? Whatever happened to the *good* McCain? Remember him, the maverick of the 2000 primaries?"

"After the primaries, he hired all the old Bush/Rove apparatchiks," Washington said, "the same hit men who slimed him in the 2000 primaries with nasty rumors about his war record and his love life. The same assholes who helped smear Kerry with that whole swift boat thing."

When Russell went to fetch another bottle of wine, Washington followed him to the kitchen.

"Listen, Crash, I hate to bring it up now, but I couldn't catch you at the office. It's nothing definite, but Anderson called me in today and gave a big speech about retrenchment and cost cutting. He hasn't made up his mind yet, but he said we shouldn't be making any capital expenditures in this climate. I made a strong case for you all over again. He told me he'll give me a decision next week."

"I thought it was your decision."

"Under normal circumstances, yeah, but these are extraordinary times. Everybody's scared shitless. Nobody knows what's happening next. Credit markets freezing up, banks going under."

"Well, we're reprinting Jack's book every other week, five thousand a pop. And what if I told you *Salon* and *McSweeney's* are both coming out with pieces on Jeff next month? I've never seen anything like this. Sales are doubling every six months."

"Can't hurt. What about the movie?"

"You'd have to ask Corrine about that."

"You guys talking?"

"We communicate. Logistics. Bills."

"I mean—about your marriage."

"Couple of summits, a few fraught phone calls."

"Have you thought about counseling?"

"She has. I don't really see the point, and I certainly never thought I'd hear you recommend it."

"Look, man, I know you're hurt and angry. But we all know you belong together. It's not like you've been—excuse the phrase—lily white through all these years. You need to forgive her."

"Easier said than done. How am I ever going to trust her again? When she says she's going to a business dinner, or a baby shower? How am I supposed to forget that she lied to me repeatedly?"

"Like I said, she's not the first, or the only one."

"I never loved anyone else."

"What makes you think she loves this guy?"

"Because she won't deny it."

"See, she's honest to a fault. I don't think you need to worry about her lying to you again."

"What are you guys doing over there?" Veronica called out.

"Seriously, though," Russell said, "if we don't make this deal, I'm well and truly fucked."

"Hey, man, I hear you. Our monthly nut's higher than my salary. Without Veronica's paycheck, we're going to burn through our savings pronto." He drained his glass and held it out for a refill. "Carpe diem, I say. Let's see if a black motherfucker can get elected president."

Soon they were talking about the meltdown. Veronica said, "If the Fed had stepped in and backstopped Lehman, we wouldn't be in this mess."

"Or if Lehman hadn't been so reckless," Russell interjected.

"Granted there were bad decisions, but J.P. Morgan and AIG were reckless, too, and they got bailouts."

"If I go to Vegas and lose my life savings," Russell said, "should my fellow taxpayers cover the losses?"

"That's a dumb analogy," Veronica said.

"I think it's a perfectly good one."

"That's so simplistic. There were so many factors at play."

"Sure, like greed, stupidity, incompetence."

"Russell, please," Washington said. "No need to get ad hominem."

"I'm just saying it wasn't some confluence of impersonal market forces that wrecked Lehman. It was a whole bunch of bad decisions made by people who worked there."

"Are you implying that *I'm* greedy, stupid and incompetent?" Veronica asked.

"No, only there has to be some accountability."

"Whoa! Shut the fuck up," Washington said, reaching for the remote control.

" . . . *the State of Ohio*," Brian Williams was saying, "*and can you name one that was fought over with more force?*"

"What? Who got it?"

"Obama."

"That's huge," Washington said. A quick check of other stations confirmed the call, including a brief stop on Fox News, where a rueful Brit Hume commiserated with Karl Rove, who seemed stunned.

"Ohio was key," Russell said as they waited for new results. "Along with Pennsylvania, I think we've got it."

But Washington wasn't ready to concede victory. "Let's see what those crackers in Virginia do."

"You can't say that about the state of Jefferson and Madison."

"Both slave owners. Two honky hypocrites."

"The latest polls had Obama ahead in Virginia," Veronica said.

"Those rednecks *really* won't admit it'll be a cold day in hell before they vote for a black man," Washington said. "And you got those Hillary Democrats sulking, sitting out the election. How about you, Russell? Did you get over your sulk and vote for the brother today?"

"I've got nothing against Obama. I just thought Hillary was better-qualified."

"Better a white chick than a black dude any day."

"Are you accusing me of racism?"

"Why not? What makes you so special?"

"I'm tired of you always being right because you're not white."

"What the fuck's that mean?"

"Hey, shut up, both of you," Veronica said. "Listen."

"*An African-American has just broken a barrier as old as the republic,* Brian Williams announced. "*An astonishing candidate. An astonishing campaign. A seismic shift in American politics.*"

"God*damn*," Washington said. "Is that shit even possible?"

Veronica embraced him, even as he continued to stare at the screen in disbelief.

Russell, too, was stunned. He'd grown so accustomed to thinking of himself as representing the minority opinion in his homeland that it was hard to believe that a majority of his fellow Americans had chosen as he had.

The kids poured in from the bedrooms, cheering. It had been weeks since Russell had seen his own kids so buoyant.

Washington advanced on Russell and crushed him in a bear hug. Through the open windows could be heard the sounds of celebration from West Broadway, which blended with those from the crowd in Chicago's Grant Park, coming from the television set.

"I wish Mom was here," Jeremy said.

Storey said, "You've been texting her all night."

"You wish Mom *were* here," Russell said.

"Don't be a dick, Russell," Washington said.

After listening to Obama's speech, they went down to the street to mingle with their neighbors. The kids found some of their former classmates; Jeremy and Mingus disappeared and came back with sparklers. A heavily freckled young woman who walked her fox terrier in the morning when Russell was taking the kids to school threw her arms around him, alarming the dog, who started barking.

"Isn't it amazing?" she said. "I'm Zoe, by the way."

"I'm Russell. Pleased to meet you."

"Stop it, Zeke. He's our neighbor."

Like nervous laughter, the cheers and cries of victory echoing through the streets of Manhattan and beyond seemed to him to mask a deep sense of anxiety. The prosperity of the past two decades appeared to be coming to an end and the country was still at war. It was hard to believe that any individual of any color could lead them out of the dark woods into which they'd stumbled. But for the moment, Russell and his friends and neighbors were willing to believe.

Corrine called shortly after midnight.

"Isn't it amazing?"

"It is."

"It gives me hope."

"We could all use some of that."

"I spoke to the kids earlier."

"I know."

"Is there any hope for us, Russell?"

"I guess anything's possible."

"Can I see you soon?"

"Soon. Maybe."

45

THE CITY WAS HOLDING ITS BREATH. It seemed as if a seismic event was in progress, shifting the tectonic plates beneath the island, toppling monuments and sucking rivers of wealth into the sewers. Billions had somehow disappeared. One heard rumors of overnight cash transactions, of Picassos and Southampton beachfront homes dumped by investors to make margin calls, of moving trucks arriving at town houses in the middle of the night.

"This is beginning to look like a bloodbath," Casey said.

They were sitting on flimsy chairs near the back of a crowded room at Christie's. The auctioneer stood at the front of the room, beneath a screen displaying the paintings on offer, the estimates, and up-to-the-minute bids. Casey had insisted that Corrine accompany her to the auction, out of a professed desire to get her out of the house, though, in fact, she didn't want to appear unaccompanied at such an important social event, and the two walkers she sometimes relied on were otherwise engaged. Although Corrine had been initially reluctant to come along, she had an ulterior motive for relenting.

Casey was selling a small *Mao* by Warhol, which she'd consigned this past summer, after Tom left her, when the market was still robust. Corrine had never failed to marvel at the irony of this gaudy image of the Great Helmsman hanging on the wall of an Upper East Side town house, but in the wake of one of those violent contractions that he would have recognized as revealing the internal contradictions of capitalism, he was about to find a new, possibly even more opulent home.

The trouble started early. The third lot, a small red-and-yellow Rothko oil on paper from 1958, estimated at four to six million, hammered for three and a half. The Roy Lichtenstein self-portrait that followed likewise failed to reach the low estimate. The room was increasingly hushed. "Purchased from the artist by a distinguished collector," Corrine read in the catalog, and remembered a moment—ten, twelve years ago—when Russell had been flipping through one from Sotheby's, reciting the text to her, mocking the descriptions of the consigners: "'From the collection of a distinguished New York gentleman, a longtime friend and former consigner,'" he'd read. "Wouldn't it be nice for once to read a noneuphemistic version, like 'From the collection of a scumbag arbitrageur whose wife is divorcing him for sleeping with the yoga instructor.' That would make for some diverting reading," he'd said. She hadn't thought of that day since, Russell stretched out on the couch in the loft, reading a catalog, laughing at the prices and the faux Brit gentility of it all.

Ten minutes into the auction, most of the lots had hammered below the low estimate and five had failed to find bidders.

The depression was alleviated briefly with a manic burst of bidding on lot nineteen, when Jean-Michel Basquiat's *Untitled (Boxer)* burst through the high estimate of fifteen million, as Corrine recalled meeting him once with Jeff. But the next lot failed to sell.

Meanwhile, she'd recognized many of the faces in the room, familiar from the society and business pages, although much of the bidding, tepid as it was, came from the ranks of Christie's employees manning the phones along one wall of the room, raising their hands as they pressed receivers to their ears. The identity of these phantom buyers in Asia and Russia was the source of fevered speculation. As the auction progressed, it became clear that their mood was subdued, to say the least.

Casey was becoming increasingly agitated as her own lot approached. The announcement of a de Kooning drawing from an important private collection inspired boos in the room.

"What could anybody have against de Kooning?" Corrine asked.

"That's one of the drawings from the collection of Dick and Kathy Fuld."

"Who?"

"Jesus, Corrine. He was the head of Lehman Brothers, the man who single-handedly flushed it down the drain. Or at least that's what the people who are booing believe. The Fulds have sixteen drawings in this sale, and whatever happens, they can't lose, because Christie's supposedly guaranteed twenty million. And no one's really happy with that except, presumably, the Fulds."

Casey clutched Corrine's knee as her painting appeared on the screen with an estimate of four to six million. Corrine tried not to imagine all the productive uses for that kind of cash.

The auctioneer described the painting as a small but brilliant example of the series, recently featured in a major show at the Asia Society. "Shall we start the bidding at three million?"

The room was silent.

It was hard to feel sorry for Casey, really, though at that moment, Corrine couldn't help doing so. She was embarrassed for her friend, even though it was unlikely that many people in the room knew the source of the painting.

"Shall we say two seven five?"

The silence persisted, punctuated by coughs and whispers.

The auctioneer brought down his gavel. "Pass."

"I'm sorry," Corrine said.

"Don't feel too bad," Casey said. "Christie's guaranteed three million, so I'm not that upset." She shrugged. "Shall we go?"

"Let's just stay for another few lots. I want to see what happens with the Tony Duplex."

"Ah, yes. First public sale since he shuffled off this mortal coil, I believe."

Corrine nodded.

"Though I have no idea what a fucking coil is."

"It basically meant 'cares' or 'worries' in Shakespeare's time."

"You're such a nerd. Why are you so interested in Duplex?"

Corrine debated whether to reveal her interest or not, concluding that her possession of a Duplex gave her something in common with her friend. "I own one."

"Oh, excellent. Duplex paintings are probably the only assets that have appreciated since September. The only thing better than death for the career of an enfant terrible is death by misadventure. I imagine Russell's doing pretty well on Jack Carson's posthumous book sales."

"Will you please not make me feel any worse about this?"

"Why should you feel bad? You didn't sell him the drugs."

"Shh, here it comes."

"Next up," the auctioneer said, "a work by the late Tony Duplex, one of the leading neo-Expressionists of the eighties, a confederate of Keith Haring and Jean-Michel Basquiat. This large oil on canvas from 1984 is a stunning example of his work from the period when he took his art from the street to the studio. Estimated at three hundred to five hundred thousand, who will start the bidding at just two hundred and fifty thousand dollars? . . . Thank you. Do I hear two seventy-five? . . . Thank you, sir. . . . Lorna has it with her phone bidder now at three hundred thousand. Do I hear three twenty-five?"

"In this sale, that still counts as a bargain," Casey said.

"Three fifty to the phone bidder. Who will give me four hundred thousand?"

A man near the front in a black suit and wearing bright pink reading glasses raised his hand.

"Why would Gary Arkadian be bidding?" Corrine asked. "He was Duplex's dealer."

"Well, *duh,* he wants to set a new level for all the paintings."

Corrine's heart began to pound as the bidding went past half a million dollars. The painting finally hammered at $800,000, which, with the addition of the buyer's premium, meant that someone had just paid almost a million. It was the only artwork of the night to sell for significantly more than the high estimate, the sale itself netting exactly half the low estimate—still enough, Corrine reckoned, to feed a million hungry New Yorkers for a month—inspiring much journalistic commentary about the collapse of the art market, along with the other major asset classes.

46

WHETHER OUT OF FINANCIAL DISTRESS or a desire not to appear extravagant in the midst of the crisis, many companies and individuals were scaling back or canceling their holiday festivities, leaving thousands of waiters and cooks and bartenders and coat checkers idle. The panhandlers, who'd almost disappeared from the city streets in recent years, seemed to multiply overnight, and the importunate year-end letters from nonprofit organizations to their patrons manifested a shrill, apocalyptic tone. When, two weeks before Christmas, a prominent money manager confessed that his business was a fifty-billion-dollar Ponzi scheme, half a dozen charities were forced to close their doors, and thousands of New Yorkers discovered that their wealth was illusory. What made this story so resonant was the widespread suspicion that it was emblematic of the economy in general, that the financial markets were houses of cards, built on sand.

Russell had his own liquidity crisis. The spike in sales on Jack's book was staving off the inevitable, but McCane, Slade was still foundering. If he didn't buy any books, and didn't pay himself, he would just have enough money to meet the January payroll, and then, if he didn't find a buyer or an infusion of capital, he'd have to declare bankruptcy. In the wake of the crisis, Corbin, Dern's interest in buying the company had evaporated, despite Washington's best efforts. At this moment, no one was sure what anything was worth.

His emotional coffers were similarly dry. His discussions with Corrine always ended at the same impasse. He'd endured two sessions of marriage counseling before bailing; the more she told him, the less he felt inclined to forgive her. Thanksgiving and Christmas, fraught as they were with emotional significance, required some sort of détente and accommodation, although Russell wasn't ready to perpetrate the illusion of normalcy, or to be alone with Corrine and their kids. For the moment, Storey and Jeremy were shuttling between the loft and Casey's town house, and they were both showing the strain. After a series of complex negotiations, it was decided that Corrine would take Storey and Jeremy to her mother's for Thanksgiving, while Russell joined the Lee clan in their loft, where, with his best friend, he watched the Tennessee Titans annihilate the Detroit Lions.

"Jack would've been pleased," Russell said afterward. "He was a big Titans fan."

"Was there ever a memorial service?"

"I was thinking about organizing something in the spring," Russell said. "A reading, maybe. Nobody else seems to be stepping up. Of course, there's no money for that at the moment."

After the feast, Washington suggested they cut through the ensuing torpor by taking a walk.

"How'd you like a partner?" Washington asked as he lit a cigarette just outside the door of his building.

"Like a drowning man would like a rope."

"I had a little windfall."

"You're saying that you *personally* want to be my partner?"

He nodded, exhaling a vast cloud of smoke."

"What kind of windfall?" Russell asked.

"I shorted the market back in September."

"And you're just telling me this now?"

"It's unseemly to flaunt your Kiton suit when everyone around you is losing his shirt. Also, it would look really bad if it got out that my biggest short was Lehman Brothers."

Russell had no idea how one shorted a stock, or even, exactly, what it meant, but Washington had always had a great head for business. "Jesus, that's rich. And Veronica doesn't know?"

"What do you think?"

"You'd really do this?"

"It's not like I'm giving you the money. It's an investment. Publishing's my business. I already did the due diligence for Corbin, Dern, and I know you're a great publisher. It'll be like old times, chief, and I expect an excellent return on my investment."

"I'm not sure you realize how much I need. It's gotten worse since you saw those numbers."

"I'm willing to kick in five large."

"Five hundred thousand?"

Wash nodded.

"Holy shit, really? That could get me through to the summer. What kind of piece would you want?"

"We can work that out later," he said.

"I don't know what to say."

"Let's not get all sentimental here," Washington said, taking a last drag from his cigarette. "It's an investment."

If only his domestic crisis had a comparable resolution, Russell thought. Christmas remained a dilemma, the negotiations fraught. "I don't understand why we can't all be together," Jeremy had said on several occasions. He refused to accompany Russell and Storey on the search for a Christmas tree. Storey did her best to act as if nothing was really amiss, but as the weeks of separation dragged on, she seemed to grow weary of the effort, becoming increasingly withdrawn and sullen. Finally it was agreed that Corrine and the kids would spend Christmas Eve together with Casey and her daughter at the Reyneses' town house. The young Calloways would be dropped off at the loft Christmas morning to spend the day with Russell, and on the day after, Corrine and the kids would drive up to Stockbridge to spend a few days with Corrine's mother.

Two days before Christmas, Hilary called to thank Russell for helping her get the job at HBO. She'd come by a couple of times lately, watching the kids when Russell needed a sitter. He asked her about her Christmas plans.

"Don't have any," she said.

"You're not going up to see your mother?"

"We're not exactly getting along at the moment. I'll just stay home, watch *It's a Wonderful Life* and drink myself senseless."

"You're welcome to come here," Russell said. Over the past few weeks, he'd found that he actually enjoyed her company. She'd picked the kids up at school several times and stayed for supper afterward. As different as she was from Corrine, she was a kind of surrogate for her sister.

"Really?" she said. "Actually, that would be great."

After he hung up, he realized that Corrine would probably be furious when she found out that Hilary was spending Christmas with him and the kids, which made the idea all the more appealing.

"So what's the plan?" Storey asked, after they'd been dropped off at the loft on Christmas morning.

"Presents," Jeremy said, pointing at the pile under the tree.

"Well, yes, presents. And then I'm cooking a goose for the carnivores and a Tofurkey for our resident vegetarian."

"Gross," said Jeremy.

"What's gross," Storey said, "is slaughtering innocent animals when there are lots of humane, nonanimal sources of protein and fat."

Russell shrugged and said, "Aunt Hilary's going to join us."

"Really?"

"Is that okay?"

"That seems kind of weird," Storey said. "I mean, it's Christmas."

"Well, she *is* family."

"I like her," Jeremy said.

"Does Mom know about this?" Storey asked.

Russell couldn't help being surprised that Storey was suddenly looking out for her mother's interests, after being instrumental in her exposure.

"I haven't mentioned it to her, no."

"I don't think she'll like it."

He almost said "Tough luck," but thought better of it. "Well, I don't suppose she has to know."

"It would've been nice if you'd talked to us first."

"She called to see how you guys were and sounded kind of lonely. I thought it was the right thing to do. As you yourself pointed out, honey, it *is* Christmas."

"Fine," Storey said as Jeremy rummaged under the tree for his presents.

Hilary arrived at five, wearing a Santa hat and bearing gifts. Underneath her coat she was wearing a short red dress with white faux-fur trim.

"I wanted to look festive," she said.

"I'd say you succeeded," Russell said.

Storey was decidedly chilly in her greeting, while her brother seemed determined to make up for his sister's reserve.

Russell opened a bottle of champagne, giving each of the kids a small glass. Storey had no choice but to turn civil after opening her aunt's present—a pink ensemble from Juicy Couture—but both she and Jeremy became mute at the dinner table, and Russell felt that his attempt to conduct a pleasant conversation wasn't succeeding in convincing anyone that this was just another Christmas. After dinner, both kids seemed to welcome his reading from "A Child's Christmas in Wales," a Calloway Christmas ritual that went back as far as either could remember, but after fifteen minutes Jeremy stood up and said, "Mom should be here," before retreating to his room. Storey, at least, had waited till the end of the reading before leaving the two adults and retreating to her room.

"Well, you tried," Hilary said as Russell poured more wine into her glass.

"It wasn't that bad, was it?"

"Not for me. For them, though, it's heartbreaking. They'll never be okay with you and Corrine not being together."

"They're probably going to have to get used to it."

"Oh, come on. Get over yourself. You think you're the first husband who's been cheated on? It happens every day. Wives are supposed to get over it somehow, but when husbands get cuckolded, it's like the laws of nature have been suspended. With you guys, it's all about pride.

"You know, I'm kind of an expert on affairs," she continued, "if I do say so myself. And if there's one thing I can say with certainty, it's that if somebody cheats, it's usually because the other party isn't giving them what they need. Think about it, Russell. Have you been there for Corrine? Have you been taking care of her needs?"

"If you mean sex, things were fine between us," he said, immediately registering how hollow it sounded.

"I'm not talking about sex. When a woman goes looking outside the home, she's looking more for seduction and understanding. She wants to be desired, not just used."

"And you're saying I used Corrine?"

"I'm saying it's something for you to think about. It's not just about having sex every few weeks."

"This was a long-term thing; it happened over a couple of years."

"Maybe you had your head up your ass for a couple of years. Wake up, Russell. Can't you just forgive her?"

"I don't know. I'd like to, maybe, but so far I can't. She lied to me."

"You're being such a hypocrite. It's not like you haven't cheated on her."

"Who says I did?"

"You're saying you never cheated on her?"

He saw no reason to confess to Hilary. "No."

"Jesus, Russell. What about that banker chick you worked with on your stupid leveraged buyout? And then there was that girl who worked for you, the one who confronted you at Talese's Christmas party."

Russell couldn't believe she knew about these prehistoric transgressions—couldn't believe that Corrine had confided in her. It felt like yet another betrayal.

"That's ancient history."

"And then there was your jaunt to Madam Gretchen's house a few months ago. So let's not get too righteous here. She doesn't even know about that one, but she told me about the others. Maybe she forgave you, but that doesn't mean she forgot. The point is, she let you off the fucking hook. So maybe you should just get over yourself and think about doing the same for her."

While he called a car for her, she said good night to the kids, who were sprawled on the bed in Jeremy's room, watching *A Christmas Story*.

Perhaps it was the influence of a not inconsiderable amount of champagne, but his good-night kiss must have been more intimate than Hilary might have expected from her brother-in-law, because she pushed him away gently, saying, "That's enough of that."

When he returned to Jeremy's room, Ralphie had just opened his yearned-for Red Ryder BB gun.

"Mind if join you?"

He took the silence as assent.

"This is, like, the crappiest Christmas ever," Jeremy eventually said.

"Sorry, guys."

"It's not Dad's fault." Storey said.

"I don't care whose fault it is," Jeremy said. "I'm mad at Mom *and* Dad."

Washington made his investment through an LLC formed specifically for the purchase of part of McCane, Slade. They signed the papers on January 13 in Washington's lawyer's office, and afterward walked a few blocks south, bundled against the cold, to the Old Town Bar, a former hangout from the old days, where they'd once plotted to take over Corbin, Dern, their erstwhile employer, with borrowed money.

"When I saw the name you used," Russell said, "I have to say, it aroused my suspicions. Art and Love, LLC?"

"That's your shtick, isn't it? An homage to your big theory about the two teams in life. Love and Art, Power and Money. We're the former, right? What's to be suspicious?"

"I don't know. For some reason, I thought I sensed the hand of my wife. Did she, by any chance, give you the money?"

"Where would Corrine find a half mil?"

"That's what I can't figure out."

"You know she's looking at real estate in Harlem?"

"Still?"

"I'm not sure I approve of white people in Harlem."

"Not sure I do, either."

"She wants us to split a town house with you guys."

"There is no *us guys*."

"Fuck that. You know, you're way less fun without her. You two are like a hyphenate: Russell-Corrine. You've always been the couple that made the rest of us think marriage was even possible. She loves you, not the other guy. But the hell with it—the papers are signed, so you should know, the money *is* from Corrine. She's the one who's saving your ass."

"Where the fuck would she get that kind of money?"

"She told me it was an inheritance."

"What inheritance? Her father left what little money he had to his second wife."

"So maybe she had a rich uncle."

Russell shook his head, because suddenly, it was perfectly clear. "No, but she does have a boyfriend who's rich as Croesus."

"That would be whack. I thought it was over and done."

"Where else could she find that kind of cash?"

"Does it really matter?"

"Of course it matters. Why do you think she didn't want me to know it was from her?"

"Because she's good people. And because she was afraid you wouldn't take it if you knew it was coming from her."

"She knew I wouldn't take it because it's from that asshole."

"Either way, Crash, the salient point is, she wanted to save your ass."

His first inclination was to give the money back; the option of accepting a bailout from Corrine's lover was completely unacceptable. Walking through an icy Union Square, he contemplated the situation. The company was out of cash and his personal savings would last another month at best. If he returned the money, his employees would be out of work in a couple of weeks and he and his children would be on the street within months. At the moment, it was nothing less than a lifeline, and he waffled over it for the next few days, alternately grateful to Corrine and furious at her for putting him in this position, his vast relief that his company had been saved eroded by the feeling that he'd been compromised.

They spoke frequently, their conversations focused on the minutiae of household finances and the logistics of shuttling Storey and Jeremy hither and yon. Corrine's attempts to initiate discussions about their marital issues had inevitably ended in the same dead end.

The day before Valentine's Day, after they'd worked out the schedule for the coming weekend, he asked, "What are you doing tomorrow night?"

"Nothing," she said.

"No romantic dinner?"

"For God's sake, Russell. With whom would I have a romantic dinner?"

"I'd prefer not to say his name."

"I haven't seen him in five months. I told you, I broke it off in September."

"He didn't give you half a million dollars?"

"What are you talking about?"

"Does Art and Love, LLC, ring a bell? Wash told me."

"Told you what?"

"That the money came from you. But, I asked myself, where the hell would you get five hundred K?"

"I sold a painting."

"That's a good one. We don't have a painting worth five *thousand*."

"*We* didn't, maybe. But I did." She paused. "Twenty-plus years ago, when you were in Frankfurt, Tony Duplex gave me a painting. . . ."

"Why would Tony Duplex give you a painting?"

"Because I did him a big favor."

"What favor—you fucked him?"

"If that's what you want to think," she said before hanging up on him.

He was looking over the sales figures for *Youth and Beauty* the next morning at work when Gita brought in an envelope messengered over from Corrine's office. Inside were two handwritten sheets on Corrine's crisp stationery, and several sheets of yellowing, brittle onionskin:

February 14, 2009

Dear Russell:

When I was at my mother's house for Thanksgiving, I found this letter pressed inside my old copy of *House of Mirth*. Reading it all these years later made me cry. (Your letter, not *House of Mirth*.) It made me incredibly sad to think of all the years that have passed, and all that we've shared since you wrote this, and sad most of all to think that our story might be over, and that I would spend the rest of my life with the guilt of knowing that I was to blame. Perhaps you can't forgive me, or ever be able to entirely trust me again. But isn't it possible that even in this diminished form, our marriage is still worth preserving, that however damaged, it's better than most other marriages at their best, that ours is still one of the great love stories, especially if we can survive this crisis? I've never forgotten that quote from your thesis, was it from *Julius Caesar*? ". . . when the sea was calm, all boats alike/show'd mastership in floating . . ." Which I take to mean that nobody should get undue credit for doing well during the good times. It's the storms that truly test us.

I'm sorry that I sailed us into a storm. You didn't deserve it. And I don't deserve to be forgiven, but I hope you will anyway.

I love you.

I'm sorry.

Corrine.

PS. You would have written this letter a few years before I got the painting. Jeff and Tony were in a jam with a drug dealer and I sacrificed a few of my grandfather's twenty-dollar gold pieces to bail them out. I should have told you at the time. I'm sorry. On the other hand, it turned out to be a pretty good investment.

He carefully unfolded the brittle onionskin, recognizing his own loopy youthful cursive script.

Cloisters Attic
Oxford
March 2, 1979

Dear Corrine,

Feeling very restless tonight. It's already spring here, one of those days when you can smell the earth thawing, the ferment of the soil, when you can almost hear the dormant vegetable life awakening, stirring and thrusting upward, and unlike some of the uniquely Limey odors of recent experience, like that of the fish and chip shop on the High Street, this is the universal scent of renewal and change and migration—and it inspires the desire to get out and do something, to go go go, like Kerouac's Dean Moriarty. I am so restless, but unlike the south-wintering birds, whose instincts are urging them northward to their summer breeding grounds, I don't know what it is I want to do. I certainly don't want to be sitting here reading Coleridge's *Biographia Literaria,* no offense to that august gentleman, but I can't concentrate tonight. "Books! 'tis a dull and endless strife," as his friend and bookish colleague Wordsworth said. Not usually, but that's how I feel right this moment. In fact, I do know where I want to go. Hearing of you and Jeff and Caitlin and everyone in New York, I feel that you're all moving ahead without me, while I'm back in school, in a backwater eddy, stuck in the nineteenth century. Meanwhile, Jeff writes to tell me that he met Norman Mailer at the Lion's Head and they thumb-wrestled while arguing about Hemingway. I feel my life is passing me by. I miss you. I want to come home tonight and crawl into your bed. I want to be inside of you. Enough. Enough of this allegedly fond-making absence. What are we waiting for? I want my life to start now. I knew the first time I saw you at the top of that staircase at the party at Phi Psi that my life would be lived for you. You were like a goddess looking down from Olympus, not unbenevolently, but with a certain amused detachment at the roiling mob of beer-soaked mortals, of which I was a part. The Aphrodite of Phi Psi. I vowed at that moment that I would find out who you were and I would spend the rest of my days at Brown pursuing you. It wasn't easy, but then, I wouldn't have wanted it to be. Nothing truly worthwhile is easy, and nothing in my life has ever been so worthwhile as loving you. I would have waited for you for as long as it took to win your affections, and yet tonight I'm so restless, and even fearful, worrying suddenly that perhaps this is the night that your heart finally begins, out of weariness, to drift away or that you lose faith in our intertwined destinies or that you'll meet someone in New York who has the unfair advantage of physical proximity, and I can't stand it, it makes me crazy. Yes I've had a few drams of Bushmills tonight, but I've never been so certain of anything as I am of my devotion to you. Tell me you'll wait, and I will be able to last this term out, though I want to fly to you now. I'm going to stick this out for the year, but I don't have it in me to come back for a second year. I hope you won't think less of me, but I've thought long and hard about this, and among other things I realize that I don't want to teach; I don't want to spend five or six more years in grad school in Cambridge or Palo Alto (if I'm lucky) in the hope of getting an assistant professorship in Duluth or Des Moines, only to hope at the end of another five or six years that I might get tenure and the privilege of spending the rest of my life there—and hope that's something you might be willing to do. I don't want to spend a decade writing yet another scholarly study of some minor aspect of Keats that nobody but my thesis advisers will read. I want to go to New York and start my life with you and I want to be a part of the history and literature of my time. By that I mean not only that I want to be to my era what Max Perkins was to his but I want to be part of the greatest love story of our time, of all time. Corrine and Russell. Russell and Corrine. Forget Troilus and Cressida or Romeo and Juliet, or Pyramus and Thisbe with their tragic fates. Ours will have a happy ending. We'll create a love story for the ages. So please wait for me. A few short months and then we will have the rest of our lives.

"Grow old along with me. The best is yet to be."

All my love,

Russell

When he finished reading, he realized there were tears in his eyes. He didn't know if he had ever felt so bereft in his life—perhaps when his mother died of cancer, almost thirty years before, slipping away when Russell was only twenty-three. He was so sad, now, to think that she'd never gotten to meet her grandchildren. He was sad for the innocence he'd lost since he wrote that letter, for the ways he'd been careless with his life and of his romance with Corrine, and for all the damage it had sustained. Remembering the boy who'd written that callow and idealistic letter, he felt acutely that he'd let him down somehow, just as he'd failed to live up to all the sweet sentiments expressed in it. He was sad that the girl to whom that letter was addressed had betrayed him, and that he'd never feel quite the same way about her again. But the storm had passed. Maybe, or, in fact, definitely, it was time to try to patch the leaks in the ship and sail onward.

For a long time Russell stared out the back window at the naked trees in the courtyard and then he turned back to his desk, found a piece of stationery in the top drawer and started to write.

14 February, 2009

Dear Corrine,

The quote was from *Coriolanus*, actually, not *Julius Caesar*, but your reading of the line was spot-on. . . .

47

GOING OUT OF BUSINESS signs on Madison—not the fake, permanent signs on the electronics stores on Fifth Avenue, catnip to tourists. These were real, right here in the retail heart of the plutocracy, Madison in the 70s, the high street of the haute monde, where the acquisitive wives of the titans of finance could find four-figure pairs of shoes, five-figure purses and six-figure watches. Luke knew as well as anyone how badly things stood in the markets, but still, this came as a bit of a surprise; he'd somehow expected the Upper East Side to remain as he remembered it from the fat days of his first marriage, years that were prosperous, if not entirely blissful. It made him melancholy, this feeling that his city was gone.

In between meetings, he'd decided to take in the Georgia O'Keeffe show at the Whitney, that great granite bunker of modernism plunked down in the midst of the stately brick apartment towers, where he found himself standing behind a woman with strawberry blond hair who immediately attracted his interest. When she turned her head to take in the canvas from another angle, he was astonished to see that it was Corrine, standing there just a few feet away from him.

He felt paralyzed, uncertain whether to greet her or try to slip away unnoticed.

"Oh my God, Luke. What are you doing here?" she asked, blushing as she walked over, smiling and finally kissing him to cover her confusion. Drawing back, cocking her head to examine him more closely, she said, "I didn't know you were a Georgia O'Keeffe fan."

"Who isn't?" he said.

"You look great," she said after an awkward pause.

"So do you," he said, though in fact she looked a little older than he remembered, her eyes webbed with tiny lines.

"Are you still in SoHo?"

"I'm still renting the loft, but I've been in Europe and Africa the last few months."

All at once, they seemed to have run out of things to say. She lifted the corners of her mouth in an exaggerated smile before turning back to the painting in front of them, surging waves of gorgeous pink and yellow and turquoise. "It's amazing that she was painting pure abstractions so early," she said. "I mean Kandinsky was still painting figuratively when she did this. Have you seen the Kandinsky show at the Guggenheim?"

He shook his head.

"You should; it's great. Although even with these abstract O'Keeffes, there's a way in which they *suggest* the figurative. Of course, maybe that's just us, our tendency to seek the familiar, to find meaning, pattern. This one's kind of intrauterine." She laughed nervously. "I'm sorry, am I babbling? I'm babbling."

He shook his head. "No, it's . . . great. I always loved listening to you hold forth on subjects that inspire you." As soon as he said this, he wondered if it was true. Listening to her extemporize, he initially felt a fond rush of nostalgia, which was almost immediately tempered by a rising irritation. While these free-associative flights of erudition had once been unequivocally charming, he now found himself losing patience—the eccentricities cherished in a lover transformed into character flaws in those we're no longer sleeping with.

He was studying her, Luke realized, with the critical eye of a scorned lover, of a man presently dating a woman twenty-three years his junior. She was still beautiful, in his eyes, though; he was surprised to feel the stirring of the old desire, a visceral response to her proximity, despite the visible arc of her decline. He could imagine the changes to come, the inevitable sagging and shriveling, as if he were fast-forwarding through time. But he was aging, as well—perhaps he also looked older to her. He was sixty. They were both getting older, and they would continue to do so, separately, shrinking and wrinkling, as would their store of collective memories—becoming less and less real to each other all the while. Though for months he'd been crushed by her rejection and at times almost hated her, he had to admit that what had seemed unbearable at first had become tolerable, until finally he'd convinced himself it was for the best.

"How's the foundation?" she asked.

"Limping along. Donations cratered last year, but we're hanging on. How about yours?"

"Same. More hungry people, fewer benefactors. Contributions down thirty percent. We've laid people off. It's scary. Surely the economy's got to recover, right? I mean, it won't be like this forever, will it?"

"It'll come back, sooner or later," he said. "It always does. How's Russell?" He needed only to utter the name of his former rival to prove it held no power over him.

"He's fine," she said. "We're fine."

This declaration sounded halfhearted and even rueful, though Luke supposed she wouldn't have been eager to sound too goddamn happy. He waited.

"We moved," she said. "To Harlem."

His face must have betrayed his concern, his supposition that the move was indicative of severe economic distress.

"No, it's great, actually. We have a nice house, an Italianate brownstone with amazing architectural details. Well, actually it's kind of a wreck, but we're fixing it up slowly. It'll be great when we finish sometime in the next century or two. We're renting out the bottom floor to defray the mortgage. But it's really so much better than our old loft. I mean, it's so great to have so much space, and the neighborhood is really cool. You'd be surprised. You should—" She stopped short, laughed mirthlessly.

"Come for a visit?"

"Well, I nearly said that, but obviously, I don't think . . ." She sighed theatrically. "This is awkward on so many levels, isn't it?"

He nodded. "Yes, it is."

She shook her head sadly.

He was at a loss for parting words. For months after she left his loft that night, he'd yearned to talk to her, to woo her back, or at least to hear her explain her abrupt change of heart. Not used to being thwarted in his desires, he'd been hurt and confused and angry, and he'd felt he deserved an explanation. But now, more than a year later, he realized the futility of that wounded compulsion. The heart didn't have explanations, any more than the painting hanging in front of them did; it had impulses, tides and currents.

"How's Ashley?"

"She's good. Applying to grad schools." He would not tell her about the relapse, the rehab, the nightmare of having to negotiate the crisis with his ex-wife. They were no longer on those terms.

"Your kids are well?" he asked.

"Except for the fact that they're teenagers."

He remembered her once saying that asking after someone's kids was the highest form of social banality. He still found himself recalling these things she'd said, still thought fondly of her, and missed her for many, various reasons, though he understood that now he would miss her a little less intensely and supposed that was a good thing.

"Do you want to grab a coffee or something?" she asked.

"I'd love to, but I've got a meeting downtown." In truth, there was time before the meeting, but the prospect of sitting down with her and exchanging small talk depressed him.

Their parting cheek-grazing kiss was a pale imitation of earlier kisses.

"Take care, Luke."

"You, too."

Neither one of them seemed to know what to do next; they were in the middle of the gallery, where, under normal circumstances, they would have continued a leisurely perusal of the paintings; before he could decide what to do, she waved, smiling ruefully, and bolted from the room, leaving him with a feeling that he'd failed to be as gracious as he might have been, a sense that would nag at him in the years to come when he thought about Corrine.

That night, at dinner, he was short-tempered with his girlfriend, bringing tears to her eyes; he broke up with her a few days later.

48

HER LOVER, ULTIMATELY, dies in a fiery crash, his beloved Austin-Healey wrapped around a tree in East Hampton, just a few miles from the spot where Jackson Pollock, whose grave they once visited together, met his own death in a car crash many years before. And her husband, who asked her to leave their home after he discovered their affair, is about to take her back, after a long separation, in which they both seemed to be in mourning, walking the gloomy canyons of Manhattan separately, against the backdrop of indifferent skyscrapers. On their anniversary, she calls to hear his voice, and when he tells her he misses her, she admits that she's out on the sidewalk, just outside his art gallery. He is, for all his faults, a good man and she realizes that they are meant to be together. Though easily entranced and distracted by shiny surfaces, by glamour and fleeting pleasures, he loves art and artists; he loves his friends and his wife. When he steps out of the gallery to meet her on the sidewalk, he's holding a painting of her, done the year before, by her deceased lover—his best friend.

In Corrine's first five drafts, this penultimate scene was more subtle, becoming increasingly rom-com and clichéd after every meeting with the studio, but now, seeing it on the screen, she feels it has a certain power and it draws tears from her eyes, which, she supposes, is good, though, of course, she is hardly an objective viewer. The final scene undercuts the easy resolution of the sidewalk reunion. Short as it is, it wasn't easy to write, but she knows from bitter experience that trust, once breached, can never be fully restored. The reunited couple is at a gallery opening, one of those big ratfucks in West Chelsea, the Cure's "Just Like Heaven" blaring away, the film's music director having intuitively chosen Jeff's second-favorite band. She asked Jeff once, "The cure for what?" and he looked at her as if to say, You really need to ask?

The camera pans the room, gradually picking out the wife, who's chatting up a handsome young artist, and then pans farther to pick up her husband, who's watching her; his expression not exactly suspicious, but wary, perhaps—cautious, wistful and sad, as if he were yearning for the time when his trust in her was absolute. That's Corrine's written stage direction. She has to admit, Jess Colter, the actor, really nailed it, and even though she wrote the scene, she knew it would all come down to whether the actor could translate her intentions, and now it's all she can do to keep herself from sobbing.

The expression on Colter's face is not so different from the one that Russell turns on her when the houselights go up.

"Well?" she says hopefully.

"It's good," he says, having already seen a rough cut without the final, gallery-opening scene. "The last scene was . . . powerful." It can't have been easy for him to watch this, and she admires his stoicism; more than that, his active support over the years, his encouraging her to persevere on a project that would inevitably revive painful memories, and at this moment she feels a great upwelling of affection for her husband.

The well-wishers approach shyly, obliquely, uncertain of the etiquette of congratulating a couple on the movie adaptation of a novel based on their marriage, written by their dead friend, who possibly—definitely in this version—slept with the wife. The fact that the wife wrote the screenplay makes it an even more complicated equation.

The screening room is womblike, as are the dark, pillowy seats, which seem to soak up the light and swallow the sitter, sucking her down into the imaginary realm, making it hard for her to stand up and regain her sense of place. It's a chapel of make-believe, an intermediate space between the dream world of the screen and the chaotic quotidian tumult of the world, which serves as an endless source of raw material, to be reshaped and interpreted and improved upon. As long as you're here, daily life can seem subsidiary to its transubstantiated representation. In the immediate afterglow, the images on the screen are more real than whatever's waiting for her outside. They linger. For this instant, she's free, suspended between her own life and the lives that might have been. In her imagination, writing the screenplay and now watching the film, the two men had become one, Luke becoming Jeff, or perhaps Jeff had become Luke, and the years separating them had fallen away and she was forever twenty-two and forever in love.

But the other life, her actual life, is coming at her like a wave, coming to reclaim her and obliterate the imagined one, washing over her and pulling her back to solid but shifting ground—friends, colleagues, a producer and two of the actors, even a sister she's been trying to discard.

Here's Casey, her oldest friend, looking a little tight around the eyes from her face-lift, dry-eyed, taut cheeks, coming over, arms open wide to sweep her in. "Oh my God, I was sobbing, it was so beautiful."

Veronica and Washington are holding back, keeping their distance while pretending not to be noticing Casey, waiting for her to disappear. Already it has been negotiated that Casey, in deference to Veronica's feelings, will not be going to the after party, which is why she gets primacy here. Among the negotiating points was the promise that her ex wouldn't be invited to either event. The present is littered with wreckage from their past.

"Well, it's wonderful you came," Corrine says, unfurling herself.

Nancy Tanner squirms through the scrum—easily done, since she is skinnier than ever—and materializes in front of Corrine. "For an amateur," she says, "you're not a bad screenwriter. Gotta say, you really captured those entitled, overeducated New Yorkers."

"I'll take that as a tribute to my vast imaginative powers. But seriously, Jeff and Cody deserve most of the credit."

And indeed, Cody Erhardt is mobbed over in the other corner, the director accepting tribute from some of the more fashionable members of the audience.

"But seriously, can you please introduce me to Tug Barkley? He was amazing playing Jeff. Is he coming to the party? He's so hot. Did you get to know him at all?"

"I can't say that we're close—I wasn't on the set."

"You absolutely must introduce me."

"I'll try to at the party."

The fluid comportment of her sister, wobbling in place, artfully tilting her head as she rests an arm on Corrine's shoulder, suggests that she didn't stint on the cheap wine served before the screening.

"So proud of you, sis."

"Thank you, Hilary."

"I mean it. S'wonderful."

"I'm paralyzed with happiness."

"I know you don't think I'm smart."

"I don't think any such thing."

"Yes, you do. But I was smart enough to know what to say to make Russell forgive you."

"You mean Russell, my husband, who's standing right there, within earshot?"

Fortunately, he's absorbed in conversation with Carlo Russi, the chef, who is hosting the after-party at his new restaurant.

"I know I shouldn't say anything."

"You're quite right about that, so don't. Have you met Michael, our exec producer? Michael, this is my sister, Hilary."

Michael, a dark, chiseled prince with a fiercely intelligent gaze, tall and handsome enough that he might have made a career in front of the camera, succeeds in distracting Hilary from whatever revelation was quivering on her lips, taking her hand and ducking his head gallantly. "A pleasure to meet you."

"Likewise. Are you going to the party? Maybe we could share a cab? I work at HBO, but I have a script I'd love to tell you about."

Michael's visibly stricken by this revelation. But he's a big boy who will have to take care of himself, and Corrine is grateful to be rid of her sister, who is towing him toward the exit.

"Corrine, this is Astrid Kladstrup," Russell is saying, presenting this voluptuous Betty Boop babe with a bobbed do, cartoon lips and a vintage dress. "Astrid's at least partly responsible for the whole Jeff Pierce revival—she curates that Web site."

"It's so amazing to meet you," the girl says as Corrine looks her over, then glances back at Russell, suddenly wondering if it's possible, and indeed he seems a little flustered. "I thought the movie was great," she continues, "although I was sorry it wasn't faithful to the drug over-dose. But I suppose there was no way that was going to fly."

The publicist has slipped behind them and is urging them forward toward the exit.

"You still weepy?" Russell asks, putting his arm around her.

"I'm fine," she says, her voice catching in her throat.

"Well, let's join Wash and Veronica, who've been waiting patiently to pay homage."

She remembers then that they're a couple; that she is, in addition to being a lover and a mother, half of this unit: Russell & Corrine.

She exchanges kisses with the Lees, and together they walk out into the anteroom, redolent of popcorn, which is glowing yellow in the glass case of the bright red machine.

They collect their coats, share the elevator down to the lobby and walk out into the cold.

"If we still lived here, we'd be home now," Russell says, looking down West Broadway. They live a hundred and forty blocks north now, in Harlem.

"What was that expression of yours?" Corrine says. "'If wishes were Porsches, beggars would drive'?"

"A clever refashioning of the old adage, I think."

"I think we'll all be a whole lot cleverer after a cocktail or two," Washington says, flagging a cab.

"It's only a few blocks," Corrine tells him. "You guys go ahead. We're going to walk." Russell gives her a quizzical look before nodding—one of those tiny empathetic exchanges of which a marriage of long dura-tion is compounded. Corrine was ready to jump in the cab, but she realizes now that she wants more than anything to walk, and she takes Russell's hand. It's an important night and she intends to savor it.

Such moments are too often lost, the private interludes between the tribal gatherings, the transit between destinations, when the city becomes an intimate landscape, a secret shared by two. This was once their neighborhood and she wants to reclaim it for a little while, to walk past the apartment where they spent so much of their lives, even if it makes her sad thinking of all that transpired there, and all that's lost. It makes her melancholy to imagine that she might never be here again, that these blocks, their former haunts, and their old building will outlast them; that the city is supremely indifferent to their transit through its arteries, and to their ultimate destination. For now, she wants just to be in between. She knows that later it won't be the party she will remember so much as this, the walk with her husband in the crisp autumn air, bathed in the yellow metropolitan light spilling from thousands of windows, this suspended moment of anticipation before arrival.

Acknowledgments

I'm very grateful to Alexandra Pringle, Elizabeth Robinson and Donna Tartt for reading early drafts of the novel and making valuable suggestions. Binky Urban read every draft and was, as always, incredibly helpful and supportive. Gary Fisketjon read the book with his usual close, critical and sympathetic scrutiny and this novel is all the better for it. Ruthie Reisner made the system at Knopf work for us. Thanks to Chip Kidd for another killer book jacket design. I'd also like to thank Lydia Buechler for her sharp eye, Carol Edwards for her sensitive copyediting and Kathleen Fridella for turning the manuscript into a book. Beverly Burris, my much-missed assistant, performed dozens of research and fact-checking missions, great and small. I'd also like to thank Ben Frischer, who did the initial research for the novel. Special thanks to Morgan Entrekin, coach of the Art & Love team. And finally I want to thank my wife, Anne, for her encouragement and support.

A NOTE ON THE TYPE

This book was set in Legacy Serif. Inspired by the 1470 edition of
Eusebius set in the roman type of Nicolas Jenson, this revival type
maintains much of the character of the original.